FOR
CHRIS —
    A   WONDERFUL
PERSON! *

Jack Olsen

* LIE!

ALPHABET JACKSON

AMONG THE BOOKS WRITTEN BY JACK OLSEN:

The Climb Up to Hell
Black Is Best: The Riddle of Cassius Clay
The Black Athlete
Better Scramble than Lose (with Fran Tarkenton)
Night of the Grizzlies
Aphrodite: Desperate Mission
Over the Fence Is Out
     (as Jonathan Rhoades)
Alphabet Jackson

ALPHABET JACKSON

A NOVEL BY JACK OLSEN

A Playboy Press Book

Published simultaneously in the United States and Canada by
Playboy Press, Chicago, Illinois. Printed in the United States of
America. Library of Congress Catalog Card Number: 74-82483.
ISBN 87223-418-5. First edition.

PLAYBOY and Rabbit Head design are trademarks of Playboy, 919
North Michigan Avenue, Chicago, Illinois 60611 (U.S.A.), Reg. U.S.
Pat. Off., marca registrada, marque deposeé.

For Edward Kuhn, Jr.

CONTENTS

BILLYGOATS OFFENSE

POS.	NO.	NAME	AGE	HT.	WT.	HOME TOWN	COLLEGE	YR.
WR	#28	Custer Fox	27	6' 1"	191	Salt Lake City, Utah	Univ. of Montana	6th
LT	#74	J. R. Rodenheimer	34	6' 5"	270	Aliquippa, Pa.	Slippery Rock State	13th
LG	#77	Thaymon Harris	30	6' 3"	250	New York, N.Y.	Lincoln Univ.	8th
C	#50	A. B. C. Jackson	31	6' 1½"	230	Upper Darby, Pa.	Penn State	10th
C	#53	Chester Zawatski	22	6' 1"	240	Jersey City, N.J.	Villanova	1st
RG	#66	Buford Bullivant	29	6' 2"	250	New Orleans, La.	L.S.U.	8th
RT	#75	Robert Boggs	32	6' 7"	285	Chicago, Ill.	Univ. of Illinois	10th
TE	#84	Luke Hairston	26	6' 10"	250	Slidell, La.	Florida A & M	5th
WR	#89	Ray Roy Jenkins	28	6'	188	Houston, Texas	Univ. of Oklahoma	6th
QB	#8	Alvin Frasch	34	5' 11½"	180	Wilmington, Del.	Georgetown	12th
RB	#41	Wing Choy	32	6'	225	San Francisco, Calif.	Univ. of California	11th
RB	#30	Jay Cox	21	5' 11"	210	Schoolcraft, Mich.	Michigan State	1st
K	#1	John Lovesey	34	5' 8"	127	Newcastle, England	Somerdale School	8th

BILLYGOATS DEFENSE

POS.	NO.	NAME	AGE	HT.	WT.	HOME TOWN	COLLEGE	YR.
LE	#83	Allen Johnson	27	6' 3"	250	Toad Suck, Ark.	No College	4th
LT	#72	Arlington Pomroy	25	6' 3"	255	Newton, Kan.	Univ. of Kansas	3rd
RT	#65	Tony Damiano	31	6' 4"	255	St. Louis, Mo.	Notre Dame	8th
RE	#69	J. R. Jones	24	6' 6"	270	Flatonia, Texas	Univ. of Texas	3rd
LLB	#58	Roosevelt Langley	23	6' 2"	235	Alexandria, Va.	Virginia State	2nd
MLB	#52	J. W. Ramwell	33	6' 2"	230	Lubbock, Texas	Texas Tech	12th
RLB	#56	Ernest Oakes	25	6' 1"	225	Atlanta, Ga.	Grambling College	3rd
LC	#31	John Black	24	6'	185	Compton, Calif.	Weber State	2nd
RC	#24	Oliver Urquhart	28	5' 11"	170	Scarsdale, N.Y.	Columbia	6th
SS	#27	Leroy Harmony	25	6' 2"	210	New Roads, La.	UTEP	3rd
FS*	#20	Malley Tietjens	29	6' 1"	190	Rollinsville, Colo.	Univ. of Colorado	7th

*also punts

THE FLIGHT

I

NOBODY'S PSYCHO BUT HIS OWN

RIDING AROUND AT GUNPOINT LIKE THAT, HOUR AFTER *hour, I began to get this weird feeling that we were hanging motionless in the sky. It was like some great big spider was dangling us from his web by a single thread, "up above the world so high, like a diamond in the sky," to quote from the classics. There was 42 players, 10 coaches, the whole front office, 6 or 8 sportswriters and a mess of hangers-on all peeing their pants in our long silver compressed-air tube and not a single thing we could do about it.*

I looked over at him, our own personal spider with his own personal submachine gun, his eyes half closed as usual, but I knew that if anybody even looked sideways at him, he'd be ready, the same as he is in games, just kind of loafing along, not seeming to do much till we really need him, and then destroying anything that gets between him and the football. We always said he's a psycho but he's our psycho. But now he wasn't anybody's psycho but his own, just a plain crazy son of a bitch, out of control, killing himself the hard way, and the rest of us along for the ride.

Well, you gamble and you lose, that's all. We knew exactly what we were doing when we picked this guy up, and we had nobody else to blame. He was always nuts, anybody could see it; standing over there on the sidelines 10 yards from his nearest teammate, never saying anything to anybody, never acknowledging your existence till you needed him out in front of you, and then he'd slam that cast-iron body of his into anything up to a Diesel truck, and when you'd say "nice block" he'd turn away. Malley and myself used to talk about him by the hour, long before he even came to the Billygoats, back when he was being traded from team to team because nobody could get on his wavelength. A 24-carat mental addict, if there ever was one. All-Conference, All-Pro and all-nuts.

The pilot had throttled back on the engines, to save fuel I guess, though the way things were going it wouldn't make any difference, we weren't going anywhere, just hanging in space from that long silver thread till the last drop oozed through the engines and then—down and dirty, like the last card in a game of 7-card stud, and watch out for that first step.

The guy had made up his mind in his own disturbed way, and how do you reason with a dude that doesn't reason? Do you say, "Hey, man, this is highly wasteful. I mean, if you're gonna kill yourself, well, that's your problem, but why take the best football team in the NFL with you?" We'd tried that approach, and all it did was make him mad. He just didn't give a hill of shit about the other people on the plane. I guess, in his twisted way of looking at things, we were expandable.

"Hey, Alphabet."

"Huh?" I turned my head to see what Malley wanted.

"How's your leg feel?"

"About as good as the rest of me," I whispered back.

"That crazy bastard," Mal said softly. "I can't get that line out of my head. 'Show me a hero and I'll write you a tragedy'—F. Scott Fitzgerald."

"I can't get a line out of my own head," I said. " 'We're fucked'—Alphabet Jackson."

I closed my eyes and tried to forget the thump-thump of the heartbeat in my knee, not really painful but aggravating as hell because it never quit. Jeez, I said to myself, who'd've ever thought? Back in July, it looked like the Billygoats all the way.

Late in the afternoon, I was sitting up in the window enjoying the oak trees and the bright green of the quadrangle and the feisty brown squirrels of the Shackley School for Boys, which is our training camp while the little turds are off enjoying their summer hiatus. In the distance I heard this sputtering and snapping, and I knew that the late Robert Boggs had turned off the highway and was about to appear on the twisting road to the dorms, panicking the swans and fouling the air with exhaust from his Porsche Carrera. A bunch of rooks were standing around the front portico, giving it the old nonchalant but actually frothing at the mouth to get their first closeup glimpse of their heroes.

The late Robert Boggs tore-ass around the last turn in a 4-wheel power drift and made 2 complete circuits of the quadrangle, scattering rooks and pigeons. He stood on his brakes about 50 feet from the door and laid rubber for the whole distance while the car lurched and yawed and finally came to a full stop on the lawn. The late Robert Boggs stepped outside and took a bow.

"Please, please," he said, "no applause. Hold yo' applause till the final selection." I could see he'd grown sparser on top, though nowheres near as bald as me. The sun gleamed down and made his head look like an unhusked coconut wearing thick black-rim glasses. The car looked the same as last year—lollipop yellow outside, zebra skin inside, and a sticker on the back saying, NO HONKIES. There were 3 different sets of driving lights scattered across the front. If an oncoming driver didn't dim, the late Robert Boggs could fry his ass. The sunroof was open, and I imagined that he still had the same inscribed silver plate on the dash: THIS BAUBLE PROPERTY OF THE LATE ROBERT BOGGS, NO. 75. PROTECTED BY THE SYMBIONESE LIBERATION ARMY.

Standing there in the hot sun, while the rooks gazed at him with their mouths open and their eyes bugged out, the late Robert Boggs looked like a whole offensive line or a battleship, one. He was wearing platform soles and heels, making him around 7 feet, and he looked like he was 5 or 10 pounds over his playing weight of 285. The only thing that didn't look scary was that big ear-to-ear Terry-Thomas grin, with about a half-inch of air between his 2 front teeth.

"Come, come, my man," the late Robert Boggs said to a rook named Jay Cox, standing goggle-eyed to one side. "Snap yo' ass and hustle these bags to Room 3." He pointed to a matched set of 4 aluminum suitcases stacked on the roof rack.

The rook looked around checking the exits, and said huffily, "I'm not your employee."

Robert's eyes narrowed slightly, but then he smiled even bigger, and he said, "What position you play, honky?"

Cox just stood there and looked fidgety, like a marshal when he doesn't know which direction the trouble's coming from. A blond-headed kid next to him blurted out,

"He's a running black, I mean he's a running black—*a running back!*"

"Well, listen at me," the late Robert Boggs said, still smiling that wide smile but pointing a thick, menacing finger in the direction of Jay Cox. "Don't come near the 3 hole, unnerstan'? 'Cause if you do, you ain't gettin' no blockin'. You dig what I'm sayin', candy ass? You come near the 3 hole, the other team gone have yo' hat 'n' ass."

He turned to the blond kid. "Pick up my bags, rook, and shag-ass."

"Yes, sir, Mr. Boggs," the kid said, and began humping all 4 bags at once.

"Good attitude," Robert said. "I'm please to see we got one whitey that know his place. My, my, if only you grays didn't have that cha'acteristic odor. Tell me, my man, you got a innate sense of rhythm?"

The blond kid smiled and pushed through the swinging doors. I called down, "Hey, Robert, what're you doing here? You're 4 hours early. You're going against your name."

The late Robert Boggs saw me in the 2d story window and clapped his big hammy hands together. "Hey, what it is, brother man?" he hollered. "How long's yo' black ass been here?"

Robert has this quaint idea that certain black men are put on earth with white skin to fool the rest of the honkies, and he thinks I'm one of these secret blacks, which would come as a surprise to my mother and father back in Upper Darby, P.A. Robert says I'm the only black center in the league, which would be true if I wasn't white. When I make a good play, he'll pull me up one-handed in front of 65,000 screaming people and he'll say, "Way to go, you black honky spook you!"

Sometimes he'll think he's grabbing me and he's actually grabbing somebody else, because Robert can't see too

5

good and plays his position by grope. Off the field, he wears great big horn-rimmed glasses, and without them his field of vision reaches out for about 3 inches. He tried contacts for a while, but one popped out in a big game and an enemy player named Duke Senz found it. "You lose something?" Duke said.

"Yeh," Robert said, reeling around pawing at his eye and blinking.

"This it?" Senz asked, holding the lens up in Robert's face.

"Yeh, man, thanks a lot," Robert said.

Senz reached back and flang the lens a half a mile, and *we* got the penalty after the riot. Robert practically tore his hair out by the roots, which he doesn't have that much hair to begin with, and he wears it close-cropped in the old-fashioned way they used to back when blacks were called Negroes. "Look like a old nigger skullcap, don't it?" Robert said to me one night. "Well, it's too late to change. That's the way my daddy looked, and I liked my daddy, the few times I seen him."

I told Robert I'd been in camp since the day before, when we held free-agent tryouts. I guess I should have known right then, in that very first conversation, that something weird was in the air or the stars or someplace. Any time the late Robert Boggs shows up 4 hours early instead of 6 hours late, you know the moon has ricochetted clean out of phrase, and everything that happens till it rights itself is bound to be dubious. The late Robert Boggs earned his name by never showing up on time to any event, including his own birth, which his cousin once told me took place a month late. Robert didn't have the slightest interest in entering the world in Meridian, Mississippi, so he just hung in there till the family moved to Chicago, and then checked in at 12 pounds, 11 ounces. "His mama never forgive him fo' that," Robert's cousin

Roosevelt Boggs told me, grinning through his snaggle teeth.

The late Robert Boggs earns 60 grand a year as our right tackle on offense, and every season he gives back 10 grand in fines, which still leaves him making about what he's worth as an all-conference player. Robert wouldn't have it any other way, and Coach loves to be able to stand up in front of the whole squad and say, "All right, Boggs, you were 7 minutes late. That'll cost you 140."

"Suck mah black cock," the late Robert Boggs will say under his breath, but he pays, knowing that his salary is inflated for such events.

He crashed into my room and we began the official Billygoats' handshake, which is a series of bumps and grinds ending with smacks on both shoulders, similar to the way we slap our pads into place just before a game, only when Robert Boggs slaps your shoulders, you better duck. You need pads just to say hello to him.

"How's my main man?" he said. But before I could answer, his eyes caught the terrible sight hanging over in the corner of my room, and he said, "Whuzzat?"

"What's that?" I said. "It's a jersey."

"What kinda jersey?"

"Our jersey. Our new jersey. Which you will be wearing soon."

Robert Boggs gasped, smacked his forehead and pretended to fall backward in a faint, almost collapsing my bed. "That's *ours?*" he said. "Oh, my po' black ass."

We have the kind of front office that believes in image. Never mind whether we win or lose, it's how we look that counts. This year's new image was fuchsia jerseys with ivory numbers, ivory pants, fuchsia stockings and ivory sox and shoes. The front office explained that the new colors were more compatible with our new name, the Billygoats, which I myself never saw a fuchsia goat, but it made as much sense as some of the other strokes by the front office. Last year they finally gave up calling us the Stags and changed our name to the Billygoats, because the whole city was already calling us Goats, owing to the fact that the Stag decals on our helmets looked more like goats' horns, and also, most of the Stags acted more like goats, off and on the field. Some of the wives resisted the change. They wanted a name like the Ospreys or the Owls or some other graceful bird, but the name Billygoats seemed to match our style, which is straight-ahead basic football and leave the flea-flicking to the Cowboys and the Rams. We use an end-around about once a season, a half-back option maybe twice, but really just showing the plays, giving the opposition something to think about. The rest of the time it's execute, execute, execute, no matter what the Supreme Court says, except that when Coach first saw the new fuchsia jerseys, he said maybe we should change our style and work some pirouttes into our attack and change our name to the Fruitcakes. If Coach had his way, we'd wear basic black and concentrate on hitting.

"That ain't *mah* football uniform, baby," the late Robert Boggs snapped at me. "Ain't no money could get me into that thing. I seen a daid hog purtier'n that. I seen a 4-car collision purtier."

"Robert, you in shape?" I said to change the subject, because I knew we would all wear the fuchsia jersey whether we liked it or not, because professional football players have a fundamental right to do exactly what the front office tells them.

"The late Robert Boggs *always* in shape," Robert said.

"Good," I said, " 'cause Coach says we start 2-a-days tomorrow."

Robert looked stunned again. "We start 2-a-days on the first mothafuckin' day of camp?"

"That's what he said."

"Well, he can suck mah righteous cock," Robert said, and slank down the hall toward his room, ducking to avoid the low ceiling.

"How come you're so early?" I called after him.

"I missed y'all too much. How come you so nosy?"

"I'm the snapper. The snapper's supposed to be nosy."

"You suppose to be dumb, too?"

"Yeh. Isn't a center supposed to be dumb?"

The late Robert Boggs's deep bass laugh came echoing down the hall. "Yeh," he said. "And you sho' enthusiastic about your work!"

A few minutes later I heard double-whistling up the corridor like kids with nickle fifes, and I knew that Malley Tietjens was on the scene. Mal always produced his own fanfare, humming and whistling that weirdo music of his, Bartock and Beethoven and a guy named Mailer or something like that. His records sounded like they were running at the wrong speed, and if you ever tried to dance to that stuff, you'd fracture your ass.

When he reached the door, I pretended not to notice. "Hey, Robert!" I yelled. "Shut your window! A bird flew in."

Mal whistled a long credenza and I turned around and acted surprised, and we did the Billygoats' handshake, and then I stepped back and took a good look at him, and I said, "Well, Malley, Coach is just gonna love that hairdo. Who did that, your regular hairdresser, Mr. Helen?" His bangs were thick and brown all the way down to his eyelids, and in the back his hair hung to the middle of his shoulder blades. "Turn around," I said. With that little cracker ass of his, he looked like Brigitte Bardot. "Jeez," I said, "if you go in the shower like that, somebody's gonna fuck you."

"Have no fear, Rooms," Mal said. "I'll cut an inch or 2 and ameliorate the situation." That's the way Malley talks, he never uses 1 syllable when 3 or 4 will suffice. Your safeties and kickers are all a little odd. You don't expect normal responses out of them, but sometimes I think that Malley broke the mold. He's always making these weirdo comments, like when we were invited to tea at the owner's mansion and he told the butler, "No, thanks. Lapsang souchong is not my cup of tea," and another time we were sitting around reading and I said, "Hey, Mal, what's an extern?" and he said, "A former bird" and kept right on reading. Or he'd say some mysterious phrase like, "Come see, come sigh," and when I'd ask him what it meant, he'd say it was a very subtle French phrase and I probably wouldn't understand. Very subtle French phrase! I knew a little French myself, and up his *merde!*

I love old Mal, but I just wish he'd learn to speak simple English. He's always so deep. He says him and I understand each other better than any of the other roomies in the club, but I'm not so sure. Like he's always pushing me to read some author named Yates. All he talks about is Yates, Yates, Yates. Last year I drew a 15-yard penalty for holding that lunatic Beast Barlow in a big game, and Mal grabbed my arm and said, "Things fall apart, the center will not hold—Yates." I asked him could he quote me something from Lombardi or Shula once in a while, I didn't want to hear from any more pansy poets, but he just snickered and got off a 65-yard punt that got us out of the hole. So you had to love the guy, and just keep hoping he'd straighten up some day.

Malley graduated with honors and also UPI All-America from the University of Colorado, which he was from Rollinsville, Colorado, a little crossroads village up in the mountains and cold enough to freeze a bear's ass in August. He didn't want people to know he had graduated tops in his class, but I kept bringing it up to annoy him. Once he recited a poem:

Summa cum laude
And summa come softly.
But either is better
Than never at all.

"What's that mean?" I asked.

"It means that no matter how bad things get on the stock market, we can always dip into our reservoir of carnal knowledge."

"Who wrote it? Yates?"

"Wolf."

"Thomas Wolf?"

"No, Wolf Rachlin, the ticket-taker."

Mal was always talking like that. He was probably the deepest person it has ever been my pleasure to know personally. He'd majored in polysci with a heavy minor in lit., and his favorite authors were Russo, Candide and Carl Lyle, but he would read anything you handed him. He knew the rulebook by heart. He knew the statistics and history of pro football back to the Decatur Staleys. If you happened to mention that your father took you to the championship game in 1950 and you saw Lou Groza kick a field goal with 26 seconds left to beat the Rams 30–27, Mal would say, "The score was 30–28, and Groza kicked the field goal with 28 seconds left, not 26," and you'd get all hot and bothered and threaten to look it up, and Mal would say, "Don't bother," and he was right; don't bother.

"How about a little gin?" he asked.

"No, thanks," I said. "I'd rather have a root canal."

Malley had a great rote memory, and he'd beat anybody in the club in gin or the card game of your choice. When he first made the team 7 years ago, he challenged Spider Brown, who was then the special teams' captain and considered himself the greatest gin player on earth, and after they'd turned about 6 cards, Mal says, "Spider, it's silly to go on with this travestry. You're finished."

"Shut up and play the cards," Spider said. "You ramble them lips an awful lot for a rook."

"You got 3 3's, the 6, 7, 8 of diamonds and the ace, deuce, trey of spades," Mal said calmly. "I got the 4 of spades in my hand, the 5 of diamonds is gone, and I got the 9. So your ass is sucking buttermilk, and also you lose. Now I will accept a compromise renumeration of 2 dollars."

"Play on, mouth," Spider said, but he didn't sound quite so sure of himself. A few flips later, Malley ginned for a total take of 3 dollars and 85 cents, and Spider claimed he cheated. But that's just the way Malley is. In my considerate opinion, he's a computer-brain. A little strange on words, maybe, but very bright on memory. Like, he'd come into the defensive huddle and say, "The slingshot back's coming sideways this time. It's the same situation they had us in last year." Sure enough, the slingshot would head around the end and 9 Goats'd be waiting for him. Wing Choy called it our "memory blitz."

Speak of the devil, Wing came bursting into the room and grabbed us and started waltzing us around like we're long-lost brothers, and Malley said, "Wing Back! Great to see you, baby." He always calls Wing by his position instead of his name. "How's your yellow ass?" Mal said.

Wing said, "Plick!" which puzzled me, because Wing Choy majored in Romance languages at the University of California and later took a master's in etymology or entomology or something like that, and if there is anything in the world Wing doesn't have, it's a Chinese accent. The whole thing is too ridiculous to think about, when you think about it, but any time you put Wing and Malley together, it sounds like you've stepped through the looking glass in Dickens's *Alice in Wonderland*. Wing comes from Galileo High School in San Francisco with a student body 70% Oriental, and Mal likes to kid him. "I drove past Galileo the other day," Malley'll say, "and an hour later I was hungry."

"Allee samee you pay bill," Wing'd say. I told you they were weird.

The day Wing broke the Billygoats' individual-rushing record, 187 yards behind the blocks of guys like Jackson and Harris and Boggs, a reporter asked him how he did it, and Mal piped up, "Occidentally."

Wing was crazy about the female bazoomba, which we all enjoy but don't make such a fuss over. He had his apartment walls papered with pictures of naked bustlines, bra ads, before-and-after ads, *Playboy* centerfolds and anything that showed the female 2d story. "Wing Back, there's a certain lack of programmatic content to your walls," Malley told him one night when we were sitting around drinking wine.

"Well," Wing said, "the way I feel is when you've seen a million of 'em, you've seen 'em all. I'm about half way."

His bath mat was made of foam rubber in the shape of bazoombas, little round flat ones, big droopy ones and everything in between. It felt like you were walking on the beach at Atlantic City. "You're in trouble when you start dreaming about your bath mat," Malley said. "Do you heathen Chinks dream about white ladies, too?"

"Go fuck yourself," Wing said. "I dream about my girl."

"Is it true what they say?" Mal asked.

"Not about mine. Mine's 45 degrees. She's Hawaiian."

After a while the 3 of us, me and Wing and Mal, we wandered over to the chow hall, and the guys were beginning to arrive thick and fast now, not wishing to miss the first delicious free poison, and there were so many monsters rocking around giving each other the Billygoats' official handshake and greeting, it looked like an audition for a core de ballet. Over against the wall I caught a glimpse of Ray Roy Jenkins, our wide receiver, with his hair all frizzed out in an Afro that wouldn't quit, and I knew the barber was in for a busy day. Ray Roy was standing next to Luke Hairston, our new tight end which we traded from the Jets. Hairston had been All-Pro 4 years before, a 6-foot-10 monster out of Florida A & M, and after that he just seemed to retire. On the field he went through the motions, but barely, and 3 teams tried him out and dropped him before the Jets unloaded him on us. There was a story that he'd broken a girl's arms in a fight, and that he took dope and stole motorcycles. There was 2 things he was crazy about: guns and bikes. I'd seen his yellow Suzuki parked outside of the mess hall. They said he took it to bed with him. And he was supposed to own 100 guns, all of them in working order. Well, when you're 6-foot-10 and black with a shaved head and a broad flat nose with nostrils big enough to accommodate a pair of ripe olives, you are entitled to be a little flaky, especially if you can block and catch passes and intimidate the opposition at the same time. And he certainly *was* a flake. He hated anybody that was in a position to give orders. Imagine not being able to get along with John Mackey of the Colts, the first black head coach and one of the nicest guys you'll ever meet, which Luke Hairston pulled a gun on him. Before that, he'd lasted a month at Cleveland. The rumor was that he thought the Browns' coaching staff was racist, but another rumor was that he thinks the whole world is racist and he's totally unreasonable on the subject. I know for a fact he calls the new Mau-Mau terrorists "those Toms."

When Hairston was traded to us, the word was that he was finished, he was just going through the motions, and we were crazy to even pay the waiver price for him. Well, I guess Coach couldn't resist the gamble. It's like betting the numbers—if you win, you win $600; if you lose, you lose a buck. I understand that Coach called Hairston in when he joined the club and told him to just do his job and everything would be all right. He wasn't expected to socialize or be a team leader, just as long as he puts out on the field. Coach told him there's no racism on the Billygoats, which is really about 87% true.

Now I watched as the late Robert Boggs walked over to Hairston, and they slapped hands, conventional style, but after a few minutes of noncommunication Robert walked off shaking his head.

J. R. Rodenheimer showed up and kept as far away from the brothers as he possibly could and still be in the same chow hall. J. R.'s the guy who once told a reporter, "I don't think of my black teammates as niggers. I think of 'em as Billygoats. *Then* I think of 'em as niggers." J. R. is our starting left tackle on offense, 270 pounds out of Slippery Rock State in P.A., not far from the anthracite mines where his father went down every morning and took a lesson in bitterness that he passed onto J. R. and the other 6 boys, and they never forgot it. The old man also taught them to be tough. J. R. is built like one of those stubby iron cannons that you see on the village greens around Valley Forge. If you smack J. R. across the shoulders, he bends just like one of those cannons.

In a few minutes, he was joined by our starting right guard, Buford Bullivant, No. 66 if you'll check your program, out of New Orleans and L.S.U. Now Buford isn't necessarily beloved by everybody on the team—he makes Mal see purple—but you have to figure him for a steadying influence on J. R. Old Buford was studying to be a banker, and he spent his off hours reading charts and figuring out percentages, but he was also the team's religious nut, and he was always saying things like, "Christ should be a part of everything we do, including our football." He made up a slogan that he said was going to be the slogan of his bank, when he got one: "Jesus Saves. Why Not Open *Your* Account Today?" Every morning and night, Buford said his prayers religiously.

Somewhere under that pious front, Bull had a mean streak, which you could see out on the field and sometimes you could see it other places too. He had absolutely no sense of humor, which always makes me suspicious. You could tell him the funniest joke in the world, the one that ends "I am peeing on your fur coat!" or the one that ends "dose Fokkers vas Messerschmidts!" and he'd just stand there waiting for the punch line. But if somebody fell off a wall at training camp and broke his ankle, Bull would break up laughing. He was like that line by Simon and Garfinkel: "They say he was a most peculiar man."

Our other offensive guard was Thaymon "Bad-ass" Harris, No. 77, 6-foot-3 out of Lincoln University and one of the craziest players in football, an all-out wild man that would fit right in with a herd of gorillas in Borneo. When anybody asked how much Bad-ass weighed, the correct answer was "250, *roughly.*" In the off-season he wrestled bears at carnivals to promote his chain of restaurants, and when he'd make an especially vicious tackle in a game, somebody in the stands would always holler, "Bring on another bear!" For a while, him and his brother had an old 4-wheel-drive Jeep Wagoneer, and their hobby was taking it out in the woods and running into trees. One brother would keep butting the tree with the car while the other brother stood in the top of the tree to ride it down. That was their idea of a pleasant outing.

On the field Bad-ass was a one-man typhoon, barely under control, ready to go completely bananas at the slightest provocation. Part of this was natural behavior, and part of it was courtesy of the Squibb Pharmaceutical Co., which made some refreshments that Bad-ass enjoyed before each game, and sometimes in-between. He'd run around and scream and froth at the mouth and bite and fart and curse and call everybody "cocksuckers" and "pussies." Well, he wasn't out there to elevate the moral tone, and he certainly didn't. But off the field—a perfect gentleman and the sharpest dresser in football, black division.

We slid through the chow line, myself and Malley and Wing, and it was the usual poison masquerading as food, full of steroids and caffeine and hydrogen fats and sorbic acids and other foreign objects, things that I ordinarily wouldn't touch with a 10-foot fork. You could just see the stilbestrol oozing out of the meat, but then stilbestrol is fed directly to some of our players in tablet form, to boost their weight up to where Coach wants it. The cancer won't come till later, after they retire. I gave up fighting this battle long ago, and in the off-season I stuff myself with organic meats and fresh unsprayed vegetables and vitamins and minerals to make up for all the crap they feed me on the Billygoats. Hell, real goats get a better diet than us.

The soup was about the only thing with any flavor. It was a spiky consomme, probably full of saltpeter. Mal called it "a consomme devoutly to be wished," whatever that's supposed to mean, but after the soup the meal went downhill and died. I mean, how can you consider yourself nourished when the dessert is some kind of gelatinous stuff the color of our jerseys and reeking with Red No. 2 and topped with artificial whipped cream that probably began life as Diesel oil? Well, they say I'm a crank on the subject, but I'd like to live past 35, if my knees hold out, provided my ankles don't collapse, assuming that my skull doesn't get fractured again.

That first gathering at camp is always exciting. The guys are suffering from St. Vitus, jerking and dancing around with energy they've been storing up since January, and they say things like, "I can't wait to get out on that field tomorrow." There is only 1 day in the life of a professional football player when he is absolutely in love with the game, and that's the day before camp opens. "Jesus, I want to start hitting!" Thaymon "Bad-ass" Harris said. 24 hours later he'd be pissing and moaning about why he didn't remain in civilian life, which in his case would mean pushing grass or horse on the streetcorners of the greater Bronx. Then Q. B. said, "Men, there's nothing as satisfying as kickin' somebody's ass," but in a few days Q. B.'ll be greatly disturbed because one of the defensive linemen will drill Q. B.'s elbows about 6 inches deep in the turf and breathe in his face and holler, *"Yah yah yah, it sure is nice to kick ass!"* and then Q. B.'ll have a different complexion. Even old Malley gets carried away by the early feeling at camp. Here he was with me and Wing Choy and 2 or 3 of the other offensive players, eating our chow and gurgling about this great game of football, and I said, "I hurt in 6 different places the day *before* camp opens, but you couldn't keep me away with a 10-ton truck," and Mal says, "Yeh, I understand the appeal, Alphabet, but I'm not sure you do."

"What's that mean?" I asked, which is the same question I'm always asking Malley.

"The appeal of this game is that quivery feeling when you go out there with your peers and tangle-ass," he said. "It's vestigial, but it's a good feeling just the same."

"Who's vestigial when he's at home?" asked John Lovesey, our superstar placekicker out of Newcastle, England, somewhere near London.

"Limey," I said, addressing him by our team nickname which he detested, "you talk funny."

Limey flared up, as usual. *"I* talk funny?" he said, sparks coming out of his chalky British ears. *"I talk funny?* Why, you whole bloody lot talk funny!"

"Hey, John," the late Robert Boggs chimed in, "lighten up, baby. We only jackin' around."

"Piss off!" Limey muttered, and buried his long British nose in the Diesel oil.

"I mean for a half a million years men have been butting heads," Malley went on after the interruption, "and for most of that time it's been a matter of survival. Take a typical Neanderthal family group, maybe 30 or 40 people. Everything's going beautiful for them, the crops are in, the animals are fat, and then they look up one morning to see a strange band marching up the hill. That other gang's coming to murder the men, rape the women and enslave the kids, and everybody's terrified. There's a big fight and the enemy's repulsed, and now the Neanderthal family feels terrific, exhilarated."

"Meaning?" I said.

"Meaning that we get exactly the same relieved, ecstatic feeling today after winning a football game. It's deep inside the genes. If we beat Dallas, then symbolically those big bastards from Dallas aren't gonna enslave our kids and rape our wives and kill our men. The spectators admire us because we've protected them from death and mutilation. The act is symbolic, but the feeling's real."

"Gee, Mal," I said, "that's deep."

"Yeh," Robert Boggs said, "about a inch and a half." He leaned over and grabbed 2 more slices of bread with his pie-plate hand. "We go for the money, that's all. I don't even know how to play no fuckin' cymbals."

Wing Choy piped up, "The thing I like about the game is there's a beginning, a middle and an end."

"And guards and tackles," I said helpfully.

"When it's over, it's over," Wing said. "Not like politics or marriage or religion or anything else I can think of."

"Oh, sure," the late Robert Boggs said sarcastically, "you dudes just in love with the game of football, ain't chew? Well, tell me about it tomorrow. *After* the grass drills. *After* the wind sprints. *After* the ropes. Let's see how much you love it after a li'l righteous workout."

"Yesterday they were falling like flies out there," I said. "Nobody loved the game yesterday by the time Coach got through with them."

"Yesterday?" Mal asked. "What was yesterday?"

"Final tryout camp for free agents," I said. "That's how come I was here early, to help with the snapping."

"Anybody look good?" Wing asked.

"Well, there was a kid that *thought* he looked good. Robert met him coming in. Kid named Jay Cox, fullback outa Michigan State. He played behind Pellington for 3 years, so nobody ever heard of him, but he looks like he can cut it, if he can just zip his mouth."

I told them how Cox reported to Coach by saying, "Of course, you know who I am?"

Coach looked him up and down and said, "Don't tell me. Let me guess. Senator Abzug?"

"I'm Jay Cox," the kid told Coach in a tone that said he would grant forgiveness just this once. "You can win with me."

The other rooks looked like they hoped the earth would swallow them. Some of them actually flinched, but you never know how Coach is gonna react, and he was surprisingly patient with the new man. "Show me what you can do, son," Coach said, and Cox ran through the whole 30 series, and damned if he didn't bang a few heads. He was the only one of the 51 free agents that survived.

"Nothin' else looked good?" the late Robert Boggs inquired.

"Well, there was two guys came in, Mutt and Jeff, one of 'em about an inch taller than you, Robert, and the other one about 150 pounds in diving weights, and Coach says to the big guy, 'Okay, what position you trying out for?'

and the big guy, he says in this soprano voice, 'Oh, I'm not the athlete, I'm the agent. *He's* the athlete.' "

"What can he do?" Coach says.

The agent says, "Well, he can run like Secretariat and he can hit like Dick Butkus and he can whistle 'Melancholy Baby,' all at the same time."

"Well," Coach says, "I don't know about that 'Melancholy Baby' part, but we can use the rest. What's his position?"

"Scatback," the agent says.

Coach looked funny, but he put the guy on the track and he stumbled through the 40 yards in 5.6 seconds, and Coach says, "So you're a scatback, huh? Well, scat the fuck outa here!"

Another guy claimed he was an offensive guard, so they put him one-on-one with a 300-pound kid from Arkansas and the Arkie kid squashed his ass. It sounded like a draft horse falling on a duck. Poor guy, he unpeeled himself like a cartoon character and he limped over to the sidelines and said, "He hit me. *He hit me!* That big sumbitch hit me."

"Oh, dear me," Coach said. "Did he break your parasol?"

"I don't know about that," the kid said, "but my shoulder sure do hurt."

The guys laughed. "It's the same every year," Malley said. "All that time and energy wasted on walk-ons, and you never get a sintilla of help out of any of them."

"That Cox might be a sintilla," I said. "If we can get him a muzzle."

How little I knew.

I went down the road to a phone booth to make my weekly call to my ex-son, A.B.C. Jackson III, living with his mom and stepdad in Augusta, Ga., and then it was time for the evening meeting, the 1st serious event of the summer training season. If you were late, it was your ass. Between the dinner at 6 and the meeting at 8, the late Robert Boggs managed to line up a foxy mama and escort her to the weeds, and he showed up at the meeting at 10 after 8, zipping his fly and humming the love theme from *Shaft Goes to Washington.*

"Where you been, Boggs?" Coach snapped.

"Pers'nal business," the late Robert Boggs said.

"100 dollars," Coach said.

"Lick my black cock," the late Robert Boggs muttered. Camp was back to normal.

"All right, men," Coach said. "Give me your attention." You could hear 80 of those cheap folding chairs scraping around on the cement floor of the gym. "Attention. Your attention, please." A few more chairs scraped, and some guys in the back kept on chattering, and Coach hit the button on his freon can and hollered, "I WANT YOUR FUCKING ATTENTION RIGHT NOW!" and everybody gave Coach their fucking attention.

"I'll get right to the point," Coach said, which I knew better. He tried to smile, but Coach really doesn't have a smile, it comes out as a leer. Mal says that whenever Coach smiles it reminds him of the original meaning of the smile back in cave-man days: To warn you that if you took one more step it was your ass.

Coach has one of those typical football faces that look like they were finished off in a trash compactor and dropped from a tall building. He wears a deep black toupee with red highlights, parted in the middle like an 1870 Laguerrotype. He has close-set black eyes like spiders, and a broken nose that curves in about 4 different directions before it ends in a point suitable for juicing oranges. The best description of Coach was provided by Bad-ass Harris one night when he got drunk and said,

adio commercial, and the last time the company
checked, Coach was ordering $350 worth of dairy prod-
ucts a month. They figured he must be using it for fertili-
zer, but if I know Coach, he was probably selling auto-
graphed quarts.

There's people around town who think that the Bil-
ygoats represent the city, but don't tell that to Coach. He
thinks of the team as an expression of his own personality,
just like his family. You should hear him. "I beat Green
Bay last week." "Boston's tough, but I think I can handle
em." "Miami doesn't give me any problems." Once he
was being interviewed on network TV after a game, and
he said, "Never in doubt, never in doubt. I knew I had 'em
from the opening kickoff."

Mal and Robert Boggs were interviewed next, and Mal
said, "Hey, Coach played a great game, didn't he?"

Robert said, "Yeh, never even tripped over the phone
wire."

If you're a veteran player, you can get away with a little
kidding like that, and if you really stand up to Coach, he'll
usually give ground. But if you're weak or vulnerable, like
maybe you're a 13th-round draft choice or your knees are
going, then watch out. "When did you first learn to play
football, Jackson?" Coach'll ask me. "I know it was today,
but what time today?" He'll tell me I snap the ball like
Mama Cass, and he'll tell Mal he punts like Sid Charisse.
"*Yah yah yah,*" he'll comment. "You look like a fucking
belly dancer out there." When the team was going horseshit, he'd say, "Now I know you girls can hit harder'n
that," or "Whatsa matter, ladies, having your monthlies?"
You can see why we all love Coach and would sacrifice
anything to please him.

"Men," Coach said at the meeting, "and I call you men
because men is what you're gonna be when this camp's
over. You veterans know what I mean." Sure, we knew

"Hey, Coach, was anybody else hurt in the acc

The main personality factor about Coach is hi
or lack of it. Wearing his elevator football shoes
¾-inch cleats, he stands about 5-foot-9, and he n
any of the rest of us forget that nature handed h
sandwich. "Coach is 5-foot-9," Robert Boggs said
mouth is 6-foot-2." Coach drives around the prac
in one of those telephone company extender tr
kind that you sit in a can and it raises 15 feet so
get at the wires. He races up and down the fiel
thing, blowing the freon and blaring out orders
bullhorn. One day Tony Damiano missed a si
Coach reamed him out from 100 yards away, a
turned his back and raised a finger. "Up yours,
bullhorn blared, and we always figured Coach n
mirrors.

I guess he meets the standard job description
ball coach: "Smart enough to do the work ar
enough to think it matters." He's certainly con
and that's 96% of the battle. He comes from th
and he still thinks of the rest of the world as a
extension of New York City. "Istanbul," he'll sa
far is that from Grand Concourse?" He stole a
favorite expressions from Red Smith, with a slip
"Everything outside of New York is Bridgepor
Bridgeport, which is Secaucus." If you can ur
Coach, you can understand integral calculus. He
anything into a con or a competition, always hap
you 4 nickels for a quarter. One day Q. B. walke
office with a dozen golf balls he'd been given, a
bounces a few, and he says, "Hey, don't play the
wreck your game. Here, give 'em to me. I'll
home and give 'em to the kids." Then he wen
played the balls himself. When he was at Detroit
a deal with a dairy for free milk in return for doi

what he meant. Every season for 10 years he opened the same way. "Some of you might think we're running a boys' camp for you pussies. Well, you'll learn different starting tomorrow morning." Blah blah, and 100% is not enough, and blah blah, and you get lucky when you work hard, and blah blah blah, and the other team's studying, too, and blah blah blah.

Coach lives on slogans. He has one on his wall that says, "The difficult we do right away, the impossible may take a few minutes longer." Every year somebody sneaks in and changes it to "the impossible is impossible." We also changed his poem, "Somebody said that it couldn't be done." We made it read,

> And he tackled the task that couldn't be done,
> And couldn't do it.

Coach has so many slogans and framed speeches and old bromines and plaques in his office, you can barely see the wall. "Coach," Mal said to him one day, "a plaque on both your houses."

Coach laughed politely, but I said, "Coach, don't encourage him. I've got to live with that all winter."

I guess the main thing about Coach is he's so intense, so excitable. One practice we messed up the handoff twice in a row. Coach let out a roar—

AAAARRRRGHHHHHHH!

and his face turned white and he said, "Edquist, you take over," and he walked to the locker room in this little mincy walk, with his feet turned outward and his spine as straight as a linemarker and leaning slightly backward like an old Charlie Chaplin movie. That night we found out he'd shit his pants when he said:

AAAARRRRGHHHHHHH!

That's how excitable Coach was. The next day we put

a roll of pink toilet paper and a card in front of his locker: TO THE NEW MOTHER. The card had a puff of satin stitched to it, and the border was pink flowers and curlicues, and it had a nice verse congratulating him on the "blessed gift from heaven." It cost us 6 bits and 10 extra laps, but it was worth it.

At the meeting, I nodded off, reminiscing. Mal gave me the elbow. "Huh?" I said.

"Wake up! He's coming to the fines."

"We're starting a whole new system this year," Coach was saying. "It's $1000 for a woman in your room. Curfew is $250 and $10 a minute, and late to practice is $500 plus $10 a minute, and there's no excuses. If you're on the way to practice and 6 bandits hold you up and tie you to a tree and make you 15 minutes late, well, that's $650 and don't bother mentioning about the bandits."

A groan went up. "Quiet!" Coach said. "Don't waste your energy griping at every single thing. Wait till you hear it all. I got a few more new rules. There's gonna be a new team image—no long hair, no moustaches, no beards and no excessively long sideburns."

"Cawch," Leroy Harmony called out in his Louisiana twang, "what chew mean no moustaches? Ah had a moustache since Ah was tin years old. Moustache pawt of mah black pride."

"We don't have black pride around here, No. 27," Coach said. "We have Billygoat pride, and Billygoat pride means we act alike, think alike and look alike."

"Ain't no way we gonna look alike, Massa," the late Robert Boggs said, laughing.

"Coach," Wing Choy said, "how do you define excessively long sideburns?"

Coach touched his own, trimmed neatly about an inch above the ear lobe. "Anything longer'n mine," he said.

"They might change from day to day. You pussies'll just have to pay attention."

Then Billy Bob Bunker, owner and general manager and all-around indoor sportsman, strolled out in a doubleknit gabardine suit, just like Billy Graham, scowling as if he didn't own the Billygoats and half of Oklahoma. Billy Bob was about 50 years old, but he was already senile from whiskey, and he never could remember our names from one year to the next, unless we were wearing uniforms and numbers. He called me "Tiger," and Bad-ass Harris was "Big Fellow," and Robert Boggs was "Sport." We were his favorites. The rest of the team he just called Pal, like "Hey, Pal, you had a bum day today."

The most important thing that ever happened to Billy Bob Bunker, aside from owning a shriveled up Oklahoma farm that turned into the Waldrop No. 2 oil field, was making 2d lieutenant in World War II and fighting heroically on the battlefields of St. Louis, Seattle and Fort Dix. He'd say things like "Hubba hubba!" and ask if he could punch your T. S. card. One day Lacklustre missed a tackle and Billy Bob hollered, "Buckle down, Winsocki!" I told you he never got a name right in his life. Malley said he was an anachronism, but he looked human enough to me.

Mr. Bunker cleared the Chivas Regal from his throat and announced that the trouble with the world was the lack of discipline and by God he had the solution and he was putting it into effect right now, and we would all be grateful at the end of the year when we split up the Superbowl winnings. "This is the year of the Goat," Billy Bob announced dramatically.

"That'll be news in Chinatown," Wing Choy whispered.

"The year of the Billygoats!" Billy Bob repeated, waggling his arms like the former Richard Millhouse Nixon, the gestures one beat behind the words. "This is the year we go the route, because this is the year we're gonna have the help of the greatest general in American history."

We all looked around, but no uniforms were in sight.

"I refer to the great General George S. Patton," Billy Bob went on. There was another groan. Every year one pro team or another discovers General Patton. It usually lasts about 3 days. Then some player takes a poke at the coach and sanity is restored. Now it was our turn. Our beloved owner pulled a sheath of papers out of his inside coat pocket and read: " 'All human beings have an innate resistance to obedience. Discipline removes this resistance and by constant repetition makes obedience habitual and unconscious.' Who said that?"

"Lennie Bruce?" Q. B. inquired under his voice.

"George S. Patton, Major General, U.S. Army," Mr. Bunker said. "And listen to this: 'An army is a team. . . . This individual heroic stuff is a lot of crap.' George S. Patton again. Isn't that great stuff? Doesn't that get you right here?" Billy Bob placed his hand over his heart. Robert Boggs placed his own hand over his balls and said, "Rat own!"

Moisture filled Billy Bob's eyes, and he was unable to continue. He sat back down amid a credenza of silence. A few of the rooks started to clap, but they stopped. Coach jumped up and said, "Any questions?"

J. W. Ramwell, our bulldogging middle linebacker out of Texas Tech, made one of his rare public speeches. "Coach, I was just wonderin'. Do you thank you could cut down on the saltpeter this year? Mah wife's here and she gets awful squirrely on the weekends."

"Send her home, J. W.," Coach said, "and you won't have the problem. Any other questions?"

"How about smoking in public?" Q. B. asked.

"Only if you're on fire," Coach said, and Billy Bob Bunker, almost hidden behind a black cloud from a corona, nodded. "When you put on your new fuchsia blazers and ivory pants, you're not representing yourself, you're representing the Billygoats. Uphold the image."

"What's the fine?" Q. B. asked.

"$200."

When Allen Johnson got up, which he is known to us as Oop because of his big feet, I *knew* there was a full moon. Oop is out of Toad Suck, Arkansas, and he talks like a man who learned English the day before from an Arab. I once asked him, "What language do they speak down there in Toad Suck?"

He said, "Jes' talk woids. Woids, 'at's all."

Oop is asshole buddies with Ray Roy Jenkins, No. 89, the wide receiver, although nobody's ever been able to figure out what they have in common, unless it's that they both come from the United States. Ray Roy is black and speaks perfect English, and Oop is white and talks with a mouthful of harmony grits, when he talks at all, and I have heard J. R. Rodenheimer say that Ray Roy talks like a white man and Oop talks like a nigger, which is the quaint way J. R. has of expressing himself.

Oop's main distinction is he's never passed a single defensive quiz in 3 years, and he's been All-Conference end twice and All-Pro once. When you ask him a question, he frames it in his mind, and then he repeats your last 3 or 4 words, like a minor bird. I'll say, "Oop, what's your responsibility on a 40 dog off a spread?"

"Oaf a spray-ed?" Oop says, while his forehead turns into a map of Colorado.

"Right. Off a spread."

Oop thinks for a couple of minutes, then he'll say, "Oaf a spray-ed?"

"Yeh. A 40 dog off a spread."

"Doag oaf a spray-ed." This can go on for hours, if you're patient. The only time I ever heard him give a direct and simple answer was when a big-time TV interviewer asked him on the air, "Allen Johnson, you have the reputation of not studying your playbook, of not knowing your responsibilities, and yet you're demonstrably a great player. Allen, can you expound on that?"

"*Pound on that,*" Oop said, repeating the last 3 words.

After a long period of dead air, the interviewer said, "How come you play so good?"

"Oh, yeh," Oop said, a light crossing his face. "Well, Ah jes' hit the ones that's dressed diff'urnt."

"And that is the entire sum and substance of your respective philosophy?" the TV man said, throwing his arm around Oop's broad shoulders.

"*Osophy,*" Oop said. "Well, yeh. Ah jes' bang they aceholes."

That was the longest speech any of us ever heard Oop make, and the network wasn't too pleased with it, because they cut away to something else and then put on some kind of apology that made it sound like all jocks were jack-offs and the station couldn't be responsible for what we said.

Anyway, Oop got up on his size 16s at the meeting and asked, "We gone have them quizzes?"

"Certainly," Coach said. "The quizzes are a vital part of our program, Johnson."

"Ain't takin' none."

"You'll take 'em," Coach snapped, "and you'll pass 'em, too."

"*Pass 'em, too,*" Oop echoed. "Crocka shit," and sat down. Coach chose not to take up this challenge, I guess owing to the fact that Oop represented about 78% of our pass rush on the left side. That's the way Coach is. Selectively stern.

"Coach? May I say a word?" It was a high voice way in

the back with the rooks, and we all turned to look, and there was Jay Cox on his feet.

"Siddown!" the late Robert Boggs said. "Rooks got no mouth here."

"Coach," Jay Cox squeaked, "speaking on behalf of the first year men—"

There were murmurs and grumbles from the other rooks. "Speaking on behalf of those of us which has the honor to be here for the first time," Jay Cox went on, "we thank you for the opportunity to play for such a great coach and a great team, and each one of us pledge to give our darndest. Thank you, Coach, for this privilege."

He sat down amid paltry applause from the rooks. Lacklustre Jones, our defensive right end out of Flatonia, Texas, broke off a thunderous rose that rattled the windows. "Hey, Daddy," Robert Boggs called out, "what crawled up your ass and died?"

"Sing those last 4 bars again," Mal said. "You were a little flatulent."

Coach blew his freon can. "Settle down there!" he said. "Lacklustre, try to save your comments for those who appreciate them."

"Who is *they?*" Robert Boggs inquired, but Coach was already informing us that wake-up would be at 6, breakfast at 7, "and on the field at 9, taped and ready. *Taped and ready!*"

Lacklustre squeezed off another American beauty, and we all hurried toward the door. In the vestibule, Malley and I spotted Father Galvin, shaking hands and sucking on one of Mr. Bunker's cigars. In all the years I've known him I've never seen Matthew J. Galvin, O.J., pay for anything which he can get a free sample. He gets meat off Uncle Maxie, the guy that gives the players their 50% meat deal, he bums his pharmaceuticals off "The Connection," which is our nickname for Jimmy Strepey, our trainer, and as far as any of us can tell he never drinks anything but free booze in the press box and Gatorade on the field.

"Well, a good evenin' and a good season to you, Mr. A.B.C. Alphabet Jackson," he said to me, smiling that porcelain grin and blowing smoke like the Lock Ness Monster.

"Evening, father," I said, trying to be polite, although I always find it hard to call another man father, being raised a Methodist and all.

"And who's this little fella with you?" Father Galvin said, pointing at Mal, which he's had a few words with Malley in the past.

"Well, feeth and bejaysus," Mal said, putting on his Barry Fitzgerald face. "If it ain't the wrong reverent Matthew Galvin ministerin' to the rich again."

"God's work must be done, my son," the priest said, smiling.

"Feeth, the Lard loves a winner, don't he now, father?"

"There's nothing unholy about winning, my boy," Father Galvin answered, the smile still on his lips but fading fast around the eyes. "It's not unchristian to win, you know. Winners are Christians, and Christians are winners."

"Yeh," Mal said. "That's what Sid Luckman used to say."

The moon was beginning to climb up behind the grandstands, and you could make out the field through the slats, all blue and gray and crosshatched in shadow. "Hey, look," I said. "A real gridiron."

"Let's go!" Mal hollered, and before I could say a word he was sprinting down the concrete toward the field. I came following after, but more like an over-the-road truck, with my knee still stiff from the operation, and caught up to him around the 50. He was running little curls and hooks, and laughing like a bufflehead duck. "Send for help," I said. "The poor man's cracked under the strain."

Mal came running full speed right at me, jerked his head to the right and his shoulders to the left and ran right through the hole I made when I took the 2d fake. All I could hear was this silly giggle. Then he ran back with that eggbeater leg action of his and said, "Snap the ball!"

I leaned over and pretended to center a ball to him, and he held it out in front of him with his left hand on top of the laces like he was getting ready to arch a punt and then quickly tucked the ball into his armpit and took off—our 97 fake punt, the one that beat Pittsburgh at 3 Rivers 2 seasons ago. He came back breathing like a steam engine.

"You're in great shape," I said. "If you live."

"Don't remind me," he said. "I'm 29, almost 30. Getting up there. But the trouble is, the older I get, the more I love to play. Explain that one."

This was pure Malley Tietjens, if ever I heard it. Sometimes I think it's better to be dumb. He loves football and he hates football, depending on the date of the month and the phrase of the moon. I never could figure him out. Like one night toward the end of last season, we were laying in bed after curfew and doing what he calls "ruminating," just chewing the rag about something that happened in our game at Detroit. The Lions had been back in their defensive huddle and we were in our offensive huddle, and this drunk comes lurching out of the stands and picks up the football and runs, falling all over himself. Buford Bullivant, 250 pounds, our right guard, lays him out with a block you could hear up in the "Z" row, and they have to peel the poor drunk off the field with a blotter and rush him to the hospital in one of those ambulances that Sick Transit Co. keeps under the exit sign. "Why'd you do that?" Malley asked Bullivant after the game.

"He was in my territory," Bullivant said. "Nobody comes into *my* territory."

Later that night laying in bed, Malley couldn't shut up about it. "Pathetic!" he kept saying. "Just pathetic! The man's an animal."

"Yeh," I said. "Well, good night, Rooms."

"Goddamn game combines every negative value that the human race has been trying to breed out for 10,000 years," Mal was saying. "And look who plays it best—the dumbest dummies, the guys that get down on their knees and ask the great spirit to help 'em hurt people. Look at the big heroes—guys who can chugalug the most beer, guys who can screw the most women. It's enough to make you sick. Jesus Christ!"

"You got me mistaken for somebody else," I said. "It's me. *Alph.* Your roommate. Good night, Mal."

"I saw the look on Bullivant's face," Malley went on, just as though I hadn't said a word. "He loved it. So fucking self-righteous. 'Nobody comes into *my* territory.' What bullshit! Sometimes I think this game's for infants. The coaches're all child psychologists, and the show's geared to infantile violence. Songs, patriotism, religion. Reward and punishment. The trappings of war. Game starts with the national anthem and ends with a gun. What can you expect?"

"Good night, Mal," I said sleepily. "Final notice."

"Hitting people before they hit you, and running away so they can't get you back. That's childish! Dodging and twisting so the big boys can't tag you. And the slogans: Fight harder! Kill 'em! Murder 'em! Babies in their cradles. Why, the whole success of a pro football franchise hangs on keeping the players and the fans in diapers."

"And you're out there in your diapers and having a hell of a good time," I said, giving up on sleep for a while.

"Yeh, I'm out there. Yeh. For 42.5 a year. It's a pact with the devil. It's Foust."

"It's what?"

"F-a-u-s-t. That's a work by Gaiety."

"Who?"

"G-o-e-t-h-e." Mal and I are always having these little spelling sessions, mostly when I'm trying to sleep.

"I keep waiting for the game to grow up," he went right on. "I'm getting sick of this kill, kill stuff. I can't accept it. I hear it from the coaches and I hear it from the fans, and I don't want to hear it anymore. Why doesn't somebody get up in the stands and holler, 'Outwit him! Outsmart him!' Fuck this kill, kill shit."

That was last year, and Mal played out the season and had a great day in the playoff game, not only knocking down 5 balls and intercepting 2, but laying a hit on Elgin Thorenson that you could hear a mile and a half away, not a bad shot for somebody that was getting sick of the kill, kill shit, even though we lost the game on a fumble.

Mal and I kept walking back toward the dorm in the moonlight, and I had to admit I wasn't feeling too optimistic myself about the coming season. He asked me if I'd thought of retiring, and I said I wanted to get in my 10th year and pick up that extra pension money to help out with the child support and maybe enable me to marry Dorris Gene in 10 or 20 years, when I had the money. The knee was responding but I could still feel the soreness, and I was having a hell of a time learning the new reflexes you have to develop after a "pes" transplant, which is when they give up on your old ligaments and split one of the tendons attached to the hamstring muscle and attach it to the patellar tendon over the top of the kneecap, and you have to learn how to move all over again. The "pes" transplant used to be rare, but medical science had to perfect it after artificial turf came in and everybody began losing cartilage and ligaments the way most people lose their hair. What a joke on me: I lost both.

"That must've been some operation," Mal said.

"The operation was easier than the post-op," I said. "Mr. Evans went in from the wrong side of the knee, so he had to take out the cartilage on both sides." Mr. Evans is our team physician; he works for nothing for the publicity. His full name is Rollie B. Evans, M.D., but we call him mister so as not to insult all the other doctors in the world. He's the guy that ended Timmy Bird's career by operating on the wrong ankle, and he left Jim Lansing dead on the table. You also may recall the Russ Trombley case, except you may not, too, because the league managed to hush it up, although every player in football knows the details. Russ Trombley was on our special teams, and he ran under a kickoff and got his bell rung. Mr. Evans checked him over and told him he was okay. 5 minutes later Russ said he was getting numb in the chest and hands, and Mr. Evans gave him a neck adjustment and sent him back into the game. The next day the pain was so bad that Russ went to the hospital, and when the X-rays came back, the technician screamed out, "Don't move! You got a broken neck!"

That's the guy that operated on my knee.

"What'd he find when he cut in?" Malley was asking.

"Well, you know those ligaments and cartilages, the ones they call the miserable triad of O'Donohue or something like that? The whole thing was shot, 2 of the ligaments gone completely, rips and tears in the cartilage, and calcium deposits all over the place. When he opened my knee, the medial collateral ligaments rolled up like a windowshade. You could swing my leg from side to side like a door."

"You watched all this?"

"Sure. It's the only right knee I'll ever have."

Mal said a friend at the University of Colorado had a
"pes" transfer, and it took 3 hours to do the operation.
I laughed. "Mine took 5," I said. "Mr. Evans was dying
of a hangover. I think he took a greenie in the middle.
Anyway, his hands were shaking when he closed me up
and put me in a hip-to-toe cast and gave me a shot. When
I woke up, he said, 'Does it hurt?' and I said, 'No,' but an
hour later it felt like the whole squad was running across
my bare leg with track shoes. From then on it was aspirin,
codeine, Empirin No. 3, morphine, Demerol, anything I
could get down. The pain never quit, and it ran from my
big toe to my ass. I didn't sleep for 3 days."

"When did the cast come off?"

"About a week after the operation. The pain was so bad,
they had to cut in and see what's happening. It looked like
somebody'd sewn a softball into my knee. Turned out the
cast was on wrong. He'd hyperextended the leg, and I had
blood poisoning."

"Jesus Christ," Mal said. "That fucking butcher ought to
be banned for life."

"They brought in a consultant, and they talked about
amputation. They stuck a 10-gauge needle into the joint
and drained off 150 ccs of stink, blood and synovial fluid,
and then they put a new cast on, and for the next 2
months the cast had to be cracked off and the knee
drained every 5 or 6 days. Now it's supposed to be ready,
but it still feels stiff and sore."

"No wonder," Malley said. "On top of everything else,
there's bound to be adhesions in there. You'll snap those."

"I hope so. You're supposed to have 130 degrees flexion
in the knee. I got 90. My right leg's an inch shorter than
my left, and I can't even go into a full squat yet, and
already I can feel the old arthuritis coming on."

"Yeh, well, we'll all end up with that."

"But I'm not ready for it. I gotta get another year in, and

I'll have that one little word written after my knee in all the scouting reports."

"What one little word?"

" 'Knee,' " I said.

Back at the dorms, a knot of players were standing in front under the yellow buglight and the bronze plate that said HERBERT J. ZIMMERMAN ATHLETIC DORMI-TORY.

"Rooks," Mal muttered. In camp, nobody trusts rookies. They're either after your job or your buddy's job. Until it's definite that a rook has made the club, you don't even associate with them. They're social leopards, ignored by the regulars except for slave duty and the annual rookie show.

"Okay, rooks," Mal said. "Time for beddy-by."

"Any of you kids play center?" I asked.

A big bugger with about 20 pounds on me held up his hand and said, "Me. I'm Zawatski from Villanova."

"Good luck," I said, lying out loud.

"All right," Mal said. "You rooks stand back and let 2 fine old veterans come through."

"Yes, sir," several rooks called out.

"Remember one thing, Zawatski," Mal said over his shoulder. "When you're snapping tomorrow, don't spread your legs too far. The quarterback's fruit." He waited to let that sink in, and then he said, "But stay loose out there. Don't be nervous. We could use a good snapper—in 8 or 10 years."

The kid put on a sickly smile, and I waggled my thumb in Mal's direction, as if to say don't mind him, he's a little weird, but I wouldn't have objected if Zawatski was shook up a little bit. You need every edge when you're 31 years old and starting out your 10th season and your knee is made of catgut and Nu-skin and transplanted tendons. So I didn't mind when Mal threw in a last resort. "Coach hates Polocks," he said, and we climbed on up to bed.

THE FLIGHT

II

THIS IS A SKYFUCK

COACH HATES POLOCKS. BUT THAT WAS BEFORE THE *fit hit the shan, and right now I'd bet Coach hated blacks more, or one particular black, anyway. But who did Coach have to blame but himself? Who signed the guy after every other team in the league had waived on him? Who wanted the Superbowl so bad he'd make a deal with the devil, sign a known lunatic just on the off chance that he could play himself sane and maybe make us $30,000 apiece while he was at it? Coach is who, and now the whole team was 30,000 feet up in the shit.*

I'd gone out to the freight terminal scrunched into the back of Malley's VW van, which was about the only transportation big enough to accommodate all the crazy things he carried around, from surf boards and fishing tackle to a portable hi-fi rig with its own loudspeakers for jiving at picnics. I made my way up the rear-end steps of our chartered 727, and when I paused half way, I noticed that Hairston was right behind, carrying that big traveling bag of his.

"How they hanging, Luke?" I asked. He looked at me with those moist black eyes and didn't even acknowledge that I'd opened my mouth. That's the way he was. I didn't get mad about it, anymore than you'd get mad at a St. Bernard that didn't want to carry on a conversation. Some organisms are different. Custer Fox, our other starting wide receiver with Malley, was like that. He just plain didn't talk. But at least Custer'd give you a nice broad smile and a pat on the ass once in a while. With Hairston, it was more a case of resigning from the human race. He did everything alone. When there was a break at practice, he'd walk over to the sidelines and stand by himself, and if you came up and stood next to him, he'd walk 10 yards away. The same during games. You learned to let him alone and let him do his thing, which he was beautiful at it, and who could ask for more? We were a professional football club, not the fucking Ladies' Aid.

After the plane took off, the guys jacked around for a while, and then they settled into the typical routine, a few card games, some muffled conversations, Bullivant and J. W. Ramwell reading their Bibles, some of the other guys studying their playbooks or looking at magazines. I noticed Hairston get up and go back to the head several times, and I wondered if maybe he'd been drinking the night before, but then I remembered that he never drank, which was only one of the suspicious things about him, but really none of my business. About the 3d time he came back from the head, I took a good look at him across the aisle from me and he was staring out the window, quiet and withdrawn as usual, and nobody sitting in the other 2 seats in his rack. Sometimes Custer Fox sat with him on flights, if the plane was extracrowded, but we had plenty of room on this 727, so we both had a full rack to ourselves up in the front row of economy, where there's a little more room because there's no seats in front of you and you can stretch out. I needed the room because of my cast, and Hairston needed it because he was 6-foot-10 and he just needed space, that's all. He turned that massive black head of his toward me, slow motion like the Frankenstein monster, and the overhead light bounced off his gleaming bald skull, and he did what he always does— just looked right through me as though I wasn't even there, and then slowly turned away. I might have been imagining things, but I thought I saw a little line of drool going down his chin, but I couldn't be sure, and it wouldn't have meant anything to me if I had been sure. How dumb I was, but then hindsight is always better than 4.

For a while I dozed, and then I looked up and saw the pilot walking down the aisle, followed by the engineer and the co-pilot. It looked like the beginning of the old rookie pilot gag, so I said real loud, "Who's flying the plane?" and turned to see if anybody bit.

Jay Cox and Chet Zawatski turned pale. "Hey," Zawatski said, licking his lips and jerking his head around for a better look, "who's flying the plane?"

The pilot said, "Why, the co-pilot, of course."

"Then who're you?" Cox said to the 3-striper behind the pilot.

"I'm the co-pilot," the co-pilot said, "and this is my friend Mr. Cays, the flight engineer."

Then the 3 of them pretended to be in a state of shock at their terrible mix-up and sprinted back to the cockpit with Cox and Zawatski right behind. I didn't go, because I'd seen the gag 100 times before. They'd fling open the door to the cockpit, and there would be the late Robert Boggs, earphones pulled down over his head, a pilot's hat cocked to one side, pretending to be driving. Robert would say something like, "Good afternoon, mah men, and welcome to the Spook Airlines," and explain that he was a multiengine pilot in his spare time and to remain calm, that he had only crashed 2 jet planes but there was nothing to worry about because Spook Airlines has no-fault insurance.

I dozed for a while and let the scenario play itself out, and then I felt the call of nature, a Joseph E. Levine production in my case, because I had to struggle down the aisle on crutches and leave the bathroom door open so my cast would fit, and, naturally, the second I got comfortable one of the guys sent a stewardess hurtling down the aisle to catch my act, embarrassing me to death and thrilling the stew no end.

I was just finishing when I noticed something in the corner. I stretched over and grabbed the business end of a hypodermic syringe, still wet. For a second, I thought that Mr. Evans or The Connection, our trainer, might have drained somebody's knee, but this needle was too small for that and besides Mr. Evans and The Connection didn't do things like that on flights. The needle made no sense at all, and the only conclusion I could draw was that a certain member of the Billygoats was shooting up. That's all we needed, a 6-foot 10-inch junkie.

I finally reached my row and strapped myself in and peeked across at Luke Hairston. He was staring at the ceiling with thse great big liquid black eyes, and except for the fact that he was slowly tapping his chest with his index finger, he could have been dead. I watched for a few minutes till he took a deep shuddering breath and shook his head violently from side to side.

As casually as I could, I pulled myself up and went through the galley and into first class, looking for "The Connection," our trainer. He was sitting next to the young punk that helps him out, and I gave him a signal to get up and join me. "What's the skinny?" Assistant Coach Ziggy Guminski called out from across the aisle.

"Oh, nothing," I said. "My knee's a little out of joint, that's all."

"I'm hep," Ziggy said. "I'm hep," which, if you're really hep, you don't say hep, you say hip, and Ziggy was about as hip as a 1937 Terraplane, but I had to smile anyway.

"Whatsa matter, kid?" The Connection said.

"Don't make a production out of it," I said, "but I think Hairston's going back to the head and shooting up."

"Shooting up?" The Connection said. "You mean hard stuff?"

"I don't know what he's shooting, but I found a needle back there and he's been up and down the aisle about 4 times already."

"How's he look?"

"Glassy-eyed. Antisocial. Strange."

"Same as usual, huh?"

"Right."

"Maybe I'll talk to him."

I told The Connection to give it 5 minutes, till I could get back to my seat and pretend that I didn't know nuttin' about nuttin', and I settled down and got myself all strapped in again, and The Connection appeared through the curtain and plopped down next to Luke. I watched out of the corner of my eyes.

The first thing I noticed was that Luke didn't even turn his head. "You okay, big fella?" The Connection said.

No comment.

"Hey, man, I just came back to see how you're feeling," The Connection said.

Silence.

"Anything I can do for you?"

The 5th amendment. Jeez, what a peculiar guy!

The Connection reached out and touched Hairston's shoulder, and this time there was an instant reaction. Luke snapped his body around and grabbed The Connec-

tion by the shirtfront and almost lifted him out of the seat. "You go back up front and mind yo' own fuckin' bidness," he said in a slow, slurred voice. "If you come back here, Daddy, I'll punch you out."

The Connection jumped up, gave me a look as though to say, "Well, what can I do with a guy like this?" and scurried back into 1st class.

By this time we were about an hour out, and I was drowsy from my pain-killers, so I just leaned my head back and took a nap. When I woke up, maybe 10, 20 minutes later, the stewardess was wheeling a cart loaded with finger sandwiches, a great big gooey chocolate cake, pastries, fruit, liquers, beer and wine down the aisle. I grabbed a couple apples and 4 B&Bs in case we got stuck in a holding pattern. Hairston just grunted when she asked if he wanted anything, and I noticed his lips were loose and flappy and his lower jaw wobbled as though it was hanging from rubber bands. The stew wheeled the cart to the 2d row and I was tucking my emergency provisions under the rack when I heard the shout:

"All right, you mothajackas, this is a skyfuck!"

That first night of training camp, I didn't get to sleep till around 2 a.m., tossing and turning and thinking about the next day and wondering whether my knee would hold up, and then I had a nightmare about arriving at camp and this big kid Zawatski hollering at me, "Grab my bags, rook, and take 'em up to Room 3," and I said, "That's not your room, that's the late Robert Boggs's," and he grabbed me by the scuff of the neck and spun me around and said, "I'm takin' over here, rook, and you better get your ass in gear!" Naturally the dream woke me up, and I sat on the edge of my bed listening to Mal snore and wiped my eyes and thought how lucky I was to get off to such a wonderful start for my 10th season, with 3 hours sleep and all. Outside the window the birds were chortling, and I figured I'd never be able to get back to sleep with that racket going on, so I went down the hall and performed the 3 S's and got back just in time to hear Assistant Coach Zigmund Guminski blow his whistle and announce, "All right, men, 6 o'clock! Drop your cocks and grab your socks!" Malley said he'd be willing to bet that's the way George Halas used to wake up the Decatur Staleys. Ziggy was a Billygoat player up until 6 years ago, and he still remembered every sharp expression he'd ever heard. Like he'd begin his sentences by saying, "For openers," and he used the word "hopefully" a lot.

"How do you feel about the game, Mr. Guminski?"

"Well, for openers we'll have to contain their rush, hopefully."

"Would you say you're hopeful?"

"Hopefully."

Some of the guys joke about Ziggy's expressions, but I always enjoy them. At least the guy is trying. He has a whole itinerary of favorite remarks: "You better believe it." "No way." "Get it on." "Are you ready for this?" With Ziggy, nobody ever died or passed away; they "bought the farm." Nothing ended bad; it was "all she wrote." He never said a simple yes; he said "you fuckin' A." When Ziggy heard a good expression, he knew what to do with it. Once he asked somebody what time it was, and they said, "6 o'clock straight up," so Ziggy added that to his vocabulary.

"What time is it, Ziggy?"

"Quarter of 4, straight up."

And if you asked Ziggy if it was Monday, he would answer, "All day."

Once Malley asked him what he thought of our new automatic blocking dummy, "Madame Defarge," and

Ziggy said, "It's the greatest thing since sliced bread."

Mal thought for a minute and then he said, "Ziggy, what's so great about sliced bread?"

Ziggy acted annoyed. "Fuck you, Mr. Wise-guy," he said in simple English. That was one of the few times Assistant Coach Guminski failed to come up with a sharp comeback or a colorful expression. You better believe it.

That first morning, a lot of the guys didn't want breakfast—they were too hyped up and excited—but it was a $50 fine if you didn't show, so the whole bunch of Billygoat players, 37 veterans and 41 rooks, sat down to eat the usual soggy oatmeal, over-fried eggs and bacon, canned orange juice, charred white toast, coffee or tea and milk. At first nobody said much, but then Mr. Alvin Frasch, Q. B. in the trade, rapped his glass. "Bein's this is our first day together," Q. B. said, "and some of us don't know all the names, why don't you new fellows kind of stand up and identify yourself?"

Let me say right here that Q. B. was another one of those guys that were not universally loved, and yet most of us would follow him into the lion's cave or even the 49ers. The thing I personally admired about Q. B. was that he really cared about doing his job right. I mean there's too many people that don't give a shit about their work, all they're interested in is the paycheck and the benefits, and getting home as fast as they can after the 4 o'clock whistle. I don't care if you're a bank president or a stevedore or a football snapper, get it right! Give it all you've got! That's how I survived 9 years, and that's how Q. B. survived 11.

Some quarterbacks make a specialty of doing a swan dive after they release the ball, but not Q. B. He wants to see where it went, and he'll stand in the face of a ton of rushing linemen till he's knocked on his ass. And you don't see Q. B. making any of those ballerina sprints toward the sidelines when he's caught with the ball, like some of the pussies that play the game nowadays. He lifts those knobby knees and lowers his head and charges like a full-back, and every once in a while he'll break one for 30, 40 yards and win a game. He told me, "I learned when I was a little kid I wasn't gonna make it unless I kicked ass. Been kicking ass ever since."

Sometimes the ass he kicks belongs to the Billygoats. Once in front of 90,000 people at Bunker Stadium, Buford Bullivant missed a snap count and went offsides on a 3d and 1 play against the Broncos. When Buford moped back to the huddle, Q. B. kicked him as hard as he could. "That's for dumbness, motherfucker!" he hollered.

"Hey, you can't kick me!" Buford said.

"Shut up!" Q. B. said. "Nobody talks in the huddle but me. One more fucking word and I'll kick you again. Right in the nuts. If any."

Bullivant muttered something under his breath, and he hasn't been offsides since. That was 4 years ago.

Q. B. looks a little like Bobby Layne, and plays a little like the old cowpoke, too, all slump-shouldered and bow-legged out there like something that came off the reject pile when they passed out the physiques. He has hair the color of straw, thin lips, little mean green eyes, big red freckles and a strange looking item in the middle of his face that some people call a nose and some people aren't sure, which it's been broken so many times that Q. B. himself has lost count. You could look at that face all day and never see a hint of what passes for character—the long thin noble face, the wide eyes, the high cheekbones. Everything about him looked devious, the way his eyes were always jacking around, counting the house, follow-ing the action. Malley said that Q. B. looked like a preacher in a whorehouse, checking for the nearest exit and listening for sirens. No, he didn't look like he had much character, but he wasn't a scoutmaster, he was a professional quarterback and he did his job. He hated to make a mistake, and he had a simple technique for handling the few mistakes he did make: He just never admitted them. His own errors were unacceptable to him, so he'd put the blame on somebody else, or claim it never happened. It was a small defect in a pro quarterback, and nobody's perfect.

One by one the rookies got up and recited their names, and Zawatski looked bigger than ever when he rose and said, "Zawatski, Chester J., Villanova." But the big attraction of the morning was the legendary 2d-string Jay Cox of Michigan State. "Jay Cox of Michigan State," he said, smiling and bowing left and right, as though everybody was cheering, which we weren't. "You can win with me."

"We can win without you, too, mothafucka," the late Robert Boggs called out.

"What was that?" Coach asked, but Robert buried his nose in his 3d cup of nourishing black coffee. The way Coach reacted, it looked as though Jay Cox was going to be his pet project this summer, which Coach always has one pet out of all the rooks.

After chow, the locker room looked like the beach at Waikiki to me. Thomas W. Dunlap, our equipment man, kept the place as clean as a hospital. The lockers were separated by chicken wire, and along the top our helmets all faced the same direction. Thomas W. Dunlap would go berserk if a helmet was an inch out of line, and last year he almost had a nervous breakdown when he found that one had been replaced by a gorilla head. Inside the lockers, on this first day of camp, our fuchsia jerseys were on a shelf in back, on top of our stockings. The sanitary items —jock, sox and t-shirt—were alongside, folded into a neat rectangle. We liked to get in there and mix them around and annoy Thomas W. Dunlap.

I slipped over to the training room and hustled right out again when The Connection saw me and hollered, "God-damn it, Jackson, can't you read?" He pointed to a Dayglo sign: REQUIRED TRAINING ROOM DRESS: CLEAN JOCK AND T-SHIRT. THIS MEANS YOU. I went back to my stall and bumped into Mal, standing in front of his locker doing toe-ups, just as if we wouldn't have to do about 600 more out on the field. "How's your hammer hanging, Rooms?" he said, and gave my jock a tweak.

"Jeez," I said. "You're feeling silly today."

"Yeh," he said, "I'm wearing my jocular strap."

3 guys were ahead of me to be taped, so I wandered around the training room enjoying the sights and smells. It was really 3 large alcoves: 1 strictly for taping, with a slanted table built out of the wall where 4 players could lie back while The Connection slapped on the tape, an-other room loaded with ultrasonic and diathermy and whirlpools, and one way in the rear with a sauna and a Universal Gym and weight machines and other torture devices. Till my knee came around, I'd be spending 2 hours a day, maybe 3, back in there. I was supposed to do leg-extension exercises to build up my quadriceps, flex exercises for my hamstring, and about 6 other maneuvers for the knee, including a couple of ballbreakers with the weight boot raising 60 pounds of lead up and down 90 times, and after that 30 minutes in the whirlpool, while all the idiots walked by saying, "You can't make the club in the tub," and Coach complaining, "*Yah yah yah,* Jackson, you're not hurt. You're a mama's boy, Jackson. Get out there on the field and play your way out of it like the rest of the guys." Sure, Coach, I'm not hurt. It's all psychose-mantic. Those 3 rows of embroidery across my knee are beauty marks.

The Connection finished taping me into an X support and a Y strap, good and firm, and barked at me, "Now

don't go messin' with that wrap!" and I walked back into
the locker room, but it was still only 8:30, so I decided to
say a word to the equipment man to get off to a good start.
"Morning, Thomas W. Dunlap," I said. "How's the season
look to you so far?"

Thomas W. Dunlap never stood in one place more than
a 5th of a second. He has to keep in constant motion,
folding towels, rearranging his stocks, taking chewing
gum out of the packages and putting them in the open
box, always flying around like a scalded cat, which is not
entirely his fault because the front office gives him so
many things to do that he could use 3 assistants, but instead he's only got a teen-age kid with acne all over his
face from jacking off. Right now Thomas W. Dunlap was
checking supplies: bottles of Tuf-skin and Nu-skin, cans of
Gym-Fresh'ner, glycerine, disinfectants, ant and roach
killer, 2 different colors of Vaseline to fool the officials, all
the little household items a pro team uses. I grabbed a jar
of Hold-Tite and read the label: "Cuts down fumbling. A
nonslip paste used by ballhandlers on tips of fingers and
thumbs to prevent fumbling, thus bolstering team's confi-
dence and morale. Increase accuracy of ballhandling in
fair or foul weather."

"Hey, Thomas W.," I said. "They oughta give this to the
wives."

"Put that down, for Chrissakes!" Thomas W. Dunlap
exploded. "Can't you see I got everything arranged?"

I put the Hold-tite back where it belonged, and Thomas
W. Dunlap turned it around so the label faced front. Mal's
theory was early toilet training.

The only thing that was different about the locker-room
layout this year was certain changes Coach made in the
johns, so that you sat right out in the open for all your
teammates to observe. Not that our crappers had ever
been completely private, like with normal people. There

never were any doors on the front, and this used to drive certain parties nuts, especially Buzz Urquhart and John Lovesey. Buzz said he'd turn to stone before he'd ever take a dump in public, and Lovesey used to go in and build a little screen out of the Sunday papers, and the other guys would sneak up on their bellies and set the papers on fire and poor Limey'd be sitting there behind a wall of flame wiping himself about 800 strokes a minute.

In case you're thinking that this lack of privacy represents the height of vulgarity, let me be quick to explain that there is method in the madness, as Malley once explained to me. "Didn't you ever wonder why there's not a single private toilet in a single shower room in the whole fucking NFL?" he said.

"No," I said. "I hadn't given it a lot of thought."

"Well, there's a reason. It's elementary sociology, or the coaches think it is. The team that dumps together wins together. There's supposed to be something fraternal about sitting side by side moving your bowels. It's a military concept, and since football's paramilitary, we follow the same principle."

That was last year when the toilets were separated by partitions. This year, under the reign of the late Gen. George S. Patton, Coach went all out and tore down the partitions, and now Limey had to buy 3 Sunday papers to build his little fortress. The high cost of living.

I walked into the toilet area and it was old-home week. Lacklustre Jones was perched on Bowl No. 3, his personal office, and already putting the needle to poor Buzz Urquhart. Lacklustre is 6-foot-6, 270 pounds, No. 69 in your program, and when he squats on the toilet, it looks like a Hampshire hog sitting on a toadstool, except that a Hampshire hog has better manners. Lacklustre has pop-eyes like a mink and the same sex habits. He always makes it a point to have his ashes hauled before every game, contrary to the rules. He explains, "I wouldn't want to go into a game with all them squiggly things bouncin' around in my nuts, would you?" His real name is James Robinson Jones, but he hasn't been called anything but "Lacklustre" or "Lack" since his sophomore year at Texas. He'd been dogging it at practice and one of the coaching assistants said, "Boy, that sure is a lacklustre lineman." When Lack heard the news, he quit screwing for 3 days and sent 2 guys on the offense to the infirmary for repairs.

Personally, I like old Lack, but he's the vulgarest player on our squad, an all-pro rosedropper and slob, and when he heads for the head, people take to the hills. Especially Buzz Urquhart, which Buzzie can't stand filth and ranky odors. Buzz has a thing on the subject and the whole team knows it, and we usually manage to drop our roses in the vicinity of Buzz's locker, so he won't be wasting that Airwick that he keeps open all season. He also keeps a spray can of Lysol and every once in a while he'll run into the toilet holding his nose, fill the place with spray and then run out still holding his nose. This is his editorial comment on Lacklustre Jones, and Lack then responds, "One of these days I'm gonna stick that thang up your ass."

"Disgusting!" Buzz will say. "Just disgusting! I don't know how you can stand yourself." Buzz is the kind of guy who goes around with a toothbrush sticking out of his shirt pocket, and on the slightest provocation he'll shove it in his mouth and start grinding away. His father calls him Bozzie, through clenched teeth, and the whole family's in stocks and bonds. One day Lacklustre asked him, "What're you gonna do when you quit football?"

"I suppose I'll go on the street," Buzz said.

"Yeh," Lack said. "Just like your sister."

Nobody fools with old Buzz on the field, though. His first year in the league, which was my 4th full season, some big horse on the Cardinals busted through the 6 hole clean and, instead of taking him head on, Buzz turned a little sideways and the horse broke right into the end zone. Buzz was benched for 3 games and everybody on the team rode him unmercilessly. They'd say, "Hey, it's Manolete!" or they'd sing "The Toreador Song," or they'd holler, *"Ole, baby!"* They called him Pussy, which is the worst thing you can call a pro football player because it means he can be intimidated.

The way Buzz got over the shame was to transform himself into the hardest hitter in the league, including in practice. He didn't care who it was—Wing Choy or Bad-ass Harris or Robert Boggs or who—Buzzie would try to break him in half at the kneecaps. He only weighs 170, 5-foot-11 tall, but he can run and he can hit. He is probably the 2d best defensive back in football, after Dreamer Tatum of the Jets.

Buzz rooms with Hyphen B-l-a-c-k, our left cornerback, which is another odd combination because Hyphen comes from a tough section of Compton, California, and Buzzie comes from Scarsdale, N.Y., and Coral Grables, Fla. Hyphen went to Weber State and Buzzie went to Columbia, and of course they are of different complexions to boot. You wouldn't think they'd have much to talk about, except football, which they manage to talk day and night, night and day, how to cover this receiver and read that receiver, how to key the pulling guard, how to roll up in a zone without tipping it, constantly, forever.

Hyphen got his name on the advice of me and Mal. He told us one day that it was tough getting noticed in the NFL. "Who can remember a spook named John Black?" he said.

At that time, some of the brothers were taking Moslem names, hard to remember but very distinctive, so Mal came up with the idea that John should rename himself "Ali Baba au Rhum."

"Hmmmm," Black said. *"Ali Baby au Rhum.* Got a nice ring to it. But I don't want nobody to think I'm one of them black Muslim crazies."

"How about doing what that guy at Washington did?" I suggested. "Stick a hyphen in your name. That'll make it stand out."

"Where the fuck you gone stick a hyphen in John Black?" John Black asked.

"Everywhere!" I said. And that's how it happened. He legally changed his name, and the sportswriters hung the nickname "Hyphen" on him, and now the whole world knows who Hyphen B-l-a-c-k is, especially on the field, where he is a star. A cornerback's job is to chase people, and Hyphen can chase them frontways, sideways and backways, all at the same speed. It's a sight to see him stick with a receiver, reflecting everything the receiver does, and getting his index finger into the action at the last minute, either in the other guy's eye or into the flight of the ball, and sometimes picking off the throw himself. When a defensive back makes an interception, he's supposed to holler "Gate!" to tell the downed linemen to get off their asses and start blocking the other way, but Hyphen has a tendency to holler "I got the mothafucka!" Then when he's running down the field, he gets paranoid about being tackled, and he'll usually pick up 10, 20 extra yards out of sheer terror. Between him and Buzz Urquhart, the opponents have to respect our corners, and our 2 safetymen, Malley and Leroy Harmony, are no campfire girls themselves.

"Hey, Rooms," Mal said when I walked past his locker. "I changed the slogan for Lacklustre."

I looked up at the fading old sign that said, WHAT YOU SEE HERE, WHAT YOU HEAR HERE, LET IT STAY HERE, WHEN YOU LEAVE HERE. Malley had crossed out "hear" and inserted "smell."

It was mid-July and by the time we hit the field at 9, the big Pepsi thermometer above the stands said 81, but we were comfortable in our fuchsia jerseys and ivory shorts. For 2 weeks the schedule would be the same: breakfast at 7, workout at 9, lunch at 12:30, afternoon drill at 3:30, supper at 6:15, meetings from 8 till 9:30, and curfew at 11. When 2-a-days were over we'd have it a little easier, but then the coaches would begin to stretch out the meetings, and practice might go on for 3, 4 hours, and on top of all that I had a minimum of 2 hours a day therapy for my knee. Or 3, or 6, or 8, it didn't matter. I'd have sneaked over to the training room at midnight and worked out if I thought it would help. There were 2 things I needed: 10 years for my full pension, and a Superbowl ring for my pride, which had been close but no cigar for straight seasons.

Out on the field, Coach gave a short talk about every journey starting with a single walk, and then we went right into 20 minutes of calisthenics under the direction of Warren Edquist, Mr. Adonis himself, our offensive coordinator and in certain ways the laughing stop of the team. Edquist will say things like, "All right, men, pair off in 3s!" Or he'll tell us to bend our knees and raise our arms "simon-taneously." Mal says Edquist's 2 favorite tenses are the prepositional tense, like "we would of won if they hadn't of blocked that kick," and the suppository tense, like "suppose it's 3d and 2, and they're in a double-double." The day Coach named Edquist offensive coordinator, the joke went around the league: "Well, he's not very well coordinated, but he's sure offensive enough." He'd been in the navy, and some of the guys called him our postnaval drip. Myself, I never had a bit of trouble with him.

The knee felt pretty good through the stretching exercises, but when we began the bends I could feel some tightening and stirring against the wrap. Nothing serious, but it still didn't feel supple and flexible, the way a snapper's knee has to feel. I kept waiting for it to rip apart, which is the constant fear you have after 3 or 4 injuries like mine. The knee may never give out again but you're convinced it'll happen any second. You have to be careful not to flinch or cover up because you can't play professional football that way. Every year the guys that try to protect their knees get a call from the Coach: "Come over to my office, and bring your playbook," or else they get racked up and measured for crutches.

There's no way to protect your knees and your ankles on artificial turf, which we have both at camp and back at Bunker Stadium. It looks so soft and green from up in the stands, but it's really just a thin rug over a skinny sheet of sponge rubber, with asphalt underneath. When you fall, it gives like an anvil. You plant your foot and your foot stops on a dime. The shock goes up to your knee, which is the weakest part of your leg and was never intended to bend any way but front and back, and the next thing you feel is *R-r-r-rp* and they turn on the air conditioning in the operating room.

The owners solve all kinds of practical problems with artificial turf, and they can always replace players. Every year they draft 500 new ones, and every year 30 or 40 retire on account of their hurts, and there's many a man in the league that'll have arthuritis and maybe walk with a cane when he's 60. Well, that's the life we chose when we signed up, and we get paid well for it. Like Billy Bob Bunker said, "Nobody pole-axed you boys to come here. You came frothing at the mouth to get a job. Don't complain about the price." Or like Harry F. Truman once said, "If you can't stand the heat, get out of the whirlpool." Besides, playing pro ball beats any other job.

After calisthenics, we split into teams and went through

light workouts, which The Adonis calls "light works-out," improving his grammar, and we finished off with a couple of wind sprints, 40 yards each, and went back in. We barely broke a sweat. That afternoon we had our first practice in full uniforms, and Coach said we were uniformly lousy. At the evening meeting, we ran into a new wrinkle: I.Q. tests. There was some bowl-legged psychologist there and she handed out papers, and for 2 hours we stabbed at multiple-choice problems, and all you could hear was Oop Johnson moaning and saying, "Fuck thee-is, fuck thee-is," over and over. When the tests were graded, 4 rooks were cut. "How'd Oop do?" I asked the offensive coordinator.

"He passed before he sat down," Edquist said, laughing.

"How about the rest of us?" I asked.

"I'm not suppose to tell," Edquist said, "but you got nothin' to worry about. The way I heard it, half the club scored high, half scored average, and half were below par."

"That's 3 halves," I said.

"Yeh, right," The Adonis said. "Well, they score them things different, ya know?"

The early thrill of the training camp was Jay Cox, the dough-faced kid from Michigan State. Everybody loved him except the players and the assistants. The 1st time we scrimmaged, Coach had Wing Choy run the 20 series, which calls for the 3 back (Cox subbing for Rolf Dale on the injured list) to throw a few blocks. Cox blocked half-heartedly, and then he held up his hand and said, "Coach, don't waste me. Gimme the ball. I'm a running back."

Anybody else, Coach would have kicked him in the ass, but instead he called for the 30 series, which is the 3 back running the ball and the 2 back faking or blocking, and Cox ran hard, and Coach hollered, "Looking good in there. *Looking good!*" I told you he was playing a favorite.

The other rooks hated Cox's ass. They circulated all kinds of stories about him at Michigan State, how his uncle had been the A.D.'s roommate, how he'd sucked his way onto the team, how he kissed the coach's ass and sent flowers to the athletic office. He drove around the campus in a black Cadillac Eldorado convert with the license plate COX 28, and he was always making speeches about the Spartans and their great traditions and how college football builds character, which college football builds character like the atom bomb builds cities. They say the night of the draft he invited a group of students over to his apartment and bought domestic champagne and had streamers painted saying, "Good luck, Jay!" Then he wasn't drafted. A couple days later he made a speech telling the students not to worry, that he'd made a deal to go into the NFL and they could still see him just by driving 100 miles or so whenever his team played in Chicago or Detroit or Cleveland, as though the poor kids should buck up because old Jay, the 2d-string fullback behind Willie Pellington, wasn't leaving them forever. They say there wasn't a wet eye in the house.

The odd thing was, Jay Cox could *go*. You wouldn't think it, to look at him. What a piece of work! He had sallow skin and kind of eggyolk yellow hair that dropped around his head as though it was glued on in patches, and his chin sloped away till it just disappeared, and his shoulders were angled down about 60 degrees, and he had banty legs. He was only about 5-foot-11, 210 pounds, but he could run through a linebacker's ass and out the other side. He had a way of sniffing the daylight, like he would hit the 2 hole and it'd be closed tight, and all of a sudden he'd pop up in the 4 hole without even making a big move, just zip-zip with his hips and a slight change of angle and off he'd go like a wet bar of soap into the secondary. From about the 3d scrimmage, it was obvious that good old Rolf Dale was out of a job, although he would always be welcome as a 2d-string back.

Me, I couldn't get all upset about Rolf Dale's problems. I had too many of my own. Coach very seldom worked me with the 1st-string line for the rest of July and early August. He said, "Alphabet, you're too important to this club to push that knee too fast." He had me snapping on the special teams. "Your turn'll come," he said with his forked tongue. In the meantime, we used Zawatski, which meant that 2 rooks were working with the 1st-string offense, Zawatski and Cox. And that's usually 1 rook too many for a serious contender.

Day by day the cutting went on, a hard time for everybody. There were foul remarks in the dorm every evening when the notices went up. Being cut is what Malley calls "a self-fulfilling judgment." As soon as a team says you're not good enough, why, you're not good enough. Maybe you can catch on with another club, but probably not. They've all heard the news, and if you're not good enough for the Goats, you're not good enough for anybody else. From then on, you're tainted meat.

Cutting is always toughest on the brothers. Some bank their whole futures on making it in the pros, and they have no cushion to fall back on. While the white college kids are studying math, the blacks are learning how to cut-block and crab-block and read a sweep off the pulling guard. That's why so many black kids make it into the pros, and that's why they have no place else to turn, no skills in reserve. It's all or nothing: fame and big money in the pros, or slopping the hogs back home. When a player gets cut, the expression is "they gave him a road map and a hamburger," meaning a map to the other training camps and a final meal. Some of the guys can't handle it emotionally. We had a linebacker that trashed his whole room the night he was cut, picked up the furniture and threw it out the 3d-floor window, bed, shiffer robe, every-thing, left it all laying in the quadrangle like a broken box of toothpicks. His last words were "Ain't no mothafuckin' mothafucker gonna mothafuck me!" But some mother-fucker had.

I don't know, there's something about Malley and me that attracts rooks to us and it can get to be an aggrava-tion, though you don't want to complain and hurt their tender feelings. I can understand the way they hero-worship Mal, with his record and all, but I can't under-stand why they flock around me, which after all I'm just a journeyman snapper, nothing special but certainly competent, at least before the knee. Some of these young rooks, I don't even understand their language any more. Every 3 words are "ya know?" Like they'll say, "I played right guard ya know for Illinois ya know against ya know Iowa ya know and it was a hot day ya know and we ya know beat em ya know 64 ya know to 7." They all smoke grass, and they think that music began with the Rolling Stones, and they can't even take a dump without having the radio on full blast. I crashed into one of these rooks' rooms one night and snapped his radio off, and he looked up at me like I'm some kind of a fanatic and he says, "Hey, man, don't *do* that, man! Like ya know I need the radio on. I'm ya know studyin' my playbook."

But I have to sympathize with the rooks, too. That's a pretty rough way to go, breaking into the lineup against 40 guys that have fought and bled together for years, guys that you know each other's wives and kids and girlfriends, and here comes this fresh-faced punk trying to put you on the welfare. I never take part in rookie hazing because I always feel too sorry for them. The veterans make them sing their alma maters at lunch, or stand on a chair and lecture about "Why I Am a Great Pass Receiver," or "How I Masturbated in Church." Some of the veterans can get downright nasty. Like one day I heard Bad-ass Harris complain, "Jesus Fuckin' Christ," and one of the black rooks said, "Now hold it right there, 77. You takin' the Lord's name in vain."

"What should I say when you fuck up my block, Chump?" Bad-ass said. "Holy Mothafucka?"

"No, that's an insult to my mother."

The late Robert Boggs interrupted. "Bad-ass, you can't say cocksucker either, 'cause that'd still be insultin' his mama."

Everybody hooted and howled, but the rook just turned away and sulked, and he kept on sulking till he got cut, which was about 2 days later. I heard he went to Canada. Well, that's what rookies are—raw material, a labor pool, and when they get cut, nobody holds funeral services. We'd end up keeping 2 or 3 on the squad, and we'd taxi maybe 4 or 5 of the rest, and the others would go back to the Continental League or try the WHL or head north or just pack it in altogether, which isn't as easy as it sounds, since most of them have built their lives around football for 8, 10 years.

After a couple weeks, Buford Bullivant circulated a false rumor that we were invited to the grain store on Hiram Road to pick up our free geese, and the other veterans kept talking it up, how big and fat and delicious the geese were, and how we'd all pick them up Friday after practice, and sure enough, 2 rooks went on down and demanded their free geese, and the store manager threw them out, and the rooks broke the front window and the cops escorted them back to camp. "What seems to be the trouble, officers?" Buford said.

"These 2 guys was screaming about geese."

"Right!" one of the rooks said excitedly. "The free geese ya know that the manager ya know gives the rest of you dudes ya know every ya know year?"

"Officer," Bullivant said, "I don't know what these young men are talking about. They certainly don't belong here."

The next morning at breakfast, another rook called down the table, "Pass the milk, will you please?" just as Bullivant happened to be walking by with a pitcher, and Bull said, "You want some milk? Hold out your glass," and poured the whole pitcher on the kid's arm. The rook jumped up like he was ready to fight, but Bullivant is 6 foot 2250 pounds without his Bible, and one of the other rooks grabbed the kid and said, "Hey, lighten up, man!" and Bullivant went back with the regulars. Me, I never could dig that kind of behavior. Here's these rooks all alone in a strange land, and I can't see the point in making things worse for them. A little kidding, yes. I can accept that. Like one of the rooks asked Ray Roy Jenkins one day, "What do you do with them Texas oil wells when they're used up?"

"Oh," Ray Roy said, "we just pull 'em back outa the ground and cut 'em up for fence holes."

Or when Lacklustre Jones peed on a rook's feet in the shower. The kid jumped back and said, "Hey, don't do that in here!"

Lack said, "Okay, get dressed and I'll do it outside," and everybody snickered, and the rook just looked embarrassed. Then when the kid leaned over to pick up the soap, Lacklustre snuggled up behind him and pretended to commit an unnatural act, and the kid jumped about 4 feet. "Hey, holt still there, honey!" Lack hollered. "Ain't you never been taken aback?" The guys all giggled their fool heads off, and the rook grabbed his towel and tore out of there fast. I guess he's still not sure about Lacklustre, and come to think of it, who is? But I don't think old Lack would attack anything except men, women and sheep. He has his principals.

THE FLIGHT

III

10 ROUNDS A SECOND

IF YOU TOLD ME BACK THEN THAT WE'D ALL WIND UP *sealed in a tube 32,000 feet in the air and taking orders from a prime candidate for a frontal lobotomy, I'd have said you were a candidate yourself. But then there was nothing about this season that was normal or ordinary, as it turned out. After I heard the scream that this was a "skyfuck," I turned and saw Luke Hairston standing there with his shaved black head pressed back against the ceiling and his arms cradling a funny-looking gun. Q. B. laughed and said, "Hey, you fuckin' idiot, put that thing down before you hurt somebody!"*

"Who you callin' idiot?" Hairston shouted, the veins standing out on his gleaming forehead. "You don't know me that well."

"Well, I know you that well," the late Robert Boggs interrupted, "and I'm tellin' you to lighten up, you big jive turkey!"

Several of the players started up the aisle, but their path was blocked by the cart and the stewardess standing there

65

with her eyes wide open and her white glove over her mouth, watching that gun like a snake watching a cobra.

"You guys that's readin'," Hairston shouted, "throw them books up here!" Some paperback pornies and a Jackie Susann flew through the air, and Hairston propped them against the back of the seat and squeezed off a round that almost fractured my eardrums. "That's single fire," he said, and fiddled with the gun again. "Now it's on rapid fire," he said. "10 rounds a second." I held my breath, but he didn't demonstrate. The smell of powder was already curling around the cabin, and Coach's head appeared at the curtain.

"Get yo' ass back up front, General!" Hairston said. "The next head I see, I shoot it off." Coach blinked and disappeared. Hairston said, "This here's a Schmeisser machine pistol. Any questions?"

I looked around. Nobody had a question. J. R. sat in the 1st seat behind Luke, and he was still shaking. I guess he figured God was getting even with him for all those clever remarks about jee-grows and jigaboos and the poor, dumb dinges.

"Hey, Luke," I said, "come on, now, man. Put that thing down."

"Shut up!" Hairston said, waving the snout of the weapon across the aisle toward me. "You nothin' special, man!" He looked down at my cast and seemed to be pondering something. "Stand up!" he said to me. I unbuckled and pulled myself to my feet. "You gone be the messenger boy," he said. "Now go tell the pilot the K.A.H. is takin' over."

"Sure, Luke, sure. What's the K.A.H.?"

He laughed that girlish high cackle again. "That's the 'Kill All Honkies,' " he said. While he was talking, I got a close look at his face, and his eyes weren't focusing right, he seemed to be looking at something just above and beyond me as he talked, and the muzzle of the gun kept wobbling as if it was alive. But that firing demonstration scared me. Maybe he was just jacking around, but that kind of jacking around can be deadly.

I went up front and gave the pilot the news, and he went ape. I thought those guys were picked for their cool, but when I told him we had a psycho waving a submachine gun at us, he spluttered, "For God's sake, keep the man calm! Go back and coddle him along. Don't let him fire that gun, no matter what you have to do to stop him. I'll try to lose some altitude. Oh, my God, my God stop . . ."

"Hey, man!" I said. "Stay cool! He's just a harmless junkie, he won't do anything. I sincerely hope."

"If he fires that submachine gun," the pilot said in a voice that sounded like he was about to break into hysterics, "the whole goddamn plane could split open. There's tons of air pressure inside here. Tons! Put a little crack in our skin and that air'd rush out like a goddamn Niagara Falls and we'd all go with it."

"Jesus Christ," I said. "What can we do?"

"Whatever you do, keep him calm, keep him quiet. Kiss his ass, anything. Does he like to shoot guns?"

"Loves it. Shoots 'em all the time."

"Oh, my God! Go back and humor him. Tell him he's the boss, we'll take him wherever he wants to go. I'll try to lose some altitude to equalize. If I can get us down below 10,000 feet it won't make much difference if he shoots a hole in the side."

"Yeh," I said. "Then all we'll have to worry about is if he shoots a hole in us."

On the way back, I stopped off in 1st class and broke the wonderful news. Coach raged. He stomped up and down and said that for 2 cents he'd go back and hand-wrestle the fucking gun away. Billy Bob Bunker waved *his arms and griped about the money he'd lose and all the people that'd bought tickets to the game and how he'd worked and sweated for 13 years to create a successful franchise, and now one crazy spook was jeopardizing the whole operation. "Why, if this plane goes down I lose $10,000,000 worth of players!" Mr. Bunker fumed. That's why he's a success, I guess. Skyjacked, he's still counting nickels. The Rev. Matthew Galvin steadied his arm and said something about Hail Mary and another lady named Grace, and drained a whole bottle of Scotch, airline size.*

I hobbled through the galley door and into the economy section, and Luke was kneeling in his rack, facing the rear, with the gun pointed halfway up to the ceiling. "Luke," I said, sounding calmer than I felt, "the pilot says you're the boss. If you want to fly to Cuba, we'll fly to Cuba. Or Mexico. Jamaica. Whatever you want. Only don't *play around with that trigger."*

As usual, he didn't answer.

After a while, I began to hear a little chatter from the rear. "Come on, Luke, we always been tight," Bad-ass said, and Robert Boggs put in, "Lighten up, Lucius, lighten up. We yo' brothers." J. R. crunched down in his seat and whimpered.

Instead of responding, Hairston cradled the Schmeisser in his left arm and reached into his traveling bag. He pulled out a hypodermic and a vial of some clear liquid and pumped it in his gun arm. "Come on and rush me," he kept muttering in a low voice. "Come on, come on!" *Nobody made a move. The gun was too close.*

After a few minutes he shook himself like a Labrador just coming out of the water with a duck in its mouth, and he hollered, "All right, you jive mothafuckas, clear these 1st 5 rows! Move on back! *That's it. Hustle yo' ass! Jackson, shove 'em on back there!" He didn't seem to feel threatened by me. I guess he figured he could handle a snapper, especially one with an anchor on his leg. After everybody moved, the plane was arranged like this:*

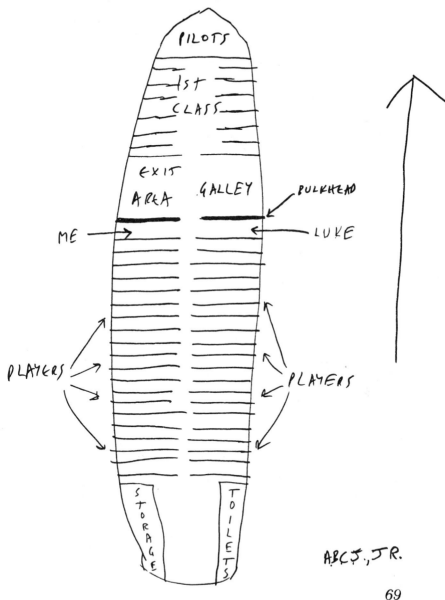

ABCJ., JR.

I looked out the window and saw that we'd lost some altitude, and then I felt the telltale popping in the ears that means you're headed down.

Hairston said, "Jackson? Get yo' ass up front! Tell the driver to climb back to where he was at and stop jivin' around. Got it?"

I said I had it.

"Tell him the next time he try to land I'll stick this gun up his ass."

"I don't think he was trying—"

"Do what you told!" He waved the snout of the gun at me and I pulled myself together and headed forward again. The pilot asked me what the skyjacker wanted, and I told him I wished to Christ I knew. When I walked back through 1st class, the Rev. Matthew Galvin was surrounded by people trying to give first aid. "What happened?" I asked.

"He thought he could talk sense into that crazy asshole," Coach said. "All he got was a gunbutt across the scalp. Vicious fucker!"

"Father," I said, leaning over the seat, "are you okay?"

He looked at me through glazy eyes, and I could see a bump already rising through his thin, wispy hairs. Hairston must have dinged him pretty good. "Hang in there, father," I said, and the priest managed a weak grin, and I kind of admired him for his guts.

I limped back to economy just as Hairston was sticking his shaved black head in the opening between the sections. "I tol' yeh!" he hollered into 1st class. "Nobody comes back here! You assholes stay in yo' place. In the front of the bus!" Something made him laugh and bend over practically double at his own cleverness. I personally didn't see anything too hilarious about clubbing an old man, but you never know what'll set off any given person. Humor is a funny thing.

In training camp, Coach sets arbitrary weights, just pulls them out of his hat, and from then on we have to measure up or pay $10 a pound. When the new charts went up, Mal took one look and said that Coach must think we're the Jeffrey Ballet or something. He had Oop Johnson down for 235, which Oop never weighed below 240 in his life and usually comes to camp around 250 or 260. Oop went to The Connection for help and was told to eat more cottage cheese, and at the next weigh-in he was fatter than ever. "Ah dunno," he complained. "Ah musta eat 6 gallons of that shit."

Malley's mother always sent us carloads of brownies and fudge cookies, which Malley liked to brag are "relatively good," but this year we just handed them out to the kids that hung around. Coach seemed intense on turning us all into wood sprites. It was pathetic to watch guys like Dooley Bethea. Dooley'd been a Goat for 5 seasons, and every year he'd come in around 315 pounds, and every year Coach would list him at 285 and somehow Dooley would make the weight, which always amazed me because Dooley is the kind of guy that can polish off 4 giant pizzas and a gallon of beer and an hour later sit down to our regular meal. But this year Dooley reported at 325, and Coach ordered him to slim to 275, and from the beginning it was plain that Dooley would never make the weight, even if he could afford the fines every Saturday morning at weigh-in. Not that he didn't try. He skipped 2 meals a day. He ran extra laps before and after practice. He did wind sprints till you thought his heart would burst through his fuchsia jersey. He even tried to keep up with the backs and the ends at grass drills, which are the deadliest form of exercise. For grass drills, The Adonis makes us run in place, knees as high as we can lift them, 20 or 30 seconds at a time, top speed, and then he'll holler, "Down!" and we have to throw ourselves forward on our faces, and then when he says "Up" again, we jump up and start churning our legs till he says quit, which might not be for 2 or 3 minutes. Dooley would try, but he just wasn't built for grass drills. One hot day he went down and stayed down. His eyes rolled back in his head, and his tongue stuck straight out, and he was shuddering instead of breathing. The sight scared me half to death, but Coach came driving over and screamed, "Don't touch him. *Don't touch him!* He's not a Billygoat! Leave him lay!" That night Dooley was optioned out. He went straight to the chow hall and got a gallon of vanilla ice cream and a quart of chocolate syrup and mixed it all together and began slurping it down, sitting there in the shadows with the tears rolling down his cheeks and myself and the late Robert Boggs trying to console him and Dooley just shoveling it all in and sniffling. Then he climbed into his Mark V and drove away for the last time. Some of us got together and broke his dinner plate in a little ceremony. Good luck to you, Dooley, wherever you are. I imagine you must go about 415 by now.

We also had the usual players that dominoed in the middle of the night. Either they knew they were blowing it or they couldn't stand the pace, and they'd just split. After our 1st nutcracker drill, we had about 4 dominoes. Another kid quit when we made Madame Defarge too tough for him. Poor guy, he didn't stop to find out it was a joke. Madame Defarge is a new type blocking dummy that hits back. It's spring-loaded, set up on two big steel runners, and you can adjust it for any force from 50 pounds on up. You bang into Madame Defarge, and she gives a foot or 2, and then she slams right back at you and you have to hold her off or get knocked on your ass. The 1st day we used her, Ziggy sent 6 straight crackerass rookies into her, and they hit pretty good, but just before the 7th rook came sprinting down the sawdust, Bullivant tightened the springs to 300 pounds, and that rook hit Madame Defarge and bounced 5 yards through the air and skidded another 5 yards on his nose and kept right on out the gate.

Coach used to enjoy watching us break our asses like that. He'd stand there like the Dolly Lama and holler *"Yah yah yah! Hit hit hit! Little Sisters of the Poor! C'mon now, hit!"* When he didn't approve of our attitude, which was every day but Ash Thursday, he'd say, "Now girls, your Tampax is in too tight!" One day after the late Robert Boggs had been out in the weeds all night with a fox and was having a very bad practice, Coach handed him a bottle of Midol in front of the whole squad. That was his idea of how to motivate. But then he also had techniques for sucking in with the players, for making us think he was strictly on our side and it was the Billygoats against the world. Like one day he saw our press agent sitting in the grass on the sidelines, and Coach hollered across the field, "Stand on your feet when you watch our men at work! They're out here sweating and you're laying on your ass!" A remark like that has 2 effects: It makes the press agent jump up and start talking to himself, and it makes some of our dumber players think that Coach is really behind them. We veterans know better. It's just Coach's way. He'd turn on you in a second. I challenged him about it last year, and he said, "Alphabet, there's got to be discipline, there's got to be hostility, there's got to be downright hatred out there. Now which do you prefer: Working for a prick like me, or should I trade you to that dear, sweet, lovable Coach Stan Frederickson, the one with the 3 and 11 record?" I never brought up the subject again.

Sometimes Ziggy Guminski, our offensive line coach, entertains his own delusions of grander and tries to out-prick Coach, but we'll only take so much. One day he made us run wind sprints for 30 minutes after the defense went in and showered. Ziggy explained that wind sprints build up the kind of unquestioning discipline that General Patton recommends. He asked how would it look if we marched up and down the field in close-order drill, like the general instructed. Didn't we prefer wind sprints? No, several of the guys insisted. We preferred close-order drill. Ziggy made us holler "kill, kill, kill!" as we ran, and I believe this is found on page 154 of the army handbook, but it is not found in any book on football. So on cue we chanted "kill, kill, kill!" and wind-sprinted right off the field and into the locker room.

J. R. Rodenheimer told me the same thing happened in New York at a Saturday morning practice. J. R. said the Giants hollered "raw meat" and ran out the nearest exit, and the split end got mugged.

I wish I could say my knee kept getting better and better, between the wind sprints and the hours in the training room and all the good hot sun and diathermy and whirlpools, but after the first adhesions popped and the joint loosened up, the improvement seemed to tail off. There were moves I could make and moves I couldn't. I could fire out and slam the middle linebacker pretty good, I could set and fill, and I could drop back to help protect Q. B., but when it came to things like C-blocking, I was off. The C-block is when the snapper slants hard and tries to dump a defensive tackle, and the offensive guard cuts around the snapper and flattens the middle linebacker, which can be very confusing to a team that is expecting normal blocking. Every time I tried to fire out to the left, I'd feel the right knee start to go and I'd hold back, and our timing would break down. Ziggy knew what I was going through, but he wouldn't give me an inch. "C'mon, now, Alph," he'd scream at me. "It's now or never." Which was bullshit, like a lot of things the coaches scream at you. But they only have a month to get you up for the pre-season games, and they don't have time to do things naturally. If you can't cut it right away, *zoom*—you drop your hat, meaning you give up your position.

In our final workouts before the first pre-season game, they had me snapping on special teams and Zawatski doing all the rest, which is like supporting your wife while she sleeps with somebody else, which I also remember. Coach said, "Alph, you're important to our game and we have every intention of using you when your knee comes around. In the meantime you can be an inspiration to the younger players, and some of them can benefit from your guidance and experience." Well, I never hired out at $38,500 a year to babysit the kiddies, but Coach made his intentions plain. So I worked twice as hard, to keep up my end of the bargain, and I exercised like a maniac, while Coach Edquist was still exercising everybody's ass off anyway. Some days he'd have us do 100 yards of front somersalts and 100 yards of back somersalts, followed by maybe 4 100-yard sprints, and then 15 minutes of pushups and situps and grass drills, and just when I'd think my lungs were breaking, he'd order us to roll on our sides for the width of the field, 160 feet, and somersalt back, and finish up with 6 or 8 wind sprints.

Ziggy'd set up behind the 7-foot tackling dummy, Big Mama, which is 500 pounds of canvas-covered sawdust suspended 2 feet above the ground by a chain, and he'd get Big Mama swinging slowly and make us do forearm shivers, whack her with our forearm pads as hard as we could, hit hit hit and then hit again, and make Big Mama swing high and then *whack!* clout her with everything you had when she swung back. I used to look forward to that, because my arms and shoulders were still strong, and I figured if I ever got back in the regular lineup, I could use forearm shivers to help make up for my knee. By the time we began drilling for the pre-season opener, the knee was flaming up and I was back on Demerol. Not only that, but I was doing something I'd never done before: popping greenies before practice. Coach and The Connection always handed out pills before the games, but when you had to take them for practice, you were in trouble. But if I went to Mr. Evans, M.D., and told him about the pain, I'd risk being dropped completely, and since everybody in the league had already waived on me, that'd be goodbye. So I just did my 2 hours a day in the tubs and lifted my weight boot and ate my pills and kept on trucking. Sometimes I felt a little woozy, but I'd take a few deep breaths and snap back to normal. I was hoping for a miracle, hoping that I'd wake up some morning and find that poor Zawatski had suffered an injury, nothing too serious, just a multiple fracture of the tibia, or black measles complicated by pneumonia, and old Alexander Barrie Crispin Jackson Jr., Alphabet to you, would be off and running again with the 1st-string line. Well, off and limping, anyway.

Zawatski started our first 2 pre-season games and we won them both easy. We took Dallas 24–7 and it could've been 64–7 except Coach tried out about 100 rooks, or 10 anyway, and then we shoved it up Boston's ass 26–6 with John Lovesey blasting 4 field goals from behind the 35-yard line, which means close to 60 yards in the air, and every kick perfect. Well, that was no surprise, you expected perfection out of Limey, but what we didn't expect was the way Luke Hairston played, charging out there like they were championship games and he was about to be waivered. He caught so many passes against Dallas that they had to double on him, and when was the last time you ever saw a team double on a tight end? Against Boston, he wiped out their outside linebackers and their cornerbacks so many times it looked like an army hospital on the sidelines.

After the Boston game, Coach said, "Boys, I think we can do it. I think with a little show of character and discipline we can go all the way." The papers were already trumpeting us after a mere 2 games. That was the signal for the Football Annies to descend like locusts. They're like Father Galvin; they love a winner, and they drive to camp from miles around when they sniff a good season coming up. It's wise to avoid them, and they should all have a sign on their cars: "Honk if you love gonorrhea," but try telling a horny rookie. There was a Football Annie in Texas went to a prostitute to learn some special techniques, and I better not name the team involved because she wound up blowing half of them, and one night a jealous suiter caught her in the back of a Volkswagen van with a famous quarterback and blew her brains out, and the front office had to hush it up. I always remember that case when some unknown crease telephones me from the lobby and says she got my name from the program, and I likewise remember the case of the baseball player that let a girl come up to his room to chat. They chatted for about 30 seconds and then she emptied a gun into him.

One time Malley and I were in Las Vegas as the guest of the Caesar's Palace, and a couple of big buxom Football Annies started following us everywhere but the men's room. We were in town for the opening of the hottest act in show biz, "22 legs," which was their cute way of advertising the June Taylor dancers plus Joe Namath. I figured some of those June Taylors had to be at least in their 50s, but Malley explained that they keep replacing them every year, like football players, and they'd be around long after the rest of us. Now if they can just figure out how to replace Namath. Imagine a guy that old, barely able to walk on those gimbly knees of his, and still chasing crease. It's enough to make you wonder.

Anyway, the two Football Annies pestered us and pestered us till finally Lacklustre Jones got to town and we did a fast shuffle and turned them over to Lack, and he hustled them right to his suite at poolside. That night he was tear-ass. "Why didn't y'all *warn* me?" he said. "Why didn't y'all *say* somethin'?"

"We thought we were doing you a favor, Lack," Malley said. "You told us you were looking for ginch."

"*Ginch?*" Lacklustre complained. "Shit, them was guys!"

Malley and I were shocked. "They were *men?*" I said. "Are you sure?"

"Am I sure?" Lack exploded. "Yeh, I'm sure. I helt 2 great big hairy nuts in my hand to prove it!"

"Not for long, I hope," Malley said.

"About 2-5ths of a second," Lack said. "Jes' long enough to kick they asses out mah room and call the manager."

The main thing about Football Annies is they're usually ugly. The L.A. Rams had a beauty contest with their own jocksniffers and one girl almost made 5th runner-up but came 3 votes short. Nobody else placed. The average football camp follower is built like Buddy Hackett and has a face like Flipper, and sometimes vice-versa. They are not your most desirable-type crease. But then living a life of celibracy is not your most desirable-type life, either, and sometimes you take what's available. One night Ziggy Guminski thought he heard giggling in the dormitory, and he burst in and caught Hyphen B-l-a-c-k with a broad about 50 years old right in the middle of the stroke. 60 guys came running out in their underwear to take a look, and finally Ziggy the fink called Coach.

When Coach shoved into the room and saw the woman over in the corner wriggling into her clothes, he blinked. "Aren't you 2-2 Devine?" he said. "Didn't you use to hang around the Colts' camp in Westminster?"

"Fuck you," she reposted.

"Hyphen," Coach said in the general direction of a quivering lump that lay under the covers, "I told you when camp opened it'd be 1000 for having a twist in your room. Now, Hyphen, I know it's been a long time, so I'm giving you a break. I'm only charging you 200."

B-l-a-c-k's round eyes appeared slowly from the foot of the bed. "Coach," he said in a voice filled with emotion, "I 'preciate that."

"AND 800 MORE FOR YOUR TASTE!" Coach hollered. "Jesus Christ, this ain't adultery, this is necrophilia. How old are you, Moms?"

"Fuck you!" the woman went on. All I could make out over Malley's shoulder was acres of fat overflowing a dirty girdle.

"Boys," Coach said, "permit me to introduce Miss 2-2 Devine, nicknamed 4. She dances at stag parties and smokers."

"Where?" Ziggy inquired.

"Mostly from the back of trucks," Coach said.

"Fuck you!" the lady screamed out. "I appeared on Broadway."

"That's right," Coach said, "one night when the truck was parked at 125th Street. Now listen, men, Miss 2-2 Devine is off limits, hear? She use to come around the Colts' camp at Westminster, when I was playing, and if I'm not mistaken she was up at Bear Mountain servicing the Giants, and I think she works the baseball teams in the St. Petersburg area in March and April, and she's not entirely unknown to the NBA either. Hyphen, I'm ashamed of you! 1000 bucks! For Raquel Welch, yeh. But for 2-2 Devine, what a price! Show some class, son, show some class!" and he stomped down the hall.

Lacklustre was kind enough to escort Miss 2-2 Devine to the taxi stand, as if she wasn't safe on the streets with her hefty bulk, and when he came back he looked like the hawk that swallowed the canary. The late Robert Boggs said, "What chew grinnin' about?"

"Got me a date for Saturday night," Lack said.

"Where to?" Malley asked. "The Cotillion Ball?"

"Naw, under the stands."

For the rest of the week, the soup tasted spikier than ever, and Coach worked us so hard for the 3d pre-season game against the Chargers that everybody just kind of sacked out after the evening meetings. On the night of the annual rookie show, Jay Cox said to me before the curtain went up, "I'm the M.C., and the team's in for a treat."

I had an idea what kind of treat the rookie show would be, having attended 9 of them already. The whole thing is some kind of high-wire balancing act where the rooks make fun of the veterans and kiss ass at the same time, so everybody gets entertained and nobody gets sore. Year after year of the same stuff, plus rooks singing and dancing like baby hippos and always ending the same way: The 2 fattest rooks waltz out with balloons under their jerseys and sing the Billygoats' fight song in drag, while 2 of the hairiest, horniest rooks prance around and try to cop a feel.

"This here's gonna be some show," Jay Cox said. "I don't do nothing half-ass."

"Gee," Mal said, "what a credit you are to the Michigan State English department," which really wasn't fair, since Jay Cox doesn't talk that much different than the rest of us, all true-blue college men that majored in football and crease.

"I don't do nothing half-ass," Cox repeated. "With me it's whole ass or nothing."

"I think you got a couple words reversed," Malley said, but I kept quiet because I didn't want to antagonize a kid that already gained 111 yards against Dallas in our first pre-season game and 94 more against the Browns in our 2d and *Sports Pictorial* was calling him a leading candidate for rookie of the year.

When the curtain rose in the gym, Jay Cox was standing there in top hat and tails, looking like something out of *Oliver* with that pasty face of his, and behind him was this big imitation cake made from wrapping paper and yard markers. Pay attention, maybe Georgina Spellman will pop out!

The acts went ahead as usual, about on the same par as any other rookie show. A kid minced out wearing Q. B.'s number, 8, and another kid wearing mine, which is 50, and they pretended to be snapping the ball and dry-humping at the same time. Very funny. Then they locked arms and did a lispy song:

> We are mean and very nasty
> We delight in pederasty.

"Whatcha think?" I whispered to Mal.

"Needs work," he said.

Then they did some routines where No. 8 was the comedian and No. 50 kept making superstupid remarks. I began to get a little warm under the collar. Ever since the T-formation came in, centers have been the butt of the jokes. Suddenly everybody's anti-Semitic against snappers. I blame the original guy that made up the first snapper joke: "What's the most nervous athlete in the world? Answer: the center on a Greek football team." I didn't think that was funny the first 100 times I heard it, and I wish Billy Bob Bunker would stop repeating it 6 times a season for the last 10 seasons, which I always laugh out of politeness and nerves and hate myself later.

A kid from northern South Carolina or southern North Carolina, I forget which, did a reading from *Tristram Shanty,* and it reminded me of Oop Johnson's rookie year, when Malley inveigled him into doing a coupling from *Hamlet:*

> The time is out of joint; O cursed spite
> That ever I was born to set it right!

It came out:

> The tam is out of joe-eent; O cussed spat
> That ivvuh Ah was bone to sit it rat!

Lack said he liked it because it rhymed, and Malley said it was probably close to the way the original Hamlet had pronounced it, and Ray Roy said it didn't sound much like Danish to him, and Limey Lovesey told us all to shut up and piss off, ya silly twits.

This year there was only one act that showed any class at all, 3 rooks with pretty good voices singing a medley of old songs, and you could see they'd at least taken some time and trouble, and I respect anybody that puts out his best, even if it's just singing a bunch of songs at a rookie show. They started off with "The Times They Are A-Changin'," a Bob Dylan number, and when they came to the line about the "times," each one pointed at his wrist as though he had a watch on. Then they swung into "If," by The Bread, and when they came to, "If a Picture's

Worth 1000 Words," they all pretended to hold an invisible brush in their hands and paint a picture while they sang. I mean, they showed a little taste, but they were the only ones.

After a while Jay Cox came prancing out in his high hat and said, "Now, ladies and gentlemen, the piece of resistance!" and he whacked his cane into the side of the paper cake and out came who else but Miss 2-2 Devine, holding her hip where the cane hit her, and shaking the rest of her 200 pounds of avoidrupois and wearing a Billygoat helmet in her entirety. I looked across the aisle at Coach and he was the color of our new jerseys. Next to him the Rev. Matthew Galvin was smiling sheepishly, like he'd just been caught beating his meat, and next to him was Billy Bob Bunker, the only one who seemed to be enjoying himself, hollering "Take it off!" which I guess meant he wanted her skinned, or maybe it was, "Take *her* off!" I'm not sure which.

The act went on for 10 or 15 minutes, to that record "The Stripper," and for the grand finale 2-2 Devine came into the audience and twirled her bazoombas like airplane propellers, in opposite directions, till she came up the aisle where Coach was sitting with the smoke coming out of his ears like twin volcanoes, and she saw him and gave him the old double finger, turned around and gave him the old reverse grinder with her bare ass, hollered "Ya sister's!" and danced right out the door like a wrecked truck.

Malley and I cheered once or twice, and Lacklustre Jones dropped a rose, and the rest of the guys clapped nervously. Coach and Mr. Bunker and Father Galvin went out the door like they were shot from a cannon, and we all hurried back to the dorm so we wouldn't be late for bedcheck.

"What'd you think?" I asked Mal.

"I thought it was fine," he said. "Very enjoyable. A little highbrow, but relaxing nonetheless."

"Relaxing?"

"Yes, relaxing. Every once in a while it's good to see something that takes your mind off sex."

I had to admit that was very deep.

We won our 3d exhibition game (excuse me, commissioner, I mean *pre-season* game) and Zawatski played well, I'm sorry to say. Whatever bad habits he had, I was helping him get over them, at Coach's insistence. He had a little problem with his stance, but nothing serious. A T-snapper's supposed to spread his feet shoulder width, then line up the toes of the right foot with the arch of the left, and he's supposed to line up like that every time he's in the T. Not 9 times out of 10, but *every time.* Well, Chet had a slight tendency to square his feet off on pass protection, because instead of firing right out at the middle linebacker he would be dropping off to pick up the rush, and he found it easier to drop from a square stance, which is the opposite of most guys. I drilled him by the hour, till it was firmly ensconced in his head. About the only other problem he had was squeezing his hands just before the snap, which gives the defensive tackles a split-second warning. I taught him to vary his squeeze, sometimes fake a few, or squeeze 2 or 3 counts early, and then anybody that's going to school on his knuckles will end up offsides.

There are certain other fine points that the kid didn't have to be taught. He had a feel for team play, which is the name of the game on offense. Linemen don't have to love each other, they can even hate each other's guts, but they do have to be able to depend on each other and move and react together like a single unit. Remember, myself at center and Bullivant and Bad-ass Harris at the guards had played together for 7 years, and Robert Boggs and J. R. Rodenheimer at the tackles were in their 10th and 13th seasons respectfully. Many a rookie center would have choked in company like that, but the kid was a very cool Polski. He had recovery reactions like a safety-man, and he backed up the guards as dependably as I ever did. Bull and Bad-ass are 2 of your more aggressive guards, and coming up to the line Bull will often say, "Alph, I'm gonna fire out on this play, so cover for me," meaning he'll commit himself to a straight shot at the tackle, and if he misses, I've got to back him up. Sometimes we'll get up to the line and Bad-ass'll say the same thing, and I'm left covering for 2 guys, which not even Chuck Bednarik could do in his prime, and all I can do is hope that one of them will get his man and I can cut-block the other tackle before he gets to Q. B. On plays like that Zawatski showed some kind of instinct, and he kept those 2 wild-ass guards covered like a blanket. Of course it didn't hurt that he weighed 240, 10 pounds more than me, and he was 22 years old, 9 years younger, and he had 2 good knees.

Sitting on the sidelines in between the kicks and punts, I had to admire the kid's cool, but I was also pretty down, too. Doing nothing is one of the toughest things to be doing, especially after you've started 121 straight games and suddenly you can see the end of the road ahead. The trouble when you're benched is you still take your full compliment of greens, because you never know when you'll have to go in, and above all you want to be ready because it may be your last chance to show them something. There's guys that got taken out of the lineup for one play and wound up in the Continental League.

But it's tough to sit on the bench when you're full of greens. You squirm around, trying to stay calm, and all you want to do is knock somebody down. I sympathize with that guy that jumped up off the bench and made a tackle a few years ago. I'll lay you odds he was full of greens, and he just had to hit somebody.

Then when the game's over you haven't had a chance to burn up the false energy, and the pills are still popping in your stomach, so you stay high half the night. I know guys that can't sleep till the next day and then wind up sleeping for 28 or 30 hours, right up till the Tuesday meeting. And even on Tuesday, you're not 100%. Your eyes are dry, your muscles feel like they're made of cement, no snap and give. It's Wednesday or Thursday before you're really ready to go again. Of course, if you don't like it you can always write in for one of those salesman's kits and go door to door with a sack full of encyclopedias. Better a hophead football player than a healthy salesman is my motto. What the hell, there's problems in every profession.

It's like I told little Alph one time, which he's my son by my former marriage to Cathy Jackson, now Quinn. The kid and I always liked to read Pinocchio, he loved old Gepetto and the puppet and so did I, and sometimes it was hard to figure out which one of us loved the story more. Little Alph always brightened up at that part where Pinocchio said he wanted to live in a land where the candy was free and all a boy had to do was play. He asked me if football was like that, and I said, "No, not quite. But close." So he said he wanted to be a football player when he grew up, and Cathy said over her dead body. That was one of her ways of keeping me from getting a swelled head, hinting around that being a ballplayer really wasn't very much, and I didn't argue the point, because I lost all the arguments anyway, and how the fuck was I supposed to explain to an ex-college beauty queen what the football life-style was really like, how you could do your whole job in 6, 7 hours a day maximum, usually less, and be jacking around with the guys at the same time, and how good it felt to walk off the field with every bone in your body aching after you beat the Vikings 21–20. I couldn't explain that any better than Cathy could explain the feeling of bearing little Alph.

The other thing that Cathy couldn't understand was my language, and who could blame her? All day long I'd be around ballplayers and ex-marine coaches, and every other word out of their mouth is either vulgar or religious. One night I practically broke my toe on her sewing machine, which she'd neglected to put it away when we went to bed, and I said, "Shit!"

Cathy said, "Ssshhh! The baby!"

Little Alph was 2 months old and I guess she was afraid his first words would be "shit!"

When I crawled back into bed with my toe on fire and probably broken in about 6 places, I said, "Honey, let me whisper in your ear," and when she tilted up I whispered, "If you ever leave that fucking thing out again, I'll break the fucking thing into little fucking pieces."

She didn't talk to me for 2 weeks, till the night the minister called on us and she had to fake it, and we got into a discussion about the book of Revelations and the scorpions and I blurted out, "I don't believe all that scorpion bullshit."

Cathy inhaled deep, and then she said, "Do you know what you just *said?*"

"Yeh," I said. "I don't believe about the scorpions."

"Quite all right, Mrs. Jackson," the minister said, smiling. "We all slip once in a while. The other day I told the choir, 'That's a hell of a note!' " He sat there beaming proudly, and I thought he never stood so tall.

With Zawatski playing ahead of me, I had a lot of time to think about things like that. I liked to lay in my bed at night and relive the past, the great games in the career of

A.B.C. Jackson, never an All-Pro but almost once or twice. I heard the old sounds and smelled the old smells, and I tried to regain my self-respect between the sheets. I can hear certain parties saying, "What does a snapper ever do that makes any difference?" which is just another example of how bigoted people can be. Your center is your key man in football. The other 10 guys can execute perfectly, but if the snapper fucks up, the play is dead before it gets off. Did you ever stop to wonder why there's no starting black centers in pro ball? Well, it's very simple, and very ridiculous, too. The coaches hand out all this crap about how they don't play favorites racially and it's what you do on the field that matters, but the truth is there's not a coach in the game that would trust a black man to snap the ball. They figure the job's too important to entrust to a spook. Sick? Sure, it's sick, but that's the way coaches think. They're becoming more enlightened, and I predict you'll see a starting black snapper in another 80, 90 years. Right after you see a starting black quarterback.

Mostly, I missed the sounds, the rhythms, the feel. I'd hunch over the ball with my arm locked and straight, my right thumb touching the front end of the laces and my left hand just resting against the back of the ball, and I'd hear Q. B. call the signals, and then I'd get the count, "Hut 1! Hut 2! H—" and I'd whip that ball back into Q. B.'s hands, giving it a quick quarter turn so the laces would come up against his fingers, and I'd hear the leather thunk in there solid. From then on it'd be like the start of an avalanche, first the crack of the defensive linemen smashing their taped hands against our helmets, then the clatter of the shoulder pads crashing up and down the line, and Buford Bullivant giving out his rebel yell and the late Robert Boggs roaring like a stuck lion and Bad-ass Harris cussing and screaming and J. R. spluttering his breath like a big old whale coming up for air.

I missed it so bad, I even missed getting held, which happens every play and you better get used to it. That big bugger at Cincinnati—Coulbourn? Colburn? something like that, first name Don—he kept holding me in a game last year, and I finally had to tell him if he kept it up I'd kick the shit out of him, and he kept it up and I smacked him in the stomach, kicked him in the balls and stepped on his hands, and the ref was standing right over us and didn't say a word. He knew what was happening.

I'd lay in bed at night and think about the time Q. B. said, "Okay, men, we're going on the 1st sound, *the 1st sound*," and the 1st sound was the middle linebacker dropping a rose, and 3 of our guys broke their stance, and the middle linebacker told the zebra, "I couldn't help it, ref. I dined Mexican last night," and the ref stepped off 5 yards against *us!* Memories like that just tumbled through my head every night like a newsreel, things that I normally wouldn't even be thinking about, because normally I'd be too busy worrying about games coming up instead of games already played. Silly things like the time I missed the snap count and gave Q. B. the ball right in the protective cup that he forgot to put on, and he called signals in the key of H sharp the rest of the day, and the time the late Robert Boggs crumpled up holding his shoulder, and when Mr. Evans ran out on the field with his little black bag, Robert said, "He kneed me in the nuts," and Mr. Evans said, "What're you holding your shoulder for?" and Robert said, "What the fuck you want me to hold?"

In the 4th pre-season game, Zawatski made one of his few mistakes. All through the 1st quarter Wilbur Thomason, "The Burro of Buffalo," kept lining up odd and telling the kid, "I'm comin' inside! I'm comin' inside! I'm gonna blow right around you and smash that honky quarterback." Then he'd come straight up, mashing his helmet into Zawatski's Adam's apple, and the kid would hold him off. But just before the half ended, Thomason got right up over the kid's head and said, "I'm comin' inside! Look out, here I come again!" and then he looped inside and almost broke Q. B.'s back. Zawatski came off the field saying, "I'll never believe *him* again."

Ziggy said, "For openers, you shudna believe him the first time." Ziggy said that the kid had learned his lesson, hopefully. Maybe he had. He played a strong 2d half, and we won the game 21–16, which was the Bills 1st loss of the pre-season, and made us the early chalk.

By this time, we'd been in camp almost 2 months, and the club had begun to jell. Most of the rooks were long gone, because Coach puts a premium on experience and he likes to let the other clubs develop the rooks and then trade them for it. "Another Brink's job," he'll say, and we wind up with a fireball like Wing Choy, who came from the 49ers, or Q. B., out of the Oiler system.

The religious click was going full swing, like it did every year, with Buford Bullivant as the main honcho. The Billygoats' chapter of the BPB, the Brotherhood of Professional Believers, met 3 nights a week in Buford's room, which was right across the hall from Lack's, where pornie films were projected live against the wall almost every night, except on Saturdays, when Lack was usually out chasing real crease under the stands or in the weeds. Guest speakers would come in and address the BPB group: rapists who'd found God in prison, preachers that liked to be around jocks, sometimes holy-roller types that would chant and speak in tongues— *"Nyahh yah riggadoo riggadee,* your voice in me, O, Lord, *ratata datata satata,* O hear me Lord"—which they claimed was ancient dead Hebrew and Malley kept saying was doubletalk, him being unreligious, as he'd confessed to me when we first began rooming together.

"I'm a pantheistic hedonist," he said. "What're you?"

"I'm Welsh and English on my father's side and French and Dago on my mother's."

"No," Malley said. "I mean what's your religious belief?"

"Oh. Well, I'm a Methodist, but I don't work at it."

"I'm an agnostic," Mal said, "but I don't work at my religion either."

Every year the BPB guys would try to recruit us, and every year there'd be these weirdo discussions. Buford would grab me in the hall and say, "Why not come to our meeting tonight? Brother Allan of the Nazarenes is bringing some spiritual food."

"Well, no, thanks, Bull," I would say, not wishing to hurt his feelings. "I already ate, and I think I'll be studying films in Lack's room tonight."

"Brother, have you found God?" he asked Mal one night.

"I didn't know he was lost," Malley said.

"God's not lost," Bullivant said, "but apparently you are," and he went into his room and slammed the door. Sometimes we listened outside, and sometimes it got so righteous that you didn't have to go to any special pains to listen, you could hear them a half a block away. The BPBs would have these long discussions about how a simple man with a Mexican name had become the savior of Jerusalem and the whole world, and what was Christ's middle name or did he have a middle name at all? One of the rooks said that he thought the full name might be Jesus Harold Christ, because he had heard his father refer several times to Jesus H. Christ. Bullivant told him that he doubted it, as it would make all the hymns come out wrong.

Sometimes the BPB meetings would get as loud as the yelps at Lack's movie sessions, and you would walk down the hall and hear this weird combination of religious and pornographic noises mingling with each other in stereo. One night Bullivant stomped across the hall and banged on Lack's door and hollered, "Could you hold down those filthy noises?"

" 'Pyours," Lack said.

"We're engaged in worship," Bull called in.

"Piss off!" Limey said.

Bullivant kicked in the door just as the female star was taking on a horny police dog on Lack's wall. "I hope you degenerates realize," he said through teeth that must have been wired together, "someday God is coming to judge the quick and the dead."

"Then you don't have to worry, Bullivant, you ain't neither one," Lack said.

Sometimes we'd sit around and play boo-ray, which is the official card game of the pros, although I wouldn't play boo-ray with Mal, or any other card game, for that matter. He's as tough in boo-ray as he is in gin or canasta or pinochle. In boo-ray everybody gets 5 cards, and you turn 1 card up for trumps, and right at the outset you make your choice: either you stay in and play or drop out and lose your ante. If you stay and you don't take a trick, you've been boo-rayed, and you have to match the pot. Cheating is allowed, but getting caught isn't.

After 2 months in camp, Jay Cox started showing up on the regulars' floor, and it got to be hard to keep him out, since he was picking up an average of 100 yards every game and had a lock on one of the running back slots. He'd come up behind you when you're playing solitary, and he'd say, "Play the red 10 on the black jack," and when you ran the whole deck, he'd repeat his slogan: "You can win with me." Malley said there was nothing worse than a nagging back.

We heard the story of his college career 40 times, his

conquests, all the little chickies that used to line up and beg to give him blow-jobs, and how Michigan State won a national championship with him and so could the Goats. "We won our division last year," the late Robert Boggs snapped at him. "Where the fuck were you?"

"Yeh, but what happened in the playoffs?" Cox said in that nasal whine of his. "You blew it, didn't you?"

I forget who first got the idea of the mock trial, but it was probably 3 or 4 guys "simon-taneously," as Coach Edquist would say. The charge was "first-degree aggravation," and the whole defensive line was commissioned to take the accused to the latrine on the rooks' floor. At first, he kicked and hollered, but then he must have figured this was some kind of an initiation right, and once it was over he'd be asshole buddies with the regulars, and he shouldn't hold his breath. We tied him up without any further resistance and beat on his feet.

His Honor the late Robert Boggs was the presiding judge, and after Cox was stripped and strapped to one of the crappers, Robert said, "Now we gone open this trial fair and square. Cock," he said, addressing the accused in the singular. "Cock, how does you plead?"

"The name's Cox," Cox said.

Judge Boggs said, "Hear ye, hear ye! The defendant plead guilty. Commence the punishment!"

Ray Roy Jenkins painted Cox's cock and balls bright red with mercurochrome, and took color pictures to send back to the folks in East Lansing, and Lacklustre peed on his feet, and then we gave him a cold shower and hauled him back to his room, which Wing Choy had trashed by emptying all the drawers and exploding a firecracker inside his toothpaste tube, and Bad-ass Harris tied up his shirts.

"Now," the late Robert Boggs proclaimed, "we begin the punishment! Jay Cock, you been tried and found guilty. Lay the mothafucka on the bed! That's it. *No* mercy! Tie his hands to the head and his feet to the foot. That's it. Now Jay Cock, you got sumpin' to say before I pronounce sentence, you dirty bastard?"

Cox said, "I take 3 baths a day."

"Man, you must be a *filthy* sumbitch!" Bad-ass Harris said.

Robert said, "Show some respec' to the cote! Jay Cock, you sentence to 3 minutes of bare-ass face-sittin' by the marshal. Do you beg for mercy?"

Cox grunted, and Robert interrupted him again. "Okay, then, jive mothafucka. If you won't beg, we'll begin wit' the persecution." Lack dropped his pants and pulled off his shorts.

"Hey, chaps, wait a moment!" Limey hollered. "I don't feel this is quite sanitary."

"Yeh," Lack said. "You might have a point there. Cox, when'd you wash your face last?"

Cox turned away, paler than usual.

Hyphen B-l-a-c-k ran to the bathroom with a washrag and soaked it in cold water, and Lack scrubbed the rookie's face till it gleamed like a new cue ball, all healthy and sanitary. Then he spread his cheeks and eased down on Jay Cox's face, and Cox bit him hard.

The next day Lack was too embarrassed to go to Mr. Evans with his problem, so he looked up a rectal doctor in the yellow pages and found a young cat about 27 years old, barely out of rectal school. The doctor took one look at the injury and began to giggle. "Well, er, uh, Mr. Jones," the doc said. "How'd this happen?"

"You know how it is, Doc," Lack blurted out. "Me and my old lady. You know. Just foolin' around."

"Far out," the doctor said, smiling. He told Lack to bathe it in salt water every few hours and try a little saltpeter in his diet.

The week of our last pre-season game, Ziggy Guminski knocked on my door after the evening meeting and said Coach wished to see me right away. I held my breath and waited, but Ziggy just stood there. "Didn't he say to bring my playbook?" I asked, and he shook his head no.

Coach was downstairs in his office, smiling like a cobra, barely visible behind his oversize desk. Out on the field, his elevator shoes make him look taller, but nobody has invented elevator pants. "Jackson," he said, "we put you on waivers."

I felt like I'd been hit in the mouth by a rock. I blinked and gulped, and I felt dizzy and light-headed.

"You passed," Coach said. If the 1st blow doesn't get you, the 2d one will. *They put you on waivers and you passed.* 25 teams, some of them about as powerful as the Jones Jr. High in Toledo, had given me the old finger on account of my knee. Word gets around fast. There's no blacklist like an NFL blacklist.

The nausea passed in a few seconds, and then I was mad. "You put me on waivers and you never even told me about it?" I said. "Why, of all—"

"Calm down, Alph!" Coach said in his 6-foot-2 voice. "Don't say something you'll be sorry for. We put you on waivers as a test, that's all. If anybody'd bit, we'd've pulled you right back." He went into a long song and dance about how he had to test the waters around the league, see how high they rated me, plan for the future, but I was still a Billygoat and I figured strongly in his plans.

"I won't stay on the cab squad," I said.

"You won't be on the cab squad. You'll be playing opening day, I promise you."

"Shagging punts?"

"No. Snapping. Backing up Zawatski. Snapping on all punts and kicks. And just being there. We want you around, Alphabet. You're an institution."

Yeh, I thought as I walked out, or *in* one. What a crock of shit! In the morning every sports page in the United States would tell how A.B.C. "Alphabet" Jackson had been put on waivers and passed, the old man of the Billygoats, and wasn't it sad how good things have to end? I could imagine all my friends feeling sorry for me and whispering when I went by. There goes the old goat. The knee, you know?

Jeez, my dad would pass out! A great old guy, A.B.C. Jackson Sr., but a typical jock father, too, from the ancient era when baseball was the national pastime. All I ever heard from the cradle up was take 2 and hit to right, and get your *whole* body in front of a ground ball even if it means you spend the rest of your life in the boys' choir. Along about the 10th grade, some asshole invented the curveball, and I was a catcher by then and I couldn't catch it let alone hit it and I didn't even feel comfortable being in the same township with one of the fucking things. When I discovered that there was no such thing as a curve or a sinker in football, I knew I'd found my game. It took a while to convince my dad, but after he saw me strike out 7 times on nickel curves in a sand-lot doubleheader he accepted my limitations.

I knew my mom and dad would hate the idea of waivers. Well, it'd be something new for mom to put in the scrapbook, not that there was all that much for her to paste up in the life of her son the snapper. When she first started keeping the book, I said, "Hey, mom, centers don't get much ink, you know?"

She said that was only true of your typical center, not an all-star superplayer like her fine son, and she went out and bought 3 scrapbooks the size of newspaper pages and had the covers embossed in imitation gold: A.B.C. JACKSON JR., and it wasn't till my 8th year in the league that she had to start using the 2d book. Half the items in the

book were about mom and dad anyway. A.B.C. JACK-
SONS CELEBRATE 25TH . . . ALEX JACKSON TOPS IN
BOWLING LEAGUE . . . NAN JACKSON WINS BAKE-
OFF. Usually there was a little squiggle somewhere in the
story that the Jacksons were the well-known parents of
A.B.C. Jackson Jr., "star" center of the Billygoats. They
could only call me star in the local Upper Darby, P.A.
newspapers, because in the rest of the country nobody'd
recognize me by that description.

I wondered if Coach knew what he was risking, putting
me on waivers. When my old man found out, Coach stood
a good chance of getting a fat eye, just like that wise guy
in the bowling league that told Dad I was washed up in
my 9th season. All Dad did was hit him with a left uppercut, which your left uppercut with a bowling ball packs a
little more authority than your ordinary left uppercut,
and there was an assault charge and all kinds of hell before
the old man paid a couple of hundred dollars and
squashed the action. You could read about it on page 4 of
volume 2 of the famous 3-part work, A.B.C. JACKSON JR.

When I got back to the room, Mal was reading Shake-
speare aloud, another one of his habits. "For in that sleep
of death what dreams may come," he said. "When we
have shoveled off this mortal coil . . ." He looked up and
said, "How now, fellatio?"

I gave him the news flash and told him I'd be turning
in my fuchsia jersey in the morning. Maybe I'd go back to
Upper Darby P.A. and sell insurance and marry Dorris
Gene.

"What about your 10 years?" Malley said. "What about
your pension?"

"I'll still get a good pension," I said.

"I know, Rooms, but don't forget, man, this is the year
of the Billygoats. Don't you at least want to go along for
the ride?" As soon as the words slipped out, his face

dropped, and he said, "I didn't mean it that way, Alph. Honest to God, I didn't."

"Is that the way you guys've been looking at it all summer?" I said. "Along for the ride?"

"Of course it isn't."

" 'Cause I don't go anyplace for the ride, Mal. If this team can't use me, I'll hang 'em up."

Malley jumped up and put his hand on my shoulder and gave it a good hard jerk. "Now listen, Alph," he said, "that's quitting. That's copping. Why, there's every chance this team can use you. What'd happen if Zawatski got racked up? Shit, we don't even carry another snapper, not even on the taxi squad. It's you and Chet, and that's it."

"J. R. can snap," I said.

"J. R. can snap my ass," Malley said.

"Well, I don't know if he can snap your ass, but he can snap a football."

"When J. R. centered in college, the kids used to line up in the end-zone stands to catch his snaps."

"Well, he can center."

"No, he can't."

"Yes, he can."

We argued on and on, and I went to sleep convinced that I was quitting the next day, and in the morning when Ziggy Guminski told us to drop our cocks and grab our socks, I was already awake and so was Malley.

"I been thinking about this all night," he said, "and I'm gonna tell you what you're gonna do, and remember, I'm not asking you, I'm telling you, so keep your fucking mouth shut."

"What'm I gonna do?"

"You're gonna take this thing one step at a time. You're not gonna make a grandstand play. Just go day by day till something gives, one way or the other."

At a quarter to 4 in the morning, I had reached exactly the same conclusion.

"And furthermore," Malley said, jumping out of bed and shaking his fist in my nostrils, "if you make one move to quit this club, I'll get Lacklustre Jones to sit on your face for a month!"

"Well," I said, "I don't think that'd be sanitary."

THE FLIGHT

IV

WATER TORTURE

FOR MAYBE AN HOUR, NOBODY TALKED, INCLUDING *Hairston, sitting over there popping pills and leaning back against the bulkhead and staring down the aisles at what used to be his teammates and now I'd guess you'd call his prisoners or prisonmates or something. Once in a while he'd fiddle with his submachine gun, push a button up or down or fool around with the magazine probably making sure all the bullets were in place. As much time as that man spent playing with his artillery, you just knew there was no chance for a misfire, whether the gun came from WWI or was brand new yesterday on its way to Tasmania. Luke Hairston's armory was like Luke Hairston the football player: it worked. You could depend on it.*

Sitting across from him, all kinds of plans and strategies went through my head, and they were all horseshit. I thought of rushing him myself, but how do you rush a 6'10" stud when you're slow to begin with and you're operating on crutches behind 19½ lbs. of surgical plaster? If it was just a matter of grabbing him and staying

*out of the line of fire maybe I could handle it coming in
under the gun but as the pilot told me himself all Luke
had to do was fire one burst and the plane could come
open like a split grapefruit, which the aerodynamics of
split grapefruits are not too satisfactory.*

*The truth is, my mother raised me to be a nice boy, not
a hero.*

*I thought of passing a note back to the other heroes,
telling them to make some excuse to come up, but what
excuse would they use?*

Teacher, I have to do number 2.

Well, go on back to the toilet, Hairston would say.

*But teacher, I don't like that toilet. I like the one up
front.*

Well, then shit in your hat.

*Or maybe Q. B.: Hey, Luke, can I go ask coach some-
thing?*

What chew wanna ask him?

I got a play to ask about. Iron something out.

You won't need no play where you goin'.

But Luke—

Shut up!

*No matter how hard I strained my brains I couldn't
figure how to get his gun. For a psycho, the way he had
things worked out wasn't so dumb. With the 5 rows of no
man's land separating him from the other players, and
me to run his errands, and the whole 1st class section
neutralized, he'd made himself absolutely impregnant.
Our brains didn't make a shit. Our guts didn't make a
shit. There wasn't anything to do but wait and hope.
Maybe he'd take an overdose.*

*I leaned my head back and thought about the funny
bounces. If somebody had picked me up on waivers ... if
Coach had just traded me ... but I'd never have gone. I'd
been a Billygoat too long. Imagine spending the rest of*

your career in one of those fruity Miami uniforms in day-glo turquoise, or that plum colored thing the Cardinals wear. Fuchsia is bad enough, but at least when you're wearing Billygoat fuchsia you've got a bunch of good guys to share your embarrassment. Who do you have when you're a Cardinal? No Malley Tietjens, no late Robert Boggs, no Wing Choy or Bad-ass Harris or the rest of those crazy jack-offs. Jeez, I even think I'd miss Ziggy. Coach? Maybe I'd make an exception in his case.

"Hey, mothafucka!"

I opened my eyes and looked across the aisles. "Yeh, Luke?" I said, trying to sound like his old asshole buddy.

"Put a couple glass of water in here." He handed me a barf bag. When I looked funny, he said, "Move yo' ass!"

I limped through the curtain to the galley and found a stewardess huddled back against the wall. "Here," I said. "He wants some water."

"That bag won't hold—"

"I know, I know," I said impatiently. "Put it in anyway."

Coach bumped into the galley and whispered, "What's up?"

"He wants water," I said.

"Water?" Coach said.

"Yeh," I said, "water, H2O. The stuff you drink with Scotch."

"Shut up a second," Coach said. "I'm thinking." Then he snapped his fingers and said, "Wait!"

He came back in a few seconds with The Connection's little black bag and he cracked it open and began unscrewing a bottle cap.

"I gotta get back," I said.

Coach came up with a handful of red pills that I recognized as Seconal, our regular nighttime treatment for before-game insomnia, and began cracking them open and dropping the powder into Luke's water. After he'd opened about 6, he started to snicker to himself. "This will knock him right on his black ass," he said. "He'll drop like a dead elephant." He tapped his head with his index finger. "You gotta keep thinking, Jackson," he said. "Never forget it."

"Coach," I said, "for chrissakes, sleeping pills taste bitter. He'll catch on and it'll be my ass."

"Just do what you're told," Coach said, breaking 3 or 4 more pills into the water bag. "Leave the thinking to the people who can think."

By the time I got back to Luke, the bag was already beginning to leak and I just knew he'd catch on. But I had to admit to myself that Coach might not be so dumb after all. Like Malley said after we broke the Cleveland placekicker's leg: Desperate situations call for desperate measures. If Luke drank down all the pills, maybe we'd be out of the woods. And if he got wise, well, we were already fucked anyway.

"Here's your water, Luke," I said in my most courteous voice.

Luke took the dripping bag without a word, then looked inside. I smiled sheepishly as he peered over at me and then into the bag again. Did the powder show? Maybe it hadn't all dissolved. I waited for that gun barrel to come whipping across my face.

"What chew lookin' at, mothafucka?" Luke said in a flat voice.

"Nothin', Luke," I said.

"Well, turn your fuckin' head and look out the window and watch nothin' over there!"

I installed myself in the window seat across from him and did as I was told. We still seemed to be flying at about the same altitude, somewheres around 30,000 feet and passing over a small mountain range that kept popping

in and out of my sight through patches of grey cloud. I
tried to figure out where we were. If the pilot was still on
course to New Orleans, probably we were someplace
around Albuquerque.
"Hey, mothafucka!" It was Luke again. "Take this back
and flush it down!"
He handed me the barf bag, and it seemed a little
heavier.
I looked inside. He'd taken a leak in it.
I started to ask him why and almost bit my stupid
tongue off. Maybe he didn't like pissing in dry holes.
Maybe he was crazy. Maybe I'd live to tell Coach how
great his plan worked out. But not if I stood in the aisle
asking Luke Hairston about his toilet habits.
I crutched off down the aisle as directed.

We beat San Francisco 14–10, and broke camp with 5
straight wins behind us, although no great credit to myself, snapping on kicks and punts only, and taking the
usual beating that the defense gives the center when he
can't fight back. All game long, young Zawatski would
hack at their ankles and knees, or stick his helmet in their
sternums and try to separate their ribs, and then I'd replace him on a kick or a punt and it'd be High Noon Do
Not Forsake Me Oh My Darling.
Anybody that snaps on a kick or a punt, he's got to be
ready to sacrifice his precious ass to get the job done right.
On punts, you snap that ball clean and hard, 15 yards back
in a nice low parabola, and you discipline yourself to forget about the big linemen breathing over you, waiting for
your hand to move so they can screw you into the ground
nose first and give you something to think about the next
time. On field goals, you look back through your legs and
memorize where the holder wants the ball, you look up

to check the defense, and you snap the ball and fire out into your man, which is usually too late, because he's already fired out into you, and you pick up your head and screw it back in place and stagger back to the bench toward the oxygen. I can only think of one thing worse than snapping on kicks and punts, and that's not snapping at all. I was happy to get the chance. My knee seemed to be responding a little, and in practice I was almost making the C-block again. But Kid Zawatski was hanging tough. "Alphabet," Coach said, "I can't take him out. Sometimes a rookie'll play himself out of a position, but this young man isn't doing it. Anyway, your knee can use the rest. You're still drawing your pay, so quit bugging me."

When we came back home from camp, we were met at the airport by 5000 screaming fans, including a certain number of *hors de combat,* as Malley calls them. The papers said it was the biggest crowd ever to welcome the Billygoats, which figured, because in earlier years we were not exactly the league's No. 1 success story, with only one division championship in 14 years of campaigning, and now everybody could smell the roses. The *Journal* headline said, YEAR OF THE GOATS? and the *Daily News* said, WE'RE ON OUR WAY, which I never saw any of those *Daily News* reporters out there throwing a block or even taking a tub, but now they were calling themselves "we"—regular members of the team. Even Slim Cantwell, who had a running feud with Billy Bob Bunker and liked to put the rap on the Goats, wrote that "the experts concede the team a reasonable chance," and *Sports Pictorial* featured a cover painting of Jay Cox on their football issue, at least I think it was Jay Cox, because the putty nose down in the left corner of the cover looked like Jay's, and the scraggly hair that ran perpendicular along the right margin was the same consistency as Jay's, and the uniform number was No. 20 when you held it up to the mirror, and the story inside the magazine said something about the unheralded Spartan Jay Cox "exploding" into the opposition trenches and being the top prospect for rookie of the year, which I thought was a pretty clever way to put it, and even Ziggy agreed with me. The caption over the story said, THE NEW AGE OF CAPRICORN, which Malley explained that Capricorn is the sign of the goat, and this was *Sports Pictorial*'s way of touting us for league champions, an encouraging sign, because they had already picked the winner once before, the Decatur Staleys in 1928.

Dorris Gene was in the crowd at the airport, and so were about 6 lady friends of Mal's, and we hauled ass for Dandy Don's, our neighborhood watering hole 2 blocks from Bunker Stadium and 3 blocks from Malley and my's apartment. The Dandy Don's bar and grill was the latest in a big chain that ran from coast to coast and down to Las Cruces, New Mexico. We drank there because the booze was free to any member of the NFL, and this was the secret of Dandy Don's success. All his places were crawling with ballplayers, which attracted campfollowers and jocksniffers and others of that ilk, and the joint could get away with selling 8 oz. of beer for $1.50 and $2 a crack for a martini. That Dandy Don was no dummy, even though he couldn't hack the broadcasting business. I liked him because he always was a big spender, even in his playing days, but of course a lot of the old-timers were. I heard that Red Grange used to pick up all the tabs, too. "Well, you are looking *good!*" Dorris Gene raved.

"Yeh," I said. "A great credit to the art of Mort. Sci."

We ordered drinks, and Dorris Gene said, "Let me see your *knee!*" and I rolled up my pant leg and showed her the 3 dotted lines.

"Why, that's much *better!*" Dorris Gene said. You have to get used to Dorris Gene. With her, every statement is a happening, and she bites down on at least 1 word in every sentence. "How are *you?*" "Gee, what a *lovely* day!" "Excuse me, I have to go to the *girls'* room." It's just her way, but underneath her skin, Dorris Gene is a very superior work of art, decent and loving and built like $700, not too big in the bazoombas, but then if she was, she'd be going with a back or a sportswriter instead of a snapper. Dorris Gene walks like a virgin in those mincy little steps with her head held up and her shoulders back, and she usually wears blue sneakers, which she calls "tennies" and look very cute on her feet at the end of 2 of the finest legs in the game. There was a great tragedy in her life when her fiance married his army nurse and Dorris Gene hauled herself off to a nunnery, but fate did not ordain her and pretty soon she kicked the habit. Lately she'd gone the other extreme and started reading these books on gymnastic sex, which about drove me crazy after a hard day on the practice field. I would say, "Dorris Gene, I love you, and I love making love, and I love standing on my head, but all 3 at once is more than I can handle right now." She'd haul out one of those books and study a new chapter and get another crazy idea. One night she splashed herself with Dream-whip, but there was nothing I could do about it. I was already having trouble making the weight. Another night she asked me if I'd like to try Connie Lingus. I told her I didn't approve of sex for 3, and in the 2d place I didn't even know the girl, so how could I state an opinion? Dorris Gene said I'd better start reading some of her sex books, because the times were passing me by. I said okay, then, I would read the *Daily Post* instead.

The group of us sat around the bar sipping our beers and reminiscing about camp, and then this fat guy came out of the woodwork, he looked like a trucker, and said, "Hey, ain't you Malley Tietjens?"

"No," Dorris Gene said. "I'm Dorris Gene Salter."

"Not you," the guy said bristly. "Him!"

"I think you mistake me for my better, sir," Mal said, and the guy said, "Huh?"

Mal held up his pinky finger and tilted his head to one side. "I'm afraid I'm not this Tietjens savage you mention."

"Oh," the truck driver said, backing away. "Well, excuse me all to hell. I thought you was Tietjens, and I wanted to ask how come you muffed that punt against the Raiders."

Just then the late Robert Boggs came sauntering up, late as usual, although we didn't have an appointment, and he was still wearing his traveling togs of cherry-red jumpsuit, gold-plated buttons and black Cavalier hat with a 2-foot pheasant plume and platform shoes that made him stand about an inch taller than the Washington Monument. "Hey, you clammy pale mothas," he said out of respect to the ladies present, "let the party begin. I has arrove."

"Excuse me," the truck driver said, "but ain't you the late Robert Boggs?"

Robert turned, blinked down on the man and said in a perfect English accent, "No, my man, I think nut. I'm Thistlethwaite of British Intelligence." The truck driver scuttled away. He looked like he was half in the bag anyway, but not enough to debate with the late Robert.

"Everybody's a critic," Malley said. "We win 5 straight exhibition games and that yo-yo wants to know why I had one punt blocked."

"We oughta put Wing Choy on his case," I said, and Robert nodded. 4 seasons ago there was a boobird at Bunker Stadium that should have been shot at the stake, until Wing stepped in and solved the problem in his own Oriental way. This joker came to the games with an oversize freon can attached to a Bronx cheer, and whenever we'd do the least little thing wrong, he'd let loose a blast and crack the eardrums of the surrounding people. When the freon ran out, about the 2d quarter, he'd start booing, and he had a mouth like a fog horn. He booed all during the game, he booed the halftime activities, he booed the cheerleaders, and when the game was over he'd run down and stand at the ramp and boo us as we came off the field, which we were already feeling bad enough because 4 years ago we were running up records like 2 and 12.

One day Wing Choy came to practice grinning like a Buddha. "I got him!" he hollered. "The guy with the big mouth? He cooks hamburgers in a joint on 15th Street. I went in and ordered a hamburger and there he was, right behind the glass, the same plick."

"What'd you do?" Malley asked.

"I booed his hamburgers," Wing said. "Every time he'd finish cooking one, I'd lean over it and go, 'Boooooo!'"

"You booed his hamburgers?" I asked. "What'd the other customers do?"

"Oh, they kinda walked off."

"Yeh," Malley said. "I'm not surprised. Did you happen to notice anybody with a butterfly net?"

"No. But the manager asked me what the hell I was doing. I told him I'd paid for the right to boo when I bought my hamburger."

Wing never said a whole lot, but every now and then he'd come up with this sly sense of humor. When we played in New York, one of his traditions was to rush us over to the Itori Japanese Steakhouse on 56th Street. He'd say, "Gimme pork fried rice, one order moo goo guy pan, egg roll and reetchee nuts, and we pass all 'round." Sometimes he'd take us to the Ali Shankar Bengal restaurant just so he could say he favored their curry.

On Sunday we opened the regular season against the Chiefs at Arrowhead, and Coach was as good as his word: I was dressed and on the roster, snapping on punts and kicks, and glad to have the work. I could feel a dull pain in my knee, but the swelling was down and I was moving pretty free, although I was growing fins from all the whirlpools. To be honest, I had no medical problems that Dr. Demerol and Mr. Green couldn't cure. Now all I had to do was beat out Zawatski for my old job as regular center.

Ziggy visited the lockers one by one before the game. "Need a little something?"

"I already took mine," I said.

"Well, better safe than sorry," Ziggy said.

After he trotted on his way, servicing his dope route, Q. B. said, "What ever happened to Daprisals?"

"I heard they took 'em off the market," Mal said, slipping his pads into their pockets.

"That's too bad," I said. "They were fun while they lasted." Fun is not the word. Daprisals saved the careers of 8 or 10 great athletes I could mention, guys that were at the end of the line but salvaged maybe 2 or 3 more seasons. Daps combined 3 different drugs: an amphetamine to pick you up, aspirin to keep you from feeling pain, and something else so you wouldn't give a shit. The Goats used to take them by the bucketful, and for a while Coach even had the assistants taking Daps before games, so they could keep up their enthusiasm and also so they could understand the players, because Daps make you talk funny, like "Say fay, baby, how you hangin' in the creech out there *hahahahaha . . .*"

I never even heard of uppers or downers till I played in the East-West Shrine Game, and I asked one of the assistants for an aspirin and he gave me a couple of bennies. It was just like Popeye after he eats the spinach. I was sprinting up and down the sidelines during the national anthem and doing grass drills at halftime and hugging and squeezing my teammates like some kind of 42d street nympho, and I played a good game, too, except for 1 ball that I snapped over the punter's head and he had to run for his ass. After the game I could hardly move, and I shook for 2 days.

Since then I've seen it all: uppers and downers, mini-whites, red devils, yellowjackets, Dexxies, greens, bennies, codeine, Empirin No. 3, Dilaudid, Demerol, all the goodies that make the new national pastime possible. I've stood right next to a star athlete when he was shooting up speed in the locker room, and I've seen a few players convulse and one player die because they'd lost track of their tolerance and put their bodies under more strain than they could handle. I've seen big trucks like the late Robert Boggs and J. R. Rodenheimer and Bad-ass Harris take as much as 400 milligrams of greens before a game, and Jake Leftwich of the Redskins told me the most awesome sight he ever saw was our offensive line before our game last year, when Coach told us we *had* to win or he was going to trade the whole fucking team, and Jake said, "They used to talk about the Fearsome Foursome scaring people to death, but you guys had white rings around your mouths! It was like playing a bunch of turned-on zombies. *White rings around your mouths!* Eyes popping out of their sockets! Terrible breath!" We won the game, too, although J. R. and Bad-ass both got racked up, and I tore my knee snapping out at their middle linebacker all day like I was made of rubber bands. That's what greens'll do for you. They're as basic to pro football as pads and cleats and helmets.

Ziggy doesn't make a habit of passing pills himself, but this opener against the Chiefs was the big game right out of the starting gate, and if we won it we'd be on our way to the Superbowl. At least that's the way we felt, and that's the way the experts felt, too. Jimmy the Greek opened us at 5-to-1 to win our division, which was the lowest odds of any club in the conference.

By the time Limey Lovesey put his foot into the kickoff on a sweaty day with just a slight stockyards odor hanging over Arrowhead, we were as high as hooty owls, and our defense held Kansas City to minus 4 yards in their first sequence of downs. Then our offense went out and made every possible mistake you can make, starting with 2 offsides and an offensive holding that finally forced Mal to punt from the end zone. We spent the whole day jacking around like the junior varsity of the St. Ignatius School for the Deaf, Dumb and Fruit. We made every mistake in the book, and we even invented some historic new routines, like me snapping the ball high on a 23-yard field-goal attempt, and Limey being English he can't pick up a beanbag unless it's with his feet, so he lets the ball carom off his chest, and then he takes a couple of volleyball swipes at it in mid-air, he looks like he's trying to kill a moth, and finally bats it into the arms of that dirty linebacker of theirs, the one with the 4 arms and 2 of them always in your nuts or your eyeballs, and by the time the zebra blows the whistle and checks through about 4 volumes of rule books, it's K.C.'s ball 1st and 10 on their own 29. 5 minutes later Coach is so pissed at me that he sends in Zawatski to snap on a punt for the first time all year, and the kid lofts the ball 5 yards over Malley's head and across the end line and the Chiefs get a safety the easy way. Going off the field, Malley hollered, "Tell Coach to ask General Patton what we do now," but not too loud.

2 things saved us: our defense, which was brutal, and their offense, which stank up the joint worse than ours. Buzzie Urquhart intercepted 2 passes and took 1 of them in, and Malley dogged and sprained their quarterback's ankle, and Hyphen B-l-a-c-k recovered a fumble when the

Chiefs were 1st and goal with a minute and a half on the clock, and somehow Q. B. and the rest of us Sisters of Mercy managed to pull our heads out of our asses long enough to get off the field with a totally undeserved win, 7–2.

Flying back on our charter, it was like your mother's funeral. None of the usual balderdash and brouhaha and big loud games of boo-ray and Lacklustre Jones dropping roses and everybody trying to feel up the stews. We knew what was coming, and we cringed at the meeting on Tuesday night. Coach was incense. You'd have thought we just lost to San Diego instead of winning our first game of the season. It got so bitter at the various meetings that Malley stoop up as captain and said, "Coach, excuse me, but the football is not round. Coach, it's a prolate spheroid, and it takes some funny bounces."

Coach turned red, purple and green and told Malley to get his ass back down and shut up or goddamn it he'd be out there doing grass drills in the middle of the night and so many of them he'd think he was a petunia and on and on and on and blah blah blah.

Poor Red Cosgriff tried to present the scouting report on Atlanta, our next opponent, and Red was never the most relaxed person anyway. The tension made him stumble all over himself and drop the chalk and when he was leaning over he left a rose, and Coach's eyes were rolling toward the ceiling, and finally Red said, "Atlanta—they have a t-t-tendency—on 3d and long, you can c-c-count—well, against the Giants they—wait a minute, let me see here. Against the Giants, they—er—uh—they r-r-ran m-m-m-m-"

"That's easy for you to say," Coach said, which I thought was a little cruel.

Cosgriff stammered around a little more, and finally Coach grabbed the chalk and the pointer and said, "You call that shit a scouting report? Sit down and shut up!"

Usually after a winning game, Coach hands out 10-dollar bills for special merit, but today he wasn't handing out anything but abuse. "Harris," he said, "I use to wonder how you got your nickname. Now I know. That was the bad-ass performance of the year. Q. B., my boy, you were a beautiful sight, just beautiful. I mean for a guy playing with his shoelaces tied together, you put on a top performance. Wing Choy, you played like a Chink asshole!"

Wing turned orange. "Chinese-American," he muttered under his breath.

"WHAT WAS THAT?" Coach inquired.

"I said I played like a Chinese-American asshole," Wing said in a soft voice.

"You played like a Chink asshole!" Coach clarified. "Chinese-Americans got guts." Wing evidently decided not to argue the point any further, especially since he had screwed up 2 important handoffs and left Q. B. standing there in his jockstrap.

"Ray Roy," Coach said, "who put the butter in the Hold-Tite jar? You missed 3 balls that fucking Shirley Temple coulda handled."

"You're absolutely right, Coach," Ray Roy said.

"Shut up when I'm talking!" Coach went on. He said that he'd enjoyed watching the game Sunday, but on the whole he'd rather have spent the time watching football. He said that it had been his intention to put Superbowl rings on our fingers this year, but if the offense wasn't interested, well, he didn't give a diddely-shit either, he would just sit quietly on the sidelines and let us poor pussies stink up the place every Sunday, which was pretty clearly what we intended to do unless we got off our fat asses and began to work and hit hit hit and *yah yah yah* and where's your fucking pride?

The following Sunday we took the field like 40 express

trains coming into the same junction, and we cleaned up the Falcons 38–10, never in doubt from the opening kickoff, which Jay Cox trundled 93 yards to the 7, and then Wing followed Bullivant and Bad-ass on our patented sweep, and with the game 41 seconds old we were ahead 7–zip. On the Falcons' first play from scrimmage our left end, Allen Oop Johnson, looped inside and smacked their ballcarrier so hard that the prolate spheroid and his upper denture popped 6 feet into the air, and J. W. Ramwell caught the ball on the short hop and stepped on the denture and went straight to the posts. The air went out of Atlanta like a pricked balloon, and who can blame them—14 points behind while the tuba player's still blowing his spit key from the *Star Spangled Banner*.

That made us 2–0 on the regular season, and I was having very serious mixed emotions about the whole situation. Zawatski was playing 1st-string, and I was assigned to the special teams for the 1st time since my 2d year in the league. "That's the nature of the beast," Ziggy Guminski said with his usual depth. "It's a competitive game, Alph, dog eat dog, and sometimes the old dogs have to move over for the young ones. Hopefully we'll have you back in there before the season's over."

"Hopefully go fuck yourself," I said. "You know what's happening as well as I do, Ziggy. Coach is giving it to me up the ass, and he isn't even wearing a conundrum."

I complained to Malley by the hour, and Malley kept repeating the same thing: Take the situation one day at a time and be patient. "You're playing out your 10th season," he said, "so you're okay on your pension. And who knows? We might make it to the Superbowl, and that's a nice piece of change."

"I got my pride," I said.

"How much is your pride worth?"

"How much is the Superbowl worth?"

"Oh, about 30 grand each."

"My pride goes for about 29."

Mal laughed, and I tried to get my act together to make my regular weekly telephone call to Master A.B.C. "Alphabet" Jackson III, which maybe I told you is my son, living in Augusta, Georgia, with my ex-wife Cathy and his stepfather the doctor. Those weekly calls could be nice, but more often they were tough, because you couldn't expect a kid to keep feeling real close to a father that he almost never saw even if you called him up every day instead of every week, and I'd dial the call and try to sound upbeat but I'd just end up feeling like shit because my kid would always have less and less to say. Then I'd slouch around the apartment or bitch at Malley and he'd say, "Oh, you just talked to little Alph, huh?"

Mal got so pissed at me one night, he shoved me down in a chair and he said, "Now you listen to me, you big dumb asshole, I'm getting sick and tired of this shit. Every week you call the kid and every week you go into a state of catatonic depression."

"Yeh," I said. "Well, I guess I'm still not used to it."

"Well, goddamn it, wise up!" Malley said. "The divorce was 4 years ago, now why don't you face up to it? He's not coming back, he's never gonna be as close to you as he used to be, and that's simple fucking reality, and you better accept it!"

"Jeez, he always sounds so—I don't know—*disinterested* when I call him."

"Well, for Chrissakes, what do you want from a 12-year-old? Give it a few years and he'll talk your head off. You're no fucking Barbara Walters on the phone yourself, you know?"

I didn't get sore. I knew Malley was only trying to be helpful, in his reverse-English style.

Anyway, after Mal and I talked about how much the Superbowl could be worth, I went into my bedroom and shut the door and dialed the kid, and the doctor answered and I said, "Hi, this is Alph Jackson. Is little Alph there?"

"Just a minute," the doc said. "I'll see if Alexander can come to the phone." *Alexander?* Who the fuck was Alexander?

A few seconds later I heard little Alph's voice, and I said, "Hey, are they calling you Alexander now?"

"Well, it's my name," he said.

"Yeh," I said. "I know. I'm the one that gave it to you."

I wasn't sure who might be hanging around his elbow, so I didn't press the point, but after a while he seemed to loosen up, and I said, "Hey, how come they're calling you Alexander now?"

He said he'd told his new Sunday School teacher that his name was Alph Jackson and the lady said, "Alf for Alfred?" and the kid said, "No, Alph for my dad," and when his mother heard about it she told him she thought he was getting too old to use a baby name like Alph. "So now I'm Alexander," little Alph said, "except some of the kids still call me Alph, but I just tell people I'm Alex."

"Yeh, son," I said. "Better do what your mother tells you."

What the hell, he was still my kid, nobody could take that away. You could tell the second you looked at him. He had the same kind of curly lemon-colored hair that I used to have before I took too many hot showers. He was skinny through the waist and square through the shoulders and bird through the legs, just like his old man. And he wanted to be a football player. Well, maybe not anymore, after 4 years under new management. Last year when I went to visit him he told me he still wanted to play, but I think he might have been just telling me what I wanted to hear. Kids are good at that.

The legendary Chester Zawatski, out of Villanova University and Jersey City, N.J., started the first 7 regular-season games as the Billygoats' center, and the worst possible thing happened—we won them all. The truth is we'd stumbled into a cesspool and come up smelling like Channel No. 5. This was the year we were supposed to be hurting in the backfield, with Wing slowing down and Rolf Dale coming off major surgery and probably finished, but instead Jay Cox wanders into the walk-on camp and plays better than Rolf Dale ever played, and this inspires Wing and he begins firing through there like the Shanghai Express of old. On top of that phenomena, crazy Luke Hairston beats out Studney at tight end, which Studney was our weak link for 6, 7 years, and for some reason invisible to all the experts Hairston begins playing back to his all-pro form of a few years earlier, and if you can diagnose that case you're a regular Zigmund Freud. To be brutally blunt, we weren't even hurting at center, because Kid Zawatski was steady as the Pru on offense, and I was handling the punts and kicks. I mean, the kid didn't exactly star out there, but how does a snapper star anyway? Your snapper's in a peculiar position. If he makes 600 perfect snaps, nobody says a word. But if he blows 1, the sports pages carry his name, address, place of birth and next of kin, and demand that he be traded. So a snapper has everything to lose and nothing to gain, which is why no center since Bulldog Turner and Chuck Bednarik has become famous, and they had to play both ways to do it. Myself, I always enjoyed the responsibility out there, the feeling that you better do your job right or the whole play's shot. But to get that quiet feeling of satisfaction, you had to be starting, not just running in and out on punts and kicks. I wanted to be part of the action. How could I take the money without earning it?

My knee was still improving, except for my heart

thumping in it and an occasional shooting pain that Demerol or codeine killed and left me feeling very pleasant to boot. But practice was getting to be a grind. It was one thing when I was 1st-string, but the main function of 2d-string subs in practice is to simulate the next week's opposition, to "give us a picture, give us a pattern," as Coach was fond of screaming, and that's a drag. About the only pleasure I had was teaching special assignments, like showing John Lovesey how to be run into, how to fall as though he's really been axed, so we can pick up the penalty. He couldn't seem to get it through his Limey head. At first he'd kick the ball, watch it sail through the posts, then suddenly flop on his back like he'd been hit by a train.

"No, no, Limey!" I said. "Do it all in one motion. 1st, kick the ball. 2, the lineman comes in front of you, trying to block it. 3, you twist a little and fall down. Not flat on your back, just kind of crumple up, like he's hit you in the nuts."

The next time, Limey kicked the ball, reached down and grabbed his crotch, and slowly slipped into a kneeling position. He made 2 or 3 grimaces and toppled forward on his stomach, wriggled and writhed for a few counts, and then laid still with his eyes rolled back in his head and his tongue sticking out, quivering, like a bowl of Jello that's fallen off the table.

"15 yard penalty," the zebra shouted. We always carry a uniformed ref at our workouts.

"Great!" I said. "Attaway, Limey!"

The ref said the penalty was against us.

"What the bugger for?" Limey asked.

"Overacting," the ref said.

We finally gave up on teaching Limey how to be run into, especially when it began to disturb him that he couldn't learn. Nobody wanted to risk fucking up our field-goal game, which was by far the best in pro football, thanks to Limey and the coach back in Newcastle, England, that taught him to kick a soccer ball 80 yards in the air. It was an astonishing sight to see him propel his whole 127 pounds into the ball and kick through it like an ostrich booting a Land Rover. Nobody in the league had his power, and nobody in the league had his size, so small that he wore boy's shoulder pads and shopped in children's departments and went around wearing those Buster Brown outfits with the neat little umpire caps and the different colored shoes. We always kidded him that masturbation stunted his growth, and he'd tell us to "piss off," which was his main comment in life, but he spent a lot of time reading an English book called *Six Improved Ways of Self-Abuse*, so I guess there was some truth in what we said. The only other comments he made were peculiar things like "Bob's your Uncle" and "Sod the Wog," and he spoke in such a funny brogan that you could hardly understand him anyway. In practice he'd kick straight and true 60, 70 yards, and he'd stand back and tell Q. B., his holder, "I'll make this one, and Bob's your uncle."

"Tom's *my* uncle," Q. B. would say.

"Yeh," I'd say. "I got a Bob that's my mom's uncle."

"Piss off, why don't you?" Limey'd say, and then come out with some expression that nobody could understand. Malley said the reason that Limey was so small was because he eats lightly, and the reason he eats lightly is because he swallows his terminal T's. "How can he eat?" Malley would say. "He's got a stomach full of terminal T's." I thought that was deep.

Well, it was fun to kid Limey, or take the Mickey out of him, as he'd put it himself, but nobody in football could fault his record on the field. Look at last season: We won 5 games by 3 points or less, and in 4 of them Limey kicked at least 1 long field goal. We beat the 49ers after time had already run out and they were caught holding, which entitled us to 1 more play, and little Limey skipped in and kicked a field goal 52 yards to win 17–16. Altogether he racked up 3 new team records: most FGs in a season, 31; most in a game, 5; and longest, 63 yards. He averaged .704 overall, highest in the league, and he kicked 48 out of 48 extra points. Maybe that's why he was the All-Pro kicker, even though he couldn't speak our native tongue.

The other job that helped me pass the time in camp was handing out papers for the offensive and defensive quizzes, and helping to grade them. Somehow it worked out the same every year: Our best players got the worst marks. Before one game, Allen Oop Johnson handed in a perfect paper: 10 multiple-choice answers, all wrong. Coach tried to drill him:

"All right, Oop, what's the Oilers' probability on 2d and 10, early game, 50 yard line?"

"Dunno, Coach."

"What'd you do last night, for Chrissakes?"

"Studied mah charts, Coach. Way you say-ed."

"So what's their tendency, 2d and 10?"

Oop looked at the floor and then at the ceiling, blinked one eye and screwed up his face and bit his lip. "Ah forget, Coach," was the result of all this activity.

"Okay, now listen, you moron. Half the time they'll throw and half the time they'll run."

"Hafe the tam they'll throw and hafe the tam they'll pay'us."

"Run!"

"Run," Oop said meekly.

"So what's their probability?"

"Dunno, Coach."

But in the game that Sunday Oop had 5 sacks, batted down 2 passes and recovered a fumble, and earned himself the game ball for about the 6th time in his career.

"How do you do it, Oop?" Coach said enthusiastically, pommeling his Brontosaurus back in the locker room.

"Dunno, Coach," Oop said.

Oop was just one of those mighty mysteries, like Luke Hairston, guys that worked on some other wavelength. You never saw Oop on a date, never saw him approach a female, but he was always sitting in front when Lacklustre showed his pornie films at camp, and he'd be licking his lips and grunting at some of the climatic moments.

"Oop, how come you never go out with girls?" Malley asked him one night in the hotel.

Oop screwed up his face and echoed, *"Out with girls,"* the way he usually does, and then he said, "Too hord."

"What's too hard?"

"Tokin' to 'em."

So Malley started a tutoring service, teaching Oop how to address young women of the opposite sex. "Now we're sitting at a bar," Mal said, "and we're out on a date, you and me, and I say, 'Gee, I saw a terrific movie the other night.' What do you say?"

"Dunno," Oop said. "Ah stayed home."

"No, no!" Malley said. "You respond, 'Oh, what film did you see?'"

"What fee-ilm did yew see?"

"Well, it was a movie about animals in British Columbia," Mal went on. Oop said nothing. "About animals in British Columbia," Malley repeated. Still no comment. "Now *you* talk!" Mal instructed.

"What do Ah say?"

"Just make small talk. Keep the conversation moving. Let's try it again. 'It was about animals in British Columbia. I really enjoyed it.'"

"Mah brother fucked a sheep."

"Jesus Christ!" Mal said. "Is that anything to say to a woman you just met?"

"Ah ain't sayin' it to no woman Ah jes' may-et. Ah'm sayin' it to yew." Malley gave up.

With 12 straight wins, 5 pre-season and 7 regular, the Billygoats were the hottest item in pro football, and according to a story that Bill Legham wrote in *Sports Pictorial*, people were making fortunes betting on us. The reason was the bookies knew we were good but they didn't realize *how* good, and they consistently underdid the point spread. Legham ran a little chart with his story, covering the 1st 7 regular-season games. We'd been even money in 2 games and a slight underdog in 2 more, and won all of them. In the other 3 games, we were the favorite by 3, 7 and 13 points, and we won those games by 9, 11 and 26 points, so for the whole regular season so far, we'd beaten the spread in every game, which doesn't mean too much to a player but the bettors love it. Like Legham pointed out, if you'd put $10 on the Goats in the first game of the year and let the money ride in every game after that, you'd already run your sawbuck up to $1280.

You'd think that with a record like that, certain parties would begin to smile once in a while, but then certain parties have a permanent case of the red ass. I especially mean Coach. If anything, General Patton got meaner as the streak mounted up. J. R. Rodenheimer is the same way, and so is his alter side of the ego, Luke Hairston. Those surly bastards stayed just as surly.

J. R. has a steel-wire crewcut and one of those ruined faces, like he's been in 1000 barroom brawls or else played lacrosse, with narrow swampwater eyes that peer at you through slits like you're a dropping off a mule. Beware if you're not J. R.'s favorite color, which is white-on-white, not just ordinary white. Ordinary white would include Tony Damiano, No. 65, our right tackle on defense, but

J. R. doesn't approve of Tony because his white is a little off-color, closer to brown. J. R. also doesn't like Damian Kumjian, our 3d-string quarterback, because being Armenian is "the next nearest thing to a nigger," which is the typical gracious way J. R. puts it.

You can see that he's a very sick individual, with his hatred of anything that doesn't look ¾ths like himself. He just can't seem to keep his mouth shut on the subject, even though he plays on a team that's ½ black in a league that's ½ black in a country that has 30,000,000 blacks doing everything from chopping cotton to brain surgery. "Hey, lookee here," J. R.'ll say to one of the smaller brothers like Ray Roy Jenkins or Lincoln Marbley, "I got me a Nigro bankroll," and he'll flash a roll of dollar bills with a 20 at both ends.

"Leave it lay, will yeh?" I'll pop in, being the chief oiler of troubled waters, but once J. R. gets started it's hard to shoot him down. He'll holler to a bartender, "Hey, bring me a *jee-gro* of bourbon." He calls Leroy Kelly "Washington's Irish jig," and falls all over himself appreciating his own joke, if you can call it that. One time on the plane, when he was still high from his game biphetamines, which they keep popping off in your stomach for 6 or 7 hours, he said, "Hey, you guys, you know what's the 3 biggest lies in the world? 'The check is in the mail, I won't come in your mouth, and I'm proud I'm a nigger.' " The late Robert Boggs was sitting in the back, and he flew down that aisle and did a regular old 1938 flying tackle into J. R., sending him sliding past the galley like he'd been meataxed. J. R. reached back and grabbed a wine bottle, and when he did the stew grabbed another one and cold-cocked him from behind, which was a good thing for all concerned.

Luke Hairston was the only black that J. R. never made any cracks to or even talked to at all, maybe because Luke would never respond or maybe because J. R. sensed that you didn't fuck around with this party, it wasn't healthy. The newspapers always called Luke "The Quiet Man," because they weren't allowed to come right out and say he's psycho, or at least antisocial, always keeping to himself like that. The only subject that seemed to turn him on was guns, his private little hobby, which he must've had 100 weapons, from a little .25 Beretta to who knows what all, maybe a .155 howitzer from World War I. I only hoped they kept the atom bomb under lock and key. Sometimes he packed a .44 magnum that'd take out a wall, and it wasn't surprising to hear a big noise in the middle of the night and find out he was squeezing off a few test rounds. If there was no other convenient place, he'd fire into the phone book. One night he shot 6 rounds in a hotel in Cincinnati, and an unsuspecting room clerk came flying up the stairs and into the room. "What the hell was that?" the clerk asked.

"If I don't sleep," No. 84 said, "nobody sleeps."

The clerk looked into the smoking end of a .38. "Yeh," he said. "Makes sense." We changed hotels after that.

Even Billy Bob Bunker had to be careful around Hairston, or else run the risk of losing a key player and not able to brag all over the Petroleum Club about rehabilitating the problem child. Mr. Bunker imagines he has a winning way with players, dating back to his ability to get along with Pfc.s when he was a 2d lieutenant, and whenever there's a dispute, he likes to intervene and try to settle it. One night he walked into Hairston's hotel room on the road, and Luke was playing with a Luger. "Hi there, big fella," Billy Bob said, sticking out his pudgy little hand. "I hear we have a problem?"

Luke stood up like he'd been goosed by a hot poker. "What chew doin' in my room?" he said to the man who pays his salary.

Mr. Bunker settled into a chair and started to say something, but before he could get out a word Hairston screamed at him, "WHAT CHEW DOIN' IN MY ROOM, WHITEY? Did you knock, Mothafucka? WOULD YOU DO THAT TO A HONKY BALLPLAYER? You don't show me the respec' people show a dog in the street! You don't *know* me well enough!"

Mr. Bunker jumped up and backed nervously toward the door. "Hey, big fella," he said, "I didn't mean anything personal."

"Don't call me no big fella, you jive chump," Luke raved. "I got a name, and it's *Mister* Hairston to you. Got it, Mr. Bigshot?"

Billy Bob eased out the door and started toward his room. " Cause I'll shoot your candy ass if you do!" Luke hollered after him, and for emphasis he fired 6 blanks, "extra loud report." They said later that Mr. Bunker covered the last 10 feet in an infantry crouch and dove into his door screaming that he'd been shot. Everybody waited for Hairston to be cut or committed, but he stayed with us, which may tell you something about how bad this club wanted the Superbowl. Coach fined him $50 for unauthorized use of firearms and rescinded it after the next game, when he caught 2 T.D. passes.

"The onliest thing I can't figure out," the late Robert Boggs was saying one night, "is how that Hairston change on the field. I don't know another dude that'll give hisse'f up the way Hairston will. I mean he'll get hisse'f *kilt* to save your ass."

"He plays a very self-sacrificing game," Malley said, which by that he means that Hairston will decoy into the short zone 4, 5 times in a row, getting assassinated by the linebackers every time, to open up deeper patterns for the wide receivers, and he'll do it without complaint. "I think it's the effect of the adrenaline."

"He don't take no adrenaline," Robert said, "but he take somethin', 'cause I see his eyes widen up before every game."

"You don't have to take adrenaline," Mal explained. "You produce it when you're under stress, and people react in different ways, just like people react differently to booze or grass. Look at Bad-ass or Wing Back, they're nice guys off the field and wild animals on. Maybe Hairston's just the opposite, adrenaline calms him down, makes him a calmer person."

"I don't know," Robert said, "but I love the way he do his thing. Till the gun go off, and then it's Bye Bye Blackbird again."

The moods of a professional football club are as changeable as a bunch of old ladies going through the menstrual pause, but right now we were as high as a 2-year ham. Just about everybody except J. R. and Luke Hairston was pals. We ran around together, partied together, everybody knew everybody else's wives and girlfriends, and the women sat in a group at games and didn't pommel each other with their handbags, the way Bullivant's wife knocked the crap out of Wing Choy's wife 2 years ago when Wing's fumble cost us the playoffs. Mal said we were living in a fool's paradise and he hoped it would never end, and I couldn't help agreeing with him, deep as he was.

Whenever one of the Goats would be interviewed about our success, he'd make this speech about depending on each other, each player just a cog in the wheel, one guy picking up the other guy, the defense coming through in one game and the offense coming through in the next, and all that familiar old clap trap. Vince Lombardi once said that the Packers ran on love, but he left out that it can be a short romance, and when you lose, you begin to run on malice, hatred, distrust and envy. Maybe Lombardi didn't know, because his teams hardly ever bothered to lose.

When you're a winner like the Billygoats, the coaches are all geniuses, with their own radio and TV shows, and ad agencies line them up for endorsements, and Ph.D.s ask them questions like fools at the throne. But if you lose a couple, seeds of doubt begin to sprout and that's when the shit-disturbers can hurt you, sitting around the bars saying things like, "Our screens aren't designed right. Anybody that's played football knows our screens are poor," and pretty soon the players aren't putting out on the screens because they're brainwashed into thinking they won't work anyway, and then you begin to lose, and one breakdown leads to another. Then a guy like J. R. puts out the word that the team has too many niggers. "What can you expect with all them jigaboos?" he'll say, and he'll quote some crooked social researcher who can "prove" that blacks are dumber than whites because they don't score as high on tests that the whiteys make up. It's enough to make you sick. Well, I been through it all, winning and losing, loving each other and constant back-biting, and I'll take winning any day. The only thing missing was playing on the 1st team, but a man can't have everything. There was $30,000 at stake. Maybe if we'd been having one of our old-fashioned 2–12 seasons, I'd have hung up the cleats, but I had to agree with the guy that said a long time ago, "I been rich and I been poor, and I can tell you, rich is better."

Our 8th game was the return with Atlanta, and in spite of what you may think, nobody took it for granted, even though we waltzed those pussies the first time. Very few people embarrass the Dutchman twice in a row and live to tell the tale. Besides, the New Orleans Saints were just 2 games behind us in the loss column, and this was no time to start dogging it. Coach worked our asses off during the week, gave us extra films to study, and ran us silly in practice. One night Mal and I were laying on our beds breathing hard when there was a knock on the door and Lacklustre Jones, 6 foot 6 inches of sweaty pulchritude, came barging in like he owned the place. "Hey," Lack said, "I'm in trouble."

"What else is new?" Malley said. "I mean we know your life is no glorious saga of song, no medley of extemporania."

"Huh?" Lack said. "Listen, I got a problem with the missus."

"What else is new?" Mal repeated, because Lacklustre and his wife Fern are always screaming at each other.

"This tam she's got the goods on me," Lack said in his Flatonia, Texas, accent. "Some broad done squealed on me, and I didn't do a fuckin' thang!"

He told us how a person speaking in a female voice had telephoned the apartment and claimed that Lacklustre had seduced her and it was a lousy thing to do because he'd promised to only put it in an inch or so, but then he'd kept on pushing and pushing and finally went all the way, and she thought she might be pregnant with a little Lacklustre Jones, and that was more than she could bear. Fern was shocked, but she kept her wits about her and asked if this wasn't just a case of mistaken identity, because Lack had only left the house about 10 minutes before to go down to the store for cigarettes, and how could he have possibly found time? The lady said it was definitely no case of mistaken identity, that her seducer was Mr. James R. Lacklustre Jones of the Billygoats, and if Fern didn't believe her, well, Lack had a tattoo of a butterfly on his cock.

"Nothing to worry about then," I said. "You don't have a tattoo, do you?"

"Yeh, I do, but it's purty faded."

"But it's not a butterfly?" Malley said.

"Depends. Sometams it's a itty bitty moth, and sometams it's a giant butterfly."

A few hours later a woman called Q. B.'s wife with a similar tale, and the next afternoon during practice Della Zawatski got a call, the poor little bride of 8 months, 7 months pregnant and still living on love and Polish sausage, and had to listen to a long description of how her Chet was getting sandwiched between 2 naked stewardesses with lots of relish.

Well, that's all the Billygoats needed. I mean professional football is a game of concentration, and how are you supposed to concentrate on things like game plans and probabilities and concealed zones when your wives are being told that the whole club is nothing but a bunch of sex maniacs, chasing everything that moves and acting like degenerates every time their backs are turned? Not that the club *isn't* a bunch of degenerates. You're on the road 10 or 11 times a year, and the Football Annies prostate themselves, and we all have feet of clay sometimes. But the strange thing was that Q. B. and Chet and Lack were getting accused of specific things that they didn't do by women they'd never heard of, and the wives were believing it. Malley said it was a kind of poetic justice, but I didn't care whether it rhymed or not, it was queering our morale. Maybe that was the idea.

The team was supposed to leave for Atlanta on a 1 o'clock charter Saturday afternoon, but I got my annual permission to take a morning flight so I could visit my kid, A.B.C. "Alphabet" Jackson III. Excuse me, I mean Alexander. My plane landed late, and it was a long 2-hour shot across Interstate 20 from Atlanta to Augusta, and I pushed the rented Chev to 86 mph on the stretch between Covington and Madison. I thought I saw a state trooper parked on the shoulder near Swords, so I shoved the car up to nearly 100 and for some reason nobody came after me. That's the way I was on those once-a-year reunions—tear-ass to see my kid, and if anybody got between me and the ice-cream parlor where we always met, it was at his own risk, including the state speed fuzz.

When I pulled up, little Alph was already there, parked back in the corner where his mother and stepfather always deposited him and then drove off in a cloud of dust as if they'd be turned into a pillow of salt if they ever laid eyes on me. "Hey, man!" I said. "How they hanging?" and I put my arms around him and gave him a squeeze.

He got himself loose pretty quick, which I understand that boys around 12, 13 years old are not too thrilled about being hugged, even by their old man, so I didn't take offense. "Hi, Pop," he said, calling me what he always called me. "I thought you forgot."

I told him the plane was late, and he told me it was okay, he'd been eating ice cream and watching the people walk by, and then we went out and did what we always did—saw a couple of movies and drank about 6 chocolate malts in about 6 different places and I bought him a new game called "Sports Pictorial Football" and an archery set and then it was time to take him back to his house and drop him off and watch him walk across the front yard and into the house and that would be it for another year. But this time when I stuck out my hand to shake goodbye and I started to turn away, he reached up to kiss me on the cheek, the way he used to do before he got to be 12 years old, and I was embarrassed because I'd sort of left him standing there with no cheek to kiss, so I leaned over and I picked him up and lifted him above my head and I said, "That's okay, son, you just go right ahead and give your old man a kiss," which he hugged me and kissed me, and then I put him down and he ran for the door and I turned away, and if they didn't like what they'd been watching from behind the curtains, well, tough titty. It wasn't my idea to lose the kid.

A pretty broody bunch of Billygoats showed up to play Atlanta. The weird phone calls had kept up right till the last minute, and guys like Q. B. and Lack were really down. "The wife called at 3 in the morning," Q. B. said, "and she was practically hysterical. Pregnant and all, ya know?"

"Put it out of your mind, Q. B.," I said. "We got a game to win."

"How'm I gonna put it out of my mind when she sounds like she's gonna put a fucking bullet in her head?"

Lack had a simular problem, except that in his story the bullet was going in *his* head and his wife said she was hopping the next plane to do it. "You know what she told me?" he said, perched on the toilet before the game. "She said, 'When you come back, *don't come back!*' Then she hung up on me."

We took the field like a bunch of ladies from a nervous ward, and a riled-up bunch of Falcons were there to meet us. The minute Mal and Limey and I'd went out at 12:15 to practice kicks and punts, we'd seen the difference between these Falcons and the pussies we'd whipped back in September. "Hey, Charlie," I said to Charlie Kligerman as we passed their bench, "how they hanging?"

"Go fuck yourself," Charlie said, and spit in the artificial turf. The fact that we'd been roomies at Penn State for 2 years didn't seem to impress him. The Dutchman must have made one of his blood and thunder speeches, "It's them or us, and it better not be us," that sort of thing for which he was famous for around the league. A couple of our 3d-stringers went behind the posts to shag, and when one of them threw the ball over my head and it rolled to the Atlanta half of the field, those Falcons just stood there and looked at it, and I had to get it myself. Greasy kid stuff! But I guess they didn't want to risk a humanitarian gesture in front of Godzilla the coach.

It was another humid day, 68 degrees, cloudy and dark, and the way the pit action went in the 1st quarter, I was almost glad Zawatski was playing instead of me. Almost, but not quite. The Goats offensive line has a tendency to come off the ball fast and hard, in fact, about a quarter-count too early, but since we're disciplined to do it together, the officials never call the penalty. Now Atlanta was doing the same thing, just as quick and just as hard, and it sounded like Chinese New Year's, with helmets clanging and pads smashing and those hard Absorblo arm pads clacking against knuckles and ankles and bones. The average person who thinks he knows the violence of pro football really hasn't the slightest idea. You can get a hint on the sidelines, but the real impact and force only comes when you're right in the middle, hearing things that can't be heard off the field, such as "You nigger cocksucker," and "I'll break your fuckin' arms yeh fruit yeh!" Malley says there's only one way to describe pro football to the layman. He says it's exactly like being in a scheduled automobile accident every Sunday. You train and condition yourself, you prepare your body, you put on protective equipment, and then you voluntarily slam head on into the other car, and if you're lucky, you end up with bumps and bruises.

Atlanta was playing a lot of odd line defense, which put Thad Kowalczyk, their big tackle, nose to nose on Zawatski, and before the 1st quarter was over, the kid was in the fight of his life. I had to hand it to him; he stood in there. Kowalczyk was All-America out of Clemson, and Zawatski went to Villanova, and *Sports Pictorial* wrote it up later as "a titanic struggle between the North Pole and the South Pole," but it seemed more like a knife fight at the time. The kid would hold off Kowalczyk for 3 downs and then stagger to the sidelines with blood all over his face from his broken nose and also from that scab that every lineman gets where the straps cross on your forehead and scrape off the skin.

"The Polock's trying to grind you down, kid," Ziggy Guminski said, and I thought, Jeez, it's nice of you to tell him, otherwise he'd never know. By the time the 2d period was half over, 0–0, the kid's snapping arm was all bruised and yellow, and his eyes were rolling in his head, but he was still keeping Kowalczyk occupied whenever they lined up odd, and Jim Ringo couldn't have done it better.

Then Chet made a tiny mistake that only another lineman can fully appreciate. When you've got to snap the ball with a tackle hunching over you, your move is to fire out and try to drive your helmet through his throat, and if he gives a little you get in there nice and close where the officials can't see and get a grip. But if you can't get a hold, then you do the opposite: You bump and step back, bump and step back, so the tackle can't grab you and throw you down, which is what's on his mind all the time. Maybe Zawatski was groggy from the forearm shivers Kowalczyk had been rapping on his helmet, 3 or 4 per play, which you're only allowed 1 per play by official rule of the National Football League, but for some reason the kid forgot himself and threw a cut-off block at Kowalczyk, a real quick throw-out at the legs, which is exactly the wrong block under the circumstances, and of course the South Pole just lifted his dainty size 14s and stepped right over Zawatski and flopped on Q. B. like a fly on dogshit.

"Jesus Christ!" Coach screamed. "That was a fucking look-out block!" meaning that it was the kind of block where you turn and holler "Look out!" to the quarterback. The look-out block is a cousin of the "Oh, shit!"

block, where a tackle gets trapped and can't get back to the play and hollers "Oh, shit!"

"Get that dumb rook outa there!" Coach hollered, and he slapped me on the ass and sent me in. I'd already been on the field for 2 punts and a missed field goal, but this was the first time all year that I'd be snapping on a regular offensive play, and I was so elated I didn't have time to feel sorry for anybody else. I knew that big gonzo Kowalczyk from years of experience, and I knew exactly how to wrack his ass. The Falcons figured to keep on using the odd line, and on the first play I asked Q. B. to call a sweep, which would take Kowalczyk and me out of the play, and I snapped the ball and rammed into the South Pole with 230 pounds of pent-up frustration and energy and knocked him about 3 feet through the air, and when he came bouncing back I whacked him across the eyes with my wrist bandages, all toughened up with Nu-skin and about 6 times as hard as steel, and when he was falling down with me on top of him I whispered in his ear, "That's for Chet, you Polock pussy!" I don't usually indulge in racial epitaphs but my strategy was to convert him from a tough, smart defensive tackle into a tough, *sore* defensive tackle. Then he'd be through for the day.

We made the first down, and they went right back into the odd line, and on the next play Kowalczyk never even looked at Q. B., he just smashed into me and decked me solid, which probably made him feel good till he looked up and saw Wing Choy flying through the 2 hole, where Kowalczyk has responsibility, picking up 7 more yards. You'd think the dumb bastard would have sensed something, but on the next play he came at me again, and this time I stepped aside and rang his bell as he passed, and Q. B. completed a zig-out to Custer Fox for another first down. But then our drive fizzled and Atlanta took over, and when we got the ball back, they went into an even line, which left me to deal with the middle linebacker on running plays or else set and fill, which is a lot softer duty.

The half ended 0–0, and Ziggy said, "Way to go, Alph!" but Coach was tear-ass in the locker room, raving about missed chances and nobody gives a fiddler's fuck and how could he coach a bunch of pussies and if we didn't give a shit neither did he, and it made me wonder if this was still the same team that was 7–zip on the season, some bunch of pussies with a record like that. Then Billy Bob Bunker had to stick his oar in, telling us to get in there and fight like General Patton and "tell those Falcons to blow it out their barracks bag."

Kid Zawatski patched up his ailments and started the 2d half, which normally would have aggravated me, but I understood Coach's thinking because it's the standard thinking of every coach in the NFL, wrong but standard. The unwritten rule is: Don't break up a winning combination. If you're winning with 10 players and a paraplegic, why, leave the paraplegic in there till he costs you a ball game. Coach had just been reacting emotionally when he yanked Chet in the 1st half. I guess he figured the kid would get his act together, and he was right. Atlanta went back to the odd line and the kid handled Kowalczyk to a stand-off, which is all you can ask, and no harm done. Atlanta scored and we scored, and it was 7–7 in the last period, and it began to look like we were finally going to pull it out, with 3d and 4 on their 6 and a "gimme" field goal coming up even if we didn't go to the posts.

Then while we're all kneeling on the sidelines with our fingers crossed and our assholes tight enough to pull railroad spikes, we observe the Looneytunes play of the year, the all-time fuckup on your hit parade of fuckups. Q. B. breaks the huddle and comes up behind Zawatski, leans over and sticks his hands up Zawatski's ass to take the snap, and the next thing we know the ball is spurting straight toward the South Pole, which Kowalczyk jumps on it and goes fetal and it's 1st and 10, Atlanta. If you're asking did Zawatski center the ball through his own legs and back over his own head to Kowalczyk, well, I guess the answer is yes. It's a first, but it happened. He snapped the ball in that hard pendulum arc you're supposed to use, but Q. B.'s hands didn't accept it, and the ball hit Q. B. in the nipple and bounced over our own line to the Falcons.

"What the fuck was that?" Coach screamed at Q. B., grabbing him by the fuchsia as he came off and shaking him like a rat terrier.

"I don't know," Q. B. said. "I tried to call time, and the kid snapped the ball."

Zawatski came dragging-ass behind, and Coach hollered, "What's the matter with you?" but the kid just went to the bench and sucked on some oxygen and huddled under his blanket. Coach flang his 5-gallon elevator hat on the ground and kicked the bench with his elevator boot. Roosevelt Atkins, the defensive line coach, came spluttering over with his usual chaw of Red Devil and asked, "Wombatta klasser jaray?"

Ziggy answered, "He tried to call time and the kid snapped the ball."

Rosey Atkins said, "Chendora neeshetting forang mothafucka," and went back to his phones. It was hard to understand Atkins during a game, and Coach always threatened to send him to the Al DeRogatis Speech School in Philadelphia, P.A.

Things weren't bad enough, but then Atlanta went into its 2-minute drill and their horny old quarterback lofted the ball into the flooded weakside zone and hit that 1-eyed spook from Grambling and he went 66 yards to the posts and threw the ball into the stands and we had our 1st loss of the year, 14–7.

Zawatski sat in front of his locker, slowly leaking blood

on the mat, while the rest of us showered. "C'mon, kid,"
I said, "the game's over."

"Dumb," he said. "Stupid. Dumb. *Stupid!*"

"Look," I said, "nobody's arguing. Now go take your
shower."

One of the reporters caught Coach on the way out the
door. "Well, Coach," he said, "you can't win 'em all."

"Why not?" Coach snapped, and kept on walking.

THE FLIGHT

V

MAYBE I CAN TALK TO HIM

SITTING IN THE FRONT OF THE HIJACKED PLANE, *Coach looked to me like he was going up in a spurt of steam any second, or die of a heart attack from high blood pressure complicated by a heavy flow of bile. "Goddamn fucking son of a bitch cocksucker!" he said to nobody special. After that he unleashed a long string of vulgar epitaphs, till the Rev. Matt Galvin had to turn around and remind him in a weak voice that there were ladies present, which he referred to Mrs. Billy Bob Bunker and a couple of socialite friends that had bummed a free ride so they wouldn't have to dip into capital to fly to the game. Coach grabbed ahold of me as I was passing by on one of my frequent Western Union trips to the cockpit. "What the fuck're we gonna do?" he said. "What're we gonna* do?"

"Well, I don't know, Coach," I said. "There's not a whole lot you can do when the guy sits there with his finger on the trigger."

"Where's the pilot say we are?"

"We're over West Texas. Why? Does it make any difference?"

"Tell him to head for open water," Coach said.

"Why?"

"We'd have a chance if we came down at sea. We could get picked up and still make it to the game."

"From 32,000 feet, I don't think it really matters, Coach," I said.

The Connection had slipped over to listen in. "Strepey," Coach said, "what the fuck are we gonna do?"

"Maybe I can talk to him," The Connection said.

"I don't recommend it," I said. "He's not in a talking mood."

"Is he ever?" Coach asked.

The Connection said, "Lately I thought he was beginning to loosen up. He smiled at me the other day when I was taping him. First time. Maybe he feels a little friendly."

"Ask him can Strepey talk to him," Coach ordered. "Jesus Christ, we gotta try something."

A few minutes later I came back into 1st class with Hairston's answer. "He says if anybody from up here shows his face, he'll shoot it off."

"Go ahead, Jimmy," Coach told The Connection. "Stand behind the curtain and try to talk some sense into him."

The trainer looked frightened. "Coach, I think the man's mental," he said. "Maybe—"

"Look, Strepey, you only live once," Coach said. "80 lives depend on you."

"I don't really know the man, Coach," The Connection complained.

"Nobody knows the man, Jimmy," Coach said, patting him on the shoulder the way I'd seen him do so many times when he was trying to con somebody. "Go ahead, Jimmy. Try to soften him up."

Strepey started down the aisle. "Wait!" I said. "Let me get back to my seat first." I limped on down the aisle and crawled into my rack. Hairston was standing with his head against the bulkhead, taking turns fiddling with the gun and watching the players, saying his usual nothing.

In a few minutes, I heard The Connection's voice from behind the curtain. "Luke! Luke! This is the trainer."

Hairston acted as if he didn't hear a sound.

"Luke!" The Connection called out. "Can I come in?"

No reaction, except maybe a little side-flip of the eyes in the direction of the drapes.

"C'mon, man," The Connection said. "Let's talk. Let's see what's troubling you. I got greens, Demerols, codeine, I even got a few Daps left over. Whatever you want."

Hairston didn't react, but I noticed that he reached down and pushed a button on the side of the gun.

The curtain rustled, and the little round head of The Connection peeped out.

Hairston turned like a cat, raised the barrel of the gun and fired one shot. I expected to hear a scream, like in the movies, but all I heard was something bumping into something, and The Connection saying almost in a whisper, "Oh, shit!"

Hairston blew the smoke from the tip of the weapon, reset the button, and snapped, "Jackson?"

"Yes, sir, Luke," I said, and at that point if he had instructed me to kiss his ass I would have thanked him for the honor. Until he squeezed off that shot, I had no real way to figure how far he'd go.

"What can I do for you?" I begged in my best suck-up voice.

"Get on up and tell those assholes don't be comin' back here and hasslin' me!"

I clambered through the galley and into 1st class. The Connection was sprawled across a rack gushing blood down his shirt, and one of the stews was trying to treat him. "Where is it?" The Connection kept saying. "Where is it? Oh, my God, find out where it is!"

Coach grabbed a knife from the galley and began slashing at the trainer's shirt. "It's okay, Jimmy," he said after he peeled away the bloody material. "It's in the upper part of your arm."

"Much blood?" The Connection asked.

"Yeh," Coach said, "but we'll tighten it up and stop it. You'll be okay, Jimmy."

"Thanks," The Connection said, closing his eyes and looking green. "And Coach—"

"Yeh, Jimmy."

"Call my wife?"

I announced that Hairston had an instruction for everybody. "Stay up here!" I said. "Don't get any brave ideas. He's acting crazy."

"No shit?" Coach said sarcastically. "He's acting crazy, huh? Jackson, we can always depend on you for the latest news."

I went back to economy for another taste of our shit sandwich. Luke stood as before, head slightly lowered, eyes half closed and heavy lidded, probably from all the injections he'd been taking. Toward the rear, most of the guys were slouched in their seats, whispering out of the sides of their mouths and trying not to be conspicuous. I headed on back to join them, and Hairston said nothing. What a lucky guy I was, to have the run of the plane on the Billygoats' annual outing.

The whole week after Zawatski pulled his rock, Coach had him working out with the 2d team, and I guess he had it coming after a stunt like that, but I still couldn't help thinking that there was something vaguely mysterious about the whole fucked-up snap. Q. B. was going around explaining to anybody who'd listen that he tried to call time and all of a sudden the ball was caroming off his chest and the next thing he knew Kowalczyk was on top of it and it was Atlanta's ball. As for Chet, he just kept his own council. "Forget it," he told Malley when we tried to open the subject. "Just forget it."

"Well, I wish it was that easy, kid," Malley said, "but the way Q. B. tells it, that was the weirdest play of the year."

"Forget it," Zawatski said like a broken record, and turned away.

The game films were no help. Ziggy Guminski ran them about 6 times in slow motion, but all you could see was Q. B. come up to the line, stick his hands under the kid, then turn his head to the right just as the ball slowly appeared like an orange balloon and floated up into Q. B.'s chest and then over the line to Kowalczyk. "See!" Q. B. said each time it showed him turning his head to the right, "I'm trying to call time."

Chet just sat there and studied his manicure.

All week long, the kid looked dull in practice, and if we'd had the personnel, I'm sure Coach would have benched him entirely. Our next game was New Orleans at New Orleans, and we only had a 1-game lead on them after they won a squeaker against the Patriots, 24–21. Coach kept screaming at us all week that this was the game where we had to show our medal, and Ziggy added, "We gotta let it all hang out, men, and show 'em the stuff we're made of."

"Jeez," I complained, "let's not do that!"

But no amount of joking around could bring Zawatski out of the deep blue funk he had spun around himself, not talking to anybody, just going through the motions on the field, until finally I realized I'd better take the bull by the tail and turn the situation around before it dragged the whole team down.

"Zawatski," I said after the Thursday practice, which was heavy workouts with pads and a run-through of the 2d-half game plan, "you and I are gonna take a nice stroll over to the Dandy Don's and have a couple beers."

Zawatski turned away.

"All right, then," I said. "We'll go to the Warsaw Inn and have a borscht with a vodka chaser."

He turned and looked at me with a dying-swan look and said, "No, thanks, but I appreciate it."

"Appreciate what?"

"Your sympathy."

"My sympathy?" I said, trying to modulate my voice. "Jesus Christ, Chet, we're 5 or 6 games away from the big apple, man. The whole ball of yarn. The Superbowl and 30,000 skins *per man*, and you pick a time like this to get the rag on?"

He turned his back again, and when I whirled around him to keep on making my point, I could see his eyes were droopy and wet like a fresh-shot rabbit, and I began to feel bad myself. "What's the matter, kid?" I said, putting my hand on his shoulder. I steered him toward the door before any of the other guys could notice what was going on, and I walked him down the alleyway. He didn't say anything for 15, 18 blocks of hard walking, and then he mumbled something, and when I asked him to repeat, he said, "It's a bad dream. It's like that thing Joyce wrote about walking around in a nightmare, trying to wake up."

"That's deep," I said. "That's really deep."

"Do you like Joyce's work?"

"I don't know," I answered truthfully. "What does she do?" We walked another 10, 12 blocks without a word.

"Look, kid," I said finally. "My knee's hurting and I'd rather not make the whole Cook's tour of the city this afternoon. Look, I know you pulled a rock out there Sunday, but it's not the end of your life. Why, shit, let me tell you what I did in my senior year." I told him how the Nittany Lions, my good old alma-mater Penn State, worked all week on a flea-flicker where we'd line up for a field goal and I'd snap straight to the kicker and he'd lob a pass to the right tackle who was eligible after a tricky shift at the last second, except that I got my wires crossed and instead of snapping to the kicker I snapped to the holder, out of habit, and 4 unguarded rushers swarmed in there and buried the holder and the kicker under 6 feet of cowshit. "See what I mean, kid?" I said. "Anybody can pull a jack-off play like that. Even me."

Zawatski stopped and looked at me out of those moony eyes. "Sure, Alph," he said. "Anybody can make a mistake. But you're supposed to admit it, aren't you?"

"Well—"

"You're supposed to come right out and say, 'Hey, I did it! *Me!* I'm the dummy.' Right?"

"Sure, but you're not supposed to brood all week. You blew it. We all know you blew it. Now let's get ready for the Saints."

"But that's the whole trouble," the kid says. "I *didn't* blow it."

"What?"

"It wasn't my fault."

Now it was my turn to stop and look dumb. "Hey, excuse me," I said. "Aren't you the Chet Zawatski that played at Villanova and then for the Billygoats and which you snapped the ball to Thad Kowalczyk last Sunday in front of about 90,000 people at Bunker Stadium? You are that individual, aren't you?"

"Yeh, I'm that individual."

"Well, then cut the travesty."

We walked another mile or 2 and then the kid said, "I knew nobody'd understand. I could hire a hall and explain, and not one person would take my word."

"Look, Chet," I said, grabbing him by the sleeve, "I don't know what you're trying to prove, but we got a ball game coming up this Sunday, and I'll try to understand *anything* if it'll help us win. Now why don't you tell me what's on your mind, and leave it up to *me* if I understand. I'm not just your typical dumb snapper, you know." I could have torn my tongue out by the roots, but he didn't seem to take offense.

"Strictly between you and me?" he asked.

"On my mother's eyes," I promised, which is a toast I heard from my Wop grandfather.

Well, if a man can be bowled over by words, then I would have wound up on my ass in the middle of Turner Drive. Zawatski gave the whole story, told it absolutely straight, and by the time he was finished I knew it was 100% the truth. Maybe you have to be an NFL snapper to follow it, but the whole thing was as simple as syrup to me, and now nobody on earth knew what'd happened except me, the kid and Q. B.

The play was supposed to go on the 1st sound, because Atlanta was acting slow about getting set, and Q. B. thought he could steal a 1st down with a superquick call. The Goats get up to the line and the 1st sound turns out to be Q. B. calling for time, which Zawatski doesn't give a fuck, it's a sound, isn't it? He's supposed to snap the ball on the 1st *sound*, whether the 1st sound is "shift," "ready," "set," "hut," "kiss my ass" or whatever. So he slams the ball back in a hard arc the way he's supposed to do, and it hits Q. B. in the chest and the rest is history.

There's only one way that Q. B. can call time in a situation like that, and that's to release his hands, break off contact with the snapper's ass, and then the snapper knows that something's wrong, and the quarterback can call time or sing the Billygoats Fight Song or whatever he wants, and the kid won't let go of the ball. But that isn't what Q. B. did. That's the risk with plays that go on the 1st sound—you can't even audible your way out of them, because the second you start calling the audible, the center snaps and you've got a faceful of pig. Too many things can go wrong.

"Why hasn't Q. B. told anybody?" I said, but I already knew the answer, knowing that Q. B. is one of those guys that aren't too enthusiastic about admitting they make mistakes.

"I wish I knew," Zawatski said. "I was coming off the field when I heard him tell Coach it was my fault, and right then I knew it was gonna be his word against mine. Who'd believe a rook against Q. B.?"

"Nobody," I said. "But who'd ever think a quarterback with his experience would pull a jack-off stunt like that?"

Chet said he'd been wondering the same thing. It was a Pop Warner League mistake, a regular Michael M. Mouse production, made by a quarterback who was generally considered the savviest in the game, a modern Bart Starr. Q. B. doesn't have the best arm in football, he doesn't have the best moves, and he can't run much faster than Robert Boggs, but he has the guts and the brains, he's Mr. Popsicle under pressure, and the tenser the situation, the calmer he gets. He *never* blows his cool. No, that's inoperative. I misspeak myself. There's no *never* in pro football. As Zigmund Guminski puts it, "Anything can happen and usually does." He's always borrowing lines from Senator Cosell (D–N.Y.).

"How's the problem with the wife?" I asked Chet, now that we understood each other. "Any more poison-pen calls about your sex life?"

"No," the kid said. "Della got all upset for a while, mostly about the language the woman used, calling me a Polock cuntlapper and all. But then when she thought about it, she realized it was a phoney."

"*Was it?*" I asked diplomatically. "Are you sure you don't have a little poozle going on the side?"

"No, I don't, Alph," Chet swore, as if I'd accused him of birth control.

"I mean, I'll never tell. You can trust me."

"No, there's nothing to it. An obscene phone call, that's all. Somebody's idea of a joke."

"Some wonderful joke," I said.

"Yeh, and they did the same thing to Lack and Q. B., too. Same style, same voice."

"I wonder if somebody has it in for us?"

Zawatski thought for a minute. "Nobody that I know of," he said, "except every other team in pro football. Della says it must be some Football Annie that got spurned, but I don't even know any Football Annies."

"Yeh," I said, "and Lack never spurned one in his life, and neither did Q. B., at least on the road."

The kid seemed pretty relaxed now, and we back-tracked to the Dandy Don's and had a couple of refreshments and he called Della and went on home. I wasn't as sure as he was about the innocence of those phone calls, although it would be nothing new for a female jocksniffer to pull a stunt like that, I mean they're all a little nuts anyway, and there isn't a team in pro sports that hasn't had everything from phony paternity suits to blackmail and extortion. I know of one assistant coach that keeps changing jobs because things get too hot for him with the chickies, and another assistant had to retire when a film strip of him and a Football Annie was spliced into the game film and everybody kept kidding him about lunching at the Y and yodeling in the canyon. Our own 1st-string center, Harry Dabney, the guy that preceded me, got himself in trouble. One day he showed me a letter that his wife opened. It said, "Hi! I'm the secretary you fucked in Kansas City."

"Jeez, Harry," I said, "did you write her back?"

"Yeh," Harry said. "I wrote, 'Now we're even.' "

Whoever was squealing to the wives wasn't helping the Billygoats one bit. The Falcons had already showed us we weren't unbeatable, and now we were having players walking around worrying about their marital estates when their minds should have been on something important like football. When you disturb players like Q. B., Lacklustre and Zawatski, you're going straight for the jugular.

And that wasn't the end of the sabotage. On Thursday morning we came to practice and found Hyphen B-l-a-c-k stomping up and down the locker room fussing and fuming and threatening to kill the jive motherfucker if he got his hands on him.

"What jive motherfucker?" I asked.

Hyphen didn't even slow down, just kept stomping back and forth and letting out a string of cuss expressions, threatening to cut the guy's nuts off and follow him to the end of the earth if it took 99 more years.

"Hey, Hyph," Malley said. "Calm down, baby! What's the matter?"

Hyphen pointed a shaky finger up to the name tag over his locker. It read:

HYPHEN B-L-A-C-K
N-I-G-G-E-R

In the shower room, a plastic message was pasted on the mirror: DO NOT THROW CIGAR BUTTS IN URINALS AS THE JIGS MISTAKE THEM FOR TURDS AND OVER-EAT. This made every black on the club sore, which is a mere 21 players, including 3 All-League and 2 All-Pro, and the whole team was looking daggers at each other, wondering who was *it*. Naturally we first thought of J. R. Rodenheimer, but then J. R. never snuck around about his race prejudices. He was always right out front with them, and besides, J. R. needed that $30,000 Super-bowl money as bad as anybody, what with his wife's expensive habits. When Malley and I discussed the signs with him, he just smirked and said, "How could anybody accuse *me* of being prejudiced against niggers?"

"Listen, asshole," I said, calling him by his formal title. "This is no time for your sick shit about race."

"Who you callin' asshole?" he said, moving up a step closer like a 270-pound banty rooster with a hard-on.

"J. R. Rodenheimer," I said, taking a step forward myself just in case he got the idea I was turning pussy. "Excuse me," I said, "I mean J. R. Rodenheimer, *asshole.*"

Malley jumped in, not that his services were needed, and J. R. whispered something under his breath that might have been "niggerlover," and I whispered something under my breath that might have been "ignorant asshole," and we dropped the subject.

With practically the whole team pissed off at each other, we had to go to the dear old Southland and face New Orleans in the Louisiana Superdome, which is their home turf, a big poison-mushroom that seats 75,000 lunatics who throw Poor Boy sandwiches and beer cans and oyster shells and occasionally fire real weapons at you, the wildest-ass fans in football outside of Philadelphia, Denver, New York, Detroit, Chicago and the Jersey flats.

The plane ride to New Orleans turned out to be a routine flight, sure, not in the same league with the crazy ride that came later, but still it was hairy enough to suit most of the Billygoats. That's one thing about playing in the NFL, or any other pro league. You'll fly 10, 12 times a year minimum if you're a football player, 30, 40 times a year if you're a baseball player or a basketball player, and when you fly that many times something's got to happen sooner or later. It's all covered by what Malley calls the law of probability, and what I call the law of going to the well once too often. One day you'll take the wrong flight; just ask around at your neighborhood morgue.

I went to the 1st row with Malley and looked at the signs above me: NO SMOKING. A B C. FASTEN SEAT BELT. CHALECO SALVIVIDAS DEBAJO DE SU ASIENTO. "Hey, Mal," I said, "I been seeing that sign for years. What's it mean?"

"Do not flush toilet while plane is standing in station," Mal told me.

"Oh," I said. "Thanks."

After a while, Ziggy popped his head through the curtain and said he wished to read the orders of the day from the general manager's office. There were boos and whistles, and Hyphen B-l-a-c-k said, "Oh, yes, sergeant. Oh, *yessssss*. Tell us poor slaves—where—it's—at!"

" 'From the desk of William Robert Bunker, president and general manager,' " Ziggy read. " 'All personnel will wear ties and blazers in New Orleans. We are supposed to be a team. Let's look like one.' "

"Piss off!" John Lovesey commented. He was wearing a rugby shirt with broad red and blue stripes and brown kangaroo-skin tennis shoes on his valuable feet.

153

"I ain't got no tie," Bad-ass Harris called out. "But I'll wear my satin jock from the Greenwich Village Crotch Boutique."

"Hey, Zig," the late Robert Boggs called from the seat behind me, "we goin' streakin' through the French Quarters after the game. What's the *ko*-rect tie?"

Ziggy ducked his head back into the galley just as a shower clog came hurtling from the rear. "That's not funny," Ziggy's voice said from the other side of the curtain. "That thing could put somebody's eye out and hurt our chances."

"It already hurt our chances," Wing Choy said. "It missed."

When I'm old and weak and even balder than now, these are the times I'll remember best, these weird-ass hours of relaxation and ease, when there's no enemy line breathing in your face, no crucial play coming up, just a bunch of crazy assholes kidding and jacking around. If I was really honest with myself, I'd probably admit I never cared much about anything else in the world except the Goats—the Goats and my ex-son and Dorris Gene, but mostly the Goats. My ex-wife Cathy said I'd rather joke with the Goats than make love to her, and mostly she was right. Maybe that makes me a fruit on 1 level or another, I don't know, but I didn't want to fuck the Goats, I just wanted to be around them, hanging at the Dandy Don's or riding the plane or snapping towels or playing cards, abnormal things like that. If the truth was known, I'd rather stand at the bar bullshitting and playing the match game with Malley Tietjens and the late Robert Boggs and even Jay Cox than go to a seminar with Alfred Einstein. I never said I wasn't strange, did I? If I was normal, would I be playing center? That's what Cathy could never understand. She sure picked the wrong stud.

"All right, you guys, shut up!" I hollered, just to see the

reaction. "This is Old Veteran Jackson speaking."

"Piss off, Old Veteran Jackson!" Limey Lovesey called out over the general din.

Soon we were flying, the engines throttled back and the signs turned off about not flushing the toilet. I pulled myself up on the seat and cupped my hands. "Men," I said, trying to sound like Don Adams, "Coach feels that we tend to get sloppy on these long flights."

Boos and hisses.

"We're starting something new to keep our edge. In-flight calisthenics. The same ones that General Patton gave the 3d Army. We'll start with grass drills, only these are called ass drills, 'cause if you don't do 'em it'll be your ass."

More boos, more hisses, and another shower clog missed me by a few inches. Out of the corner of my eye I saw the gray head of Coach Edquist, offensive coordinator and general illiterate, appear in the curtain, and I said, "All right, men, pair off by 3s!"

Hyphen B-l-a-c-k and Q. B. must have spotted Edquist peeking, because they rolled out into the aisle with dead serious looks on their faces and began flopping up and down, up and down, just like a real grass drill. Edquist's head disappeared back in the hole, replaced by Ziggy's, and I said, "All right, men, be at ease. Drop your cocks and grab your socks."

A few minutes later Coach stalked into the compartment and asked what in the fuck was going on. "Nothing that I can see, Coach," I said.

"Edquist says some of you balloon-heads were doing grass drills."

"Oh, he must mean me," Q. B. said. "I dropped a cuff-link, and we were crawling around looking for it."

"Well, try not to break up the plane before we get there," Coach said, and stomped back to the throne room.

I joined a group of guys leaning over their seats and spilling into the aisles, all of them trying to get a peep at a notebook. "What's that?" I asked.

"That's mah life list," Lacklustre Jones replied proudly. "I just brought it up to date. It's 1st names only. 127 altogether."

Somebody asked what name came up the most often.

"Well, I fucked 6 Jennifers," Lack said. "Leastways that I know of."

"Gee," Malley said, "there sure are a lot of fucking Jennifers."

"What's the name you banged the least?" Jay Cox asked innocently.

Lack mulled that one over. "Charles, I guess," he said.

A few rows further along, Bad-ass and Q. B. were wrapped in conversation. I leaned over and listened.

"Then you ain't seen Sally McCord. She's got a little bitty one in between."

"You mean the redheaded Sally that hangs around the Chiefs?"

"Yeh, that's her. It's right in between the regular ones. They call it a super-numerary. Ugly little thing, like a eye staring up at you."

"That'd turn me right off."

"Yeh, but some guys cain't resist a mama with 3."

"You seen 3, you seen one too many."

I continued on up the aisle, and the plane wobbled lightly, and I grabbed the nearest shoulder. "Careful there, Ol' Veteran," said the late Robert Boggs. "We may need you in the game. Hit 'em with yo' purse or sumpin'."

I sat down and then I heard a "bong" and looked up and noticed that the seat belt sign was on. The plane was rocking.

"What?" I said, turning halfway around in my seat. Mal tucked in beside me and belted up. Before he could say anything, there was a *whomp,* and the whole plane seemed to drop out from under us. I jerked around and saw the boo-ray game, 4 players and a tray, suspended in midair, feet dangling down over the seatbacks, and then they dropped in a tangle of arms and legs. There was a shout from the rear, and somebody hollered about bumping the ceiling.

The P.A. clicked on and the pilot explained that we were experiencing severe turbulence and be sure to stay in the seats. There was another jolt, even rougher than the 1st one, and then the plane began careering around the sky like a moth in a wind tunnel. I turned my head and called out, "Who's hurt?"

"Fuckin' pilot gone be if he try *that* move again!" Badass Harris said.

"Did somebody hit the roof?" I asked.

"Oop hit," Ray Roy called out. "But it didn't wake him."

For a second, I wondered where Buford Bullivant was hiding. "Hey, what're you doing down there?" I said.

Bull just kept mumbling on his hands and knees, kneeling against the seat, saying, "Lord, I'm ready. Oh, Lord, call Thy servant."

"Belt up!" Malley snapped, "or the Lord's gonna call His servant right through the roof."

For a few minutes the whipsawing motions seemed to relax, and Mal turned and said, "How'd it go, Bull? Did the Lord save your ass?"

"That's disgusting," Bullivant said. "But I consider the source."

"Excuse me if I offended you," Mal said.

"Just answer me one thing," Bull went on. "Do you believe in anything at all?"

"I believe in pure reason."

"*Hmmmm.* Pure reason. Is that an organized religion, or what?"

"Sure, it's organized. Haven't you heard our hymns? 'Nearer My Pure Reason to Thee.' 'Oh, Pure Reason, Our Hope in Ages Past?' "

"I mighta known," Buford said. "That's all you do: crack wise and lie."

"If I'm lying," Malley said, "may pure reason strike me dead."

The plane hit another updraft, and we suddenly weighed 500 pounds apiece, pressed back in our seats with our lower jaws turned to lead. The plane began to lurch from side to side. I looked across at Luke Hairston, and his eyes were wide and staring. "Don't worry, Luke," I said. "We been through worse."

"I'm not worried, mothafucka," he snapped. "Jes' take care of your own red wagon." I didn't say anything back, I knew he didn't mean it the way it sounded. In the seat behind him, J. R. Rodenheimer was moaning and groaning like a little kid, and I heard Lack call over to him, "How yew, J. R.?"

J. R. looked up nervously and tried to say something but no words came out. He never did fly very good. A row behind him, Wing Choy's nose was sunk in a book. "What're you reading, Wing Back?" Malley asked. " 'The Little Engine That Could'?"

Wing didn't answer. The plane quivered and shook a few more times, and then shot out of the turbulence as quickly as it went in. For a few seconds, the only sound was the whoosh of the engines, and then a cheer went up.

"Way to go, Bussie!" the late Robert Boggs called out.

Ziggy poked his nose through the curtain. "Everything in order back here?" he asked.

"Yeh," I said. "How about the command post up front?"

"Nothing to worry about. When the going gets tough—"

"The tough shit their pants," Wing interrupted.

"Hey, Ziggy," Bad-ass hollered, "tell that fuckin' bussie to get his shit together. We ain't goin' through *that* again."

"You better believe it," Ziggy said. "That was C.A.T., clear air turbulence."

"Is it dangerous?" J. R. whined. "I mean can it wreck a plane?"

Ziggy inquired as to whether a bear shits in the woods.

Bullivant hollered, "Any you wise guys got any more sacreligious remarks to make now?"

"Yeh," Limey called from the back. "Piss off!"

"Jeez, Limey," I said, "you got a million of 'em."

"Piss off!" was all he answered.

"Hey," Lacklustre hollered in his Texas twang. "Where's the beer? Ain't it about tam?"

A stewardess peeped in and said the refreshments would be right along.

"Well, shake yo' ass, honey," Lack instructed. "And don't fo'git our slogan: 'When you outa Schlitz, you outa Schlitz!' "

Just before we landed, there was a pounding and banging from the rear of the plane, and somebody hollered that Limey was stuck in the toilet. "Big deal," I said to myself, and went on reading.

"Hey, Alph," Chet Zawatski said, interrupting a good article in *Sports Pictorial* about fishing for permit, the 6th in a series, "you better see if you can calm him down."

"Huh?" I said. I walked back to the head and it sounded like there was a pack of wildcats in there.

"Goddamn it the bleedin' fuckin' hell, get me outa here!" Limey was screaming. He banged and kicked at the door, but it wouldn't give.

I stuck my head against the door and I hollered, "Don't kick, Limey, for Chrissakes, don't kick! We'll get you out." His twinkletoes were too precious to be used on doors.

159

He was quiet for a few seconds, and then he started moaning like a sick baby. "Oh, please, *please*," he said, "get me outa here! Oh, please, I'll go 'round the bleedin' bend. Please!"

We pulled at the door, but it wouldn't give. There was no place to get a grip except a little titty sticking out, and only one of us could hold on at a time. I tried and Zawatski tried and Oop Johnson tried, which he is the strongest man on the team, and all we managed was to bust the titty off.

Limey screamed and begged for another 3, 4 minutes and the stewardess warned us that the seat-belt signs were on and we'd have to return to our seats, but I couldn't leave Limey all upset like that, so I belted up in the seat nearest the head and kept hollering to him that it'd be okay, we'd get him out, be patient. But we didn't get the door open till we landed and a ground crew came aboard, and Limey was white and shaking.

"It's okay, kid," I said, and put my arm around him, but he kept on quivering.

"I'm sorry I made such a scene," he said. "That bleedin' claustrophobia."

"Don't worry, Lime," Malley said. "Happens to the best of us," and the other players crowded around and told him to forget it. When a guy's worth 5, 6 games a year, you don't care if he's a little peculiar.

Hairston came bumping down the aisle. He found something awfully goddamn funny. Strange for him.

The Saints never were a pushover at home, even back in the days when they played at Tulane Stadium and lost every Sunday. To give people their money's worth, the old Saints engaged in violence, which may not be football, but it sells tickets—ask any hockey fan. At New Orleans, they used to keep score in broken legs and stitches, and if the Saints broke more legs and cut more stitches than the enemy, the game was considered an artistic success. The Chicago Bears used to play that way, too. You came away from Chicago or New Orleans like a platoon of infantry after a long battle, everybody full of pain-killers and greenies, and sometimes flaky things happened on the airplane going home.

After the Saints hired "Snake" Stabler as coach and developed practically a whole new team, they began coming on, and the result was now they were the 2d best team in the conference, after us, of course. When we arrived at the airport and checked into the Hilton Inn across the Airline Highway we were still only 1 game ahead of them, even with our gaudy 7–1 record on the year. New Orleans had dropped their first 2 games, to Atlanta and Dallas, and then reeled off 6 straight. It was an aggravating situation: the 2 best teams around playing in the same division and beating each other's brains out.

Which is exactly what we did all afternoon. It was like our game the week before, except that the score at the end of the 1st half was 14–14 instead of 0–0, and it was me that was bleeding instead of Zawatski. I was snapping on every play. Zawatski had looked better in practice, but I guess Coach was trying to show him who's boss. Me, I was just glad to get my regular job back.

Most of the game I was matched up with Tommy Sancton, their All-Pro middle linebacker, or Ahmad Mahli, their right tackle that usually lines up over me in the odd, and to be perfectly honest I'd have to call it a Mexican stand-off. They got one sack through the middle, but it took 2 men to move me out, Mahli hitting me low and Sancton hitting me high and the stub back creaming Q. B. on a play that'd developed too slow anyway and left time to dance the left-handed funky chicken back there. So nobody blamed me for the sack, and I kept feeling stronger and stronger as the game went on. The main thing was there was hardly a twitch in my bad knee, except for the heartbeat, which sometimes it felt like they'd transplanted my heart instead of a tendon, it pounded so hard down there, but there was no real pain, very little stiffness, and I was making the C-block almost as good as ever. Let me say right here, God bless Xylocaine. They gave me my usual 3 shots in the knee before the game and at halftime. Robert Boggs said he didn't see how I could stand the shots, and Mal told him I was like the guy that was asked if he enjoyed life and said, "Well, when you consider the alternative . . ."

The Saints took a 3-point lead early in the 4th period, but then we began a long drive that ate up 7 minutes on the clock and it looked like nothing less than the Chinese Wall could stop us, the way we were firing out clean and sharp, opening holes for the backs, moving about a quarter-count ahead of the ball and getting away with it as usual. It was 2d and 2 on their 35-yard line when we encountered another psychic phenomena like the one against Atlanta.

"Check with me," Q. B. says in the huddle. We line up tight, like we're going inside on a dive or a slant, the route you'd normally take to pick up 2 yards, and then Q. B. audibles our "splash" play, the one designed for special occasions. He hollers, "Red 38, red 38!" Then he looks to both sides and he puts on a phoney confused look and hollers, "Check!" which makes it sound like he's changing the play, only he isn't, it's just a device we practiced to give the defense something to think about. Sure enough, they draw in tighter, and the right linebacker dips in and out of the line with the cornerback about 2 steps behind him and even the weak safety cheats in about 5 yards. Then Q. B. hollers, "Blue 32, blue 32. *Set.* Hut 1! Hut 2! H—" We all fire out ahead of the ball, spearing and wedging and elbowing and trying to make it look like a dive play, and Q. B. fakes a handoff to Wing Choy, takes 3 little steps backwards and hits Ray Roy Jenkins at the sideline. Ray Roy juggles the ball and takes off toward the posts, 30 yards away, and nobody's within a half a mile.

Well, I guess part of the explanation for what happened is that it's tough to get attention if you're a black jock, because the brothers always seem to be doing something special to get noticed, like Hyphen changing his name or Luke Hairston packing an armory or the late Robert Boggs driving his lollipop-yellow Porsche Carrera. Some of the brothers work out different ways of moving, like they'll go into the end zone stutter-stepping or doing the congo or some other kind of African folk dance, or they'll throw the ball into the stands or spike it. That used to be Ray Roy's number, spiking, only now he had a new technique, his own personalized move, trademark reg. pat. pending. Ray Roy would run across the goal line and give it the old nonchalant, just let the ball kind of slip from his hands as if he'd forgotten he had it. Cool, man, far out!

So Ray Roy flies down the sideline on the secret play we practiced all week, and sees the end zone coming up, and he kicks his feet out ahead of him, the way the brothers do, lollygagging and toe-dancing, and he steams across the chalkline like a scalded gazelle and drops that ball out of his hand like a sackful of mooseshit.

On the 1-yard line. The simple shit! He thought he was in the end zone.

The ball squirts and slips around, 4 guys jump on it, it takes off again like it's coated with baby oil, and finally a Saint jumps on it and goes fetal and that's the old ball game, 17–14. Now we've lost 2 in a row, and New Orleans has tied us for the lead, and Coach is having apoplexy and angelina pectoris and a painful case of hemorrhoids at the same time.

The Saints' fans tried to grab their hero and carry him off the field, but Ray Roy was too quick, and he ran into the dressing room and got under the shower with his uniform on, so he wouldn't have to shower with anybody else, which was just fine with the rest of us. Nobody wanted to be near his black ass, not even the brothers. At last the Billygoats were united—against Ray Roy Jenkins, former honor student at the University of Oklahoma, but just a dumb turd as far as we were concerned. I remembered something he'd told me 5 years before, when he first came to the Goats, and he was explaining how him and his friends in southeast Houston used to ride the cooties, climb up on top of those big oil pumps and get bucked up and down till they lost their grip or got bored. "Texans," he told me, "we're apart from this world. We are descended from Martians, I truly believe." After the New Orleans game, I truly believed it too.

On the bus, Ray Roy moaned, "Oh, if I'd only taken one more step. One more fucking step."

"Yeh," Ziggy said. "If the queen had nuts she'd be king." I love the way he puts things.

It was 9 o'clock that night when our chartered DC–9, "The Mausoleum Special," landed after a quiet and uneventful flight. Quiet and uneventful except that Luke Hairston couldn't seem to get down from his game pills, and kept stirring up trouble. "Waitress!" he'd called, and when the stewardess didn't serve him fast enough, he told her she was prejudice. The stew brought him a beer— Coach and the ghost of General Patton allowed us 2 beers on a losing flight and as many as we could drink after a win —and he said, "Hey, bitch, how come you serve all the gray boys first?"

"I take everybody in order, Luke," the girl said patiently.

"Who you callin' Luke? You don't know me that well."

"Well enough," the stew said, and turned on her spiffy little ankles and walked away. Luke Hairston shot out of his seat like he was ejected, and he grabbed that stew and lifted her by the crotch and the hair and stuffed her in a luggage rack. "You're prejudice!" he hollered, and the late Robert Boggs threw his arms around him and eased him away. "That's enough now!" Robert said.

"Who you tellin'?" Hairston said, jerking loose.

"I'm tellin' *you*, you jive turkey," Robert snapped. "You crazy or sumpin'? You gone hurt somebody."

"That's mah business, mothafucka," Hairston said, glowering at the stew in the overhead rack.

"This is *mah* fuckin' business too, chump!" Robert said. "This is evahbody's business, up here in the air like this. Now go sit down!"

"Who the fuck you think *you* are?"

"I'm the senior fuckin' spook, that's who!" By this time 4 or 5 of the brothers had backed up behind Robert, and Malley and myself and a few of the other whiteys were there, too. Hairston stood still for a few more seconds, then went back to his seat.

Zawatski and I helped the girl down. She was crying, and mascara dripped on the front of her blouse. She turned to find Hairston and shouted, "You dirty rotten nigger prick!" and stomped off to the head and locked herself in.

"Jeez," Mal said, "I got a feeling she said the wrong thing."

Luke just stared into space, the way he does, his lower jaw hanging slack, his eyes like wet fire, and when the same stewardess hustled by later balancing 2 dinner trays, he stuck out his long leg and tripped her, and mashed potatoes and soggy meat and boiled vegetables slurped all over the aisle, and the girl came up with a carrot in her hair. "Why'd you do that?" she said. "Oh, you awful thing!"

Hairston just said quietly, "Us nigger pricks, we don't know no better." The girl had the sense not to challenge him again. He probably would have thrown her through the emergency exit. We all just sat there quietly and took the late Robert Boggs's quiet advice: "Don't fuck wid him right now, man. He's fulla sumpin', and that dude crazy enough when he's straight."

So the Billygoats and the Saints each had 7–2 records, but the difference was that they were coming on and we were playing like pussies. Then the thievery began, nothing sensational, just enough to make everybody on the club suspect everybody else, especially those of a different racial persuasion. I'd stashed 2 bottles of Bell's 12 in my locker before practice, and they were gone when I got back. Any one of 47 guys could have taken them, plus Coach and his assistants and the equipment man and The Connection and 6 or 8 others that were hanging around.

While I was wondering for the 15th time if I hadn't made a mistake and left the Scotch in the apartment, Jay Cox yelped like he'd been skewered for shish-ka-bob. "My watch!" he said, jumping all over the place. "My watch's gone!"

"That's terrible," Malley said. "Was it an heirloom?"

"You're fuckin' A," Cox said. "My dad gave it to me for graduation."

"What kind was it?" I asked.

"Timex." It figured. Jay Cox hadn't picked up a check in 6 months with the team, and now I knew his cheapness was inherited. His old man must be like Moose Gelband's old man that sent him a bill for $41,000 after Moose got his bonus from the Browns. It was marked, "Parental services for 22 years, please remit. May we hear from you promptly?"

The guys huddled around Jay Cox's locker, except I noticed that most of the brothers hung to one side, and Malley said, "Are you sure you had the watch with you?"

"Sure I'm sure," Cox said. "A fuckin' heirloom, too. Given to me by my daddy."

"Yeh," Mal said. "I heard that."

The next afternoon somebody heisted a tie pin from Q. B.'s locker, a hot comb from Lack's, and a money clip with $63 from J. R.'s. That made 5 victims altogether, and every one of us white. The club was seething like a stack of maggots. Myself and Malley dragged in from practice Friday afternoon and saw J. R. Rodenheimer standing in front of Bad-ass Harris's locker going off like Mt. Everest. "Here's the son of a bitch!" he hollered. "Here's my fuckin' money clip." He held up an empty clip in the shape of a dollar sign, and I asked him where he found it.

"Right fuckin' here!" J. R. said, pointing into Bad's locker. "I guess that solves the mystery."

"*What* mystery?" Bad-ass said, clomping in from the field on his cleats.

"The mystery of the nigger thief," J. R. said, jutting his big jaw out at Bad.

Malley jumped in between, and I backed him up, and a tag-team wrestling match began, and Coach and Ziggy and Edquist and several other assistants came flying out of their cubicles. It wasn't an ideal situation for team morale, with 270 pounds of white left tackle trying to kill 250 pounds of black left guard and vice versa, and several other 1st-stringers pairing off like hockey players just before the shit hits the fans.

"*Quit it, quit it!*" Coach screamed.

"Jive mothafucka!" Bad was saying. "Honky cock-suckah! What chew doin' in my locker in the first place?"

"It's the nigger blood!" J. R. shouted over the peace-makers. "Ya thievin' shine ya!"

"Come on now, J. R.," I said, giving his arm an extra wrench. "Settle down. Let's talk."

"Go fuck yourself, niggerlover!" he said. I guess it was inevitable.

The late Robert Boggs arrived just in time to catch the jist of the message, and he came at J. R. from the rear, where nobody was standing guard, and flipped him over backwards like a 270-pound dried cow flop. "Now lighten up on that color talk!" Robert instructed, placing his cleats on the back of J. R.'s neck. "Or you daid!"

5 more players jumped on J. R. and held him, and Mal and Hyphen B-l-a-c-k pinned Bad-ass's arms and Lack Jones grabbed him around the waist, so he couldn't move. It was an opportunistic time for Coach to holler, "Shut up! SHUT UP! The next man that talks, it's 1000."

This was the first fine I ever heard that made sense, and the din turned to mumbles. Coach jumped on the bench, which still left him about an inch shorter than most of us, and said, "This has gone far enough. Now let's get to the bottom of it."

We told him about the thefts, and somebody mentioned the poison-pen phone calls, and Hyphen pulled out his "HYPHEN B-L-A-C-K N-I-G-G-E-R" sign, and Q. B. showed the sign about blacks eating turds.

"Yeh, I heard about some of that shit," Coach said, "but I didn't know it'd went this far." He turned to the assistants. "Whatta you think, Ziggy?" he asked.

"I think we got a problem, Coach," Ziggy answered.

"*I think we got a problem,*" Coach imitated, in a squeaky, high voice. "Why, you dumb fuck, certainly we got a problem! We got a lotta problems. And you're one of 'em!"

"Jeez, Coach—"

"Shut your face!" Coach said. "Now the rest of you pussies, pay attention. You're all squaring off at each other and you can't even see what's happening."

"What's happening?" somebody muttered.

"It's the oldest story in sports," Coach said. "Somebody's trying to get to us. And you buncha dumb stupid assholes, you're taking the fake."

"Why would anybody want to do a thing like that?" Jay Cox asked.

"I wisht I knew," Coach said, shaking his head. "I wisht I knew. Maybe somebody's got a few bets down. Maybe somebody don't want us going all the way."

"Well, what're we gonna *do?*" Buford Bullivant called out in a whiny voice.

Coach put on a disgusted look and started screaming. *"What're we gonna do?"* he echoed. "Why, we're gonna act like men, that's what we're gonna do! We're gonna act like Billygoats! I say we're not gonna let this get us down. *Fuck 'em!* Whoever they are, they can't fuck up the Billygoats! If you pussies are gonna let a coupla little incidents get to you, well, you don't deserve the fucking 30 G's!" He turned and walked out, and all the little ducklings like Ziggy and Edquist followed.

For the next couple days, everybody on the team kept looking sideways at everybody else, and practice went about as smooth as a summer evening in the projects. We'd always had our problems with individual players, troublemakers like J. R. or Luke Hairston, like Jay Cox and Bullivant, but so does every other team in the NFL. It's like Coach said a long time ago, there's got to be hostility, there's even got to be hatred, just as long as you can depend on each other once the game begins. But I wasn't even sure of that anymore. We were having outright personal warfare, players not covering for others, losing faith, letting each other down. "It's not a team,"

Malley said. "It's a bunch of sovereign nations fighting a civil war among themselves. What's gonna happen when we play the 49ers Sunday?"

Well, what happened is we lucked out. The way we were torn inside, we should have lost big, but San Francisco came into the game playing their 3d-string quarterback, with Mattley and Roginski both injured, and 2 or 3 of their linemen were out, and their morale was almost as bad as ours, with 6 one-sided losses in 9 games, and even with all those advantages going for us, we didn't salt the game till Limey Lovesey kicked a 51-yard field goal with a minute and 8 seconds left. Down in New Orleans, the Saints were winning a laugher from the Dolphins, 35–3. I don't know what's the matter with Miami, but they've been playing like the Bloomer Girls ever since Shula left.

So now we're 8–2, and the stage is set for our 11th game, the return match at home against the Saints, with the division lead and a cinch shot at the playoffs at stake and the whole town going ape and scalpers getting $150 for seats in the end zone. In spite of the way we'd been playing, we opened a 1-point favorite. I think the bookies must have lost their marbles.

Now here is why you absolutely can't handicap professional football the way you can handicap horses or dogs or even figure the odds against boxcars in craps. Football is played by human beings, the ball's shaped funny, and on some days you get all the breaks, which is why every once in a while a pisscutting club will play a Michael M. Mouse team and lose their ass 63–0. The way things were going for the Billygoats, there was no conceivable way we could beat the Saints, home or away, but just look what happened.

On our 3d play from scrimmage, Wing Choy dives into the line behind straight-wedge blocking, trying to pick up

2 yards and a 1st down, and for one of the few times all year he fumbles, and the ball squiggles out sideways and Luke Hairston looks up from a little fake and grabs the ball for a 6-yard gain, when we should have lost the ball completely and left the Saints in position for a field goal or a touch.

New Orleans holds us on downs, and Malley goes in to punt and that little crackerass No. 28 slices through and blocks it. Wing Choy is standing there with egg foo young on his face for not picking up No. 28, and he sees the ball bouncing around and picks it up and runs 54 yards. Then the Saints get called for interfering with Ray Roy on the next play, which they weren't interfering at all, and it's our ball 1st and goal on the 1, and then Cox drops the hand-off and Q. B. grabs the ball and runs for his life and accidentally scores. You figure it out: 3 straight fuckups equals 1 touchdown. 2 minutes later the Saints' punter slips in the mud and shanks a 16-yard punt and Limey kicks a field goal to put us ahead 10–zip, which we should be losing by the same score at the least.

In any other football game, 10–zip is not what you would call an overwhelming lead, you can catch up with a touch and an onside kick in about 38 seconds playing time. But the Goats and the Saints were so evenly matched that even a 3-point lead was crucial. Look at our 1st game with them: we lose 17–14 when Ray Roy spikes on the 1.

The rest of the 1st half, it was slug and punt, slug and punt, and we went in at halftime with the score still 10–0. They came out passing in the 2d half, and you can't blame them because their ground game wasn't going any better than ours, but all they could pick up was a field goal in the middle of the 3d quarter, and then it was back to the trenches again. Our defense was bleeding, and every time the offense went in, Ziggy would holler, "For Chris-

171

sakes, give the defense a break! They're draggin'. If they quit, that's all she wrote!" Then we'd go out and run 3 plays and turn over the ball, and those poor defensive bastards would have to quit sucking oxygen and Gatorade and stagger back on the field, while the crowd would roar, "DEE-fense! DEE-fense!"

There was 6 minutes left to play when the Saints made another field goal from the 7, creeping up on us 10–6 now, and then they kicked off and Jay Cox brought it out to our 43 behind an open-field block by Zawatski that you could hear in Walla Walla, Washington. In the huddle, Q. B. says, "All right, I'm sicka this shit! Now this play's goin' to the posts. *To the posts!*" He called our red-diamond pass, the Saints came on a blitz, and Q. B. threw over the middle to Jay Cox in full stride and Cox went to the posts untrammeled by human hand.

Our defense was pissed! They were actually screaming at us as we came off the field! Q. B. grabbed Cox by the shoulder pad and pretended to be mad and said, "Hey, man, why'd you go and upset the defense?"

Cox has the sense of humor of an ardvark. He snapped back at Q. B., "If you want to rest the defense, then say so. You said the posts, man. If you don't mean the posts, *don't say the posts!*"

New Orleans kept fighting till the last seconds, but we won the game 17–16, and we were back in the lead by a full game and the sun was shining on the Billygoats, world headquarters for racial tolerance and brotherhood of men. Q. B. gave the game ball to Cox, his 1st, even though Jay could just as easily have had 2 or 3 in the earlier games, but you don't like to hand out game balls to mouthy rooks. For the life of me, I can't understand why grown men get so excited over a hunk of dried hog that anybody can buy at a sporting-goods store for $35.50. And who wants to get hugged by Jay Cox anyway? I mean I was trying my best to like him, but I wished he'd give me something to go on. "Feel good, kid?" I said.

"Great," he said. "I told you guys at the beginning of the season, 'You can win with me.' "

"Yeh," I said, "you did. You did that." Some guys don't ever change. When things are going against them, they're 1st-class assholes. But when things start to go their way, they're 1st-class assholes.

Amidst all the whooping and hollering and snapping of towels against bare asses, Ziggy Guminski came out and climbed on a bench and hollered, "Boys!"

"You mean men, don't you?" Luke Hairston said, making his 1st and only contribution to the post-game festivities.

"Men!" Ziggy hollered again. "Have no fear, Ziggy's here!"

"Go fuck yo'self," Leroy Harmony called out. "You was suppose to get some 1st downs."

"Men," Ziggy plowed on, "There's a party at one of Mr. Bunker's friends, and we're all invited."

"What kinda party?" Lacklustre Jones inquired. "Down in the cavern at the brewery like the last one, or a block party in Woptown like the one before?"

"No," Ziggy said. "This is a high-society affair. The Arthur A. Clamages III."

"The Arthur A. Clamages III?" Q. B. said, as though he couldn't believe his ears, and neither could the rest of us. We'd all read about the Clamages, Art and Vickie—their champagne breakfasts for visiting royalty, their moonlight cruises in honor of various diseases, their masquerade balls and fancy-dress parties and formals and all that shit. I couldn't imagine the Billygoats at a Clamage party; it'd be like inviting a dump truck to Le Mans.

"You sure you got the name right?" Malley asked.

"I can read, can't I?" Ziggy said, holding up a slip of paper.

"That's debatable," Malley said. He grabbed the paper and read aloud:

Billy Bob, Dearest—
I think it would be just *darling* if your "Billygoats" (ugh—whoever gave them such an *icky* name!) could come to our little "do" tonight—*provided they win, of course*—I'm sure they'd rather just go home and *brood* if they lose—see you all "9-ish" . . .

Love,
Vickie

"Hey, all you sloppy dicks!" Bad-ass Harris hollered. "Let's meet at Vickie's 9-ish, sling some shit!"

"Right on, baby!" the late Robert Boggs said in a high, squealy voice. "That'd be just *dahling.*"

On the way back to the apartment to get ready, I told Malley I had my misgivings about the Clamages's party. "I mean, we're not in their league," I said.

"What's their league?" Mal said.

"You know what I mean. They're high society, and we're—"

"You checked the standings lately?"

"I mean our whole history we been losers. We never saw the inside of a place like the Clamages. Why're they all of a sudden inviting us now?"

"You checked the standings lately?" Malley loved that trick of repeating his own lines as if you're some kind of a deaf mute. But he had a point. Strange things were happening all over town now that the old 2-and-12 team was enjoying its 2d straight season at the top of the division. I guess everybody loves a winner, even the society assholes. If we went all the way to the Superbowl, we'd be the biggest thing in town since the nitrate plant blew up. Nobody wanted to be left out of the action.

"How do you act at these fancy deals?" I said.

"Just be yourself," Malley said.

"What about Lack and Boggs and J. R. Rodenheimer?" I said.

"Oh, yeh," Malley said. "That's a problem."

The real problem was we just weren't a glamour team. We could bust your ass on the playing field, but the social world was another country. We weren't even a good-*looking* team, except maybe for Malley and Buzz Urquhart and Hyphen B-l-a-c-k and a few others. Who'd invite uglies like me with my prematurely bald skull and Q. B. with his Santa Claus nose and Wing Choy with his puffy eyes and J. R. with the pimples all over his ass? Ugliness was almost a tradition on the Goats. Even when we got new players, they were ugly. Jay Cox could hire out as a crossing guard at the zoo, and Chester Zawatski was a big hulk with a complexion like a walrus.

In all my 10 seasons, I'd never been to a single one of those real high-class orgies. The way I heard it, everybody fucks the hostess and a good time is had by all, at least that's the way the Clamage parties turned out. But that could be bullshit, too. I mean, I keep reading books that tell how NFL players are chased by all the society ginch and there's a round of hot parties after every game and if you work it right you can get 3 or 4 bluebook blow-jobs without obligation, but that's only stories to me. I asked Malley what he knew about the Clamages.

"Well, I heard they invited the Wheel one night and it got pretty wild," he said. The Wheel is our local pro basketball team.

"Why'd they invite the Wheel?"

"You checked the standings lately?" Jeez, he'd repeated on me again! That was 3. The Wheel had won the league last year and they looked strong again for this season.

In the apartment, I got to thinking about jocks and jocksniffers and society parties. Guys like Frank Gifford, Kyle Rote, Crazylegs Hirsh, Fran Tarkenton, Paul Horning, all those good-looking dudes from the old days, I guess they could just pick their spot. Joe Namath, now, there was a stud! I never knew what made him so attractive to women. To me, he always looked like a short-order Greek cook that needed a haircut. But he had that easy way of talking, kind of a half-ass southern accent that he picked up at Alabama, and they tell me the crease used to collapse in his path and throw him rose petals. I bet he banged 20, 30 different women before he married that June Taylor dancer and went on the road.

"You think Namath went to these high-society things?" I asked Malley. "And don't ask me if I checked the standings."

"Yeh, he went to a few," Mal said. "I imagine maybe 8 or 10,000."

"Well, if that hunky asshole can handle it, so can we," I said.

"That's the spirit," Mal said. "Get your ass in gear."

"Dorris Gene'll be here in about 15 minutes," I said.

Malley slapped his forehead. "You're taking Dorris Gene?" he said.

"Why not?"

Mal didn't answer for a few minutes. Then he said, "Sure, why not? And by the way, Alph, Coach said we'd have a few bottles of champagne after we win the championship game. Be sure to pick up some Ripple to go along with it, will you?" He kind of laughed to himself, but like I said, I gave up a long time ago understanding everything that came out of *that* crazy mouth.

The party turned out to be in a colonial mansion on one of those streets where every house is tucked away at the end of a long winding driveway and the garbage is put outside in sunken containers and you couldn't imagine any of the residents ever taking a dump. There were no streetlights, just gas flares on the lawn, lighting up giant oak trees and maples that must've been planted by Thomas Alva Jefferson, and for an extra added attraction about 18 fountains all bathed in colored lights. "Hey," I said to Mal, "isn't there supposed to be an energy shortage?"

"Not in this part of town," Malley said.

2 huge gas torches sent flickering patterns across the front of the house and we walked under a tall arch and into a hallway with a rug like a new-mown wheat field and then into a room big enough to conduct grass drills for the whole squad. The furniture was walnut and gold and bronze, old looking but you could tell somebody had spent many an hour polishing it to look new, although there was a chip here and there. "Louie says," Malley said, but then he turned away and never did tell me what Louie says, or even who Louie is. There were about a dozen different sofas, 6-man sofas, loveseats, curving sofas, sexual sofas, every kind of sofa you could imagine, and all covered in red velvet and matched by dark maroon curtains hanging down from a 2-story ceiling and gold tassels on each side. The only off beat in the place was that the beams weren't finished yet. They were 30 feet up, criss-crossing in a high vault full of shadows and probably bats, and you could still see axe marks on them; the carpenters hadn't had time to plane and sand them down. "Gothic," Mal said, and I said, "Yeh, awful!" But the builders certainly had done a nice job on everything else.

There couldn't have been more than 2 or 300 people there, huddled in clumps, sprawled all over the davenports, seated half way up a wide spiral staircase, lounging on another staircase on the other side of the room, and spilling out into the entranceways and the halls. I saw Q. B. leaning against the bannisters trying to put the make on a redhead dressed for tropic climbs, with a halter top and about 2 square feet of bare skin reaching down to her public hairs and a tight-fitting pair of pants that Q. B. had his index finger hooked into in his usual subtle way. Class! Right from the brewery! I wondered where his pregnant wife Rodna was.

"Well, hello, thayuh, dahlings!" The female voice came out of the bottom of a well, like a frog. "How *nice* of you to come."

I turned and saw this gold-plated crease standing with her arm linked in Billy Bob Bunker's, and Mr. Bunker was saying, "Boys, this is Mrs. Arthur Clamage III."

Mrs. Arthur Clamage III had the kind of bazoombas that drive some guys ape, spilling out of a black V-neck sweater that ran down to Annapolis, 2 bowls of fresh whipped cream under there. "Oh, how subtle," Dorris Gene whispered to me, and it surprised me to hear her praise another woman's look because usually the sight of big-busted women annoys Dorris Gene, owing to the fact that she herself is a 30-A. My ballpark estimate of Mrs. Clamage was about 38-C on the right and maybe a 40-C on the left, which nobody's perfect. She was probably 35 years old, but with all her skillful make-up she looked more like 33 or 34, and she was wearing some kind of perfume that you could feel all the way down in your feet. She was built fairly small otherwise, with hair as black as a G. M.'s heart, bobbed like Mal's before the age of Patton. Her nose was short and pug, and her lips were wet and moist, probably because she kept licking them.

"Nice to meet you, Mrs. Cleavage," I said. "I'm Alphabet—"

"*Clamage,*" Mr. Bunker interrupted.

"Call me Vickie," she said with that voice from the bottom of the sea.

"I'd rather call you Tuesday," Malley said.

"Please *do!*" She smiled widely and showed a set of teeth that would light up Soldier Field.

"Vickie's our hostess," Billy Bob said.

"Oh," Dorris Gene said. "Is there a host?"

"Yes, that's Art over there." He pointed to a fireplug in the corner, maybe the only male adult in town shorter than Coach, depending on whether Coach was wearing his elevator cleats. The match-ups in life always amaze me. How did this busty broad wind up with a little guy like Clamage? A look at her jewels gave me a hint. The Kohinoor diamond hung from her neck and there was enough assorted baubles on her wrists to fill Tiffany's window and leave enough for Elizabeth Taylor and Jackie O. combined.

"Yes," Mrs. Clamage said in a bored voice, "that's Mr. Clamage. Call him Art."

"I'd rather call him a *year* from Tuesday," Mal cracked.

"Oh, Malley," Dorris Gene said, "stop doing Groucho!" But that's the way Malley is after his game pills, and sometimes before.

"I'd like you to meet my friend Dorris Gene Salter," I said, and everybody shook hands, although I noticed Dorris Gene kept her distance from Mr. Bunker. She's had trouble with him in the past and she said she would kick him in the balls if he tried it again. "I'm Alph Jackson and this is my roomie Malley Tietjens."

Billy Bob said, "Art and Vickie arranged this soiree for the team." I looked around at a sea of strange faces, except for Q. B.

"Soiree, wrong number," Malley said. "What team?"

"Oh, the Billygoats, silly!" Vickie said. "My husband

says the Goats are just fn-tastic!" She has a funny way of saying fantastic, as though the first syllable is a sack of shit and you want to throw it away quick so you can get the fun of emphasizing, *"Tastic!"*

"You still don't follow football, Vickie?" Mr. Bunker asked politely.

"Oh, my, no," she said from the bottom of her well. "My dear, when would I have *time?* You *know* how crammed my schedule is, Ducks."

Mrs. Arthur Clamage III gave us to understand that she knew nothing about sports, but occasionally indulged her husband's tastes by holding a saloon for athletes, preferably tennis players, but the NFL guys were welcome provided they knew their place, since so many of them were —you know—eh, black, or vulgar, or both. She didn't put it just that way, but she made her message plain. Her own life, she informed us, was devoted to "the awts," and she swept her upraised palm toward a wall of paintings that looked like the collected works of A.B.C. Jackson III, my divorced son. "Polock, Clay, Buffet," she said. I started to ask if her kids had any other paintings around, but there was a racket behind us at the door, and the late Robert Boggs clomped into the room grinning ear to ear and smelling like a bar rag. He counted the house through glazed eyes with little black pupils like points and then he spotted me and lurched over with the grace of a hippopotamus on roller skates.

"Hey, there you are, you black fuckah!" he announced for the whole room to hear, and held out his hands for slapping. "Hey, babe," he said, "what it is?"

I nudged him about 4 feet to the side and said, "You been drinking."

"Sure, baby, I been drinkin'. What the fuck you expec' me to do after runnin' around all day like a swirlin' dervish. I already had me a fit of Scotch—a fif—"

"Robert," I said, "if you don't cool it you're *really* gonna be the late Robert Boggs. You must have had 6 greenies today, and now you're boozing on top of it."

"Hey, brother man," Robert said, yanking at my arm and almost toppling us both, "I didn't take no greens. That's a fuckin' false lie." A gleam came into his eye. "I took Dexxies!" he said.

"How many?"

"I don't 'member. I dunno. 2, 3. 11."

"Well, try to pull yourself together," I said. "I'm gonna introduce you to Mrs.—Mrs. Clamage." I led him back to the group and supported him with an arm while I made the introduction. "Vickie, this is Robert Boggs, our right tackle on offense. He had a good game today. He's been celebrating."

Mrs. Arthur Clamage III turned 5 shades paler under her make-up, but she stepped forward like a trooper and stuck out a hand bristling with diamonds and fingernails 4 inches long. "How do you *do?*" she said.

"How do *you* do, Mama?" the late Robert Boggs said. "Le's fuck!"

"Perhaps later," Mrs. Clamage answered without batting an eye. I looked at Mal and Mal looked at me, and then we both looked at Robert and Robert looked at us, and what we were all saying with those looks was—

"!?!"

Then I remembered Dorris Gene. "Well, er, uh, Honey," I said, putting my hand on her elbow, "maybe we should mingle a little."

"Go mingle by *yourself!*" Dorris Gene said, and flounced into the other room. Mrs. Clamage slipped away, and there was another commotion at the door, and in pranced Thaymon "Bad-ass" Harris, resplendid in a gold suede cavalier hat with 2 heavy gold hatpins that looked like they were speared clear through his head, a floor-length purple suede coat belted by 2 sets of gold chains, and purple lizard-skin shoes with 6-inch heels made of clear plastic and each heel filled with water and a single Siamese fighting fish that made hostile gestures at the other whenever Bad stood in one place long enough. I'd seen those shoes on him once before, at the Mother's March for Polio stag party, and Malley had advised him to scrap them. The fish turned red when they squared off to fight, and it upset the color scheme.

"My gracious, Thaymon," Malley said. "You certainly got your drag together tonight."

The late Robert Boggs elbowed Malley and me aside, stood swaying lightly in the lack of breeze, and said, "Lawdee, this dude sho' do look nice in my hand-me-downs!"

"I admire that drag of yours, too," Bad said. "Is it the Good Will, or the Salvation Army?"

"What a clever repost, my man!" Robert said, laughing and slobbering slightly on his one-piece Velours jumpsuit, zebra-striped with a rhinestone-studded codpiece bulging in the front.

"Hey, brother," Bad-ass said, pointing at the codpiece. "You got John Lovesey in there? You better hang a light on that thing, my man, or you liable to cause a accident."

Robert turned to me. "Hey, man," he said, "where'd that fox go?"

"You mean Vickie Clamage? I think you scared her away."

Robert whispered confidentially, "I guess she ain't use to so much class."

Bad-ass said, "Hey, where's the juice?" and him and Robert staggered away arm in arm, looking like the winning float at Mardi Gras. Malley clucked his tongue. "Those two guys," he said. "They got all the style and taste of a Marine latrine."

Malley had selected a Lance Loud tie and a pair of dark-brown Gucci boots, and I was wearing a tweed jacket and slacks. It was too much of a pain to put on fancy clothes after a game. Mal passed me a nice compliment. He said I was dressed to the 5s.

After a while, Dorris Gene wandered back, and we were introduced to Art Clamage himself, a monkey-faced dude as bald as me and as ugly as a Billygoat. He held up his cocked arm to give me and Mal the hipster's handshake, and when we didn't respond, he turned palms up as though he'd just scored a touch, and finally he just stuck his hand out and shook hands the way God intended for civilians. We chatted for a while, but Art Clamage didn't seem to know anything but jock expressions that we'd dropped years before—"no way," "get it on," "let it all hang out," dumb things like that. Finally he just wandered off looking for some jocks to sniff.

I was surprised to see Luke Hairston arrive—"the quiet man" rarely showed up at our social functions—but I wasn't surprised to see him grab a drink and stand over in the corner and not talk to anybody, just peering down at the crowd from his 6-foot 10-inch loft and looking like he was thoroughly disgusted. Limey Lovesey showed up with 2 rank Football Annies by the name of Mabel and Myra Longthatch, twin sisters that were working on the project of blowing every rostered player in the NFL. Coach once tried to declare the Longthatch twins off-limits, like 2-2 Devine. "Those twins are giving blow-jobs a bad name," Coach complained. Lately Limey had taken an interest in their project and was squiring them around so they could meet players, and Malley said he had to admire John for helping out. "I happen to know that both the Longthatches had shaky marriages," Mal explained. "By setting up a worthwhile goal, they're putting some meaning back in their lives."

"Yeh, but what a goal," I said.

"Don't make snap judgments just because you're a snapper. Sure, their goal sounds impossible. There's 1000 players in the league, and so far they've only blown about 300 of them. But the Panama Canal sounded impossible, too, and the transatlantic cable, and putting men on the moon. A lady's grasp must exceed her reach." So far the Longthatches had made good progress with the Goats, except for a few die-hards. Buzz Urquhart said he felt that blow-jobs were too suggestive, and J. W. Ramwell, our middle linebacker, was also reluctant, him being a one-woman man married to a one-man woman. "I love roses," J. W. explained, "and she loves mine." Buford Bullivant turned the twins down before they could even state their proposition, but promised to pray for their continued success, and the late Robert Boggs said he wouldn't mind helping the twins but he had a couple of hemorrhoids that were cuter than the Longthatches and he was already getting all the leg he could handle and the Longthatches were probably bulldaggers.

When you tell it flat-out like this, I guess it sounds like pro football players don't do anything but get sucked off and drink Gatorade, but it's not that radical. As NBA President Bill Russell once said, "There's no more sex in sport than there is in any other group of healthy young men," or something like that. I mean, you're constantly on the road, and after you've seen the zoo in San Diego and the Franklin Institute in Philly and the Stockyards in K.C. and the packing plants in Green Bay, what's left? You're out every other night and pretty soon you've seen all the movies, so you wind up chasing crease. Or getting chased. And some of those crease can run! I've seen 'em that can spot old Malley 8 yards along the bar and still tear his pants off.

Soon J. R. Rodenheimer arrived, under the private

cloud that always travels with him like a personal representative of the monsoon season. Bullivant dropped in and stayed about 11 seconds. Zawatski showed up in a neat gabardine suit and glossy-shined shoes and Malley said, "Hey, look at Chet! All spit and Polish." Lacklustre rushed in and said breathlessly, "Where's the cooz?" We pointed him toward Mrs. Clamage. Wing Choy turned up with a shiner that he got in a pile-up in the 4th quarter, and J. R. said, "Hey, Wing, I can't tell where the bruise leaves off and the yellow begins."

"Go fuck yourself," Wing said pleasantly, and J. R. bored right back in with his typical sloppy hostility. "Hey, Wing," he said, "you know why my mother only had 3 kids?"

" 'Cause she gave up after looking at you?"

"No," J. R. said, " 'Cause she read somewhere that every 4th kid born on earth is a Chink."

"Jeez," I said sarcastically, "that's really funny, Rodenheimer."

"Yeh," Dorris Gene intertwined. "On the whole, you're at *least* as funny as Bergen-Belsen."

"Or multiple sclerosis," Malley said.

There's always a little tension at postgame get-togethers, no matter where they are. Half the players are just coming off greenies or biphetamine spansules that keep popping in your blood stream till 4 o'clock in the morning or muscle relaxants that some experts say are the most dangerous thing you can take with booze. Turn loose a bunch of healthy animals full of weird chemicals like that and you're asking for trouble. At the Clamage affair some of the younger members of the audience were smoking lettuce or parsley or maybe even joints, but this didn't phrase me in the slightest. If you've played 10 years in the NFL and never smelled grass, you're either retarded or you're Buford Bullivant. But then somebody knocked on a loud gong and a servant came in carrying a shallow white saucer at arm's length.

"Bali high!" Art Clamage hollered, and everybody crowded around, and a blonde in a mini-skirt held a little silver spoon up to my nose and said, "Sniff!"

I sniffed and my whole nose went dead, and a few minutes later I began to feel like I'd just taken 4 bennies, and for a while I seemed to move faster and everybody else moved slower. People talked funny and floated around the floor without moving their feet. Vickie Clamage came up and tweaked my balls and I said, "Thank you very much I'm sure," and she waltzed away and blew me a kiss and turned into a man. Then the clothes began to fly around, shirts and socks and bras and sweaters, and pretty soon the whole room was half naked. I sat in the corner and tried to focus, and after a while I began to feel better, and I just leaned back and shut my eyes and kind of listened to the noises swirling around me. It sounded like 2 guys were talking:

"Jeez, that's the best legs I ever saw."

"No tits, though."

"Who gives a fuck? With a nice little ass like that, who needs tits?"

"What's her name?"

"I don't know, but I'd like to fuck her from here to Tuesday."

The music got louder, and somebody screamed "Take it off!" and somebody else said, "Sock it to us, you foxy bitch!" and then I heard Jay Cox hollering, "Viola! Viola!"

"Hey, man," I heard Malley say. "That's no Viola. That's Dorris Gene."

I started to open my eyes just as Cox said, "I know, man. I'm just cheering her act, the way the French do. Viola! Viola!"

"That's *voila*, dummy," Mal said disgustedly.

I looked over in the corner and there was Dorris Gene dancing on top of a table with nothing on but panty hoses, I mean Dorris Gene, not the table. I crossed that room in about 3 strides and threw her over my shoulder like a well-built sack of flour and hustled her off to the clothes closet and told her she should be ashamed of herself.

"Who're *you*, honey?" Dorris Gene said. She grabbed my hand and began licking it, and I took a good look at her and she looked like she had cataracts, her eyes were filmy and out of focus and she didn't know whether she was at the Clamages's party or on a safari in Alaska. I told her to stay put for a minute, and when I let go she plopped down like a day-old souffle.

When I came back with a pitcher of ice and a bath towel, she'd pulled herself together and was back in front of the closet door, doing a boogaloo for 6 or 8 interested studs, and I just shoved my way through and said, "Close your eyes, you fucking fruits! The next guy that looks, call the ambulance!" and I don't know when I was ever any madder.

Dorris Gene settled down after a while, and I found her clothes over in the corner and got her dressed, and when the little blonde with the white powder came around again, I told her thanks, but the lady and myself would pass this round. Out in the middle of the room, Bad-ass Harris was doing a funky rooster that shook the unfinished beams and Mal sang in German to the tune of *Falling Leaves* and drew a polite round of applause. Then Lacklustre Jones announced that he was going to sing and the room quieted as he made several attempts to mount a mahogany table.

"My god, no!" a woman's voice rang out, but too late. The table broke, and Lack went down like a clubbed owl, and Vickie Clamage screamed out, *"Whoopee!* Who gives a fuck?" Lack pulled himself up and began to croon softly:

'Twas on a pile of debris that I found her.
'Twas on the top of an old garbage truck.
Oh, how she sighed when I laid down beside her.
Censored, censored, censored, censored, censored.
Fuck.

When he turned in our direction I saw that one of his ingredients was dangling out the front of his pants. Vickie Clamage shoved past me for a better look, and then she hollered, "Art's is bigger! *Whoopee!*"

"I don't know Art's," Dorris Gene said, "but I know what I *like*," and she slipped her arm in mine. Then she covered her mouth with her hand and said, "Oops! Did I say *that?*"

A machismo contest began, based on the penal sizes of the various machos in the audience. "Great idea!" Malley said. "A closed contest, for members only."

It didn't take long for the women to pick out their "knights" for the big contest. The Longthatches sponsored the late Robert Boggs and Q. B.'s redhead sponsored Q. B. I'd been in the shower room with those 2 guys, and when Q. B. showered, somebody'd always holler, "Hey, get him outa here! He stops up the drain," and some of the guys called Robert "Spearchucker," after the football player in *Mash,* only Robert's spear wasn't detachable.

An ugly brunette sauntered over to Malley and said in a Marilyn Monroe tenor, "Don't you want to enter?"

"Well, ma'am," Malley said apologetically. "I'm more renowned for my speed and dexterity than I am for my size."

"And you?" she said to me.

I just nodded my head toward Dorris Gene. "I'm with her," I said hazily.

"He's with *me,*" Dorris Gene said. She was getting a little jelly-legged again.

"Yeh," Mal said. "He's with him."

The finals came down to Q. B. and the late Robert Boggs, as expected, and Q. B. measured out at a full 11 inches and there were lots of ooh's and ah's but I heard one frightened lady whisper, "My God, you can hurt a girl with a thing like that," and another lady said, "Yeh, with a little luck."

In spite of all kinds of help from the Longthatch twins, Robert couldn't break 10½, and Bad-ass hollered, "Too bad you couldn't get a hard-on." Robert just smiled like a good loser. A good stoned loser.

"Hey, Mal," I said to the old roomie wobbling across the floor. "These society parties aren't so bad, hey, man?"

"Not bad at all," Malley said, and I could tell that he had about 92% of a heat on. "About the same as the ones at the brewery, except the place smells better."

"Yeh," I said. "The broads, too." Old Malley pommeled me on the shoulder, and then Limey stepped up on a chair and said, "Ladies and gentlemen, enough vulgarity! I propose a gentlemen's contest."

"A *what?*" Vickie Clamage shrieked.

"A contest for the smallest," Limey said, and dropped his pants and exposed his famous one-incher, the smallest dong in the NFL. Lying there at rest, with its usual soft-on, it looked like a circumcised tulip, and everybody crowded around.

Malley hollered, "Remember, folks, less is more!" and some strange stud said, "Hey, man, you can't fuck a *mouse* with a tool like that," and all the society assholes laughed.

Limey looked offended and leaned down and whipped out his wallet. "Oh, I cawn't, cawn't I, you greasy cunt?" he said, and flashed a picture of his wife, about twice his size, and 5 assorted kids and every one of them the mirror image of Limey. "Does that answer your question, arsehole?" Limey asked.

"Right on!" Malley said to the smart-ass stranger. "You made the same mistake they used to make about De-Gaulle. You confused bigness with greatness."

"Precisely," Limey said, and zipped up his pants on a note of pride.

J. R. was walking around looking kind of lost. "Whatsa matter, Rodenheimer?" Bad-ass asked. "Doesn't anybody like your nigger jokes?"

"Go fuck yourself," J. R. said, once again showing his speed with the quick repost.

"Look at him," I said to Malley after J. R. walked away. "He's cruising for tail and he can't find any. That guy'd go hungry at a free banquet."

"Maybe we can fix him up," Malley said.

He dragged me over to where Ziggy was standing, and he said, "Hey, Zig, there's a big tall redhead wants to fuck you."

"Don't put me on, Tietjens," Ziggy said.

"No!" Malley said in his sincerest voice. "No shit. She asked me who you were, and she said she'd like to make it with you but she's too shy. Listen, Zig, I fixed it up. Go down the hall and into the 2d bedroom on the right. But for Chrissakes, don't turn on the light."

"Hot to trot, huh?" Ziggy said, and you could see he was beginning to be convinced. He disappeared down the hall.

Malley and I raced over to J. R. and gave him the same story about the tall redhead waiting for him in the 2d bedroom on the right. That horny old bigot didn't have to be told twice. "Don't turn on the light!" Mal hollered after him.

About 20 seconds later J. R. came flying out and raced

through the hall without breaking stride. Ziggy walked into the living room about a minute behind him. "Jeez," I said, "that was quick, Zig. You must have a little rabbit blood."

"Aw, no, man, nothing happened," Ziggy said. "Man, that broad is *shy!*"

"Why?" Mal said. "What'd she do?"

"Well, we were just starting to hold hands when I asked her what her name was, and *whoosh*—that's all she wrote."

"Musta got cold feet," I said.

"Probably married," Malley said.

"Yeh," Ziggy said. "Well, some days you can't make a nickel."

Oop Johnson strolled by with a regular Brunhilda, about 6 feet 2, wearing a wig that had turned around so that her hair hung over her nose. We heard Oop say, "Then mah brother fucked a goat."

"Do tell!" the woman said through her hair.

Suddenly there's a banshee yell from the next room, and here comes the tag-team of the late Robert Boggs and Mrs. Arthur Clamage III, both ass naked, and Robert is riding her across the rug and our hostess is making rubbery faces and moaning.

And I'd thought that the Goats wouldn't know how to act at a high-class party!

"2d prize!" Robert was shouting. "I won the 2d prize!"

"Robert," Dorris Gene said, "I think you've made a *conquest!*"

Art Clamage looked up from where he'd slumped to the rug, and said, "Nice time, Hon? That's good. Try to mix," and slipped back down.

Several hours and a quart or 2 later, I saw Q. B. and Ziggy, both of them looking like they'd been on a 3-month drunk and I'm sure I looked the same. Something real mean came up inside me, which happens sometimes when I drink and take greens, and I said, "You 2 girls got a lot to confess together, *don't you, Q. B.?*"

"Whuzzat?" Q. B. said.

"You know fucking well whuzzat," I said, really getting righteous and hot behind my pills and booze. "A little matter of a missed snap—"

Ziggy spotted a tall redhead and lurched away, probably to ask her why she was so shy.

"What chew talkin'?" Q. B. muttered.

"I'm talking about you, our beloved leader, Mr. Alvin Frasch, Mr. Q. B. himself, the asshole that fucked up a handoff and blamed it on a dumb rookie."

"I did not!"

"You did so!"

"You callin' me a liar?" Q. B. said, lifting his fists up to his chest and cocking his head to one side and almost toppling over on the rug.

"No," I said, "I'm calling you a *fucking* liar."

"Why, you muh-fucka!" Q. B. slurred. "Le's go outside and se'l this. Here, wait a minute, gimme a fuckin' hand."

He held onto my shoulder and we went out the big front door and turned right and walked through a pool that was only a foot or 2 deep and ended in a garden.

"Okay," Q. B. said, detaching himself, "now jes' repeat y'self what you jes' said."

I thought and thought and I couldn't remember. Besides, the one cardinal rule on all football teams is you never *never* beat up your quarterback.

"I don't remember," I said. "What was it?"

Q. B. fell in a hydrangea bush and blinked his eyes. "Don't 'member," he said. "Alls I 'member is we're s'pose to fight."

He stood up and took a long swing courtesy of Western Union, and your mother could have blocked it. Then he stepped back and began throwing jabs that landed a little short, maybe 16, 18 inches, and then he wound up one of those old-fashioned Kid Gavilan bolo punches and whacked the shit out of a chrysanthemum.

"Hey," I said, "the fight's over here!"

Q. B. peered out of his mean little green eyes and lowered his head and butted me right in the *la bonza*. I grunted and slapped him in the upper arm and he sat down like he'd been hit by a train and started to rub his eyes and cry like a kid.

"All right for *you*, Alph," he blubbered. "You hit me in the *passing* arm."

"Oh, gee, I'm sorry," I said. I really was.

"You're gonna get it when I tell Coach!"

"Here," I said, sitting down next to him. "Lemme see."

We were squatting in some trailing arbutus, and he started to laugh. "You hit like a fuckin' old lady!" he said, and laughed some more, and then I started to laugh, everything he said just sounded hilarious to me.

"A fuckin' old *lady*!" he said, and I broke up. Jeez, nobody could get off a funny line like Q. B.

"Man," I said between gasps and giggles, "you oughta go on the stage. Jeez, you keep me in stitches! Say something else."

"I'm gonna puke," Q. B. said, and I just collapsed with laughter. That's an amazing talent the guy has.

We went back inside and washed the used food off, and it must have been about 3 a.m. in the morning, and the party was still at its height. People were tear-assing all up and down the halls, and there was dancing and charades and screaming and hollering and the waitress in the black-and-white outfit was still wandering around giving people snorts of powder when Malley jumped up on the couch and hollered for attention and said, "Who'll accept a challenge for streaking?"

And that's when the trouble started.

A groan went up. "Fuck streaking!" somebody hollered. "That's kid stuff."

"I mean competitive streaking," Malley said. "A really quality event. I mean Olympic streaking, and a big prize for the winner, right, Mr. Clamage?"

"Big prize," Art Clamage muttered.

"Yah yah yah," Hypen B-l-a-c-k screamed, untangling himself from a stewardess. "That's mah game! I challenge the house."

Myra Longthatch, slightly bald except on her arms and legs, said she'd accept. Hyph was gone about 30 seconds. "Where'd you streak?" Mal asked.

"Out on the lawn and back," he said. "Too fuckin' cold."

The Longthatch twin lasted a few seconds longer. "I ran all the way down to the curb and back," she said, giggling.

"Shee-it," Bad-ass Harris said, already heading for the hallway and yanking at his shorts. "You 2 gone got waived out the league. Now where's a *real* streaker?"

Vickie Clamage, the hostess with the mostest, stepped out of her shoes, which was all she was wearing, and took off. 2 minutes later she flopped inside and said she'd been all the way to the corner, the streets were quiet and there was a light crosswind.

"Right on!" Bad-ass said and went out and streaked for 5 minutes.

"Where'd you go?" I asked.

"Around the whole block," Bad said. "That's the fuckin' record."

J. R. almost ruined it by muttering "Black on black, who's gonna see *that*?" but nobody heard him.

"My turn, chaps," little John Lovesey piped up, walking over in his private hole. You could see that Limey was totalled, leaning and tottering around, but he insisted he could out-streak anybody in the room. That's the way it is with short little guys at parties.

Limey disappeared into the hall, shouted "Oy'm awf!" and slammed the door. We listened but we didn't hear anything for a few minutes. Then there was a distant shriek, maybe 2 or 3 blocks away, and then quiet again, and then a faint sound way in the distance, like a baby crying, getting louder and louder till everybody in the house recognized it as a siren. We doused the lights and waited, and pretty soon we heard Limey taking the front steps 2 at a time and yanking at the door and hollering, "Let me in, you bloody sods!" Mal had trouble with the door, and by the time he got it open, Limey was standing there in his birthday suit flanked by 2 of the biggest fuzz in town. They played their flashlights up and down the miniature Lovesey frame, and then one of them said, "You folks know this subject?"

"A total stranger," Malley said.

"Mal!" Limey implored.

"Hey," the other cop said, "ain't you Malley Tietjens? Hey, you guys are the Billygoats, ain'tcha? But who's this little fruit?" He gave Limey a jerk, and shined the light down on his family jewels. "Say, ain't he your 2d-string kicker?"

"We don't carry a 2d-string kicker," Malley explained. "Our 1st-string kicker is 2d string." It seemed logical at the time.

"Oh," the cop said, taking off his hat and scratching his head. "Well, Mr. Tietjens, I'm afraid we're gonna have to take the subject in."

"Off the pigs!" Luke Hairston's voice came from down the hallway. That's the most I'd heard him say in a month.

"What's the charge?"

"Indecent exposure. A felony."

"In Limey's case shouldn't it just be a misdemeanor?" Q. B. put in.

"It's an on-view 211-E, felony all the way," the cop said, and grabbed Limey by the arm. "Come on, little fella, it's time to call it a day." Malley said this was certainly an arresting development.

"Hey," I called after them, "can we ride down to headquarters with you?"

"Only if you want to sleep there," the cop said. I graciously declined.

On the way home, the late Robert Boggs was so annoyed at the cops that he flipped on his 3 sets of driving lights and incinerated a couple of Volkswagons. Then he flang a whole bottle of J&B through the sunroof of his Porsche Carrera. The sunroof wasn't open.

You can imagine the excitement the next day, with the press and Mrs. Clamage and Billy Bob Bunker all getting involved, and Mr. Bunker telling the papers, "I arranged to have the boys invited to a respectable dinner party, but apparently they spoiled it after I left." That's what you call loyalty. Mr. Bunker, after a long-distance chat with the commissioner, wouldn't even allow the club to post Limey's bail so Mal and I snuck down and signed for $1000 and Limey came out of his cell like a ghost of himself, all quivering and haggard around the eyes and his clothes looking like they'd been put through a mangle with Limey inside. The jail was so unsanitary that his claustrophobia acted up something terrible and he spent the night beating on the bars and begging to be let out. It was pathetic to hear him talking, a grown man, his voice cracking and tears running down his cheeks and using all these funny expressions like "Bob's your Uncle" and "taking the mickey out" and "sod the wogs" and other remarks that I didn't understand, but you had to excuse the poor man's ravings in a foreign tongue. Here he'd been a star kicker just the afternoon before, and now he was wiped out. He said he was too upset to go to practice, and when he finally showed up at Bunker Stadium on Wednesday afternoon he couldn't hit a barn wall if he was kicking from the inside.

Malley and I hashed and rehashed the whole disaster, as best we could recall through our own hangovers, and there was one aspect that kept hanging us up. 4 or 5 people had streaked before Limey took off, and every one of them came bounding back through the front door at top speed. Limey was the only one that gave the cops time to collar him.

"I know it's fuzzy," I told Mal, "but you were the one who let him in. Why'd it take so long?"

Mal went into a trance and sat and meditated for hours, and he still couldn't remember anything out of the ordinary. Then at 4 o'clock in the morning, it came to him. "Rooms!" he said. "Wake up!"

"Huh?" I said. *"Gesorn under the nernbull ha ha ha,"* quoting Assistant Coach Roosevelt Atkins.

"I see it," Mal said. "I remember now."

"Remember what?" I said.

"The snap lock was locked. The bolt was bolted. 2 fucking locks on that door, and they were both locked!"

For an hour we discussed this new revelation but still it didn't make much sense. Why should the door have been locked for Limey and unlocked for everybody else?

"One thing for sure," Malley said, sitting on the edge of his bed rubbing his eyes. "This whole thing's getting like murder in the cathedral." Poor Mal, he didn't even know where he was.

THE FLIGHT

VI

WHERE WILL YOU SPEND ETERNITY?

THE SKYJACK WAS 3 HOURS OLD, WITH HAIRSTON HIT-
*ting up and eating handfuls of pills the whole time, and
still he held his ground like a black statue, appearing to
doze and stand guard over us at the same time, which is
a trick I wish I'd known in the Guard. Gradually the
other players got over their shock at seeing The Connection shot and began to talk in low voices, and Hairston
didn't seem to object, although one word out of him and
every one of us would have shut up in a second.*

"What the fuck does he wont?" Lacklustre asked.

"He didn't say," I said.

"Money?" Wing asked.

"No, he never mentioned money."

"Well, what's the fuckin' point?" the late Robert asked.

"The point is, he's flipped his lid," Malley said.

*"Yeh," Robert insisted, "but what do he have in
mind?"*

*"A psychotic doesn't have to have anything in mind,"
Malley said.*

199

"Oh, Jesus," J. R. Rodenheimer was whimpering, his mouth curled up like a kid on the way to the dentist. "That black bastard, he's gonna kill us all just 'cause he's nuts. Oh, that bastard." He started crying softly.

"Shut up, chump!" Robert said, "or I'll take care of you my own self."

"I tried *to* change *him," Buford Bullivant said in a sing-song voice like Muhammad Ali's. "I* tried *to bring him to* Christ. *But he* told *me to go—to go—go—*fuck *myself. Now we're* all *in the* grip *of a* devil. *"*

"You got everything backwards as usual," Mal said. "Luke's no devil. He's just a poor mentally ill guy that shoulda been put away a long time ago. It didn't take a psychiatrist to see what was coming. But we wanted the money, didn't we?"

"If he 'uz nuts, how come he played so good?" Lack asked.

"There's no connection," Wing Choy put in. "Lots of psychos do a job, and nobody knows they're sick till they flip."

"Anyway, bein' nuts don't show in the NFL," Robert said. "Right, Rosenheiser?"

Hairston stirred around, and we could see he was fixing again. "Hey, brother man, lemme help you with that!" Bad-ass called out.

Luke ignored the offer and finally got the needle in his arm after about 6 false starts. The way his hand was shaking and the point was jerking around, it's a wonder he didn't stab himself to death. Once again the injection seemed to give him strength, and he called out, "Start prayin', mothafuckas!" He lifted the machine pistol to his eyes and sighted down the barrel. The sweat gleamed on his shaved head like beads of mercury.

"Uh-uh-uh-uh-uh-uh-uh-uh!" he said, his lips flapping as he made the sound that boys make when they play

machine gunner, and then he threw his head back and laughed a big old Emperor Jones laugh.

Bullivant shook a long finger at the rest of us and said, "Where will you *spend eternity?" I halfway expected to hear the Schmeisser start burping bullets, real ones this time, but Hairston just leaned back against the bulkhead and watched through heavy-lidded eyes. "Where will* you *spend* eternity? Fall down and repent!"

"This whole plane gone fall down and repent if you don't lighten up!" Bad-ass said, pulling at Buford's arm.

"I repent, I repent!" Lacklustre called out. "If it'll do the least li'l good, I repent rat now."

"Do you accept the Lord Jesus Christ as your personal savior?" Bull said.

"I hope so," Lack said, dropping to his 2 good knees.

"Then you're saved, *brother!* Hallalejuah!"

"Oh, I hope so!" Lack said in a sickly voice.

"Brother," Bull said, "Ye are bornagain."

"Bornagain?" Wing Choy interrupted. "What the fuck is bornagain?"

"COOL IT!" Luke Hairston's voice hit like a cannon shot. "That's enough jivin' around! Siddown there, Holy Roller, and stop yammerin'."

We sat for a while, and the plane droned on, and nobody spoke except in whispers. I stayed in the back with the guys and leaned my head against the pillow and shut my eyes and wondered why I was so tired. I felt like I'd played a whole game, and I remembered other rides years ago, in the days when we'd lose 10, 12 times a season, and we'd have to make the long flight home with battered arms and legs propped on pillows and eyes bloodshot from greens and some of the guys dropping off in a half-sleep and babbling and grunting and playing the whole football game over again, and other guys begging The Connection for codeine or Demerol or a shot.

I looked out the window, and we still seemed to be flying straight and level around 30,000 feet, and way down below there was a turnpike or a freeway that just looked like a long white worm, you couldn't even make out a truck or a car on it, and I thought how small we really were, all of us human beings, the Billygoats and President Nader and Pope Dominick and Carly Simon and everybody else, and how we were invisible to each other till it's too late. Here we were, 42 ballplayers, which there's 40 regulars and 2 back-ups from the taxi squad in case there's a last-minute injury, and up front maybe 30 more people plus the crew. Let's see, that made about 80 in all, average weight let's say 200 pounds, that's 16,000 pounds of meat on the wing, 8 tons of muscle and bones and tissue and fat, and nobody down below could even see us. Well, we'd be plenty visible if we went down. We'd come into sharp fucking focus then. We'd all be big men again for our final appearances, big dead men, and somebody'd make a fortune in camellias.

"Alph," the voice said. "Hey, Alph!"

I turned my head and saw Chet Zawatski leaning against my seat from the next rack.

"Keep it down, man," I whispered.

"Q. B. apologized," he said.

"Huh?"

"Q. B. said he was sorry he got me in trouble. He said he'd tell Coach and bring it out in the open."

"What'd you say?"

"I told him to forget it. I understood. You can't be a quarterback and admit you fucked up."

"Not during a game, anyway."

"Yeh, that's what Q. B. said. He said he couldn't admit his mistake, and then he got locked in. He said he felt lousy about it, couldn't sleep. Said you wanted to fight him about it."

*"The battle of the century," I said. "I hit him with a
snapdragon."*

*"He's got a lotta balls," Zawatski said. "He coulda just
kept quiet."*

"Nobody ever wondered about Q. B.'s balls," I said.

*I looked up ahead at Hairston. His head was slumped
on his chest, but somehow or other he was still standing
with his back against the bulkhead, still cradling the gun
in those long arms. "Hey, Z," I whispered, "just tell the
guys to keep on talking naturally."*

*I grabbed my crutches and started slowly up the aisle.
I hadn't taken 5 steps when Hairston slowly raised his
head and the gun at the same time and swung the barrel
into line with me, like one of those heat-seeking missiles
that locks right onto a fighter plane's exhaust. "Just coming back to see if I can help," I said nervously. "Just
coming back to my rack. Okay?"*

*He waved the snout of the machine pistol toward the
seat. "Thanks," I said. "I'll rest a while."*

The Friday after the Clamage party there was a message for me and Mal to see Coach in his private office
immediately or sooner. We rushed over and found a 3-
judge tribunal, all looking like their mothers had just been
gang-banged and we were the bangers. Personally, I
didn't see why Malley and I should have to take any more
blame than the other studs at the party, and if they were
giving a trial, why, they should bring in Billy Bob Bunker
himself, the guy that arranged the whole affair.

"Siddown, ya assholes ya!" Coach said with his usual
savoir-fair.

"Right," Ziggy echoed. "Let's get this show on the
road."

"This is Jerry Stein of the commissioner's office," Coach

said. "Shake hands with Malley Tietjens and Alphabet Jackson." I remembered Stein from a few years back when he'd made the annual pre-season speech about don't associate with gamblers and be sure to report anybody that tries to suck up to you for inside information. He had an extrastrong handshake—every office worker in the world tries to break a football player's hand—and I began to wonder what the charges would be.

"Just a minute," Malley said. "Before you go on with the hanging, I want a lawyer. I know my rights."

Coach jumped out of his seat. "*You* know *your* rights?" he said. "You got no fucking rights, understand?"

Mal jumped up himself, and I moved right alongside him in case somebody started swinging, and Malley said, "Don't tell me I don't have rights, you fucking Nazi you! I—"

"SIDDOWN!" Coach said, turning red and blowing steam out his nose holes. "You got rights, yeh. You got the right to siddown and shut up, and you got the right to pay attention. Don't you know who this man is?"

"Yeh," Mal said, "I know who this man is. He's the commissioner's pimp, and you're the pimp's pimp."

"Right!" I said, and I was sorry I said it but I wanted to back up my roomie.

"Gentlemen! Gentlemen!" Stein said. "Relax! This is no inquisition. We're all good people here."

"Don't include him," Malley said, pointing to General Patton standing there in his elevator jockstrap.

"*No* exceptions," Stein said. "I know Coach and I know you boys and I know the Goats, and I say you're all gentlemen. Now just one thing—before we go any further, I want to remind you of the sign in your locker room, the one about talking out of turn."

"Everything that's said here today," Coach put in,

"comes under the heading of league business, top security, understand? *Top security!*"

If the NFL intended to lower the boom on me just for going to a party, I reserved the right to speak up in the future. I crossed my fingers and nodded.

Stein started to talk in a low voice, the way you would imagine an FBI man would talk, which he probably was an ex like most of the guys in Commissioner Summerall's office. "Gentlemen," he said, "we called you in because we have reason to trust you, and because you're alert and intelligent, and because you're respected by the other players."

I nodded. That was a pretty good description of Mal.

"But mostly we called you in because we think you have discretion, and discretion's what we need in this situation."

"Look, man," Malley said in a snotty voice, "the cocaine party wasn't *our* idea."

"We don't give a doodely-squat about the party," Coach interrupted.

"No," Ziggy said through a cloud of blue smoke from a Cigarillo, "that's water over the dam."

"Gentlemen," Jerry Stein said, drawing a deep breath like a high diver about to go off the 100-foot board, "someone is trying to shave points."

Malley leaned forward, and I almost fell off my chair. What did he think this was, basketball?

"We're absolutely certain it's happening," Stein went on.

"Yeh," Ziggy said. "You're fuckin' A!"

"They know it's the Goats," Coach said wearily. "And they're pretty sure it's somebody on our offensive line."

"If our club was shaving points," Malley said, "wouldn't Alph and I be the 1st to know?"

"Not necessarily," Jerry Stein said. "Not if the fixers are clever about it, and apparently they are. Look here." He pulled a bunch of papers out of his briefcase and slid them across the table. "There's the *prima facie* case," he said, whatever that meant. "I'll brief it for you."

He told us that the commissioner's office had begun to pick up rumors the week before the 2d Atlanta game, the one we lost 14–7. We had opened a 10-point favorite, but so much heavy money came down on the Falcons during the week that we were lowered to 3 points by game time, and when we lost the game a whole bunch of bookies were wiped out.

"The next week you played New Orleans for the first time," Stein went on, "and you opened a 2-point favorite, which was probably an overlay, because personally I don't think you're any better than pick 'em against the Saints."

"That's your opinion," Coach snapped, winning friends and influencing people as usual.

"Yeh," Ziggy echoed. "Everybody to his own taste, as the man said when he kissed the cow." I couldn't help laughing.

"The money poured in on New Orleans," Stein said, giving Ziggy and me a funny look, "and most of it from the northeast. By Wednesday you were down to even, and by game time the spread had gone the other way and the Saints were favored. You lose 17–14 and somebody makes a big killing, and more books are wiped out."

"Excuse me," I said, "but what do you care about bookies? I thought the commissioner's office had nothing to do with gambling. I thought gambling was your biggest nightmare."

"Exactly," Stein said patiently, taking out a pipe. "It *is* our biggest nightmare. We care about bookies because 50,000,000 bettors care about bookies, and 2 billion bucks goes down every Sunday. We check with big gamblers, we study how the lines are moving, see if we can sniff a fix before it happens. We've never had a point-shaving scandal in the NFL."

"Knock wood," Ziggy said, "for openers."

"But now we seem to be having a beaut," Stein said. He flipped a page and showed us a set of charts and graphs marked "GOATS vs. SAINTS, 2d GAME."

"How'd we shave points in that game?" Mal asked. "We won 17–16."

"It isn't only what happens in the game that we're concerned about," the commissioner's man said, lighting his pipe and then pointing it at us. "It's what happens to the betting line. It opened with New Orleans getting a point, though I personally think it should have been even."

"On our home field?" Coach asked. "Man, you really got a hard-on for the Goats, don't you, Stein?"

"I'm from Baton Rouge," he explained. "By Tuesday, the spread was up to 7. By Friday afternoon so much funny money was down on the Goats that the books had taken it off."

"What's that mean in English?" I asked.

"The fix was in, but the other way. The smart money knew you'd win. Maybe they bought themselves a couple of Saints."

"Or a referee," Mal put in.

"Mr. Stein," I said. "I'm not too good at numbers, but tell me one thing: Is there any doubt in your mind that somebody's shaving?"

"None. We study these lines year in, year out. We know how they flow, how they change. Point spreads change gradually, and you can always spot the reasons. Suppose your friend Tietjens here breaks a leg on a Wednesday afternoon, the spread might change a half point. Suppose 4 or 5 of your starting players come down with the flu, the spread might change 2, 3 points. And we'd know exactly why. But on your last 4 games, leaving out the 49ers game, the spread jumped around like the Dow Jones, with no logic whatever."

"Somebody's taking a dive," Coach said, sighing deeply. "That's all in the fuck we need."

"And it's the offensive line," Ziggy moaned, "Oh, man, that's all she wrote!"

"Why're you so sure it's the offensive line?" I said. "The 2 guys that can shave the easiest are the quarterback and the field-goal kicker, and they're both going horseshit."

"It's not them," Stein said.

"How do you know?" Malley said.

" 'Cause we got word, that's all I can tell you," Stein said. "I wish I could say more, but I can't. We're told it's somebody on the offensive line, and I think the word's reliable."

He got up and walked over to me and Malley. "Look," he said, "I'm trying to be as open as I can. I'm here to get information. I'm sure you guys don't want to be involved in a football scandal any more than the league does."

"No," Malley said, "especially since we were already involved in one over the weekend."

"The Clamage party was fun and games," Stein said. "I heard all about it. Happens every Sunday in one NFL city or another. No, boys, I'm talking about something serious. The whole future of the Billygoats. The whole future of the league." He jabbed his pipestem at me. "Jackson, you've been around 10 years. You know the rhythms. What's been different about the Goats lately?"

I thought for a second. "We all been pissed at each other a lot," I said, "but that's not too unusual. Win some, lose some, that's about it."

"Yeh," Ziggy piped up. "That's the name of the game."

"How do you mean, 'pissed at each other'?"

Malley and I led him through our troubles, the mix-ups

between Q. B. and Zawatski, Ray Roy spiking on the 1-yard line, the racist signs that we found in the shower room, the HYPHEN B-L-A-C-K N-I-G-G-E-R sign, the stolen stuff in Bad-ass Harris's locker, etc. We even told about the door being locked Sunday night. "If somebody was trying to make us lose," Malley said, "there wouldn't be a better way than to demoralize the field-goal kicker."

"Maybe that explains the jump this week," Stein said. "You started off a 10-point favorite over the Bears, but now you're down to 3. That means a swing of millions of dollars on Chicago. Somebody knows something."

Coach said, "One thing I don't get, Jerry. How do we fix a game we win, like the 2d New Orleans game?"

"You don't have to fix," Stein said, beginning to sound a little red-ass. "All you have to do is shave a little. Blow an assignment, drop a hand-off at a crucial time, angle a field goal a few feet to the right. If you give a big betting syndicate a 2% edge every weekend, they'll own the goddamn league."

"Coach," Malley said, "remember that interference call against LeBlanc in the 1st period Sunday? Well, it was a bad call and you knew it and I knew it and the whole Bunker Stadium knew it, right?"

"So what?" Coach said. "The bad calls even out."

"I re-ran that play on the films, and the back judge had his hand on his handkerchief before the ball was thrown."

"He *what?*" Stein said, leaning forward.

"He was ready to call a penalty before the penalty happened," Mal said.

"Why didn't you open your yap before this?" Coach said.

"I've been a little busy raising bail for Limey and a few other things," Malley said. "Besides, I didn't know it was the end of the world. Maybe the zebra just sort of sensed there'd be a penalty and he wanted to be ready."

Stein made a note. "We'll check," he said. "It may mean something, it may mean zilch." He blew a flume of smoke across Coach's desk and said, "We'll have to look into these things one by one, and we'll have to do it quietly and thoroughly. Is there any chance that Thaymon Harris is a thief?"

"No," I said quickly. "No chance. We been teammates for 7 years. If a cashier gives him too much change, he hands it back."

"Look," Stein said, "I don't want to sound ethnic, but some of these boys from deprived backgrounds, it's just their 2d nature to steal. We looked into Harris when he came into the league, and he was no Mother Cabrini back in the Bronx."

"Well," I said, heating up a little, "Mr. J. R. Rodenheimer would certainly go along with you on that. He said so himself; it's the niggers' nature to steal. But that's a lot of crap and you know it. Bad-ass got his nickname on the field, not in the shopping center."

Stein leaned back and talked through a smoke cloud. "Every 4 years there's an outbreak of thievery at the Olympic games, and every 4 years it's hushed up. The Indians and the Pakistanis and some of the other athletes from deprived countries can't resist shoplifting in the Olympic stores. It's not because they're bad or immoral. It's because they've never seen cameras and portable radios lying around at their fingertips, and they're dirt-poor to begin with. Could this be something like that?"

"Oh, sure," I said sarcastically. "Bad-ass makes 46,000 a year from the Goats and another 30,000 from his restaurant. He's just another deprived Indian."

"Okay, okay," Stein said, holding up his hand. "You sold me. Now who else could be trying to sabotage the effort. Rodenheimer?"

"He's too dumb," Mal said. "He's a big, All-Conference, *dumb* lineman."

"Buford Bullivant?"

"Bull?" I said. "Next to him, Rodenheimer's a Rhoades scholar."

"What about Hairston?" Coach put in.

"He's smart enough and he's mad enough," Malley said. "And lately he's been acting weirder and weirder. But he's the best team player we've got."

"Fuckin' A," Ziggy agreed.

"Well, let's keep our eyes on him," Coach said, "and anybody else you can think of. That's why we called you boys in here. Stein asked me to pick out our most reliable players, and you're the ones."

"We'll get together again," Stein said, and Malley and I started to leave, but Coach speared us with a pudgy finger.

"One more thing, Alph," he said. "You got a slight tendency to get things a little wrong. Nothing big, nothing important. But this time we can't afford *any* mistakes. *None whatever!* We're gonna run some poor son of a bitch clean out of the NFL and maybe into jail and probably blow our chance for the championship and maybe the Superbowl, so we have to know what we're doing. You follow me?"

I had to wince. "Coach," I said, "I'm no genius, but even a stopped clock is right once a day."

Coach looked up at the ceiling and rolled his baby-blue eyes. "A stopped clock is right *twice* a day," he said.

"Oh," I said. "I sit corrected."

We shook hands all around, as though we had just gone through a wonderful spiritual experience instead of being handed a doubledecker shit sandwich, and Stein said, "Excuse me if I sound ethnic again, but my Jewish grandfather used to say, 'A fool can throw a stone into a lake that 10 wise men can't find it.' That's what we're dealing with."

Ziggy said, "Well, it's simple then. All we gotta do is look for somebody with wet hands." When nobody laughed, he giggled nervously.

"Call the wagon," Coach said. "Dumb pussy, he practiced too much in the sun."

Mal and I drove over to the Dandy Don's just in time to catch Zawatski and Lack and Ray Roy and Cox finishing their beers. They ordered another round in our honor, and then we played the match game for a while, but my mind was so messed I lost 3 straight to Ray Roy, and Malley was even worse, and he's usually the king of any game we play.

"Whatsa matter with y'all today?" Lacklustre asked. "You look lak the wreck of the Hebrides."

"Musta been something I ate," I said. "You feel okay, don't you, Mal?"

"Yeh," Malley said, but he looked like he'd just told his mother about the explosion in the mine.

When we got back to the apartment, Malley said, "Well, it's a regular Hobson's choice, isn't it?"

"What's a Hobson's choice?" I asked.

"We can go along the way we are, with somebody sabotaging us, or we can try to expose the son of a bitch and throw the whole team into a worse turmoil than it's already in. That's a Hobson's choice. It's British for 'our ass is sucking buttermilk.'"

"Not necessarily," I said. "Suppose the fixer turns out to be The Connection's assistant or it's Florian Kumjian or somebody else that never plays. It wouldn't hurt the club's chances to expose them."

Malley told me to dream on. "A helper can't shave points and a 3d-string quarterback can't shave points," he said. "It's got to be somebody closer to the action, somebody that can do some little tiny invisible thing that messes up the whole team."

"Like fucking up a hand-off?"

"Hell, no. How many times do you think a quarterback could fuck up a hand-off intentionally and get away with it?"

I didn't have to answer. The way the game of football is studied nowadays, you can't blink your left eyeball without having one of the coaches notice it. Those guys re-run the game film 6, 8 times in *full,* and if there's a play they can't figure out, they think nothing of running it 50, 60 times till they sort things out. You could mess up a play deliberately maybe once or twice, but after that you'd be on your way to jail or maybe the Calgary Stampeders.

"Well, how would you shave points then?" I asked.

"I'm not sure," Malley said. "I never planned to go into the shaving business. But if I did, I'd think in terms of something subtle, and the last place I'd do it would be out on the field. I'd probably do what our own resident shaver's already doing: Get everybody pissed off at everybody else. That's the easiest thing in the world."

"Yeh," I said, "and nobody's filming it."

"I hope it's not Hairston," Malley said. "If it's him, we kiss the championship goodbye. Who's worth more to our offense?"

"Maybe Q. B.?" I suggested.

"Q. B. my ass! 1st off, if you take Luke Hairston out and put in Studney, you got a whole different team. Studney doesn't give himself up. Studney blocks like Golda Meir, and he doesn't even have good hands. Bench Hairston and our short passing game dies, and Q. B. turns into Lee Grosscup right before your eyes."

On that exciting analysis, we dropped off to sleep, visions of sugar tits dancing in our brains.

On Sunday, we beat the Bears, 14–6, not as big as expected, but not bad considering we have a 5th column in our midst. Malley and myself kept looking for somebody taking a dive, and we compared notes on the bench, but the only thing out of the ordinary was that Limey missed 3 straight field goals: 2 long and 1 from the 18. And Luke Hairston had a big screaming debate with The Connection at the half.

At first I hadn't known what the shouting was about in the training room, but then I heard Hairston holler, "What chew mean I had enough? Who're *you* to tell *me* I had enough?" He came stomping out in his clogs, and I went in for my shots.

"He wanted some greens," The Connection said. "I told him 300 milligrams was enough."

"300 milligrams?" I said. "I don't know about him, but that's enough for your average racehorse, right?" The Connection grunted and gave me my 3 hits of Xylocaine.

Malley and I watched Hairston close during the game, and he put on his usual performance that seemed so out of character with his attitude off the field. I can still see him loping into the short zone on one of those fake pass routes that he's famous for, bringing up one of the safeties to help cover him because he's so tall he can beat the one-man coverage every time, and just when they were all over him like flies on dogshit, he kind of shook himself like King Kong and shifted gears and converted that little curling route into a regular old-fashioned fly pattern and caught a 55–yard pass on the dead run for our first touch. We all ran down the field to hug and squeeze and act like idiots, but there wasn't any hero to hug and squeeze. He was already over at the sidelines, throwing something down his throat at the water tank and then jogging 10 yards away from the nearest player to commute with nature, the way he always does.

On the plane ride home, he shuffled up and down the aisle like a caged cheetah, his eyes narrowed to slits, and picked fights with the stewardesses. Every 5 minutes, he'd push the call button and say, "Waitress!" and if she didn't rush down the aisle with a beer for his majesty, he screamed like a stuck bull.

I nudged Mal. "I gotta believe that's our man," I said. "He's sure crazy enough."

"I gotta disbelieve it," Mal said. "Nobody can play the way he does and still be trying to mess up. But he does have a problem."

"He's hooked?" I said.

"Sure, he's hooked, but it's worse than that. I think he's a walking nervous breakdown. I think he's on the verge of being totally whacked out."

"Yeh," I said. "With a little help from his friends."

The next week we had something else to worry about: our 13th game, the next-to-last of the regular season. It was an interdivisional contest with the Jersey Giants, the same team we'd probably have to play in the championships, provided we ever got to the championships. We were still hanging on to a 1-game lead over the Saints after we both won on Sunday.

Ever since the Giants came out and admitted they weren't from New York anymore and renamed themselves the Jersey Giants, they'd worked hard to change their image away from the artsy-craftsy style of the past and toward a more physical game, with less flea-flicking and more breaking heads. They brought in that old macho Joe Kapp as coach, and he drafted every available Chicano player, and now they were drinking tequila and leading the east, a game and a half ahead of Pittsburgh. "They don't have any special talent," Coach said at the Tuesday meeting, "but they get by on bluster. They play you for pussies, but if you don't react like pussies, you can whip their ass."

"Don't worry, we're no pussies," Jay Cox spoke up from the front row.

"That remains to be seen," Coach said in his usual cheerful way. One thing about Coach, he was always behind us, 18% of the way.

You'd have to be stupid not to be a little nervous about the Giants. I don't say you should roll over and play dead for them, but I do say you have to know what they can do. You got to be hipper than Skippy Favre of the Patriots, which the Giants destroyed the poor little fellow right in front of your eyes. Skippy was only about 5-foot-7, maybe 160, and he liked to wear a helmet with a single bar, and his specialty was greasing up his pants and running back kickoffs 102 yards. Then he played against the Giants. The 1st time he carried the ball he was clotheslined, which is an old technique, but the 2d time he got hit high by Pedro Nunez and low by Cotton Armbrister, and in the split second while he was hanging there defenseless Marvin "Beast" Barlow smashed his Absorblo wristpad into the side of Skippy's face and down he went with a dislocated jaw and a broken cheekbone and the blood spurting out of his helmet hole like a drinking fountain. The Patriots tried to play him the next season with a water helmet, one of those special jobs with canals of liquid lining the inside, but the dye was already cast. The other teams began gunning for him, and Lucky Lucchesi of the Bengals broke the water helmet and screamed at the zebra, "He pissed on me! The dirty little bastard pissed on me!" A few more Absorblos to the head, and Skippy Favre went into retirement. He was 23.

If the Jersey Giants had any honest talent, other than a bunch of alley fighters and pug-uglies, it was down the middle of their defense, the part that concerns me the most. Their right tackle, the villian above-mentioned, was Marvin "Beast" Barlow, 6-foot-5 and a hard 240, with hands like machetes and very bad breath. Their right tackle was "Little Jack" Herner, 250 pounds, 6-foot-4 in cleats and 6-foot-7 in heels, a guy that would press a ton and then make a pass at the P.R. man. On a bet, Beast Barlow and Jack Herner once pushed an 18-wheel tractor-trailer a mile and a half in the Macy's parade and didn't even get winded, and Jack finished out the parade wrapped in a sable coat blowing kisses to the crowd. Mal said he was a practicing homosexual, but to me he looked like an expert.

The middle linebacker was Pancho Peterson, a half-Chicano like Kapp and just as tough. He was out of USC, rangy and tall, built like Ted Hendricks, which is why he got dubbed "The Mad Heron," because Hendricks used to be called "The Mad Stork" before he retired and went into the bail-bond business. Peterson's specialty was the screaming dog. Beast and Little Jack would clear out the middle and Pancho'd come crunching through with those carbon-steel knees pumping like pistons and squash the runner before he could get out of the backfield. Then he'd scream, "*Yah yah yah* ya pussy ya! Don't ever come my way. Don't you *ever* come my way!" If that wasn't aggravating enough, he had a habit of pulling the hairs out of your arms in the pile-ups. At first I thought it was a bee sting, but the next time he did it I caught him and kicked him in the helmet, but as Malley says, "No sense, no feeling," and Pancho kept right on coming the rest of the game.

Between Peterson and Beast Barlow and Little Jack Herner, you couldn't do much up the middle against the Giants, but it was no waltz running around the ends either, because their other 2 linebackers, Felix Hernandez and Peaches Morales, were mobile and aggressive, and they just stood there spouting hot sauce and chile peppers and daring you to try them. That left a very simple approach, and Coach spelled it out in the offensive game plan:

No. 1. Don't let them intimidate you, or you're already beat. If they hold, gouge their eyes. If they kick, kick back twice as hard. If they try to break your arm, go for their nuts.

No. 2. Use play-action, to bring those fire-eating linebackers in and set up the short pass.

No. 3. Play with patience and see what happens later. These wild-ass aggressive teams usually fizzle out around the end of the 3d quarter. You can't give everything you've got on every single play in an NFL game, no matter what the public's been led to believe. Every player dogs it maybe 1 play out of 4. If you don't, you got nothing left at the end. We figured to let the Giants do their thing for a while, and then we'd do *our* thing and finesse them to death.

The 1st quarter went about as expected. They didn't cross our 40, and we didn't cross theirs. Pancho Peterson slugged Wing Choy and drew a flag and screamed, "Whatsa matter, can't you arm-tackle a man in this league?"

"Yeh," the zebra said, stepping off 15, "but you can't throw a left hook. Don't try it again."

A few plays later he tried it again, but the officials didn't see it, and Wing wobbled off the field for ammonia and oxygen. When the Giants got the ball on the next sequence, Lacklustre Jones fell on their little scooter Marcus Hess in the open field and collapsed his lung. Then Buzz Urquhart got his bell rung and carried off on a stretcher, and when he opened his eyes, he looked up at the Rev. Matthew Galvin, our faithful team chaplain, and Buzzie was still groggy and said, "Father, how much more time?"

The priest peeked at the clock and said, "About 2½ minutes, my son."

"Father," Buzz gulped, "I'll have to talk fast. Can I just confess the high points?"

All this time I was having my hands full with the Mad Heron and the Beast and Little Jack Herner, and I was calling every blocking variation in the book to try to move them out. Once I called a scissors block, where our 2 guards, Bad-ass and Bullivant, are supposed to crisscross and take out the opposite tackles, and I'm supposed to fire straight out on the middle linebacker, which some coaches call a great maneuver and others call a useless bit of deception that usually fools the offense more than anybody else, which is exactly what happened. Bull completely forgot his assignment and put a crab block on Herner, and Bad-ass came crossing over and plowed into the 2 of them, and this left nobody in front of Beast Barlow, and the Beast descended on Q. B. like an eagle on a mouse and almost tore his head off. For a second I wondered if Bullivant could be the fixer. But that was impossible. It was like mistaking the Holy Ghost for Pontius Pilot, and I perished the thought.

Just before the half, we tried a fly pattern, to show it and set something up for later, and their weak safety tripped over his own feet and Ray Roy caught the ball on their 30 and headed for the end zone. "Don't spike," I hollered. *"Don't spike!"* But instead of spiking Ray Roy got caught on the 6 by the other safety.

We ran 3 plays to their 4, and then John Lovesey came in with that same anxious look around his eyes that we'd all noticed ever since he was thrown in jail. In the huddle, Q. B. said calmly, "Okay, men, this is just like an extra point. Just a point-after, that's all. Play starts when the kicker's ready."

I looked back through my legs and memorized where

Q. B. wanted the ball, lifted my head to check the defense, and when I heard the signal I snapped clean and hard, to give Q. B. plenty of time to get it down and turn the laces. The ball slurped off his fingers like a peeled avocado and bounced over to Limey, and Limey looked at it like it was a sack of scorpions. He reached down and picked it up just as the 1st blocker came flying past, taking himself out of the play, followed by Pancho Peterson gallomping in like a tidal wave with his arms outstretched to a 6-foot width. Limey cocked his arm back in sheer terror, to pass the ball, to get rid of it, but instead of making the tackle the Mad Heron plucked the ball from Limey's outstretched hand and ran 20 yards before J. W. Ramwell got him from behind.

I pulled myself up from where Jack Herner had trompled all over me and felt me up, and looked frantically for the handkerchief. There *had* to be a flag on this play. It was only a matter of life and death. But there was no flag, and the Jersey fans were going pomegranite.

When I got back to the bench, Coach was tearing patches out of his toupee. "What was wrong with that snap?" he hollered at Q. B., elbowing me out of the way. I stuck my nose right in where I could hear the answer, and I made sure Q. B. saw me.

"Nothing," he said. "I fucked up." Sure, but why? This made 2 horses on Q. B., counting the goof with Zawatski. He was better than that.

Limey kicked off to start the 2d half and bodies went flying through the air, and when just about everybody was flat on his ass there was one terrible, awful, paralyzing sight at the middle of the field, which was the sight of their kick returner Amos Allen toe-dancing along with nobody but Limey to beat, and Allen did a dainty sidestep and Limey did a dying swan and Allen went to the posts waving bye-bye. We're the team that's supposed to come on in the 2d half, but somebody neglected to tell the Giants.

There's about 20 teams in the NFL that would have quit right there. I mean any time you go out to play the Jersey Giants you're due for a pounding, you're in pain for 60 minutes of playing time and for 2 or 3 days after, but it's well worth it as long as you pound right back and kick the shit out of them and win the game. But if your special teams just hand points away, what's the incentive to go out and get beat up? Why suffer?

Well, there's something called pride, that's why suffer. The Billygoats were disorganized and hurting, and we even had a sabotager somewhere, but we still had enough discipline and pride to stick to our game plan, Point No. 3, which was to be patient and see what happens later. What happened later was that Hyphen B-l-a-c-k put a hit on the Giants' quarterback that almost snapped his spine, and the quarterback coughed up the ball to end a Giant drive on our 2. Then Wing Choy broke 3 tackles singlefootedly and picked up 12 yards to get us out of the end zone. All of a sudden the whole club seemed to pick up, matching the wild-ass Jersey Giants crunch for crunch, and in the end it was the Giants that gave, not the Billygoats, and up Joe Kapp's Chicano ass. Cox scored on a dive play from the 2, and ten minutes later Custer Fox faked the corner out of his hat, ass and jock and scored on a 15-yard curl, and I almost tore my lungs out hollering.

That's what the game of football is all about, that's why you play when you hurt and play when you're demoralized and play even when you suspect that there's a rattlesnake on your own side. Maybe it's like a gambler betting long shots, he loses race after race day after day and it's agony, and then one of his horses pays 60 to 1 and makes everything worthwhile. A game like this against the Giants, where we had the crap knocked out of us and didn't get a break and then came back and whipped their ass—that's worth years of frustration. You'll tell your great-grandchildren about it. At the gun, with the score Billygoats 14, Giants 7, we sprinted and hobbled and staggered toward the tunnel, and nobody took his helmet off, because those crazy Jersey fans were throwing beer cans and ice-balls and everything hard they could get their hands on, and even though they were aiming at the Giants, once in a while they would hit us.

On the bus to Newark Airport, we were all high on greens and pain killers and muscle relaxants and happy as though we were in our right minds. Crossing the hog flats, Ziggy Guminski hollered to the driver, "Hey, Bussie, would you stop and let my little brother Jack off?" Oh, that Ziggy!

Buzz Urquhart was saying, "I dunno how it happened, I just put my head down and smashed into him and everything went black."

"Jeez," J. R. Rodenheimer said, "we musta been playin' Kansas City."

The late Robert Boggs jumped up and shouted, "That's a racist remark, Mr. Hitler," but I could see he really wasn't mad. He leaned over and gave J. R. a friendly Dutch rub on his crewcut, only ripping out a few of the short blond hairs, and then he said, "Even *you* can't make me mad today, Rosenheiser. Poor thing, you don't know what chew sayin'. You just a ignorant Honky, and I forgives you."

We passed through a residential area lined with trees and fancy houses and I looked around to see Bad-ass Harris hanging a B.A. out a back window. I nudged Ziggy, and Ziggy hollered, "Hey, knock it off!" and Bad stopped waving his naked mahogany ass in the open air.

"What'sa matter, Ziggy?" Bad-ass whined. "The defense is hangin' B.A.s in the next bus."

"Oh, those assholes been hangin' B.A.s for years," Ziggy said. "No class."

I turned and looked back. "Oh, yeh?" I said. "Lack and the coaches? The chaplain?"

"Lack would never do a thing like that," Malley said.

On the plane home, we heard the news that New Orleans had walloped Minnesota 35–7. We were still in 1st place by a game. 1 more win and we're in the playoffs.

When you win, you're liberated for 2, 3 days. You can sleep, your mind is easy, you don't wake up at 3 in the morning and think you're a shit. On Tuesday when you look at the game films, everybody's loose and relaxed, and there's a lot of jacking around. This time Coach kept re-running a play where the late Robert Boggs tripped over his own cleats and fell on his face mask and the end just stepped over him and slapped Q. B. down like a ragdoll. After Coach ran it for the 4th time, without comment, Lacklustre Jones said, "Hey, Coach, one of these times he's gonna get hurt."

After the 5th replay, the late Robert Boggs called out, "One more once, Coach. I'll get the mothafucka this time!"

The 6th replay was in slo-mo, and Robert sort of floated through the air, hit the turf softly, bounced once and then oozed back to the ground. "Mothafucka can fly, too!" Bad-ass hollered.

"Oh, yeh," said Wing Choy. "He flies on *green* fuel."

The only unpleasant note was little John Lovesey, sitting back in the shadows and performing his regular chore at the film sessions, which is to turn the light switch off and on at Coach's instruction. Coach called out, "Lights!" and nothing happened. "Lights!" Coach repeated, and still nothing happened. We turned around and looked and Limey was sitting there staring at the floor, with his head around his belt.

"Hey, Lovesey, wake up, for Chrissakes!" Coach hollered, and Limey raised his head and hit the switch all in one reflex. "Well, at least you're good for something," Coach said, which was definitely unfair. Here's all the guys sharing the biggest win of the year, the most important game we'd played, and just because Limey hadn't kicked a field goal since he went to jail he had to be singled out for abuse. Anybody with half a brain could see that criticism was something the kid didn't need, since he was already so down on himself he could hardly function. Coming home on the plane, he'd been the only player to refuse his beers, just sitting in the last row by himself pretending to doze, and I knew he was wide awake, because I went back there and whispered, "Limey?" and I saw him shudder, so I just left him alone.

After practice on Tuesday, Malley and myself hung back and waited for Limey, and we cornered him in the locker room. Mostly I kept quiet while Mal tried to worm the truth. Finally Limey admitted that he couldn't shake a terrible fear of being enclosed or held down or trapped. "I've always had it," he told us, "but I never realized how bad it was till that night in jail. Now it's the only thing I think about, 'round the clock. I'm afraid to lock the door in me own bawth."

"That's serious business," Mal said. "We got to get you some help."

"No, no, no!" Limey insisted. "I'll face it meself," but he broke out in a cold sweat just talking about it.

A couple of days later, our team doctor, Mr. Evans, got on the case and gave Limey a thorough work-up, blood pressure and heart rate and internal exams and the whole smear.

"What's the diagnosis, Doc?" Mal asked.

"Nothing to worry about," Mr. Evans said, smiling. "It's all in his mind."

For the finishing straw, *Sports Pictorial* ran a picture of Limey just after Pancho Peterson took the ball from his outstretched hand, and it looked like Limey was saying goodbye to a friend, and the caption said, "They also serve who only stand and wave," followed by a dumb story on how the Goats had lucked out and had no chance for "the laurels" unless the team got its act together. Well, who ever wanted any laurels anyway? All we wanted was to win the Superbowl and 30,000 bucks apiece, and some other club could keep the fucking greenery.

All week Malley and I kept buying the morning papers to check the spread for our game with Washington. We opened a 17-point favorite, which is a terrific spread but not out of line in this case. The Redskins were completely wrecked and had been for ages, ever since they traded away 5 years of future draft choices, and the team had nothing to play for but pride, and not much of that. But the Goats had to win to clinch the division. If we blew the game, New Orleans could take it all by winning over the Bears. So we had plenty of motivation. We had so much motivation, in fact, that Coach dressed one of our ticket men as a plumber and sent him to observe an enemy workout and bring us back a few helpful hints. After that, there was no way we could possibly lose.

But you'd never know it as the week went on. By Wednesday the spread was down to 10, then it dropped to 7, and by game time it was 4. Tons of money was being bet against us. It was ridiculous. Our 3d string could have handled the Redskins. I asked Mal what he made of it.

"Somebody knows something," he said.

"How could we lose?" I said.

"Well, we could tie our shoelaces together, the way we did against Chicago," Malley said. "Otherwise I don't see how."

About 2 hours before the game, Ziggy came around and asked each player, "Need a little extra?" and ladled out greenies from his pocket. He'd already given me one an hour or so before and it'd done absolutely nothing for me, so I popped another one, and still there was no reaction. Usually you can feel a green in 20, 30 minutes, and you get kind of dry-mouthed and pop-eyed and excitable, and you want to throw your arms around everybody in the world, or else kill them. But I wasn't the least bit high and neither was anybody else I could see. I looked up and down the lockers and I thought maybe I'd wandered into the Benedictine monkery by mistake. Players sat in their jockstraps and looked straight ahead with their mouths open. There was none of the usual pizazz, with guys whacking each other on the pads and whipping each other with towels and generally jacking around. "Come on, guys, let's get it up!" Q. B. hollered, but the only response was a soft rose from Lacklustre Jones, carrying out his customary pre-game assignment of sitting on his throne reading *Penthouse.*

I climbed up on the bench and said, "Hey, let's hear a little chatter," but I felt silly doing it because I didn't even feel like chattering myself. Then "the quiet man," Luke Hairston, blurted out, "Yeh! Come on, ya buncha fuckin' pussies!" I wondered what had gotten into him, but I found out when I looked his way. He had the telltale white wash around his mouth, and his feet were tapping out a little dance. The rest of the guys kept on dressing for the funeral. We were a fine-looking ballclub: 1 lunatic pill-freak and 39 members of the Ladies Aid.

The zebra stuck his head in the door and hollered, "5

minutes, Coach," and I hunted up Ziggy. "Hey," I said, "gimme another green."

"That's 3, isn't it?" Ziggy asked.

"Come on!" I said. "Gimme another one." I swallowed the pill and went outside for the introductions. My legs felt unsteady, and my right knee was numb from Xylocaine, and I barely had the strength to sing the national anthem along with the several other guys on the club that Billy Bob Bunker asked us to sing so the TV cameras would have a couple of patriots to pan across.

Then we went into our customary pre-game beeswarm, where everybody's supposed to crowd around and bang each other on the pads and slap ass and say things like "Come on, men!" "You can do it!" "Hit hit *hit!*" "Stick 'em quick!" and the other brilliant remarks that have been jacking teams up since Romulus and Ramos. The only trouble was that we looked like a bunch of zombies, no enthusiasm, no vitality, all but Luke Hairston, which he was slamming into people and acting like a high-school cheerleader, completely out of character for "the quiet man." I wondered how many he'd had. Not how many pills; how many *bottles* of pills. He was so turned-on his feet barely touched the ground. I didn't see how he could last the 1st period.

Against any other team in the NFL, we'd have lost 50–0, the way we played. We dragged so bad that Coach turned into a screaming meemie, slapping and kicking at us to wake us up. "Little Sisters of the Poor!" he kept saying. "You must all got the rag on!" But Washington looked even worse, if you can imagine. They played 2d and 3d stringers, they tried out a couple guys nobody ever heard of, and we ended up the half tied at 10. The only bright note was that Limey kicked his 1st field goal in 4 games, from 9 yards out. He shanked it and almost blew it, and I swear he kicked with his eyes closed and ran off the field like he was persued by dragons.

Before we split into units for the halftime strategy sessions, Ziggy handed out more greens.

"Hey, Mal!" I said. "You take a pill before the game?"

"Yeh," Malley said. "But you'd never know it."

"I took 3 of the fucking things," I said, "and I can hardly stay awake."

"They're just plain not working."

"Maybe we're getting too used to 'em."

I took 2 more this time, that made 5 pills working away in my bloodstream and they might as well have been chalk. "Hey, Ziggy," I said. "Whatsa matter with these greens? They ain't doing fuck all."

"You just play football," Ziggy said, as if I'd insulted his grandmother. "I'll take care of the pills."

Luke Hairston was still the only player up for the game, and he kept mumbling and humming to himself while Offensive Coordinator Edquist tried to diagram adjustments on the blackboard. "Shut up, Hairston, for Chrissakes!" Edquist finally hollered, but Luke kept right on as if he didn't hear.

We scored early in the 2d half when a Redskin fumbled and Hyphen B-l-a-c-k stumbled 10 yards unmolested before almost falling on his face in the end zone. Then a few minutes later Limey had a chance to salt the game with a 14-yard kick, but he delayed too long and the ball bounced off a lineman and straight up in the air. Limey watched it coming down, like a fat balloon, and instinctively took another swipe at it with his kicking foot, and the ball sailed square between the posts, the most perfect 2d effort of the year. What a way to salt the game!

When I got up, the zebra was crisscrossing his palms flat in front of his belt. I jumped 3 feet, and then I joined about 6 other Goats jawing at the ref. "No good," he kept saying. "No good!"

"Why no good?" Q. B. screamed.

"Because I say so," the ref said, looking slightly upset.

"Listen," Lacklustre Jones said, running up and parting the backs of the players with his big hands to get to the zebra, "that bullshit don't go around here. 'Because I say so' ain't good enough. Now why's the kick no good?"

"The rules," the ref said, gulping hard.

"What mothafuckin' rule you got in mind?" Robert Boggs put in. "Sight the rule!"

"Wait a minute. Lemme think."

"Fuck you, zebra," Bad-ass Harris said, his spit flying at the official's shirt. "You zebras always tryin' to fuck us."

"I don't *know* the rule," the ref said frantically, walking toward the sideline, "but I know that kick's no good." We all let out a cry like we'd been hit in the ass by a freight train. "No, wait!" the zeeb said, and turned back. "It's a loose ball. *That's right!* You can't kick a loose ball."

It went down as a blocked kick and a touchback, if you're scoring, and the 'Skins took over on their 20. A few minutes later, the pressbox sent word that New Orleans was beating the Bears 19–zip at the end of the half. "Jesus Christ," Ziggy said, "if we lose this, it's Katy bar the door."

Washington's drive went 50 yards before their kicker blew a field goal, and we were still ahead, 17–10. Then on 3d and 4, Q. B. blooped a banana ball end over end to Luke Hairston, which he had already caught 6 passes for good yardage, and he gathered it in and started to run and all of a sudden crashed to the rug like somebody had clubbed him with a sledge. His feet did a regular St. Vitus dance, churning away like he was running for a touchdown, except that he was laying on his side and the ball was being carried the other way, all the way to the posts by the 'Skins' left corner.

Even after the official's hands went straight up and the scoreboard flashed the 6 for Washington, Luke Hairston was still shaking his feet, but more trembly now, the way you see a fish's fins quiver after he's out of the water. Then his whole body began to heave and writhe around.

"Convulsions!" The Connection said as he ran up with the medical tray, closely followed by Mr. Evans and his black bag. After 5 or 10 minutes they sent for a stretcher and carried 6 foot 10 inches of tight end off the field. Mr. Evans walked alongside, wringing his hands.

"What's that in his mouth?" I asked The Connection.

"My wallet," the trainer said. "Keeps him from biting off his tongue."

"Jesus," Coach said. "He was our whole offense."

Our rushing team dragged onto the field with instructions for an all-out rush, but the 'Skins managed to fuck up the extra point all by themselves with a bad snap just as word came down that the Saints had won. We were still ahead, 17–16. "Come on, men!" Ziggy shouted when he sent the offense back on the field. "It's now or never! There's no tomorrow!"

With Luke Hairston out of our lineup and Bill Studney in his place, Washington went into a quick adjustment that stopped us cold. At the warning, the 'Skins had the ball on their own 35. They went into their 2-minute drill, but we ran out the clock and held onto the win, the sorriest way any NFL team ever backed into a division championship.

In the dressing room, where there should have been a wild party, the only real noisemakers were Billy Bob Bunker, the Rev. Matthew Galvin and a few of the front-office people. The players sat in front of our lockers, stunned and quiet, and thanking our stars we hadn't blown it all. "We sure stank up the joint," Lacklustre Jones said after a while. The honest opinion of an expert in the field.

"If we play that way next week," Malley said, "the season's over."

I said, "You know, that's the flattest I felt since I had mono in college. I took 5 greens and I'm still in a coma."

"How's Hairston?" somebody asked The Connection.

"He'll be okay," the trainer said. "He's sleeping in the whirlpool."

"What'd you give him?" I asked.

"300 milligrams of sodium amytal right in the ass."

"Will that keep him out?"

"Only for a day or 2."

THE FLIGHT
VII
NO PLACE FOR BOXIN'

WHAT ANY OF US WOULD'VE GIVEN TO STICK 300 MILLI-*grams in Luke Hairston's ass now, after 4 hours in the air and one shooting and about 16 cases of the dry heaves and the wet pants from the fright and the worry. Maybe pro football players are brave, resourceful men, and maybe we're not, but nobody can be very brave hanging up in the sky like that, while a whacked-out junkie watches you through the sights of a gun that can fire 10 rounds before you bat an eye. It was 6 o'clock at night, dark now, and we were still flying the same course, dead ahead toward New Orleans, and Luke was still hanging in there, refreshing himself every hour or so with one kind of fix or another, either in the mouth or in the vein, and the rest of the time just watching us through those big, wet, owl eyes of his, halfway daring us to make a move. On my latest trip up front, the pilot said we were 30 minutes away from New Orleans and we had about 2 hours' reserve of fuel. I passed the message to Hairston, but he didn't seem to hear me. I repeated in a louder voice:*

*"WE'RE ALMOST TO NEW ORLEANS AND WE'RE
GETTING LOW ON FUEL."*

"Sit—down," Hairston said, spacing the words about 2
seconds apart, as though he was having trouble talking.
The drugs were slowing his action, and I hoped he would
finally lose control and we could jump him. His eyes
seemed heavy, and he kept bobbing his head up every
second or 2 as though it was getting heavy. But he still
held the gun in his arm, and he still kept his finger on the
trigger.

Just when I thought he was on the verge of nodding out,
he shuddered again like a wet dog and sidestepped into
the aisle and hollered, "Hey, you dudes in the back of the
bus, pay attention!"

Everybody looked up.

"Times fo' the Tuesday night fights," he said. "Now le's
see, who should we have on the card? How 'bout Jones
against Bullivant?" Nobody answered him. "That'd be a
very heavy fight," he raved on. "Lacklustre Jones versus
Buford Bullivant, yes suh! Bullivant could hit him with
his Bible and Jones could whack him with his butterfly."
I glanced at Malley and Malley had on that "I'm thinking" look. Hairston kept his distance but he knew about
Lack's little moth that sometimes turned into a butterfly?
Probably said it in the shower. It's tough to keep a secret
on a pro football team.

"Naw, wait a minute!" Hairston hollered, "I got it! The
perfec' main event. You, Rodenheimer! Stand up, you
fuckin' honky chump! Boggs, on yo' feet! Now le's see y'all
mix it up."

Neither player moved. I guess they couldn't believe
their ears.

"Ain't no place for boxin'," Lacklustre understated for
the year.

"Hey," Hairston hollered, "I said on yo' feet and mix it

up. *FIGHT!" He raised the submachine gun to his shoulder, and J. R. quickly stepped into the aisle. "Go own, go own!" Hairston said. "You 2 pussies always makin' noise. Now let's see kin you back it up."*

Robert climbed into the aisle almost at the last row, and J. R. moved slowly toward him. "Go own!*" Hairston commanded. "Slap him one! He s'pose to be the senior spook."*

I could see J. R.'s heart wasn't in it, but his heart wasn't in getting his ass shot off either, so he kept advancing toward the late Robert. "Better not try slappin' no Robert Boggs," Robert said softly. He posed like a sumo wrestler in that one-piece jumpsuit he always flies in. "Don't come near me, Rosenheiser!" he said, but J. R. kept coming.

All I could think of was the time Roman Gabriel and David Jones started to tango on a Rams' flight and some of the Rams jumped in and broke it up before it really got started, and the players talked about it for years after. "Nothing that ever happened on the field scared me as much as that," one of their players was quoted. No wonder. With 2 powerful dudes like Gabe and Deacon slugging it out in the aisle at 36,000 feet, it only takes one wild swing or one wild kick to take out a window.

I turned and sat halfway up on my seat and tried to get Robert's attention, which wasn't easy because he was staring at the advancing form of J. R. Rodenheimer, slowly lurching down the aisle, turning around every few steps to give Hairston these sickly looks, as if to say, "Do I have to go through with this?" and Hairston giving him looks that said, "Fuck, yes!"

When I finally caught Robert's eye, they were only about 4 or 5 feet apart, and I winked broadly as hard as I could, and just kept winking over and over again, and hoped he got my meaning.

J. R. put out a sickly left jab, and Robert ducked. "Go ahead, fight!*" Hairston ordered, and walked a few steps down the aisle himself, cackling and slobbering. When J. R. stuck out his fist again, Robert grabbed it and threw him down on the aisle, and the 2 of them rolled around and squeezed each other and grunted and groaned. I could only hope that the right information was being exchanged. After a minute or so of jacking around, they jumped back up and began slamming each other with lefts and rights, which the expert eye could tell that the blows were not quite landing or were being slipped or faked. It looked like Saturday night on a smalltown boxing card when the local gamblers are throwing a benefit for themselves. But Hairston was too far gone catch it. The simulated fight was good enough for him, and he laughed out loud when J. R. went down and Robert straddled him and began raining "punches" on his unprotected face and head. "Stop!" Malley hollered. "You'll kill him. Don't hit him again! He's out already."*

Robert pulled himself to his feet and strutted back to his place, wiping imaginary blood off his hands, while J. R. lay in a big heap. "Satisfied?" I said to Hairston. He just wobbled back to his rack and drooled, like all the rest of your fight fans. I limped up to ringside just as Bad-ass Harris threw a cup of water into J. R.'s face.

"Hey, spook, cut that out!" J. R. whispered.

Bad-ass went for more water and sloshed it up J. R.'s nostrils. "Mothafucka," Bad said. "This as good a time as any to drown you."

The night after the Washington win, there was a victory party, but Malley and I begged off. "If those guys party the way they played," Mal said, "they'll all be asleep by 8 o'clock."

It turned out to be a good thing we went home early,

because the phone rang around 9 and it was Coach.

"You guys up?" he asked.

"I'm watching TV," I said. "Mal's in his room. I don't know if he's asleep or—"

"Don't tell me your life story," Coach said. "Just get your asses down here right away."

Once again we found Coach and Ziggy and Jerry Stein in a conference with the room reeking of tobacco. "Siddown, you assholes," Coach said. "You must be all wore out from that terrific effort on Sunday."

"How can 40 guys be so flat?" Malley said. "I can't figure it out."

"Flat?" Coach mimicked. "Shit, it was more like the fucking typhoid fever. Buncha fucking pussies out there."

"Well, Coach, we won," I said, sticking up for my roomie.

"You won, my ass! Washington lost."

Malley said, "It looks the same in the standings."

"Tietjens," Coach said, twirling his cigar and studying the disgusting sloppy part he sticks in his mouth, "with that attitude and 10 cents you can ride all the way from the Bronx to the Battery." I had to laugh to myself. Coach's reference points are always to the New York of his childhood. That ride must cost at least a quarter now.

"Coach, excuse me," Mal said, "but did you call us down here in the middle of the night to tell us we played lousy?"

Jerry Stein said, "No, that's *not* the reason. The reason is they hit us again."

"Huh?" I said.

"The shavers. The fixers. The mob, or whoever it is."

In the excitement and confusion of backing into the division championship by barely beating the worst team in football, I'd completely forgotten about the peculiar movements the spread had made all week. "It went from

17 to 10 to 7 and finally to 4, and then most books took it down," Stein said. "The commissioner's got the red ass. You guys have to help us."

Malley looked at me and I looked at Malley. "What've you been able to find out from your end?" Mal asked. "Anything you can tell us?"

"Yeh," said the man from the commissioner's office, whacking his pipe in his palm. "We found out that those racist signs in the locker room were cut on a Dymo label-maker that anybody can buy at a hardware store. So that's a dead end. We learned that Bad-ass Harris is still singing the blues to his girlfriend every night over the phone, complaining about how Rodenheimer accused him of stealing and he's never stolen anything since he took the gym teacher's Trojans in the 9th grade."

"How'd you find that out?" I asked.

"And we learned that none of the locks on the Clamages' front door snap in place automatically," Stein went on, ignoring my question. "They have to be turned by hand. Somebody locked Lovesey out on purpose. Then he slipped upstairs and tipped off the cops from one of the extensions. Maybe they hoped there'd be a raid and the whole team'd be arrested, I don't know."

"Okay, but how'd they fix the Washington game?" Malley asked.

"I wish I knew," Jerry Stein said. "I've never seen a spread drop like that, except once or twice when Joe Namath had the knee. The bookies say they had to completely unbalance the spread to draw any Billygoat money at all."

"And even then they took the bath of the year," Coach threw in.

"Right," Stein said. "There's a coupla layoff men in Vegas that're ready to fit some shoes."

"Fit some shoes?" I said.

"Yeh. In cement."

Ziggy piped up. "It didn't look like point-shaving to me. You guys were just flat. No pizazz, no balls. You played like the Little Sisters of the Poor. Right, Coach?"

" 'B' team," Coach said.

"Coach," I said, "I been waiting for 10 seasons to get into the championships, and Mal's been waiting for 7, and all we had to do Sunday was beat the worst club in football. But we were just saying tonight both of us felt like we were playing underwater. I don't understand it. And I took—"

Ziggy gave me a quick look.

"You took what?" Stein asked evenly.

"Oh, nothing," I said, feeling my cheeks burning. "I took a dump before the game, and sometimes that tires me out."

"What'd you *really* take before the game?" Coach asked. "The usual?"

I looked over at the representative of the whole National Football League. "Can I say?" I asked Coach.

"Certainly you can say, you dizzy shit!" Coach screamed. "Do you think the league gives a fuck about a few greenies when the whole future of pro football's at stake? *What'd you take?*"

"5 greens altogether."

Stein whistled softly.

"How about you, Tietjens?" Coach asked.

"I usually take 1 about an hour before the game, and another at the half," Malley said. "But I didn't feel any reaction, so I doubled up, and I still didn't feel anything. By the looks of the way we played, nobody else did either."

"Wait a minute," Jerry Stein said, jumping up and pacing across to the projector and back. "Wait—a—*minute!* Where'd you get the pills?"

I looked at Ziggy, and Ziggy looked jumpy.

"Go ahead and answer!" Coach said.

"Coach Guminski gave 'em out," I said.

"Yeh," Malley said. "Sometimes we get 'em from The Connection, I mean the trainer, and sometimes we get 'em from Ziggy. This time it was Ziggy."

Our poor offensive-line coach looked like he wanted the floorboards to part and swallow him up, but Stein aimed his pipestem at Ziggy and said, "Listen, Guminski, I want to see one of those Dexamyls and I want to see it right now."

"I give 'em all out," Ziggy protested.

"Where'd you have 'em?"

"In the pocket of my game jacket."

"Where's your game jacket?"

"Hangin' in my locker."

"Well, get your fucking ass over there and check!" Stein screamed, his nose right up against Ziggy's. It was the 1st time I'd seen him show any heat, but then there was a lot at stake.

A few minutes later Ziggy dashed back into Coach's office, breathing like he'd just done a wind sprint, and laid a greenie on the desk. "It was way down in my pocket," he said. "I didn't know I had any left."

Stein broke it in half, along the marking, and touched one half to his tongue. Then he began shaking his head up and down the way Sir Isaac Newton must have done when he discovered figs. "You boys know how greens taste," he said.

"Sure," Malley said. "Like unripe persimmons. If you get one stuck in your mouth, you can taste it for a week."

"Try this," Stein said, shoving the other half across the table.

Mal took a taste and handed the half to me. "Like Life-Savers," he said.

"Sweeter than that," I said. "More like powdered sugar."

"Where'd you get these, Guminski?" Stein asked.

"From the trainer," Ziggy answered.

"They're sugar pills," Stein said. "You could eat 100 and they wouldn't do a thing for you."

"Oh, yeh?" Coach barked. "Then how do you explain Luke Hairston having an overdose?"

"I can explain it," I chipped in after a sweaty silence. "Hairston doesn't only use greens. He has a private stock of Dexxies, and some other items, too."

Coach said it was a fucking shame he hadn't shared.

We met Green Bay at Lambeau Field in the playoffs, and for once we had our act together, not that the Packers had ever presented the slightest problem, with us having 6 wins and a tie in our last 7 games against them. Ever since Dan Devine left to study orthopedic medicine and Bo Medley came in, we'd been cleaning up on the Pack. We'd go there in a blizzard, and Coach would say, "Billygoat weather!" and then we'd all go out and play like he was right, even though our normal weather was 75 in the shade. This time the temperature sank to 10 below for the game on Christmas day, and as usual, Medley announced before the game that his players would not be allowed to use hand-warmers. "I want 'em to keep their mind on football," he said for the 30th time, "not on their hands." Which of course is an absolute guarantee that their minds will be on their freezing hands the whole game. Just to help them concentrate, we'd holler things like, "Boy it's *cold* out here!" and Robert Boggs told the defensive end, "Cold hands, warm heart," and then speared the poor guy in the nuts.

By the end of the 1st quarter, we had the Green Bay lines ground down to dust, and we began to take control.

We were leading 7–zip when Luke Hairston put a move on the outside linebacker and left the poor guy jacking off about 5 yards from the action. Then Luke eased into the seam, but just as the ball was thrown the Green Bay safety came running full tilt and hit Hairston like a ton of rabbit-shit and knocked his feet out from under him and all you could see was this 6 foot 10 inches of tight end sailing through space. Just before he hit the ground he stuck up his hand and so help me, he caught that pass one-fucking-handed while he's in mid-fucking-air. Naturally everybody expected him to drop the ball when he hit, which he didn't, or wind up unconscious or dead, but he just flipped the ball to the zebra and walked back to the huddle like nothing had happened.

"Great grab!" Q. B. said, and the rest of the guys put in their own 2 cents, but naturally Luke didn't acknowledge them. He just went out and made a couple more beautiful plays and we win the game easy, 28–7. The spread was normal. The fixers must be in between shaves.

Coach always has his beady eyes open, looking for an edge. It's not enough for him to know that the Billygoats are, say, 5% better than the Jersey Giants. He wants more of a lock, something on the order of 95%, or as close as he can get. That's why he dresses front-office personnel as plumbers and electricians and sends them to spy on practices, or makes sure we have our greens before a big game or even a small game, and that's why he films every move we make during scrimmages and then stays up half the night studying the films to figure out how we can sharpen the edge. Coach is an over-achiever, and he's got 3 ulcers to prove it. He'll work and strain and fight and push and shove till we all fall down with total exhaustion. Then he'll say, "You're not Billygoats! You're a buncha pussies!"

Now that we were coming up on the 1st conference

championship game in Goat history, Coach ate nails and spit tacks. He moved us out of our comfortable houses and apartments and into the Lakeview Arms, a motel near the stadium. He set curfew at 11 o'clock, not that it made much difference, because he worked us so hard during the day that we didn't have enough strength to go carousing. He set $1000 fines for missing bed-check and $5000 for missing practice. Nobody got fined. Myself and Mal, we'd go to our rooms around 10 o'clock, after the evening meeting, and crap right out. Then Ziggy'd come around at 11 and open the door and flash his lights on us and holler, "All tucked in?" If we didn't answer, he'd say, "Jackson?" and I'd groan. Then he'd say, "Tietjens?" and Malley'd mutter something, and Ziggy'd say, "Nighty night, sleep tight, don't let the bed-bugs bite," and slam the door. One night Mal jumped out of bed and opened the door and called after him, "Ziggy, can't you just shine the fucking light and see that we're sleeping? Do you *have* to call our names and say 'Nighty night, sleep tight'?"

"I got my orders," Ziggy said. "I only work here."

Mal went back to bed, and a little later I heard him babbling something about a little touch of Ziggy in the night, but I might have been hearing things.

Another thing Coach did before the championship game was order half the team to watch Hairston, try to steer him off whatever he was on. One by one Coach got Malley and myself and Robert Boggs, Bad-ass Harris, Lack Jones and Custer Fox aside and told us to do what we could.

"And what's that?" I asked.

"Well, kinda encourage him away from the stuff," Coach said.

"Coach," I said, "you gotta be realistic. We're never gonna steer Luke Hairston away from anything. If anybody can steer him, it's you. Why don't you talk to him?"

"Yeh, I might do that." But we found out later he never did a thing. Knowing Coach, he didn't give a shit if Hairston was taking heroin with an opium chaser, as long as he didn't convulse again till the big game was over.

We usually got the game plan on Wednesday, but this week Coach not only passed it out, he ordered the defense to *memorize* the Giant probabilities: what they'd do on 1st and 10, 2d and 7 or more, 2d and less than 7, when they split their backs, how their backs line up, how they use their wide receivers, when they line up strong right and strong left, when they run from different formations, when they go to the weak side or the strong side, where they're likely to go out of each formation, how they handle their screens and draws, etc. Then he handed out a whole chart of keys to the offense, and another page of information on how the Giants will be keying on us and how we can confuse the picture, how to read their secondary, when they double-double and when they roll up into a semizone and when they go 4–3–3, how to tell when they're getting ready to shift into an odd defense, when to cross-cut them and scissors-block them and wedge and cut and crab them at the line. Jeez, it was like memorizing the Magna Charta.

On Thursday afternoon we had a multiple-choice quiz and Oop Johnson got 11 out of 20, which was a new record for him, and Coach called Oop up to the front and made a little speech about how anybody could teach himself to study, how Oop had been a little slow at first but now that we were getting ready to play the most important game in Billygoat history, the big game on Sunday for the championship of the National Football Conference against our hated rivals from the East, why, Oop was studying his defensive charts and playbooks and showing the world that he could keep right up there with the best of us. "It's all in here, boys," Coach said, tapping the cover of Oop's game folder. "Everything you need to know about the Jersey Giants."

"The Jersey Giants?" Oop said, looking confused as usual.

"That's right," Coach said. "The shit-eating Jersey Giants." He held up Oop's folder for all of us to see. Right across the cover you could read it in nice big letters:

BILLYGOATS VS. GREEN BAY PACKERS

That night, we got inside information that Beast Barlow, Jersey's big right tackle, had damaged his knee and might not start, he was working out in a metal brace and favoring the knee heavily. This went well with our game plan, to fire out and assassinate them right from the opening kickoff, trade them blow for blow, punch for punch. That's the way we beat them before, and that was the only way to handle Joe Kapp's hatchetmen. Ziggy told me Coach had even considered an old trick that one of the pro teams had used back in the '30s, which was to lash out on the 1st offensive series and just openly kick the shit out of the other team, punch them and slug them and twist their nuts for 3 straight downs, take the penalties and then punt. After that, the opponents would be so flustered you could walk right over them. But he knew Billy Bob Bunker wouldn't go for that approach, not with all the society and City Hall asses he had to kiss, so instead Coach modified the approach. He just instructed me and Bad-ass Harris to spend the 1st few series of downs working on Beast Barlow's bad knee. "Nothing cruel or inhuman," Coach said. "Just break it or something."

"Gee, I don't know, Coach," Bad-ass said. "I sho' hate to play that way."

"Do you like nice clothes?" Coach said, ripping Bad's $70 Abercrombie & Fitch pith helmet off his head. "Do you like nice paydays?"

"Just break it or sumpin'?" Bad said, his voice rising. He took back the helmet and gingerly put it on at the correct angle.

"How about you, Jackson?" Coach said, squinting his eyes to little slits. "You got any reservations?"

I had a few, but I wasn't about to tell him. "No, sir," I said. "I'll do my job."

By Friday, 2 days before the kickoff, some of the players were getting antsy about being confined, and Coach gave everybody the early evening off. "I know I can't keep you guys from seeing your wives and girlfriends," he said, "but remember: In 48 hours we play the most important game in Goat history. So whatever you do tonight, for Chrissakes *use your heads!*"

Lacklustre Jones streaked for the door and out into the night. *"Right own,* Coach!" he said over his shoulder.

Mal and I took Dorris Gene and a beautiful dark-haired Spanish lady to dinner and bored them to death. Our heads were so full of keys and signals and routes and blocking patterns that we couldn't talk about anything else, and the Spanish lady finally flounced off in a huff, and Malley and I drove Dorris Gene home. Her parting request was, "Don't get hurt now, *hear?"* and I told her not to worry. Famous last words.

It was still a few minutes before curfew, and some of the players were sitting around the lobby when Mal and myself got back to the Lakeview Arms. Off to one side, Ziggy was being interviewed for radio, but all I could hear was:

"Coach Guminski, would you say that anything can happen—"

"And usually does," Ziggy replied.

Jay Cox was telling Chet Zawatski and 2 or 3 other guys that his real first name was Garnet, but he'd changed it out of embarrassment. It was the kind of confession a man

makes on Death Row just before the priest comes in with
the last supper and it doesn't matter anymore what the
world knows and then the governor turns down the par-
don request and the lights go dim all over town for a
second or 2. You get this kind of feeling before a big game,
and the only way to get rid of it is to talk, and the guys you
talk to are your teammates, because anybody else would
think you'd flipped. "Yeh, Garnet W. Cox," Jay Cox was
saying. "Ain't that a pip?"

"Fuck, man," the late Robert Boggs said. "Where'd
your mama get that name?"

"I hate to say," Garnet W. Cox said.

Zawatski said, "We'll never tell."

"Well," Cox said hesitantly, "she always explained that
I was semi-precious, so she called me Garnet."

"Oh, ain't that *sweet!*" Robert Boggs said, jumping up
and clapping his hands. "I bet you was the cutest li'l thing,
too. Man, how yo' ass done changed!"

"Hey, baby," Bad-ass Harris put in, "it's a good thing
she didn't call you Ruby," and did his yuck-yuck imitation
of Amos and Andy.

"You guys!" Garnet Cox said, and for the first time I
realized there wasn't a bit of doubt about it—he was a
Billygoat all the way, for better or worse, till death do us
part. He was accepted, and if anybody tried to lay a hand
on him, there'd be 39 mean mothers to the rescue.

Malley said, "The night before a game like this, you
wonder about a lot of things."

"Like what?" I said, hoping for a simple answer but
expecting the worst, knowing good old Mal.

"Did you ever wonder why we work as hard as we do?
I don't mean just put out, I mean work our hairy asses
off?"

"No," I said. "Not since you told me we were a Neanderthal tribe protecting our kiddies."

"Yeh, well, there's another component," Malley said. "Downright fucking fear."

"Shit, I never get afraid," Lack said. "They ain't gonna hurt me, and if they do, it ain't the ind of the road."

"Not that kind of fear," Mal said. "I mean fear of fucking up, fear of being embarrassed. I think that's the biggest motivation of all."

"You're fucking right," Ray Roy Jenkins said, where he'd been sitting behind a potted palm not saying much. "We're like actors in a play, and we've got certain roles, only we're playing in front of maybe 80,000 people. And instead of a prompter to help us along, we've got 11 wildmen breathing on us across the line and doing everything they can do to make us look stupid."

"It's a contest of embarrassments," Malley said. "You're out there in front of your family and your friends and the whole world and you're trying to embarrass the other team and they're trying to embarrass you."

"Shit, I don't get embarrassed," I threw in, just to see the reaction.

"Well, try playing split end a while!" Ray Roy said with a little heat. "Try chasing that ball when it's just you and the corner and somebody's gonna wind up looking like an asshole. That's the trouble with you linemen—everything you do is hidden. Fat fuckers! You been getting away with murder for years, Jackson!"

Now I was supposed to get pissed, but I knew Ray Roy didn't mean it. Besides, I agreed with him and Mal. "A contest of embarrassments." That's the best way I know to describe pro football. A contest of embarrassments and a car wreck at the same time.

After a while, the famed radio personality Zigmund Guminski wandered over and said, "Hey, isn't it about time you girls got your beauty sleep?"

It was 1 minute to 11.

"Yeh," Mal said. "Time to drop our socks and grab our cocks."

"Remember," Ziggy said, "don't stunt your growth," and we all trooped up to bed like a bunch of obedient little kiddies from a planet of monsters.

That night I couldn't sleep for thinking about the game. All kinds of crazy plays kept running across a movie screen in my mind, and I could imagine the Billygoats winning the game in the final seconds on some great solo play by good old me. That's the trouble with being a snapper: You can always look real bad, but it's hard to look real good. I shut my eyes and let the films roll on. I saw the Goats come up to the line and start a running play. But what is this? The center has pulled out of the line to run interference. A pulling snapper! Who ever heard of anything so clever, so original? Look at him there, old Crazylegs himself, sprinting downfield like a wildebeest, bowling over the defense one by one, while Wing Choy tucks in behind, his outstretched hand barely touching the snapper's back, his slant-eyed legs churning toward the posts. It's *pathetic* what that snapper's doing to the Giants! He crashes into Beast Barlow and sends one of the Beast's legs flying up into the 3d tier. He flattens Little Jack Herner and slaps his face, and he jukes Pancho Peterson out of his jock and steps on his nose. In perfect tribute to the skills of this thrilling new breed of mobile center, Wing Choy slows down at the 1-yard line, laterals the ball, and A.B.C. "Alphabet" Jackson, No. 50 in your official program, steps across the goal line and slams the football to the ground in a tremendous spike.

"What?" I said. "What *what?*"

Malley was standing over me, shaking me hard. "Gimme a break, will ya, Rooms?" he was saying. "You're talking in your sleep, and you sound like Howard Cosell."

"What was I saying?"

"Something about spiking the ball."

"I was dreaming," I explained. "Hey, Mal, did any team ever use a pulling center?"

Malley snorted. "Want me to call Coach and ask him? I mean, it's only 2:30 in the morning. He'd probably thank me for my interest."

"I'm serious," I said. "Why can't a center pull just like a guard?"

"Because it doesn't work," Mal said. "The Bears did it a few times, years ago, and all it did was confuse their own players."

I laid back on my pillow and kept thinking about the dizzy life of a snapper. "You awake?" I said.

"Yeh, thanks to you."

"All these years at center," I said. "10 here, and 4 more in college and 6 more in high school and junior high and Pop Warner. That's 18 years I been snapping. And you know something, Mal? I never got one game ball. Not one."

"Tough shit," Mal said. "Snappers aren't supposed to get the game ball."

"Yeh, I guess you're right."

"Tell you what, though. If you let me sleep, I'll give you a play that'll make you an instant hero. All you have to do is convince Coach to put it in. Years ago the Giants lined up strong right with only the left end outside the snapper. The quarterback gave a signal and the left end stepped back a yard and the right halfback jumped up into the line. That made Mel Hein eligible for a pass, and he caught it for a touch."

"Jesus!" I said. "A center-eligible play!"

"Yeh," Mal said, laughing, "and if you suggest it to Coach, he'll think you flipped your lid."

"No chance," I said. I spent the rest of the night as a center eligible, catching quick slants and posts and flies and turn-ins and helping the Billygoats whip the Jersey Giants 86–0, the most win-sided lop in NFL history. Unfortunately, our backers lost their ass. The spread was 91.

Coach reserved the Bengal Room of the Lakeview Arms for the pre-game breakfast, and we all came streaming in at 8 a.m., owing to the fact that there was an automatic $500 fine for not showing, even if you had to get up from your death bed to be there. We had ham, Canadian bacon, dried cereal, scrambled eggs, toast, honey, coffee and juice, and there were maybe 70 people there, counting coaches, trainers, equipment men and Father Matthew Galvin and a few guys from the front office. It was the usual strained affair. You don't see much horseplay at a pre-game breakfast, and the reason is that coaches like to make remarks like, "I knew we'd lose. They were all jacking around at breakfast." You learn to put on your game face early.

On the way back to our room, Mal and I ran into The Connection. "You got good pills this week?" Malley said.

"You'll love 'em," the trainer said.

"Yeh, we loved 'em in the Washington game," I said. "They were great with bananas and cream."

Malley asked if the supply was in a safe place.

"How's Mr. Bunker's safe-deposit box grab you?" The Connection said. "They're being sent to the stadium in an armored car."

"Sounds fairly safe," Malley said.

"Not only that," the trainer went on, "but I ran a quality check right after I bought the new supply. I give 3 of 'em to my helper, and an hour later he didn't know whether he wanted to fuck or fight."

We drove right on out to the stadium and checked into the locker room at 9:30.

Some guys show up at the last minute, but Malley and

I like to sit around and jaw and watch the animals. The place gets like a 2d home to you. The equipment man had everything shiny and polished, the helmets all sitting on top of the lockers and facing the same way, like columns of infantry, and the whites neatly folded, pads ready, pants hanging on the right hook, jerseys in the middle, shoes on the bottom. He'd just finished spraying with Gym-fresh'ner and the whole place smelled like a forest glade, not at all what you might expect with Lacklustre Jones and all us other animals sweating and dropping roses 6 days a week. A helper was laying out tapes and wraps, and a light scent of wintergreen came from the training room, and for just a split second I said to myself, what am I going to do when it's all over and I'll never smell that smell again? Maybe I could go on for another year or 2. Some snappers last 14, 15 seasons. Well, I was willing, if the knee was.

The other players began to wander in around 10:30. Ray Roy Jenkins arrived with his roomie Oop Johnson, and Ray Roy came over and confided, "I don't know what to do about Oop. He's constipated. Says he hasn't moved in 3 days."

"See The Connection," Malley advised. "He has some stuff that'd flush the Sphinx."

The Connection gave Oop a glycerine suppository, and 5 minutes later he came walking out of the crapper shaking his head from side to side. "Jeez," he said, "them things is sure hard to swaller."

After a while we began to hear this *thunk thunk thunk* against the wall of the shower room, where the visiting team's washroom was next to ours. When you played the Jersey Giants, you always expected to hear that same racket: Pancho Peterson, their wild-ass middle linebacker, ramming his head against the wall, getting up for the game. He usually broke 2 or 3 helmets a year, but never his head. Too bad. We'd see what we could do after the kickoff.

Luke Hairston arrived on his Suzuki and went straight to his locker without saying a word. He didn't seem especially up, but I knew a few trips to the watercooler would straighten him out. Lack Jones took his customary station on one of the crappers and began filling the air with nauseous fumes. Buford Bullivant sat quietly in front of his locker in T-shirt and jock, reading from the monthly magazine of the Brotherhood of Professional Believers, moving his lips. The late Robert Boggs arrived at 5 minutes after 11, a mere $500 worth of lateness this time, and raced into the shower to dress, so Coach wouldn't see him.

The Connection gave me my usual 3 shots of Xylocaine, one under each side of the cap and one in the back of the knee, then taped it up and strapped a little black sponge right on top. He shook his finger at me and said, "Now don't go messin' with that wrap!" I don't know why he always said that. I never messed with a wrap in my life. I was only too glad to have that sponge on there, if it'd help me keep on playing.

At 12:15 I jogged out on the field with John Lovesey and helped him warm up, and he was deadly accurate. He started from the 25 and worked back to the 50, and he hardly missed a shot, clean and crisp and quick. That had been the pattern with him lately. If there was nobody rushing, he could kick the ball a mile and a half dead center. But under a rush, he'd tighten up. I doubted if we could rely on him in the game, except for kickoffs. He was still suffering from that crazy claustrophobia. One night in jail and he blows his season.

Just before the rest of the players ran out for calisthenics at 12:30, with the stands almost full of fans under a bright winter sun, I crossed paths with Pancho Peterson around mid-field, and I said, "Hello, there, Panch old boy.

I hope you're feeling good. How's the wife? How's that sweet little *madre* of yours?" I don't believe in antagonizing the opposition before a game, unless I think I can make somebody blow his cool, and Pancho was too savvy for that. He didn't respond to my courteous greeting. He just kept on walking and I never did find out how his wife and his *madre* were doing.

Back in the dressing room, it was Gettysburg Address time. The Rev. Matthew Galvin called on the Father, the Son and the Holy Ghost to stand by us in this our hour of need, and Mal said under his breath that he thought the Father, the Son and the Holy Ghost might have more to do than worry about the Billygoats this afternoon, and Wing Choy said he wondered if the Father, the Son and the Holy Ghost put on their togas one leg at a time. Over in a corner, the late Robert Boggs slumped to his knees and offered a post-prayer prayer of his own: "Lawd, jes' get us the fuckin' ball and we'll take it from there, Amen."

Coach made a speech that began with his days at Hofstra, outlined his entire coaching history and philosophy, and emphasized that he loved each and every one of us like sons and would hand out extra bonuses and genuine simulated leatherette wallets if we brought home the 1st league championship in Billygoat history. By the time he finished with several quotes from *Deuteronomy* and the Book of Vince Lombardi the tears were running down his stubby little cheeks, and I thought that Lacklustre's response was in very poor taste.

"Okay, men, move out!" Ziggy hollered, and we walked down the tunnel for the pre-game introductions, whooping and hollering and slapping ass. There are 95,000 seats in Bunker Stadium, and it looked like 96,000 of them were filled, with people sitting in the exit aisles and spilling over in the end zones and sneaking onto the track. When they saw us, they let up a roar that vibrated your inlays. It gave me a funny sensation. Here I was, a grown man of 31, and I knew that half these people couldn't care if I fractured my skull in 8 places, as long as the Goats won, but still it gave me the feeling that I was part of something big, almost 100,000 people, all of us old buddies and mutual admirers, our own family of Billygoats and Billygoat fans, maybe the best family I'd ever had. I knew the feeling was dumb, but I couldn't shake it off, and it kind of flowed over me and made me want to laugh and cry at the same time. Well, greens will do that to you, and I told you snappers are not your everyday normal people. And anyway, my ex-wife used to say I cried at card tricks.

We lined up along the west sideline, and the P.A. announced that the *Star Spangled Banner* would be played by the Living for Jesus Musical Saw Choir of Rockview Heights Methodist Cathedral, and then this eerie, whiny sound swelled up and filled the place, 15 musicians screeching in harmony. "That's unfair!" Malley said out of the corner of his mouth, but he couldn't say more, because the TV cameras began to sweep our faces. Every week the management tries to come up with a new and novel way of presenting the anthem, and I guess they're running out of ideas. The year before, a group from Juliard played it on flugel horns, and it was very impressive and marshal.

THE FLIGHT

VIII

LICK! 1! 2!

LUKE HAIRSTON MUST HAVE ENJOYED THE AIRBORNE *boxing show put on by J. R. and Robert Boggs, because he seemed to relax for a while. When we were somewhere around Houston, Texas, he told me to go up front and "fetch" Billy Bob Bunker, but Mr. Bunker wouldn't budge.*

"I'm not going near that nut!" he said, cringing against the wall. "Tell him you couldn't find me. Tell him I'm in the bathroom. Tell him anything!"

"Mr. Bunker," I said, "he's crazy. I guarantee you, he'll come up here and shoot you if you don't do what he says."

Billy Bob Bunker wiped his watery blue eyes with a handkerchief and shot a stricken look in the direction of poor Jimmy Strepey, The Connection, stretched across 2 seats with a bloody bandage of rags around his upper arm, his little round eyes looking straight up into the dome lights and flowing with tears.

"Look what he did to Jimmy," Mr. Bunker said.

"Aw, go on back and see what he wants," Coach whined. "He's not gonna hurt you."

"That's right, Mr. Bunker," I said. "I don't think he'll hurt you if you do what he says."

"What's that gonna be?" our beloved owner and field marshal asked.

"We're dealing with a lunatic," I said. "Who knows? Maybe he'll ask you for a raise."

Mr. Bunker didn't appreciate the joke. He kissed his wife, and they embraced, and then Coach tapped him on the shoulder and said, "Go ahead, Mr. Bunker. Try to talk some sense into him. You're good at that."

"Not with him I'm not," Mr. Bunker said. "He already hates my guts."

"C'mon," I said, and led him through the galley.

Luke Hairston stood up and smiled when he saw us. "Well, well, well," he said, sounding like the Kingfish. "If it ain't the slavemaster hisself, ol' General Patton. Ain't that yo' name, honky chump?"

"Right!" Billy Bob Bunker said, looking wildly around. "Right, Luke. Anything you say."

"Right, who?"

"Right, Mister Hairston."

"Now what's yo' name? General Patton?"

"Right!"

"Wrong! You Private Bunker."

"Private Bunker. Right!"

"You asslick Bunker."

"Right."

"Right what?"

"Right, sir! I'm asslick Bunker."

"And who'm I?"

"Mister Hairston."

"General Hairston! You asslick Bunker."

"I'm asslick Bunker."

258

"Now you gettin' it. You asslick Bunker, and you eat shit and suck cocks."

"Eat shit and suck cocks. Yes, sir, that's me. Asslick Bunker." The poor man was trembling so hard that I felt sorry for him, but then I realized he probably just had the shakes. He almost always got the shakes on our flights, he drank so much.

"Now brother asslick, this been a long flight," Hairston said, "and the aisles done picked up a little pollution. You gone police the area."

"Police the area?"

"Yeh, you gone lean yo' fat ass over and lick the carpet from this end to the back. Go on, get goin'! Lick!—1!—2! Lick!—1!—2!" He reached out and kicked Mr. Bunker hard, and the poor man went sprawling. "Now all I wonta see is asshole and elbows!" Hairston hollered. "And don't come back till yo' ready for another detail. Got that, general asslick?"

"Right," Billy Bob said, already gagging on lint, and licked on down the aisle.

"Now bring in the stewardess," Hairston said, "while I do a li'l fix."

It didn't take as long to convince the stewardess as it had taken to convince Billy Bob Bunker, because these girls are professionals and they do as they're told. But she was plenty scared, you could see that. Hairston told her to dance, and when she lifted her heels about a half inch off the floor, he screamed, "Dance, bitch! Get those ugly knees up!" She did a half-ass Charleston, and Luke said, "That dance wouldn't win a amachoor night in a Chinese whorehouse. Now take off them clothes, and le's see a real dance." The girl hesitated, and he whacked her across the ass with the gun barrel, and she started to cry. "Come own!" he said, "Le's give the boys a li'l show."

When she got down to her bikini briefs, a round dark

spot showed where she had lost control of herself, and I felt ashamed on behalf of the whole male race, which even though he was nuts Luke Hairston was still one of us, and I just wished I could crawl into a hole somewhere to keep that poor girl from blaming me. She kept on crying and flopping her body around in some kind of a clumsy silly dance, and I just wanted to reach out and pat her shoulder and tell her not to worry, that we shared her fear and shame, and probably half the guys in the back had already wet their own pants or maybe worse.

"Come on, Luke," I said after a few minutes more, "let her go. She's scared, man." He didn't acknowledge me. Instead he hollered, "Hey, how come ain't no sisters on this bus? Bring me one of the sisters!"

The stewardess looked over at me and shook her head a few inches and I said, "Luke, there's no black stewardesses on duty."

"Airlines don't have no fuckin' sisters period," Hairston said.

"No, they got 'em," I said. "We had one for the Philadelphia game last year, remember?"

Hairston ignored me. "We gone have one right now," he said. "Bitch, go get some of that chocolate cake you was servin'!"

The stew gave me another look, and I jerked my head toward the galley, trying to get her to shag-ass. She came back in a few seconds with a half a chocolate cake, and Hairston said, "Good. Good! Now you gone be one of the sisters. Rub it all over. Go on! Rub!"

The girl looked at me with a kind of beseeching look, and I just nodded my head a little. The cake would come off, but a bullet hole might be more lasting. She started to rub over her breasts and her stomach and her legs, and Hairston just sat there grinning. "Hey, you lef' sumpin' out," he said. "Le's darken up that hair a little," and he

*made the poor girl smear the gooey chocolate down there.
"Lookin' good, Bitch!" he hollered. "You really lookin'
good now, you honky whore!"*

*Then he beckoned her over to his seat and made her do
some things. It wasn't sexy, it was just sick. I don't want
to talk about it. I turned and looked out the window. I
hated Luke and I hated myself and I hated the whole
male race.*

The Goats received, and the Giants came down under
that kickoff and broke up our wedge like it was made of
peanut brittle, dumping Buzz Urquhart on the 15. They
were so fired up for the championship game that they
carried each other off the field and jumped 6 feet in the
air and screamed like a bunch of drunken seagulls. Watching them, I only hoped I could get my hands on some
pharmaceutical stock; those guys must have boosted the
market 2 or 3 points all by themselves. Our players had
only taken their usual couple of greens, except I noticed
Luke Hairston tapping his feet and beating his hands on
his helmet waiting to go in, meaning he'd dipped into his
private stock as usual.

On our 1st running play, the Giants lined up even, and
I looked up and saw the dried spit around Beast Barlow
and Little Jack Herner's mouth, and back of them Pancho
Peterson was lunging in and out, grunting and groaning
and barking out numbers and colors and other defensive
signals, and I knew the Jersey Giants were open for business.

Q. B. calls a burst up the middle and Peterson slams me
down and stops the play for a yard loss. *"Yah yah yah!"*
Pancho hollers. "Don't come my way!" Q. B. calls a screen
to the left, and Peterson sidesteps his way along the line,
cuts in behind the interference and whomps Wing Choy

the way you'd fall an oak. 2 more yards lost. On 3d and 13, Q. B. calls a play-option pass to the right, and Peterson head-fakes Luke Hairston and busts inside and dumps Q. B. for 7 yards. *"Yah yah yah!"* he screams in Q. B.'s face. "You little cocksucker! Don't you *ever* come my way!"

Q. B. kicks the rug and hollers back, "I went left and I went right and I went up the middle. *Which the fuck isn't your way?"*

"Yah yah yah!" Peterson answered. He grabbed his crotch and hollered, "Time for lunch, pussy!"

Standing at our bench, Bad-ass said, "Hey, lookee over there." On the far side of the field, I could see a cluster of men around the big right tackle, Barlow. "You see what I see?" Bad asked. The Giants' trainer was kneeling in front of the Beast, working on his knee.

"I think that's your cue," Ziggy said, and Bad-ass nodded.

On our next series, everybody could see that Barlow was favoring the knee, leaning too far forward, using too much of his upper torso, hand-fighting us to keep us away from his legs. But even wounded, he was dangerous, all hooks and angles, like an overgrown hawk. His technique is to beat you and claw you to death, finger you in the eyes, twist your arms and legs when you're down, and then run all over you when you weaken.

In the first 6 or 8 minutes of play the teams kept probing and testing and experimenting, trying to find the soft spots, but if there were many soft spots neither of us would even be here, and the 2 lines kept smashing into each other like bull elk. Usually you pace yourself, try to figure out when the play isn't coming your way and relax a little, but today every play was World War Fucking III. Match-ups that were 10 yards away from the ballcarrier kept butting and chopping at each other even after the whistle, and Ray Roy told me he was tripped and held by the cornerback almost every time till he bit a hole in the asshole's arm.

By 10 minutes of the 1st quarter, neither team had been inside the other's 40, and it was beginning to look like a gang rumble. I came off a block on Little Jack Herner with my hand all gooey, and I knew they'd laid the Vaseline on thick, about as thick as the law allows, which technically the law allows *no* Vaseline, strictly going by the rule book, but every team uses it, including us. The backs put it on their pants, around their hips and knees, and the offensive linemen put it on their shoulders and arms. It wasn't long before my hands were stained blue from the tinted stuff the Giants use on their road jerseys.

Through the whole 1st quarter, the longest gain from scrimmage was 6 yards, and the Giants totaled 2 1st downs to our 1. Mostly it was hitting and slugging, clawing and scratching, with the warnings of the officials in the background: "Get your hands off him, 73. You're hitting late. That's a warning." "Linemen, goddamn it, keep those hands in!" "Watch your feet." "Offensive linemen, hands *in!* Last warning." Every once in a while the ze-bra'd run over to the bench and holler something like, "I've got number 60. *6–0.* Holding," and the guys would let up a groan and call the zeeb a motherfucker.

At the beginning of the 2d quarter, I went after Beast Barlow on a C-block, and just as I reached him he turned sideways and I hit his thigh on an angle and he went down groaning and writhing, with his leg twisted under him, and I could hear him saying, "Ummm. *Ummmm. UMMMM!*" When a player's hurt, even one of your own let alone the enemy, you don't go near him. It's a jinx, and besides you can't keep on playing pro football unless you convince yourself that nothing bad can happen, at least not to you. But I couldn't help leaning over him, and he looked up at me with his face twisted in pain and said, "Fuck you!" I reached down to help him up and he spit on my hand and said, "I didn't expect it from you." I slank off the field, and the hometown crowd cheered when they saw that Beast was down for good. Me, I felt a little sick to my stomach. I tried to figure out whether I'd maimed him on purpose or not, but my mind was too mixed up to decide. Besides, that kind of thinking is just jacking off. We had a game to play.

With time back in, we began to move through the 2 and the 4 hole, where Beast would normally have covered, but just when we were getting our act together, Cox fumbled, and there was a big pile-up in the middle of the field, with me somewhere around the bottom, and my own bad leg doubled under me. Poetic license! I heard the referee say, "All right, you guys. Relax. Relax in there! All except you with the ball. Relax, goddamn it! *Giants' ball!*"

On the very next play, Malley was hit and left for dead. Lacklustre Jones grabbed him under the armpits and dragged him off the field, so we wouldn't get charged with a time-out. He revived when we stretched him out on the rug, but he didn't seem to know anybody. He babbled to himself and when I leaned across him he said, "Say the secret woid and win a hunnid dollahs."

"Huh?" I said.

"Any club that would let me in," he mumbled, "I wooden wanna join. Right, duck?"

Then he stood up and did a funny kind of walk along the bench, all bent forward, with his hands behind his back and his eyebrows jumping up and down like black dragonflies. I grabbed him and gave him some oxygen to suck on, and after a few minutes he regained his sanity.

I had an idea that something was pulling out in my knee, but it was hard to tell exactly what the problem was because the Xylocaine kept it numb. Maybe the "pes" transplant was working loose. When I tightened up my thigh tendons to raise my right leg, it reacted slowly, as though the split ligament might be lying slack on the kneecap. I looked at the clock. 32 more minutes to play. After those 32 minutes, I'd have 2 weeks to get the knee ready for the Superbowl. That's all I asked.

Our defense held the Giants again, and we went back on the field with 1st and 10 at our own 21. We ran a couple of slants, with simple blocking, and the knee held up. In the huddle Q. B. asked Ray Roy, "Whatcha got? You got anything over there?"

"I got a sideline at 10 yards," Ray Roy said. "He's playing off me right now. It's open."

Q. B. faded to pass, and I dropped to fill, and Pancho Peterson came over me like a bowling ball over an eggshell. The knee twisted back, and this time I felt a shock, dull and vague under the Xylocaine, but a real jolt nevertheless. Ray Roy caught the pass and we had a first down on our 33. We came out in an orange set, unbalanced right, and Peterson called out some colors of his own, and Bullivant pulled and Pancho went for the fake and gallivanted out toward the right end and Jay Cox took a delayed hand-off and sprinted straight up the middle, right where I was flat on my ass from a throw-out block at the tackle. All I could see was Cox's churning legs and then I felt a searing pain where he stepped on my outstretched hand and before I could twist away he pushed off to change directions and the cleats dug into the bone. I sat up and looked at my left hand, and it was raw meat, blood pulsing out like there was a pump inside. I could see the bone in 3 different places, 2 of the middle fingers and the palm.

The back judge said, "You want a time-out?"

"My ass," I said, and jogged back to the huddle, but somebody had already signaled Coach, and Zawatski came trotting in from the bench.

"Lemme see that!" The Connection said. He put gauze around my hand and after a few minutes it began to go numb. Coach sent me back in, and the Giants' defense held, and at the half it was 0–0 in a game that all the experts predicted would be high-scoring.

I headed straight for the training room, and Mr. Evans cleaned my hand with alcohol and told me he thought I had compound fractures of 2 fingers and maybe a few slivers of broken bone in the palm. "Lucky it's not your snapping hand," he said.

"How long will it take to stitch?" I asked.

"Too long," The Connection put in. "Coach wants you back in."

Mr. Evans closed the wound with 3 or 4 silver clips, and The Connection layered it with about 20 thicknesses of gauze to sop up the blood. "How about some Xylocaine?" I asked, but The Connection said that was out of the question, I needed to be able to feel the ball with my left hand even though my right hand did most of the work, and I realized he was right. We settled for the usual boosters under my kneecap, and by then it was time to go back. I limped after the other guys till we got out in the winter sunshine, and then I tried not to limp anymore. What the Giants didn't know wouldn't hurt me.

But football players can smell an injury a mile away. On my 1st snap of the 2d half, Pancho Peterson ignored the ballcarrier and drove me into the artificial turf, and when I was down he grabbed my right ankle and gave it a twist. "That's for Barlow, pussy!" he said, and then ran screaming to the zebra that I'd held him and pointed to a blue handprint on his clean sleeve for proof. The oldest trick in football, and the ref knew it. You scoop up a little bit of your own colored Vaseline and make a handprint where it stands out on your arm and then claim you were held. It's similar to biting yourself, then showing the toothmarks, except the last time Pancho tried that trick it didn't work, because he claimed that Bullivant had bitten him and it turned out that Bull had left his dentures back in the dressing room. Those Giants would stoop to nothing to win.

The 2d half began to look like the 1st, all pit-work, helmets and elbows, eyeballs and fingernails. I stopped feeling any pain in my hand, and my knee was just a big dead clump, you could have hit it with an ax and I'd never have known. The only trouble was that it was beginning to fail on heavy blocks, and it wasn't reacting to the signals I sent down from my brain, at least not as fast as a football player's knees have to react. After a few plays, the left hand began to throb and the blood seeped through the bandages and every time I tried to use the hand the gauze would unravel. I had a piercing headache from all the butting, but that was the least of my worries. If a lineman doesn't get a headache and also open up that running sore where the straps cross on his forehead, he's just not doing his job. The way my head felt behind that sore, there was a herd of termites digging their way out, and every once in a while I could imagine them pouring through the hole and down over my face as I snapped the ball. Those are the lovely visions that flash through the minds of your football heroes as they go about their dedicated task of giving you your $8 worth.

Q. B. started calling some quick counts, trying to upset the Giants' timing. Or he'd say, "Check with me" and break the huddle and call the play at the line, which gave me less chance to get set for my blocking assignment, and Peterson and the others racked my ass almost every play. Q. B. let them rack. "They're after you good now," he said. "Just hang in and we'll work outside." He slapped me on the ass, and I told him no sweat, I was feeling no pain, and my greens were popping off like Popeye and the spinach can.

The play whipsawed back and forth, and I began to feel like the Christian in the gladiator joke, "I can't talk right now. Here come them fuckin' lions again." Wing broke a screen for 17 yards to their 35, but on 4th and 3 Coach didn't even bother to send John Lovesey in. The way Limey was kicking lately it was safer for Malley to punt the ball out of bounds and try to stick the Giants deep in their own end. We were playing at a terrific disadvantage with a field-goal game like that, but there was nothing we could do about it.

The game was still scoreless when the 4th quarter began, and the fans were up and screaming on every play. I began to feel my heart beating in my hand and my knee both, and The Connection slipped me a fast squirt in the knee. The way things were going, I'd get about 3 minutes on the bench and then back on the field again for 4 plays, with Peterson or one of the tackles slamming me into the ground practically every time, as though it was more important to get revenge for Beast Barlow than it was to win the ball game. Q. B. kept trying to take advantage by dunking short passes and running the ends, but the rest of the Giants tightened up and back and forth we went, like the immovable force meeting the irresistible object. The blood dripped off my left hand and speckled the ball, and the officials kept calling for new balls, the way they do on a rainy day, but Coach left me in, which I was grateful for that.

With 10 minutes left, I snapped the ball on a pass play and Herner and another lineman sandwiched me after the ball was thrown and Herner clubbed me in the gut, and I almost threw up. On the next play I tried to fire out

on Pancho Peterson and cut-block him, but my knee bent
under and he elbowed me into the rug, and that artificial
stuff scratches and burns when you're pressured against it.
"Whatsa matter, pussy," I hollered, "ya blind? I'm not the
ballcarrier!"

"You ain't gonna be nothin' time I get through with ya,"
the big blond jack-off hollered in my ear, and stepped on
my groin as he got up.

When I came back to the bench, I realized my cup was
out of place and I reached in and tried to yank it around.
Bad-ass said, "Where'd he get you? In the family jewels?"

"No," I said, "in the nuts." I was beginning to feel giddy.

I went back in and just kept snapping the ball and firing
out, snapping and firing out. The bandage unraveled completely on my left hand and The Connection rewrapped
it with about 2 rolls of tape and gauze. My knee still felt
okay but it wasn't dependable, and whenever there'd be
a shoving match between me and Peterson or between
me and one of the tackles, the leg would twist under me
and down I'd go. About the best I could do was slow them
down.

Malley grabbed me on the sidelines when there was 8
minutes to play and still no score, and he said, "Somebody
called down on the phones and said to take you out,
they're killing you out there."

"Shit," I said, walking away.

"Nobody has the guts to tell Coach, and Coach wants
you in."

A few seconds later Ziggy came jogging over and put
his arm around my shoulder. "You just can't go, can you,
old horse," he said in a tender voice that I hardly recognized.

I jerked away. "Yeh, I can go," I said, and walked over
to the water.

Malley caught up and screamed at me, "Goddamn it,

take your fucking helmet off and put on a baseball cap and go tell that fucking idiot you're gonna get killed!" I just looked at him, and he ran over to where Coach was standing and said something and I saw Coach turn back to him with a face like a sliced beet and then Ziggy hollered, "Okay, offense, move out!" and we went back in the pit.

Cox managed to pick up a 1st down, but then the Giants held, and pretty soon their offense began to click. With 6 minutes left, they started at their 20—8 yards on a quarterback draw, 5 yards up the middle, a little swing pass for 8, a dive for 3. They converted on a couple of crucial 3d downs, and when I looked up from the oxygen tube, they were 1st and 10 at mid-field. The next thing I knew their quarterback spiralled the ball 60 yards in the air, and the flanker was wide open, and it looked like there was no way he could miss it for a touch, but then old Malley came out of nowhere, the way your great safetymen will do, and caught that ball one-handed, like you'd catch a baseball, actually grabbing it by the tip end, which almost seems impossible for anybody other than Kareem Abdul-Jabbar or Wilt the Stilt, and then he stumbled over his own momentum and slid out of bounds on our 1. "Okay, Alph!" Ziggy gulped. "Sock it to 'em!"

Q. B. sneaked the ball to the 3 while I wedged out on Herner and held him pretty good with my right hand. Then Wing tried a 33 buck and got dumped for a yard loss, and somebody's cleat smashed against my face-mask and I felt a tooth tear loose. On 3d down Q. B. tried to hit Luke Hairston on a crossing pattern, but the ball was batted away. Now it was 4th and 9 from our 2, and Malley had to punt from the end line. My responsibility would be to center the ball clean and hard right to his numbers, and somebody in our backfield would pick up my man. Also, I would get crunched. Ho-hum. Another busy day in the pits.

I sighted through my legs, memorized the spot, looked up at Jack Herner and Pancho Peterson breathing hot sauce on me, looked back and let fly. Something like a Greyhound bus slammed me down, bending my bad knee sidewards, and I could feel the insides popping like cords on a package, one by one, but in slow motion, and a flash of pain shot up my thigh and through my groin and into my neck, and I was laying there with my eyeballs flipped back into my head and the tears blinding my eyes like a fucking infant baby. "Oh, Jesus Christ, do something!" I said, but there was nobody there to hear. I twisted my head around and saw a big pile-up 50 yards down the field and I knew that Malley's punt must have been a beaut.

"Get *off!*" a voice was shouting. I looked over and saw Coach screaming at me through cupped hands. "Roll over the side line!" he said. He didn't want a time-out. I tried to do what he said, but when I started to move, my right knee just laid flat against the rug, like it was pinned there, and then the timekeeper called the 2-minute warning and The Connection and Mr. Evans came trotting out on the field to take care of me.

"Can you raise it?" Mr. Evans asked, and I shook my head.

He stretched me flat on my back and lifted my right foot. The pain flashed up my side, and I grunted, and he raised the foot some more, till it was 8 or 10 inches high, and my knee still laid perfectly flat on the rug. Whatever I'd been using to hold things together since the operation, it was gone now. I hopped off the field between Bad-ass and Robert Boggs, with my right leg trailing behind. They eased me down, and Coach came running over. "I hated to do that, son," he said, "but I didn't think we could win without you. I hated to do it."

Robert stuck his nose right up in Coach's face and hollered, "Then why don't you cry, you little chump!" and

Ziggy jumped in between. Coach turned pale and hurried back to the action, and the ambulance attendants brought out a stretcher and started to roll me onto it.

"Don't bother," I said. "I'm okay," which meant I was going to watch that game. I cocked a fist at one of them, and I said, "I'm okay, you son of a bitch. Leave me alone!"

Ray Roy helped prop my head, and I watched as the 2 teams kept slugging it out, and the gun went off with the Giants back on their own 30 and nobody giving an inch.

It was nearly the end of the 1st overtime, still 0–0, when Jersey had to punt from their own end zone, and Buzz Urquhart fair-caught the ball on their 45 and called time. There was 3 seconds showing on the clock, time for exactly 1 play. I saw Mal run over to Ziggy and say something, and Ziggy turned to Coach, and Coach looked up and down the bench, and right there in front of God and the Giants and 95,000 fans and a TV audience of millions, John "Limey" Lovesey trotted out on the field with Q. B. alongside him and began to line up a 55-yard field goal.

The Giants came to the line and the zebra waved them off. The ref hollered something, but all I could hear was Pancho Peterson screaming "Free kick, my ass!" The players milled around and they needed a straightjacket for Joe Kapp on the sidelines, but he finally settled down after the ref explained that we were entitled to a free kick after a fair catch, he could look it up, and Malley and Coach and Ziggy stood there shaking their heads up and down like a bunch of ducks in a rice field. I pulled myself up by my right hand, so I could see better over the bench, and I remembered how Lovesey had been pumping those practice kicks before the game, when nobody was rushing him, and I crossed my fingers and started praying right out loud.

Q. B. held the ball and not a sound came out of the stands. Limey took that funny little angled run-up of his and put his foot in the ball like he was trying to drive it all the way back to Newcastle. It went up like a balloon, slow and easy, rotating backwards but not very fast, the sign of a good kick, and hung, hung, *hung*—

Then it dropped over the goalposts with plenty to spare and as dead center as you can get without using a tape measure. The zebra nearly tore his arms out ramming his hands straight over his head.

The ceiling came off Bunker Stadium and I slumped to the ground and started to bawl, and when I lifted my head a few minutes later the guys from Sick Transit were bringing the stretcher and our whole offensive team was circling around to protect me from the crowd. Just before the back doors closed, Ziggy stuck his head in and flipped me the game ball, which I dropped. "Still got those great hands!" he hollered, and then the doors snapped shut and the siren started moaning and the ambulance lurched away. Before we got out of the stadium, one of the attendants dinged me with a needle, and I went to sleep and dreamed, and all my dreams were sweet.

When I woke up, I was in a narrow bed with my right leg wrapped and mummified and stiff. The only feeling was a tingling in my big toe, and I remembered something I'd read, that sometimes you can feel pain in your toes even after the whole leg has been amputated. "Hey!" I hollered, but no sound came out of my mouth. Then I panicked. "Help!" I yelled. "Help! HELP! Turn on the fucking light!"

A light blinked on, and a hatchet-faced figure in a white uniform and a big gold cross was sitting on a chair in the corner. "A simple request will do," it said in a voice that would chill a tamale.

"What happened, Father?" I asked.

"It's *Sister*—Sister Ruth," the figure said, "and you'll

have to wait for doctor. He'll explain."

"Doctor who?"

"Doctor Evans. Your team physician."

"Oh," I said, slapping myself on the forehead with my one good hand. "Mr. Evans again. Have I got anything left?"

"As much as Our Lord willed you," Sister Ruth said. "More than some."

After a while, Mr. Evans arrived and explained that the cartilages and ligaments in my knee were almost gone, and there were certain activities I was going to have to give up in the future. "Like breathing?" I joked.

"No," Mr. Evans said, smiling and slapping me on the cast. "Nothing *that* terminal. But you won't be playing football."

"Hey," I said, trying to pull myself up. "We only got 2 weeks till the Superbowl."

"In 2 weeks you'll still be in your cast. In 2 months you may or may not be out of it. We'll see."

I let out a low, disgusted whistle. "That's it for the year, huh?"

"That's it, period," Mr. Evans said. "You won't play again." I just shut my eyes and listened. "You'll be able to walk, but you'll never be able to run. You might need a cane, you might not. Later you could develop some secondary problems. Rheumatism, arthuritis, maybe some bone infection."

It's a funny thing about jocks. When you're young and strong you feel like a god, you're different than other men, nothing serious can ever happen to you, at least nothing that you can't heal with a whirlpool and some heat. And when you finally realize that you're wiped out, your first reaction is there's been a terrible mistake, they must mean somebody else, you're a god, don't they remember? And then you pass into a stage where you figure it's all a joke or a bad dream or a misunderstanding, and then when you get it straight, that it's no bullshit and you—are—*through* . . . Well, it's like they dropped you in the Sea of Antarctica, and you're just a punk little kid again with a snotty nose and screaming to your mama that the big kids aren't fair, and mama tells you she's busy. What can you do but bawl?

Mr. Evans and Sister Ruth left, and I just laid there for a while, trying to get my act together, and then there was a knock on the door. "Who goes there?" I said, wiping my eyes with the back of my bandaged hand. "Friend or enema?"

A green blur came rocketing through that door and practically threw herself on top of me. "Dorris Gene!" I said. Her mascara was strung all the way down to her chin and her glossy black hair looked like it had fallen into a yogurt recipe by mistake, and she was taking turns crying and letting out strangled gulps at the top of her lungs, like a seal having an orgasm.

"Oh, Alph, *Alph!*" she kept saying, hugging me and slapping my cheeks and yanking my head back hard and kissing me. "I came as soon as they'd *let* me. I waited downstairs 5 *hours*. Oh, Honey, how *are* you?" Dorris Gene is always enthusiastic, even about diarrhea, but now she was sounding out of her skull. "How *are* you?" she repeated. "Does it *hurt?*"

"Only when I do the kazotsky," I said.

"Oh, Alph, you're all right," she said when she heard my little joke. "YOU'RE ALL RIGHT!" She shrieked the words, and Sister Ruth came in and told her to please modify her voice.

"What's Mr. Evans's diagnosis?" Dorris Gene asked.

"That's *Dr.* Evans," the nun put in.

"Well," I said, "Mr. Evans said it looked like iron deficiency anemia or the heartbreak of psoriasis, I forget which."

"Oh, you *silly!*" Dorris Gene cried, and began asphyxiating me again. Then Malley and Ziggy Guminski slumped in with their chins dragging around their socks. "Whatsa matter with you guys?" I asked. "I'm the one that's hurt."

"We just saw Mr. Evans in the hall," Mal said. "He told us."

"Well, try not to have a nervous breakdown," I said. "You still got Zawatski, and I'll slip the kid some of my trade secrets."

"Here," Ziggy said, and handed me a big box of panatelas in individual glass containers. "Smoke 'em in good health."

"Hey, thanks!" I said, wondering if I should tell him I don't smoke. "Dorris Gene's favorite brand. Are they Havanas?"

Ziggy said, "You better believe it."

"The containers are Havana," Mal corrected. "The tobacco comes from East Chicago, Indiana." I knew he'd end up smoking them.

For a while, we jawed about the game. Ziggy told how Mal had suggested the free kick, and how every newspaper in the country had explained the free-kick rule in full because otherwise nobody would believe what'd happened, and he'd seen it so many times now he could recite it himself:

ON A FREE KICK *AFTER A FAIR CATCH,* captain of receiving team has the option to put the ball in play by punt, dropkick or placekick without a Tee, or by snap. If the place kick or dropkick goes between the uprights, a field goal is scored.

276

Ziggy said the sportswriters and sportscasters were billing Coach as the greatest football genius since Lombardi, and Coach accepted the compliment with his usual grace, telling one of the columnists that frankly he doubted if Lombardi would have thought up the idea and every coach in the league would be better off if they spent less time jacking around with Ouija boards and more time instilling discipline the way great generals like Patton had done.

"Still on the Patton kick, huh?" I said.

"Oh, yeh," Ziggy said. "Coach is really gung ho."

"He's coming over later to slap you," Malley put in.

"What's gung ho?" Dorris Gene asked.

Mal said, "Gung ho is a Chinese expression meaning, 'I was in the Marine Corps and I don't want you to forget it.' Right, Zig?"

Ziggy turned red and said, "You talk like a man with a paper—"

"Quiet!" I said. "Ladies present."

"Oh, don't bother about me," Sister Ruth said from the corner.

"—A paper asshole," Ziggy said, and Sister Ruth took a duck.

"The best thing about the game is how we screwed up the shavers," Mal said after a while.

"The shavers?" I said, forgetting again. "Oh, the *point-*shavers."

"Yeh," Ziggy said. "Anybody that bet against us, the whole bet went tapioca."

Dorris Gene piped up, "Don't you want to see your flowers?" She lifted my head by the chin and pointed across the room. I'd been in the hospital only a few hours and it looked like somebody had transplanted a whole summer meadow, there was everything but redwoods in there. For an hour we opened cards and read messages.

Wing Choy sent a bucket of daisies with a note: "You get well. We go Japanese restaurant, order egg foo yung pass all 'round." Bullivant sent a Bible reading, something about the last being first, which I hoped was a compliment. Lack sent a simple note: "In your honor J. R. 'Lacklustre' Jones has left a bouquet of roses at Dandy Don's restaurant. P.S. I found a place with nude fortune tellers. Get well quick!" There was a fancy envelope from Jay Cox, and inside a message: "I'm sorry I waited this long to tell you I'm one of your biggest admirers." Zawatski's card said, "I need the work, but I wish there'd been another way to get it." I liked that. It wasn't the usual hypocritical horseshit that guys hand out when they take your job. There was even a note from Coach: "Get in shape! We need you for the Superbowl, standing up, sitting down, or on your ass."

The front office sent along a bottle of Napoleon brandy and the Rev. Matthew Galvin to drink it, and we all kept chattering away till the end of visiting hours. Just after Sister Ruth shooed everybody out, an attendant brought in a big bouquet of red and white dappled carnations and a large package wrapped in yellow tissue paper. Inside the package was a football, official Pop Warner League, $11.95, and a barely legible scrawl that said I'd probably feel more at home with a football in my room, signed "Allen W. Johnson (Oop)." Now I had 2 footballs, this one and the game ball. It was really 2 more than you could use in Room 407 of Our Lady of Angels hospital.

Sister put the carnations on the floor, because there was no more room on the table or the windowsill, and handed me the envelope that came with them. It was heavily bordered in black and addressed, "Mr. Alfabet B.C. Jackson, Esquire," and it had 4 little gold stars pasted after my name. "I guess it was all he could find on a Sunday night," the nurse said helpfully, looking over my shoulder. The

message was embossed in dignified gold letters: WITH
YOU IN YOUR HOUR OF SORROW. Under it was a P.S.
scribbled in Magic Marker: "Get well, you lazy spook
motherfucker! From your friend the late Robert Boggs."

"Here," I said to the nun, "you want to read it?" But she
had already turned off the light.

I was out of the hospital in 5 days, with my leg in a cast
from the ankle to the hip, 19 1/2 pounds of plaster, dragging myself around on crutches, which was something I
learned the year before. The Goats were running light
workouts, and every morning I climbed into the back of
Mal's VW bus and rode with him to Bunker Stadium. At
first nobody knew what to do with me, but then Coach
came over and said, "How'd you like to help us out?"

"Sure, Coach. How?"

"Oh, help chart defenses, study Bronco films, stuff like
that."

"Like an assistant coach?"

"I didn't say that. I just said help us out."

The next 3 nights I helped Ziggy in the coaching offices
adjoining the locker room. We would turn off the lights
and roll films of the last 3 Denver games and try to work
up flow charts and defenses and probabilities. It wasn't
easy, figuring out the Broncos' weakness. They'd dropped
3 games all season, 2 when their quarterback had an ankle
and 1 after they'd clinched the division. Anytime they had
to roll, they rolled. For an example, they smothered the
Jersey Giants 34–10, which we beat the Giants too, but we
had to practically give blood to do it.

The Denver approach was simple. They had Dolph
Smetana running inside and little Randy Lewis running
outside and Billy D. Schwartz pitching and big Tom
Walsh catching, and everything was simple and basic,
nothing flashy, no flea-flickers, just grind grind grind till

they were standing on your throat. Smetana was probably the most dependable short-gainer since Larry Csonka, good for 4, 5 yards every time you gave him the ball. *Sports Pictorial* called him "Denver's routine Czech."

Late Monday night Ziggy and I were rolling films, working out keys for Denver's double-double to the strong side. In the morning the whole team, myself included, would fly south for the Superbowl, to give us 5 full days to get accustomed to the Superdome and the wonderful New Orleans climate, which is like being locked in a steam kitchen with somebody frying oysters.

"What was that noise?" Ziggy said.

I listened, but no sound came from the long dark hallway that led to the locker room.

"Must of been one of the players forgot his playbook or something," Ziggy said.

"Why couldn't he pick it up in the morning?" I said. "Aren't we all supposed to meet here?"

"Yeh, but maybe he wants to burn the midnight oil."

"At 1:30?" I cocked my ear again, and I thought I heard a door shut.

"Roll that film again," Ziggy instructed, "and this time keep your eye on the stub back." As I punched the rewind button, I distinctly heard popping and snarling, and then I caught the hum of a motor fading in the distance.

Ziggy and I worked till 3, and I excused myself and hobbled down the hallway to the dressing room. It was eerie in there, with a patch of cool blue moonlight coming through a high window, and I groped my way to the switch and flipped it on. About 6 athletic trunks were parked alongside the door, all packed and ready for morning, and something on one of them caught my eye. I leaned over and read a plastic tape:

BILLYGOATS BROTHERHOOD WEEK
INVITE A NIGGER TO THE SUPERBOWL

I stripped it off and jammed it in my pocket.

When Coach announced in the morning that I was going along to the game, all the guys sang, "Hooray for
Alphie, he's a horse's ass." Then I climbed into the back
of Malley's van and went out to the freight terminal to
begin the famous "Flight of the Billygoats," which is what
our ride to the Superbowl turned out to be called, and
which it will go down in sports history.

THE FLIGHT

IX

GOIN' TO GLORY

THE FLIGHT DIDN'T HAVE ANY NAME AT ALL TILL WE *were skyjacked about 4½ hours and I went up ahead to deliver some message or other from Luke and hung around for a few extra minutes with the flight engineer. He seemed calm enough. "Listen to this," he said, slipping a pair of earphones over my head. "We're famous." A lady newscaster with a shrill voice like Phyliss Diller's was telling everybody that the Goats' hijacked charter was now approaching New Orleans and "stay tuned to this station for the lastest on the Flight of the Billygoats."*

The engineer turned the dial to another station and I heard an announcer that sounded like a barker for the morgue reciting all the horrible things that had happened to athletic teams on previous airplane rides, running through the wipe-out of the Manchester United soccer team through the Boston College disaster to the mountainside crash of the Wichita University plane about 10 miles from Malley's old hometown in Colorado. It was great for our morale. Here we were living and breathing, not quite ready for embalming yet, and down on the ground they were measuring us for shrouds and black-edged jockstraps.

"Thanks," I told the flight engineer, "but that's not my favorite program." He spun the dial again and somebody started speaking French, and the flight engineer said it was hockey from Montreal. French is Greek to me, but every minute or 2 I'd hear the frog announcer say something about "Beelyguts." They were even following us in Montreal, in a foreign language. I heard the announcer say, "Supairdome," and a few minutes later I thought he said "New Orleans," even though he butchered the pronounciation. Then we caught another New Orleans station, and a guy in a southern drawl reported that 75,000 people were massed at the airport waiting to see if the Billygoats made it.

"We're all over the dial," the flight engineer said cheerfully.

"Well," I said, "I'm just as proud as you are. I never knew we had so many fans. Let me know if we crash."

I turned to the console where the pilot and the co-pilot were hunched over a Christmas tree of red and green lights. "What're those reds?" I asked.

"Empty tanks," the pilot said. He and his side-kick seemed to have regained their cool.

"How much fuel have we got?"

"An hour, give or take a few minutes. Why don't you see if that junkie's still awake back there?"

He was awake. Wide awake. Just as I came back through the curtain, Bad-ass Harris was hollering, "Hey, Luke, man, I gotta take a leak, man."

"Go own," Luke said.

Bad-ass started walking down the aisle.

"Freeze!" Hairston said. "Don't take one mo' step!"

"You said I could take a leak," Bad-ass whined.

"Yeh. Said you could take a leak. Didn't say you could git up." He gulped and began a hacking cough. He looked about ready to nod out. As I watched, he slumped over the back of the window seat and began moaning and groaning like a country preacher, and after a while his voice grew louder and you could begin to hear him all over the plane. "You know who we are? Flyspecks! We jes' flyspecks on the earth."

Robert Boggs called out, "Right own, brother!" Trying to establish some communication, I guess.

"Fuckin' flyspecks! Ain't nobody worth a shit on this whole plane, including my own self."

As I stood there in the aisle, balancing on my crutches, I noticed that his eyes were brimming with tears, and as he spoke they began rolling down his face and hanging on his chin. He looked like a big kid—a 6 foot 10 inch kid playing with a toy gun. "We just takin' up space," he went on. "Takin' up air. Wasted people. Chumps and fuck-ups. That's us. That's the Goats."

Nobody had ever heard him refer to himself as a Billygoat before, or even admit that there was such an organization. Maybe there was hope. Then I noticed Jay Cox moving up the aisle on his belly, slithering like an alligator, coming very fast for what he was doing. He was out of Luke's sight, at least for the moment, but the whole picture could change if Luke took one step toward the aisle.

"Come on, Lucius," Bad-ass called out. "We all brothers."

"Brothers," Hairston said, sounding almost completely wiped out. "No bruzh. Flyspecks. Fuckin' flyspecks."

"Amen!" Hyphen B-l-a-c-k hollered, and Robert Boggs said, "Right own, Brother Lucius!" It was beginning to

sound like the Saturday night service at the Upper Darby Tabernacle Church back home, slogan: JESUS SAVES AND SATISFIES.

Cox was 8 or 10 feet away now, and I saw that he had something in his hand, but I didn't want to stare at him for fear of giving away his action.

"We yo' teammates," *Leroy Harmony called out.*

"Yo' friends!" *Bad-ass cried.*

"We yo' brothers!" *Robert Boggs shouted.*

Hairston muttered something I couldn't make out, and the tears began rolling again.

"We wit' chew, man!"

"Shut up, fuckin' flyspeck!" *Luke screamed.* "SHUT UP! SHUT UP! SHUT UP!" *He raised the gun and they all shut up.*

Jay Cox shinnied the last few feet and jumped up and swung a full bottle of Aqua Velvet aftershave in a murderous arc toward Hairston's head. Like a tall snake, Luke slipped his head backward about 6 inches, just enough to make Cox miss, and then dropped him with the barrel of the gun. Cox fell into the aisle between me and Hairston, and a trickle of blood flowed out of his nose.

"Okay, mothafuckas," *Hairston said.* "That's it. Jackson! Go tell the pilot to blast off!"

"What's that?"

"Blast off!" *he said.* "Goin' to glory!" *He screamed out the word glory like he was trying to tell the pilot himself, and I could still hear the echoes as I climbed onto my aluminum crutches for about the 15th time and headed toward the cockpit.*

When I repeated the new flight plan, from wherever we were to glory, wherever that was, the pilot said, "Listen, you guys gotta make your move now. There's 30 minutes of fuel, and that's it. We're fresh out of time."

"He's not ready yet," *I said.* "There's a guy laying in the aisle with a broken head to prove it. We can't jump him without at least one burst being fired."

"Well, go tell him we're gonna crash then."

When I got back, I said, "Luke, we got 5 minutes fuel left. We're gonna crash."

"Shee-it!" he said. "These fuckas can fly the Atlantic and the 'Cific too."

"Yeh, but not when they're fueled for 2000 miles."

"Bullshit, bullshit, bullshit! You jivin' me."

"I'm telling you what the pilot said. He's got red lights all over his board."

"Bullshit. He jivin' you. Get up there! Tell the pilot no mo' jive! Tell him we goin' up to glory, high as we can climb, and if he don't get his ass in gear, I'm gone pick off the crew one by one, startin' with that little bitch that called me a nigger prick."

"Luke," I said, "that was 3 or 4 flights ago. This girl hasn't said a word to you, except to do what you told her to."

"Now you jivin'!" he said, turning the muzzle around and jerking it toward the cockpit. "Get on up there! Tell the pilot what I said. And I don't want no more bullshit from either one of you chumps." I took a last deep look into his eyes, and I could see they weren't focusing.

When I limped into the cockpit, the pilot didn't even wait to hear my message. "I'm going in," he said. "We've got just enough fuel to land."

"He'll shoot," I warned.

"I can't help it, Jackson," the pilot said. "We got to chance it. Otherwise we run out of fuel and crash-land anyway."

"Look, just a few more minutes. He seems to be nodding out."

"I got red lights all over the panel. We're going in."

"Okay," I said. "We'll do what we can."

"And Jackson," the pilot said, "don't bother coming back. By the time you get here, it'll be too late to make any new plans."

"The only plan he has is blast off, goin' to glory, and if you start to land, he'll shoot the crew, one by one, starting with the stewardesses."

"Yeh," the pilot said. "Well, we'll say our prayers."

"Look there!" the co-pilot said, pointing to a set of twinkling lights that flanked us at about a mile range.

"Tell him we're glad to see him," the pilot said. "He can help in the search-and-rescue."

As I started out of the cockpit, we headed into a thunderhead, and we jolted around before we came out the other side. "Can you find a few more like that?" I asked the pilot.

"All you can use," he said.

"Good," I said, opening the door to the passenger sections. "Give me all the action you can."

As I hobbled through 1st class, half a dozen people grabbed at me to ask questions, but I just kept right on rolling along on my crutches, and out of the corner of my eye I saw Ziggy get up and follow me. I found Hairston leaning against the rack of seats, breathing hard, with the barrel of the gun resting on the top level of the seatbacks.

"Luke?" I said softly, to test his reflexes, and he spun around and shoved the gun barrel at me.

"Get over there!" he snarled at me, motioning to my own rack. I eased myself down and looked out the window. We seemed to be going slower, and after a minute or 2 I realized we were headed sharply down. Luke Hairston realized it, too.

"Hey!" he hollered. "I tol' that pilot to blast off. Up, up, up!" He jumped into the aisle and swept the muzzle of the gun back and forth toward the guys. The barrel waved crazily and he seemed to be fighting to hold it still, as

288

though it was almost too much for him to control. A slow, silly smile came across his face, and he lowered the gun at the floor, and then slowly, shaking violently, he brought it up to his shoulder and aimed down the aisle.

I don't know how I knew he was going to pull the trigger, but I knew, and it didn't make a bit of difference anymore what happened to me, because whatever happened was going to happen to all of us together, the Billygoats in their final team effort.

I whipped my crutch backhand with all the strength and snap I had in my good arm and swung it in an arc that caught his gun hand right in the meat, and there was a loud Brpppppp *like somebody ripping a paper along the dotted line but about 1000 times louder, and then there was a big whoosh and whine like all the vacuum cleaners in the world turned on at once, and a hornet stung me right in the ass.*

I lost my balance and my good leg jerked out from under me and the upper part of my body spun around and my head slammed into something, eye first. I have a hazy recollection of being dragged between the seats and sticking there and watching 2 pictures, one out of each eye, like trying to see through wrecked binoculars. In one eye I saw a row of seats and a pant leg, in the other a shoe flying through the air and a magazine with the pages rippling. Then the pictures changed and I saw Malley's face out of one eye and a beer can out of the other. Then it got cold and black.

For the 2d time in a week, I woke up in a strange bed, but this time there was an improvement. The doctor wasn't Mr. Evans. The new doc told me in a soft southern accent that I'd suffered a fracture of the floor orbit of the right eye, that I wouldn't be able to take the bandage off for a few weeks but that he expected me to regain full vision. I told him that the last thing I remembered was being in an airplane and seeing one picture out of one eye and a completely different scene out of the other, and he said that's what happens in the floor orbit fracture, the broken bones trap the eye muscles and keep them from working, and you end up seeing stereo till it's fixed. He also mentioned that he'd dug one bullet out of my ass and 3 more out of my cast and I was lucky it wasn't reversed.

"Doc," I said, "if I'm not being too pushy, where the hell am I?"

"Charity Hospital."

"Where's that?"

"New Awl'yins."

"That's good," I said. "That's great! I expect to star in the Superbowl."

The doctor laughed politely and took a duck, and about an hour later in walked Malley with a stack of sports magazines and newspapers and some paperbacks by Xaviera Hollander and Joey Gallo and Linda Lovelace. "Listen, Alph," Mal said, raising his voice as though I'd lost my hearing as well as half my eyesight, "I got great news. I talked to the lady at admissions, and she says if you can guarantee 2 more major injuries this year, she'll get you the wholesale rate."

"Very funny," I said, and I asked him if he would mind filling me in on current events. He rambled on for 20 or 30 minutes. He told me that Ziggy had jumped Luke from behind after I smashed his gun hand, but one of the wild bullets nicked me in the ass and another wiped out a window on my side, and I was sucked toward the opening but my cast jammed under the seats and my eye hit the outside armrest and I was saved from taking one of the longest swan dives in the history of sports. The plane landed on a strip of foam at New Orleans International

Airport and I was rushed to the hospital while the other players flapped their arms and buttoned their collars and took about 3 hours to thaw out.

"What about Luke?" I asked.

"Luke's right in here with you," Malley said. "Up in the neuropsychiatric ward. He's quit babbling, but they got enough of the story out of him. He got hooked, he got in over his head, and he agreed to shave points. The doctors said if he'd taken a couple more hits he'd been dead."

"And we're supposed to believe Luke did all the point-shaving? Luke did the shit-disturbing?"

"Well, he had help, sure. He was coached. But most of it was pretty easy. I mean, how much trouble was it to lift Rodenheimer's money clip and put it in Bad-ass's locker?"

"What about the phone calls?"

"His girlfriend made a few and he made a few himself. None of the wives know his voice. Shit, he never talked. How would they?"

"And he fixed it up to get Limey thrown in jail?"

"Maybe, maybe not. The cops got an anonymous call at 3 in the morning complaining about the Clamage bash. That's a pretty deadly way to mess up a football team. Get one of their wild parties busted."

"So he just thought—"

"He knew it'd cause some kind of trouble. I guess it worked better than he dreamed."

"Yeh," I said. "It worked great. He's upstairs in the psycho ward, I'm flat on my ass, and the whole team's tapioca." For a second, I had a crazy impulse. "Hey," I said, "is there any chance he can play Sunday?"

"You gotta be crazy too," Mal said, laughing.

"How about Cox?" I asked.

"He'll play."

"That's something."

"Yeh," Mal said, "but the point spread's changing fast

in Denver's favor." He paused. "One good thing, though," he said. "This time we know why."

They wheeled a television into my room, and Billy Bob Bunker sent word the front office would pay for it out of the kindness of their heart, and all day long the New Orleans stations didn't carry anything but Superbowl, Superbowl, Superbowl, which was fine with me. Coach was interviewed by a panel of hotshots from *Sports Pictorial*, the New York *Times-News* and the Chicago *Sun-Times-Tribune*, just about the most high-powered sportswriters you could imagine. I remember every word, because it was exactly like all the press conferences I'd listened to since I was a kid, and I felt kind of silly and lightheaded as I watched.

"Coach, what can you tell us about your game plan?"

"Well, I'd like to get in there and score early."

(Did any team ever intend to get in there and score late?)

"Will you be practicing ball control?"

"I'll play a ball-control type game, yes. Grind out those 1st downs and try to control the clock."

(Did any team ever decide to play a *mis*control game, like maybe come up on 3d and 3 and deliberately go for 2?)

"What worries you the most about the Broncos?"

"Well, they have a powerful runner in that Smetana. I'll try to slow him down."

(Instead of trying to speed him up?)

"How do you rate the Broncos overall?"

"Just like everybody else, they put on their pants one leg at a time."

(Wrong there! I had a friend at Penn State that used to lay his pants in front of him, then jump straight up in the air, kick out his feet, and come down with his pants on, just so nobody could say he put them on one leg at a time.)

"Coach, how about Manders, their right guard?"

"Tough. *Tough!* They're all tough. I only wish I knew what they got up their sleeve."

(Several secret agents carrying monkey wrenches and plumbers' tools had probably eased his mind by now.)

"One final question, Coach. If you had to make a prediction on what's gonna happen out there Sunday, what would it be?"

"Let's just say I hope the better team wins."

(He really hoped that the Denver Club would come down with leprosy and their arms and legs would fall off.)

"Are the Goats the better team?"

"On any given Sunday—"

"Thank you."

I took a nap, and when I woke up it was time for the evening news with Roger Dirt or whatever that anchorman's name is, the one with the slanty eyes, and I watched for a while with the sound off and all of a sudden I let out a whoop and almost jumped out of bed, cast and all. There in living color was none other than Mr. A.B.C. Jackson, Sr. and his ever-loving wife my mother and Leslie Stall was interviewing them and I almost broke my finger punching that sound button.

"—And of course it came as no surprise to us," my father was saying. "We've known the boy since he was an infant."

I smacked my head. What a brilliant observation!

"He's always made us so proud," Mom said. "Look here," and she held up the 3 scrapbooks marked A.B.C. Jackson Jr., and the camera moved in real tight while Mom began turning the pages, and wouldn't you know it, she grabbed volume 3 and not a fucking clipping in it, just these huge blank white pages, and Mom turning them over and over one by one, real carefully, as if she's demonstrating a Gutenberg Bible.

Leslie Stall had the sense to cut that short, and then Pop got out the merit badges and told about the paper route, and then they cut to a commentator in New Orleans, John Philson or Phil Johnson, a big hefty guy with a beard, and he's explaining how the hero of the Superbowl has already been decided no matter what happens on the playing field, etc., etc., and I was so embarrassed I turned if off and pulled the pillow over my head.

A few minutes later, I heard a gruff voice say, "Oh, isn't that sweet? Look at that cute little fellow, pretending he's asleep. Wake up, you dumb shit!" It was Coach, with Jerry Stein.

"How you feeling?" Coach asked me.

"Oh, fine, Coach," I said. "How about you?"

"Never mind me," Coach said. "You're the man of the hour, not me. I'm sorry we didn't get here earlier, but it's been a pisser. When the papers aren't interviewing me, the cops are. I feel like a murder suspect."

Jerry Stein hurried right up to the bed and ran his fingers through my lack of hair and slapped me hard on the shoulder. "You saved us, kid" he said. "You and Ziggy saved the whole league, and Commissioner Summerall wants me to say thanks." Coach looked a little sour. I guess he was upset about being left out of the commissioner's message. After all, it'd been Coach's idea to send Ziggy back to jump Hairston.

"Oh, that's okay, Jerry," I said. "Call on me anytime. Listen, I'm still wondering about Hairston. What do you know so far?"

"Nobody knows much yet," Stein said, pulling out that smelly pipe of his and slumping into a chair in the corner. "The medics say you get somebody like that every once in a while, an unstable personality that just starts gulping everything he can get, and pretty soon he's either dead or on a psycho ward."

"But why Hairston of all people?"

"It wasn't any one thing. The fixers picked the perfect patsy. Hairston's always had a hard-on for the league 'cause he thinks we're racist. He's always been big on the pills, plus he's always been a little flaky in the 1st place. The FBI found a note, but they said you could hardly read the writing. Something about the mob paid him off a hundred grand and he was gonna start a new colony in Africa but it was just too much goddamned trouble and he was heading for the bridge."

"Heading for the *bridge?*" I said.

"Yeh, but apparently he went out and boarded the plane instead."

"He was gonna use our charter to commit suicide?"

"Yeh," Coach put in. "He thought it'd be a nice touch to take the Billygoats with him."

"Jeez, it's great to be needed," I said, "but next time I'd just as soon he'd send a card."

"Edquist talked to the lab," Coach said. "They did a blood test. He had 7 different kinds of drugs in him: Dexedrine, something called Desoxyn, methadrine, barbituric acid, 3 or 4 others I can't pronounce."

"A walking drugstore," Stein said. "The only thing that saved him is that some of the drugs canceled each other out, and even then he came close to cashing his ticket. The doc said he must have developed a terrific tolerance for dope over the years."

"Well," I said, "who hasn't? You can't play this game without the pills anymore. You'd get cut in the first scrimmage."

"Bullshit," Coach said. "How'd Sammy Baugh and Steve Van Buren and all the rest of us play the game? We didn't know what a stimulant was."

"Sammy Baugh and Steve Van Buren and the rest of you guys were a buncha pussies," I said, a little surprised at the way I was talking to General Patton, but what did I give a shit, still half weird from the ether and all. "I've seen the films. You guys hit like faggots. You even had players without helmets. If you went out there today without a helmet, you'd be dead by the end of the 1st quarter."

"Bullshit!" Coach said.

"Bullshit yourself!" I said, getting a little steamed. "The public wants hitting, so we hit, but we gotta have a little help to do it. Normal isn't good enough anymore, Coach, and you know it. Why, in that 2d Giant game—"

"Wait!" Stein said, grinning sheepishly. "Don't say it! Let me stay ignorant."

A nurse came bouncing in from the hall, all starch and authority. "Please," she said, "Hold it down, gentlemen."

After she tiptoed out, Coach took a deep breath and said he didn't know what the Billygoats and himself would have ever done without me blah blah blah and he put his arms around me and gave me a hug, just like the last scene of a movie romance, and I only wished he knew about Clorets with their miracle ingredient Retsyn.

"Jerry," I said when Coach had unleashed me, "do you really think this is the first time anyone's shaved points in the NFL? Easy as it turns out to be?"

"I just don't know," the commissioner's man said quickly.

"We just don't know," Coach echoed. "That's the truth."

"Look at what Hairston got away with, week after week," I said, "till he practically begged to be caught."

That's why we're jumpy about gambling," Stein admitted. "That's why we have all the undercover men. That's why there's an investigation every time a player wants to buy into a bar or restaurant. That's why Namath had to sell Bachelors III, years ago."

"Come on now, Jerry," I said. "You can tell me. Didn't anybody every go for the money before?"

He hesitated. "We've suspected a few," he said softly.

"What'd you do?"

"Eased 'em out."

"Who were they?"

"Don't ask me that. I can't tell you."

He didn't have to tell me. I could think of a few probables and 100 possibles. Players that retired long before their prime. The split end that quit and went to work for a big racketeer. The quarterback that never made more than $10,000 a year and then bought half the state of Arkansas when he quit. And plenty more.

"How've you kept it quiet?" I asked.

"Same way we'll keep this one quiet," Stein said. "By dealing with decent people, guys like you and Tietjens, *members of the family.*"

"Oh," I said. "Gee, I never knew I was a member of the family before."

"Well, you *are,*" Coach said. "You're one of us. We already put the word out: Luke Hairston went nuts and hijacked the plane, and you risked your ass to save us. That's all the public'll ever know. Let's keep it that way."

"What a guy!" I said, thinking back on that 6 foot 10 inch mother with the glue hands and the understated style. "Jesus, what a player he was. The only time I ever wondered was when he caught the convulsions in the Washington game, but even then he was trying."

"It's a good thing," Coach said. "The rest of you pussies was half asleep that day."

"I looked at him upstairs," Stein said, "with all the tubes and needles in him, and I couldn't help think what Churchill said, 'an enigma cloaked in a shroud wrapped in a mystery,' something like that."

297

"Yeh," Coach said, "an enigma cloaked in a shroud wrapped in a wet pack."

After a while we got to talking about the Superbowl, and Coach said the line was still 13 on Denver, which he felt was unreasonable, even considering that the Goats had been through a shattering experience just 5 days before the game. "Why 13 points?" Coach complained. "That's the biggest spread since Green Bay played Kansas City, back before the merger."

"I think the handicappers are figuring on 3 things," Jerry Stein said. "You don't have Jackson, you don't have Hairston, and your ballclub's in a state of shock."

"Well," Coach said, "maybe I'll pull one out of the hat."

"You can do it, Coach," I said. "Just hit a little harder."

He started to give me a look, but then he smiled and patted my cheek. "Alphabet," he said, "you gotta learn to watch that mouth—*Coach.*"

"I'm a coach?" I said, all flustered and stupid. "Gee, great! Gee, wow, thanks a lot, Coach." I'm embarrassed just remembering that I said those things but I did. "I'm a coach, huh? Terrific! Just what I always wanted." It wasn't exactly what I wanted, but it sounded good now. Assistant coach or waterboy, at least I could stay around the bench.

"Yeh, I thought it over and considered all the possibilities and—"

"—Got a call from the commissioner," Stein interrupted.

"Yeh, well that too," Coach said, "but that isn't what made up my mind. I always liked old Alph here. He's my kind of guy."

"Gee, thanks, Coach," I said. "Gee, great! Gee, wow, thanks a lot!"

"You said already," Coach said. "Save your stren'th."

"For what?"

"I'll tell you later."

After they left, I just closed my eye and looked at the red spots whirling around in my head and thought about Luke Hairston and the funny bounces you get from the prolate spheroid of life, and wondering how on earth we could have stopped him before it was too late and what effect the whole mess would have on the Superbowl game and whether we had even the slightest chance. The lights were turned off at 10, and my phone rang half an hour later, just as I was starting to doze.

"Coach?" the voice said.

"Yeh, Coach," I said, knowing that nobody else on earth would call me by my new title.

"Listen, I talked to your doctor," Coach said, sounding excited. "I asked him to keep you in the room till Sunday morning."

"Jesus Christ, Coach—"

"It's only a few days."

"But Coach—"

"Goddamn it, if you want that Superbowl money, do what I tell you! And if anybody asks you when you're getting out, just tell 'em you've taken a turn for the worse. Got that?"

I said I had it.

"Just relax and enjoy yourself and watch the TV. The club's paying for everything. Send out for pizza. Get the nurse to give you a blow-job. Anything you want. It's on the house."

"Coach, you had a few drinks?"

"And maybe exercise a little, when nobody's looking. Could you go 50 yards on crutches?"

"Sober up, Coach!"

"Well, get your ass in shape so you can!"

On Thursday, 3 days before the game, practically everybody on the club visited me, and I told them I knew we could win. Right before bedtime, Malley came in, and he looked like he was the one that was hurt instead of me. "Hey, Rooms," I said. "How they hanging?"

He flopped down in the chair in the corner like he'd done 1000 grass drills, and he stared at the floor and didn't answer.

"Jeez, the suspense is terrific," I said. "Give it another hour or 2 before you tell me what's wrong. I mean, I got time."

"I went upstairs to see if they'd let me visit Hairston," Mal said, "but they wouldn't let me in."

"Well," I said, "that's too bad, but I wouldn't pass out about it. That crazy bastard—"

"As I was leaving the ward office," Malley said, talking straight into the floor, "I saw a black lady sitting there, tall and skinny, maybe 6 feet, maybe 110 pounds. She was acting like she was on guard duty or something."

"Hairston's mother?" I said.

"Hairston's aunt," Malley said. "An old woman with a plantation accent. I had to strain to understand her."

"What'd she say?"

"What *didn't* she say? She rambled on and on about having to go to so much trouble, coming all the way from Slidell on the bus, sitting up all night, and for what? To wait out in the corridor and not even see the boy."

"The boy?"

"Yeh, she seems to think he's still a little kid. She raved on and on about his no-'count father and how he ruined the family and Luke was no-'count too and how she always knew it'd come to bad, she warned 'em, she told 'em over and over, but they wouldn't listen to her."

"Sounds very understanding."

"Oh, yeh, she was! She said she told the mother, that's

her sister, she said, 'You raisin' a bum, a outright bum! And you a bum yourself!' "

"She told you all this?"

"At the top of her lungs, up and down the scale, like a lamentation in a black Baptist church, except that she didn't pity anybody or anything, she just hated."

"So why'd she come to the hospital?"

"I guess she thought she had to. It was her duty. She had to see the kid one more time."

"Yeh, and tell him what a bum he was. God, that's awful."

"Then the mother died—'Nothin' lost,' the old sister said—and Luke was in and out of homes, and somewhere along the way a coach saw he was big and turned him on to football. Every black kid needs an out. Football was his. Well, it clears up one thing. It clears up why he never talked."

"Why?"

"There was nothing good to say."

I left the hospital Sunday morning, all wobbly and wearing a big bandage on my head and the cast on my leg and a compress on my ass where the slug had gone in about an inch. Ziggy Guminski and The Connection helped me into one of the 50 new Ford Ladybugs that had been provided for the team. As we drove, I asked The Connection how his arm was coming along.

"Shit, it'd take more than one bullet to hurt a old crock like me," he said, smiling bravely. I thought about how pathetic he'd looked back on the plane, with the blood all over his shirt and his wet eyes staring up at the lights, but I understood. Every man's entitled to his moment.

"Yeh," I said. "You're a plenty tough fucker, you are."

"You're no lily of the valley yourself," The Connection said. "At least you got the papers fooled. Look at this!"

He handed me a bunch of newspaper clippings about me myself and I, great big headlines like CRIPPLED CENTER SAVES AIR TRAGEDY and COACH SAYS GAME ON, THANKS TO JACKSON, stuff like that.

"You're the biggest thing in New Orleans since sliced bread," Ziggy said. "Show him, Strepey!"

The Connection handed back a page from the morning's *Times-Picayune-States-Item*, and the whole top half was a picture of me, captioned "Man of the Hour!—A.B.C. Jackson Jr. of the Billygoats!"

"Here's another one," The Connection said, and passed back a page full of pictures of the team getting off the plane, me being carried on a stretcher, entering the hospital and doing everything but taking a leak. There was even a picture of me as a 12-year-old on my bicycle. It was the only one where I wasn't bald.

We headed straight through town to the Superdome. I figured they'd fixed it up so I could watch from the press-box, along with the other interlopers, wives, girlfriends, friends of friends, clergymen and everybody but the press.

Ziggy drove through a big sliding door and down the track that surrounded the playing field. "Coach's idea is terrific," Ziggy said. "I hope you can reach back for a little extra."

"Well, Zig, I don't think I could go both ways today," I quipped.

The Connection said, "Could you walk maybe 50 yards?"

"Shit, I could *crawl* 50 yards, if it'd help us win. What does Coach have in mind? Spotting me at the sidelines so I can take a pass and go into the end zone untouched if my crutches don't break if I can see where the end zone is?"

"Never trouble trouble till trouble troubles you," Ziggy said mysteriously.

Coach came out of an office and almost knocked me down with enthusiasm. He steered me into the office and sat me down. "Alph," he said, "the kickoff's in 4 hours, and we're hurting bad. It's like everybody on the club just lost his mother." My knee was still sore as an unlanced boil and my heart was pumping melted lead into my right eye, but I understood what Coach was driving at.

"Yeh," I said, "I know it. I wish there was something I could do, but I don't think I better play."

Coach laughed, but it sounded forced. "I just wish to Christ you *could* play," he said, "but I think I know the next best thing. You ever hear of El Cid?"

"Yeh. Wasn't he in a movie?"

"Listen, El Cid wasn't *in* a movie, El Cid *was* the fucking movie. Charlton Heston played the part. El Cid was the great Spanish hero."

That was news to me. I'd always thought he was Jewish.

"He dies before he can lead his men into battle," Ziggy put in.

"Listen to me!" Coach said, jumping up and walking around the desk. "El Cid dies before the battle, so they dress his body in fighting clothes and they strap him to his horse and they kick the horse in the ass and send him out."

I was beginning to get a glimmer of what was coming.

"And the other team sees El Cid galloping toward them," Ziggy said, "and they turn and run and the Spanish win the battle."

"Against the spread?" I inquired.

"Look, this is no time to be smart-ass," Coach snapped.

"I wasn't being smart-ass. I'm just trying to head you off before you ask me to do something dumb like being in the lineup for the kickoff."

"No," Ziggy said, looking shocked. "Nothing *that* dumb!"

"Alph," Coach said, putting his hand on my shoulder, "this club needs an emotional lift, something out of the ordinary. We still got the horses, but they're all dragging ass. We need something to get the adrenaline flowing."

"How about doubling the greens?" I suggested.

"No, no," Coach said. "I don't mean something like greens. I mean something really inspiring, really dramatic."

"You don't think your pep talk's dramatic?"

"Now listen," Coach said, ignoring me. "Here's what you're gonna do. I already fixed it up with the P.A. announcer. Goddamn it, this is an order, and *you're gonna do it!* Don't shake your fucking head till you hear me out."

Coach spelled out his stroke of genius, the master plan that was going to transform the Billygoats from hang-dog underlings to wild men. I argued for 15 minutes that the idea was half-assed, and Coach told me he didn't care what I thought, he didn't care how embarrassed I'd be, we had to do something or the Goats were goners. "They were down *before* that crazy plane ride," he said. "Imagine what they're like now."

"Yeh," I said. "Most of the guys came to see me, and they didn't look like much."

"Tell me you'll do it."

I took a deep breath. "Okay, General, I'll do it."

"Hey, that's great!" Coach said just as Mr. Bunker and Father Galvin came in.

"Is he going along?" Billy Bob said, and Coach nodded.

"Wonderful news!" our beloved owner and general manager said, and grabbed my hand in his fishlike grip.

"The Lord was with us," the Rev. Matthew Galvin said. But when Coach laid the rest of his plan on me, the part about cutting a leg out of my uniform and suiting up, the conversation got a little hot and heavy, with Coach ordering me and Billy Bob Bunker threatening me and the Rev. Matthew Galvin begging me and Ziggy saying, "Can't you see it, Alph? It'll really get 'em where they live!"

"You'll do it in your fucking uniform!" Coach hollered. "That's a fucking order and you won't question it!"

"Goddamn it, *I question it!*"

"Here," Billy Bob said. "See how it looks." They had actually brought that one-legged fuchsia monstrosity with them.

"Get that amputated bastard of a uniform out of my sight!" I said. "I'll do it in my street clothes, or I won't do it at all." So we compromised.

Coach came over and tried to put his arm around me, but I held up my hand. "Jeez," I said, "I just hope I don't fall down out there."

"Fall down?" Coach said. "That'd be even better!"

I felt like an idiot sitting at the far end of the Superdome wearing a Billygoats' cap, but Coach thought I'd be less conspicuous in a wheelchair, with my cast propped out in front of me. The stitches in my left hand still flamed red and ugly, and the whole right side of my face was bandaged, and I felt like I was wearing a big neon sign that announced: MY NAME IS ALPH JACKSON AND I'M ABOUT TO DO SOMETHING DUMB. I was shaking with nerves and stagefright as it was.

Down at the other end of the field I caught a flash of fuchsia, and I knew the Billygoats must be lining up in the tunnel for the introductions. Around me all the paraplegics kept up a steady chatter, but they hushed when the announcer called for attention and told the 75,000 spectators that they were about to meet today's contestants one by one.

"First, from the National Football Conference champion Billygoats—"

My good knee buckled as I stood up, and the echoes of the P.A. bounced back and forth: *"Billygoats.* ˙Goats.*"*

"No. 50," the announcer said. *"50.* 50.*"*

Jeez, they were going through with it.

"From Pennsylvania State University. *University.* ˙Versity.*"*

A rustle went through the stands.

"The veteran center. *Center.* Center.*"*

I swallowed hard.

"The great—A.B.C.—Alphabet—JACKSON! *Jackson.* Jackson.*"*

I gulped for air and got out of my chair and pushed off on my crutches. One of the paraplegics hollered, "Down in front!" I couldn't blame him for getting pissed. He's looking all over the stadium for "The Great A.B.C. Alphabet Jackson" and here comes this asshole on crutches blocking his view.

As I took my first wobbly step onto the playing surface I happened to glance sideways into the end-zone stands, and my good eye caught a boy about 12 years old. I turned and stopped, dumb as it looked, but the kid stood out, which he had the same general built as my divorced son, A.B.C. Jackson III, and I couldn't resist giving him a little wave, and when I did, 75,000 people spotted me and began to cheer, first at my end of the Superdome and then flowing along like a tidal wave, till I felt my eardrums might burst and I could go back to the hospital for another visit, maybe at wholesale. They jumped up and threw hats and cushions, and down at the other end I could see the Goats bouncing around like they'd been goosed with a cattle prod.

At the 30, I stopped for a rest, but then I pushed off

again, and the announcer grabbed me at the 50 and kept one arm around me while he motioned for quiet with the other. I didn't think the noise could get any louder, but it did, and the bands were puffing on their instruments like I was some kind of astronaut just returned from the solar system, but you couldn't hear a note they played.

I did a kind of half-ass whirl like a crippled elephant, but other than that I didn't know what to do. I couldn't take a bow because of my cast, and I didn't want to tip my cap because the bald would show. I tried to wave a crutch, but I almost fell on my ass, so I settled for raising my right arm in a fist, and then I realized I'd given the old black power salute to 75,000 Southerners. Oh, well, the late Robert Boggs always claimed I was half spook anyway. I could imagine J. R. Rodenheimer standing over by the gate muttering to himself, "Fuckin' niggerlover!" Well, J. R., if that's the whole choice, between being a niggerlover and being a niggerhater, I guess there's no doubt where I stand, or you either.

It must have been a good 5 minutes before the M.C. finally gave a signal to the massed trombone choirs from 25 Louisiana high schools and they swung into "I Wish I Was in the Land of Cotton" and quietened things down. I dragged my sore ass over to the sidelines and flopped on the bench, and The Connection slipped me a green. For just a second, I wondered if little Alph was in the stands, not just a kid that looked like him but the genuine article, all the way from Augusta, Ga., but I knew that was too much to expect. I'd sent tickets for him and his mother and the doc, but they were always busy.

When the rest of the Goats ran out, there was another bedlam, and I realized what a card-trick our conniving coach had pulled off, converting the whole New Orleans crowd that used to hate our guts into a regular hometown nuthouse. Every Goat that was introduced the fans practi-

cally lifted the roof off the Superdome, even including
Oop Johnson, which a little while ago they'd tried to kill
him for assaulting their quarterback, and somebody'd
threw a rock after the game but luckily it caught him in
the head.

The Broncos were introduced next, and there was polite applause, and from the minute Limey teed the ball up
on the 35-yard line you could tell the way it was going to
be all day, with maybe 74,000 fans rooting for us and the
other 1000 scared to open their mouths. I've heard people
say it doesn't make any difference who cheers for who,
but any player will tell you that's bullshit. You have to
figure the hometown advantage for 3, 4 points a game,
that's what the bookies all say, and I'd say it's worth even
more.

The question was, would it make up for what we were
missing, me and Luke Hairston out entirely and Jay Cox
playing a little groggy and the whole team disorientated
from the crazy things that happened?

Limey sent the kickoff over the end line, which is only
a mere 75, 80 yards in the air, and the way our kickoff
team busted ass on that opening play, the Broncos must
have wondered where the pussies went that they were
supposed to beat by 13 points. It looked like the battle of
Damascus all over again. But there's a pattern to Superbowl games, and no changing it. We opened strong, and
the Broncs opened strong, but after 5 or 6 minutes of
playing time, the game turned into your typical dollars-
and-cents football, 3 yards and a cloud of dust like Woody
Hayes played, short passes and nobody willing to sing and
dance and take a chance till the very last seconds, when
it became a case of gamble or lose for the Goats. *Sports
Pictorial* wrote that "the only inspiring moments were at
the beginning and the end, the tremendous pre-game
ovation given to the Billygoats' heroic Alph Jackson, free-

ing the team from its cocoon of morosity, and the antic improvisation that decided the contest with less than a minute to play." How those guys could sling the words! I was embarrassed by what they wrote about me, but Dorris Gene ordered 50 copies.

The "antic improvisation" was a center-eligible play that Malley whispered to Q. B. during our last time-out after Coach ordered a 30 dive that'd already failed about 6 times. Zawatski caught a pass in the flat and fell into the end zone to win it 10–7 and Coach was tear-ass but he pulled himself together and took the credit later. Him and General Patton.

The guys voted to give me the game ball, so I have some wonderful momentoes of my career: 2 prolate spheroids, a pair of aluminum crutches and a Superbowl ring. Good old Dorris Gene, she polishes them every day, balls and all, and they're in a nice display case in our house, along with pictures of the baby and a few game scenes and a glossy of Little Alph.

They don't call him Alexander any more.